THE UTOPIAN GENERATION

PEPETELA

THE UTOPIAN GENERATION

Translated from the Portuguese

by David Brookshaw

BIBLIOASIS

Windsor, Ontario

First published as *A Geração da Utopia* by Edições Dom Quixote,
Lisbon, Portugal, 1992.

FIRST EDITION
10 9 8 7 6 5 4 3 2 1

Library and Archives Canada Cataloguing in Publication
Title: The utopian generation / Pepetela ; translated from the Portuguese
by David Brookshaw.
Other titles: Geração da utopia. English Names: Pepetela, author.
Brookshaw, David, translator.
Series: Biblioasis international translation series ; 47.
Description: Series statement: Biblioasis international translation series ; 47 |
Translation of: A geração da utopia. | In English, translated from the Portuguese.
Identifiers: Canadiana (print) 20240317475 | Canadiana (ebook)
20240321022 | ISBN 9781771965798 (softcover) | ISBN 9781771965804 (EPUB)
Subjects: LCGFT: Novels. Classification: LCC PQ9929.P46 G4713 2024 |
DDC 869.3/42—dc23

Funded by the DGLAB/Culture and the Camões, I.P. – PORTUGAL

REPÚBLICA
PORTUGUESA
CULTURA

DIREÇÃO-GERAL DO LIVRO,
DOS ARQUIVOS E DAS BIBLIOTECAS

CAMÕES
INSTITUTO
DA COOPERAÇÃO
E DA LíNGUA
PORTUGAL
MINISTÉRIO DOS NEGÓCIOS ESTRANGEIROS

Edited by Stephen Henighan and Daniel Wells
Copyedited by Crissy Boylan
Cover designed by Zoe Norvell
Typeset by Vanessa Stauffer

Cover image: Angola, Portuguese troops gathered in Luanda, 1961.
From the American Geographical Society Library,
University of Wisconsin-Milwaukee Libraries.

PRINTED AND BOUND IN CANADA

CONTENTS

Translator's Preface

Long before being invited to undertake the translation of this work, I had included a number of Pepetela's novels over the years in a unit I taught on African literatures in Portuguese at Bristol University. During that period, and indeed over the last forty years, Pepetela, the nom-de-plume of Artur Pestana dos Santos (*pepetela* is the Umbundu word for eyelash, *pestana* in Portuguese), has emerged as the most prolific and multifaceted of Angola's modern fiction writers. Born in Benguela, Southern Angola, in 1941, into a family with roots in the country going back to the nineteenth century, Pepetela played an active part in the anticolonial struggle. As a student in Portugal, he fled to Paris in 1961 to avoid being drafted into the colonial army sent to put down the uprising in his home country. From there, he moved to Algiers, where he completed a degree in sociology and set up the Centre for Angolan Studies, under the auspices of the Popular Movement for the Liberation of Angola (MPLA). He then moved to Brazzaville, where he became more involved in both the front line and the rearguard of the guerrilla war against the Portuguese. He was in Zambia from 1971 to '74, where he was active on the Eastern Front. After the independence of Angola in 1975, he became vice minister for education in the government of Agostinho Neto, and Pepetela was a founding member of the Union of Angolan Writers. In the early 1980s, he left political life in order to dedicate himself more fully to his career as a writer, while also teaching sociology at a university in Luanda. To date, he is the author of over twenty novels, in addition to short stories and plays.

The Utopian Generation is generally seen as closing a cycle of work begun by his first major novel, *Mayombe*, written in 1971 but only published in 1980 with the backing of Neto, who considered it a work that debated contentious but important issues in newly independent Angola. The setting of *Mayombe* switches between an MPLA rear base, just inside the Congolese border, and a guerrilla encampment deep inside the Mayombe rainforest in Cabinda. The guerrilla fighters are from diverse racial, ethnic, and tribal backgrounds, and through their discussions and individual memories, we are given an idea of the rivalries and animosities that need to be overcome in order for a new, socialist Angola to emerge. The novel was considered of such significance in a continent still emerging from the effects of European colonialism that it was translated into English and published in 1983 in Zimbabwe, where it was studied on courses related to African studies.

Mayombe was the first major Angolan novel to be published in the years immediately following independence, when the country was avowedly a revolutionary state with a markedly Marxist agenda. *The Utopian Generation*, first published in Portuguese in 1992—the year that was to supposedly end the civil war with the MPLA's main rival, UNITA, while also introducing multi-party elections—brought an end to Pepetela's cycle of works that had engaged, in one way or another, with the ideals held dear by the MPLA at independence, namely the struggle to create a socialist state. *Mayombe* had held out hope for the future through one of its two main characters, the young political commissar, João, whose revolutionary fervour enables him to take the struggle to the new guerrilla front opening up on the Eastern Front, after the death of his commander, Fearless, in a skirmish with the Portuguese. The death of Fearless, a kind of father figure to the young commissar, marks the end of a dream based on the notion that utopia can never be achieved because it requires never-ending revolution rather than political compromise. The understanding at the end of Pepetela's more youthful novel was that something of Fearless's unstinting commitment would live on in the new man emerging in the figure of his ideological son.

Mayombe was a novel of hope despite the difficulties faced in achieving a socially and culturally integrated country; *The Utopian Generation* ends on a note of profound disillusion over the failure of the generation which fought for and achieved Angola's political independence to deliver the society envisioned in their youthful ideals. Unlike in *Mayombe*, in *The Utopian Generation*, the figure who most resembles Fearless survives into independence and becomes a hermit living by the beach near Pepetela's own birthplace, unable and unwilling to adapt to the compromises being made by the power brokers in Luanda; the figure who most closely resembles *Mayombe*'s political commissar becomes a government minister, happy to take kickbacks in return for favours granted to the new generation of entrepreneurs emerging as the MPLA abandoned its commitment to socialism.

Mayombe was a glimpse of a historical moment, while *The Utopian Generation* is an epic set over three decades. The first section, entitled "The Casa," focuses on the emerging sense of Angolan nationalism among a group of students in Lisbon, who congregate on most days at the Casa dos Estudantes do Império (Imperial Students' House), a students' association established by the Portuguese government in 1944, designed to provide a space where students from the colonies could meet, eat, access services, and be more effectively supervised under one roof. It was closed down in 1965 at the instigation of the PIDE (the Portuguese political police) in the wake of anticolonial uprisings in Angola, Guinea, and Mozambique. In this first section of the work, we are introduced to all the novel's characters. Pepetela's evocation of Lisbon in the early 1960s will be familiar to anyone who lived in Portugal during those years: student rooms, lodging houses, and apartments in downtown Lisbon; the cafés where friends and colleagues met, always careful of what they were saying in case the person at a nearby table apparently reading a newspaper was on PIDE's payroll; the nuns' residences where girls from "good" families in the colonies or the countryside were accommodated under the watchful eye of the Mother Superior; the occasional student demonstration brutally put down by the police; and the painstaking care with which the clandestine opposition to the regime (essentially the Portuguese Communist Party) operated in the shadows in order to help their activists escape the clutches of the authorities. And over and above all this activity is the inevitability that young men would be called up for military service and dispatched to the colonies.

In the second section, "Savannah," we jump forward ten years to 1972. Here, the central figure is Vítor, now using the guerrilla sobriquet Worldly, one of the young Angolan idealists who had escaped Lisbon ten years previously. By this time, the MPLA had attempted to break out of its northern heartland, where it had been pinned back by the colonial army and a rival nationalist movement, the FNLA. It had opened up an Eastern Front, with its rear base in Zambia, and was trying to wage a guerrilla insurgency against the Portuguese forces in Central Angola. Vítor is making his way back to safety from deep within this Angolan hinterland, supposedly the only survivor of a small detachment of fighters. We follow him on this epic journey across open terrain and forest, the drama of his getting lost and ending up close to where he began, his fear of being captured by enemy forces. The most important feature of the narrative at this point are Vítor's memories—which give us glimpses into the lives of the other escapees from Lisbon ten years before, notably his fellow guerrilla fighter Aníbal, now known as Wisdom—and his inner thoughts about loyalty to the cause as opposed to the possible comforts and opportunities offered by surrender and integration into colonial society. As in *Mayombe*, the character's physical movement is also a philosophical journey through and around his conscience, as well as an evolving consideration about what Vítor sees as his role in the MPLA on its Eastern Front.

The third section, entitled "The Octopus," takes us forward another ten years. Angola is now independent under the MPLA but embroiled in a civil war with its rival movement, UNITA. The focus of the narrative here is the war hero, Aníbal, or Wisdom, whom we first met in Lisbon. In *Mayombe*, Fearless, the uncompromising guerrilla leader, had died in battle and been buried deep in the forest. In this novel, Aníbal/Wisdom, surely an iteration of Pepetela's first hero, survives, in spite of having gone missing and being assumed dead during the war. Unable to adapt to the realities of political life after independence, we find him living by the beach south of Benguela on a meagre military pension, supplementing his veteran's rations by fishing. While the central focus of this section is Aníbal's preparations to confront the monster that haunted his childhood dreams—the octopus that dwelt among the rocks when the future guerrilla leader spent his summer holidays at an uncle's house near the beach—the most important reencounter in this part is that between Aníbal and Sara, the white Angolan medical student he had known in Lisbon, for they are the couple with whom Pepetela might identify most closely. Aníbal, the Black Angolan idealist who overcame any particular regional or ethnic loyalty, who remains wedded to the ideals of equality and self-sacrifice, and who delivered his country into independence, and Sara, the doctor from a Judeo-Christian Portuguese colonial family, whose loyalty to the cause had been treated with suspicion by the MPLA leadership during the campaign against colonial rule and who had suffered accordingly. Both characters contain elements in their background and ideals that coincide with Pepetela's own personal and political experience: Aníbal's profound disillusion with the tangible results of struggle that had failed to root out individual ambition, petty corruption, and notions of hierarchy, and Sara's situation as a white Angolan.

In the final section, "The Temple," we are brought back to Luanda. The year is 1992. A peace accord has been signed, bringing to an end the civil war. (In reality, it dragged on for another ten years until the death of UNITA's leader, Jonas Savimbi). Political parties are allowed, capitalist enterprise is encouraged, and characters, some of whom we last saw thirty years before in the Casa, reappear in this nascent kleptocracy that Pepetela would go on to portray in later novels. Malongo—the former party-loving footballer, Vítor's roommate in Lisbon, and the father of Sara's child, Judite—returns as a budding entrepreneur. Elias, whom we met briefly as a student funded by a Protestant organization in Portugal, returns to Angola after years in the United States and West Africa, in order to set up his church. (It is, perhaps, no coincidence that the Brazilian Universal Church of the Kingdom of God was allowed to establish itself in Angola in the early 1990s.) Vítor is, by this time, a government minister, happy to oil the wheels of business, provided he is not exposed. And so, from *Mayombe*, which ended with the dream of a future utopia still intact, in spite of the debates over its impossibility, *The Utopian Generation* suggests a budding dystopia with some of the characteristics of the long-overthrown colonial regime re-emerging, reflected in the incident in which Malongo physically mistreats his houseboy for failing to season his scrambled eggs. Is there any hope for the future? There is a suggestion of a lingering ideal for social justice in the next generation, incarnated by Judite and her boyfriend, Orlando, but for now, the purity of belief among those who fought against colonialism has been sullied by the opportunists who have lurked among them since the beginning.

All writing represents challenges to the translator, and Pepetela is no exception. Unlike some Lusophone African writers, he is not a linguistic experimentalist, like his older compatriot, Luandino Vieira, whose work is characterized by an orality based on African storytelling techniques and a creolized Luanda speech pattern inspired by the mingling of Portuguese and Kimbundu, the main African language spoken in the area. To some extent, this tradition has been continued by other Angolan writers of a newer generation like Ondjaki, whose work is rich in the slang of Luanda. Pepetela's narrative is elliptical; his poetic imagery is simple and stripped down; his orality is that of the Socratic dialogues, or of the philosophical works they went on to inspire in the European Renaissance. Pepetela's novels of this period are replete with discussions about the intricacies of politics, about the contradictions of local and national identities, about individual ambition versus abnegation on behalf of the greater good. In many ways, the action of his novels progresses at the pace of these debates, whether held around a campfire in the middle of the forest, during lunch while overlooking the beach south of Benguela, in a student canteen back in Lisbon, or within the inner thoughts and memories of a character making his way across the savannah, deep-sea swimming, or sitting on a Lisbon bus. Debate and introspection are the lifeblood of Pepetela's novels, and nowhere more so than in *The Utopian Generation*. The challenge in translation is to preserve the vividness of this aspect of the writer's narrative technique and artistic prerogative.

At the same time, there are poetic moments in the memories of characters, such as when the young Vítor contemplates the

Angolan girl he has met at the beach in Lisbon: "Her laughter was like the sunset over the mountains of Huambo after the rain, when all the rainbows blend in with the pinkish purple and blue of the clouds, brushing the black rocks at the top of the green escarpments. Or else it was the crystal-clear water falling from the top of the Unguéria Falls mingling with the strange sounds of the pale violet-brown Namib Desert." But then sensing any mawkish intrusion, Vítor concludes, "Oh, I won't even try and describe her laughter," preferring to leave such things to those who profess to be poets. Pepetela's poetic descriptions are sparing, viewed through the characters whose attachment to Angola has gained them little or nothing in terms of political power or material gain. The two characters who reflect this spirit most closely are Sara and Aníbal. As a young girl leaving to further her studies, Sara leans on the rail of the ship carrying her away from Angola, watching the sights and sensing the smells of her homeland recede into the distance, and she wonders when she will return: "The ship had called in at Luanda for a day, and her father's relatives had taken her sightseeing. She had avidly taken in the whole atmosphere; she had tried to fix in her memory the red earth and the way it contrasted with the blueness of the sea, the tight curve of the bay and the green peninsula of the Ilha, the vast array of colours in the cloth worn by the market women, and their cries. She knew that her exile was about to begin. The unshakeable weight of exile made her weep as the ship sailed away from Luanda, the bay lit up at night. She stood for a long time at the ship's rail, gazing at and breathing in, one last time, the lights and smells of the land she was leaving behind." The scene reminds us that within less than a lifetime, the world has shrunk to a matter of hours on a jetliner rather than days or even weeks on a ship, and that separation from home was far more dramatic in the 1950s and '60s than it is now in our age of fast travel and instant communication.

At the end of the novel, as Aníbal travels up to Luanda on the back of a truck, for the first time since peace was declared, his wonder at the grandeur of Angolan nature is peppered with the sight of the relics of the long war: "We passed the mythical Keve, imagined on our right the Gabela Mountains in their eternal green, then entered the Kissama Park of all the lions, which, one must add, are no longer there, nor are the elephants or buffaloes, all eliminated by heroic weekend hunters, some of them even ferried there on helicopters. A country of plunderers, that's what we have become." In Pepetela's novel, there is always a practical purpose to poetic musings, just as there is to his storytelling. Ultimately, man's inhumanity to man is reflected in his abuse of the natural environment in which he lives, which is perhaps why the only utopia left is the sea, or as Sara puts it as she contemplates the former war hero: "She had a vision of Aníbal swimming out into the open seas, as straight as a die, in the direction of Brazil, without the strength or the will to struggle against the current that sucked him along."

In picking up this extraordinary novel set over a particular period of history in, for some, an unfamiliar part of Africa, the reader will engage with the eternal, universal questions affecting humankind in our own little corner of time: the unending quest for the purity of an ideal and a collective egalitarian spirit, amid the reality of individual ambition, greed, and the ugliness of politics.

DAVID BROOKSHAW
Bristol, January, 2024

THE UTOPIAN GENERATION

THE CASA
(1961)

I

So, only circles were eternal.

(In the oral exam for acceptance into the Arts Faculty in Lisbon, the examiner asked the future writer a question. He answered hesitantly, beginning with *so*. "Where are you from?" the professor asked, to which the writer answered from Angola. "I could see straightaway that you didn't know how to speak Portuguese; aren't you aware the word *so* can only be used to introduce a conclusion to a line of argument?" Just like that, to put the examinee at ease. That was why the author was so angry he swore he would one day start a book with this word. A promise fulfilled. And after this parenthesis, which sheds light on an unflagging thirty-year rancour, the author will now prudently and definitively conceal himself.)

It was a particularly hot, clear day for April in Lisbon. It had rained continuously since the previous evening, which was normal for this time of year, though today the sun had risen in a sky of such radiant blue that it pained one not to be able to fly. Sara opened her bare arms. It was no use; she hadn't been born a bird.

She decided to walk a bit, as far as the next bus stop, so as to enjoy the sun and the warmth. There were few people in the streets around the university hospital. Ungainly folk who were coming from or heading to the hospital. Worried about some real or imagined illness. If they are not ill, they worry about what they will catch in the future. The Portuguese are always in need of something to stoke their melancholia. And if it's not health, then it's family, or else their job. A sad people, Sara thought. Is it the political regime or people's nature? Let's not blame Salazar for everything. Salazar himself was already glum and drab before he created his drab regime. A regime full of priests and solemn military men, appropriate for a nation of peasants without much land. She shook herself, startled: weren't these ideas reactionary? She would have to ask Aníbal; he had a duty to be a specialist in such things. But it was true, the Portuguese were sad. How different from the exuberance and joy of the Africans, which make them seem irresponsible. But that wasn't true either. Aníbal, for example, ever clinging to his books and ideas, wasn't a joyful character. And he was from Luanda, the city of countless follies . . . Now Malongo, there was a cheerful soul, in fact too much so. Sara smiled up at the sky, at the people who didn't notice her, absorbed in their own selves.

She reached the bus stop. Two women were waiting, dressed in black with black headscarves. Have they come from a funeral or from the countryside? Maybe from mass. Or perhaps they are dressed like that because they are widows. Are they mourning relatives killed in Angola, during the uprising in the north? She dismissed the idea. Not as many have died as official propaganda has claimed. It is useful for Salazar to create a climate of mass hysteria, hundreds upon hundreds of whites hacked to pieces by the terrorists, Angola ablaze from end to end, the Portuguese and the fatherland had to be defended. "To Angola and in strength!" The propaganda was working, she had to admit. A dense cloud of suspicion hung over Africans in Lisbon. They started to mumble to each other, instead of arguing in loud voices punctuated by bursts of laughter. And the locals started to look at them with hostility. Not at Sara, who was white and therefore from the outset considered a good Portuguese. Black and mixed-race people were all but openly pointed at in cafés, cinemas. And in the street. They bore in their faces the stigma that denounced them as potential terrorists. These whites haven't yet invented a paint for us guys to colour ourselves and become like them, Malongo said, summoning up enough courage for a joke.

The bus arrived. Fortunately, it was a double-decker, and she was able to climb up to the top deck and get a better view of Lisbon basking in sunshine. She sat at the front and stretched out her legs. Campo Grande and the Avenida da República opened out at her feet. It's a pretty city, there's no doubt about that. She had to concede this, when almost everything about Lisbon displeased her. Then she modified her thoughts: It's not as if I know any other big cities with which I can compare it.

Born in Benguela, she had completed her secondary education at the high school in Lubango and come to Lisbon six years ago in order to study medicine. The ship had called in at Luanda for a day, and her father's relatives had taken her sightseeing. She had avidly taken in the whole atmosphere; she had tried to fix in her memory the red earth and the way it contrasted with the blueness of the sea, the tight curve of the bay and the green peninsula of the Ilha, the vast array of colours in the cloth worn by the market women, and their cries. She knew that her exile was about to begin. The unshakeable weight of exile made her weep as the ship sailed away from Luanda, the bay lit up at night. She stood for a long time at the ship's rail, gazing at and breathing in, one last time, the lights and smells of the land she was leaving behind. These impressions remained intact within her, continually rekindled by Angolans living in the capital of the empire. Do you remember Sofia from the Bairro Operário? one would ask. On her street, two houses along from her, isn't there a blue house in the BO, where Rita used to live? No, there are no blue houses in the BO; they're all yellow. Yes, there is. Rita's house is blue. And she would listen and see again the streets that she had visited only fleetingly, as if she had always lived there. The same thing happened with Benguela, Malanje, and the whole of Angola. Each person kept clutching to their memories of childhood, transmitting them to others, who then experienced them as if they were their own. And an ever more mythical idea of their distant homeland took shape, made up of jumbled impressions, in which the cadenced sound of the kissanje mingled with the fruits of the Central Highlands and the zebras of the Namib Desert. Distance endowed things with the veneer of perfection.

Those years were about discovering an absent homeland. And about her yearning for change. Conversations in the Casa dos Estudantes do Império, where the young coming from Africa met. Lectures and talks on the reality of the colonies. Her introduction to poems and short stories that suggested a different order. And right there, at the heart of the empire, Sara discovered the cultural differences between herself and the Portuguese. It was a long, disturbing journey. She came to the conclusion that the drum dances she had heard as a child pointed in another direction, which was not that of Portuguese fado. That her desire for medicine to be available to all was incompatible with the structures of colonialism, in which a few had access to everything while everyone else had nothing. That the alarming rate of child mortality in the colonies, though not a direct reflection of iniquitous policy, was nevertheless aggravated by it, while serving its purposes. She had expounded on these ideas in a joint presentation she had made with a Cape Verdean doctor the previous year. A discreet talk with carefully chosen words, which earned her loud applause at the end but also a summons from the political police, the PIDE. She was issued a warning. Now the PIDE have got a file on you, be careful, Aníbal advised. Her parents back in Benguela got wind of the incident, God knows how. And sure enough, a letter from home arrived: We're paying for you to study to be a doctor, not to defend communist ideas. Don't use such absurd adjectives; my ideas are rooted in fairness, she replied, knowing that she wouldn't convince them.

Absorbed in her recollections, she was unaware of the city around her. She got off at the corner of the Duque de Ávila and proceeded toward the Arco do Cego. She passed the Casa dos Estudantes and went into the Café Rialva, an obligatory meeting point. She greeted the owner, Senhor Evaristo, a pleasant, ruddy-faced man, and looked around at the tables. These were all taken up by students waiting for lunch hour at the Casa's canteen. Malongo wasn't there. Vítor Ramos waved to her, and she went over.

"Hello, Vítor. Have you seen Malongo?"

"Take a seat, Sara. He went off to training this morning. He should be on his way. Are you going to have lunch with us?"

"He was supposed to pick me up in front of the hospital. As usual, he got delayed. I might eat with you, though I already had something at home."

Vítor Ramos, who would one day assume the name Worldly, lived with Malongo in a shared room rented from a lady on the Rua Praia da Vitória. Malongo had arrived first some four years earlier, in order to play soccer and study. He had managed to get signed by a big club, Benfica, and had rented the room. But he wasn't able to break into the first team, and the money wasn't great. With the constant training, he stopped studying. His friends urged him to finish secondary school at least. It never happened. He regularly failed his graduation exams. Vítor arrived a year later. Malongo got on well with him and suggested they share his room, which would be cheaper for both of them. The lady accepted a small supplement to the rent, saying, I'm very fond of Black boys. Sometimes they're a bit noisy, but they're good at heart. Vítor seemed to be following in his older companion's footsteps and failed his first-year veterinary exams. He managed to pass his retake exam but failed the second year.

Looks like it's the curse of the Rua Praia da Vitória, Malongo said. We'd better burn some magic herbs to placate the evil spirits.

Sara asked how his studies were going, to which he replied, as he always did, that they were going well. Then he asked her the same question, hearing the answer he already knew: that she would graduate in July, provided there were no major disasters.

"Now we really will be able to call you doctor. And that's good because you'll be able to treat us."

Which was what she already did. Not only did she help the Casa's doctor during his regular surgery hours, but she also gave the odd friend advice right there in the café. She and the other medical students in their final year. At first, she did so apprehensively, conscious of the heavy burden of responsibility, but later she became more sure of herself. She had gained this confidence from Dr. Arménio, the Casa's doctor who, although a man who liked to laugh, knew how to be serious when required. So she did a double clinical internship, both at the hospital and at the Casa. She preferred the latter, that was for sure. Because she was treating her own people. And because of the personality of Dr. Arménio, a self-declared nationalist who didn't charge Africans for consultations.

"Malongo's very late," she said. "Training doesn't go on for so long."

"He must have had something else to do. Relax, he'll turn up for lunch."

Vítor seemed awkward when the conversation turned to Malongo. He must be hiding something. What's Malongo up to? Certainly not politics—he doesn't join in anything, just shoots his mouth off occasionally. Meeting a girl? He's perfectly capable of that, the rat. She didn't like the idea. Oh, it's probably some trivial matter; I'm not going to make a big deal out of it.

"But are you really studying, Vítor? You've got exams coming up."

"Well, I've been studying. But lately, you know, with everything going on, very few of us can really study. You can't stop thinking and thinking ... Your mind is on other things."

"Yes, it's not the best time to be preparing for exams. But we've got to. We've got to make an effort."

She wasn't finding it easy either, especially when it came to preparing the report on her internship. What's really happening back home? What's the truth and what's propaganda put out by the regime? And how are my parents back home, faced with a war? Because whatever the government says, it is all about a war. The pages of the newspapers were filled, but there was little actual information. The censors were working overtime, their scissors had never been as busy as now. The papers were full of jingoistic rhetoric—Portugal is one nation and indivisible—of declarations of support for the regime, but there was nothing concrete about what was actually happening. They were aware there had been an uprising in the north in the name of the previously unknown UPA organization, and they knew of Lumumba, which boded well for the future.

It had all begun on March 15. No, before that, on February 4, there was an attack on the prisons in Luanda to free political prisoners. This was followed by an atrocious crackdown in Luanda, with talk of thousands of nationalists being killed. But here, there was mystery as well: who had carried out these actions, and what was their objective? After that, everything blew up in the north. An uprising against the whites, in which coffee planters were killed and villages sacked. That, at least, was what government propaganda had claimed. Information gathered from other sources by students confirmed the government's version. But couldn't this just be euphoria? What was certain was that no one knew anything about this UPA group apart from its wish to expel all whites and mulatos from Angola. Sara could not agree with its aims. Neither did any of her friends; what they wanted was a political program with a clear long-term vision. They spent their days talking and swapping ideas, conjecturing. Was it really possible to do any studying? For Vítor, it was certainly worse. He came from Huambo, from where there was no news of any great upheavals. But repression must be occurring there as well. And he was suffering from the racism that had been intensified by propaganda in Portugal. Sara patted his hand.

"Of course it's not easy. But you're a greater help to your homeland by studying than by being dejected, doing nothing but speculating."

"I know," he said with a smile. "Hey, I didn't offer you anything. Do you want a coffee?"

"No, don't worry. Besides, here comes Malongo."

In he came with his familiar sauntering gait. He was tall, well built, an open smile on his face. He slapped the café owner on the back. "How are those old bones of yours, Senhor Evaristo?" And he almost made the fellow drop his tray. Keeping his balance, while holding his tray full of coffees, Evaristo smiled. "Hey, watch what you're doing or you'll smash the place up." But even if the coffees had ended up on the floor, the proprietor would have forgiven him, for weren't they both for Benfica? Malongo came over to the table and gave Sara a hearty kiss on the lips, while she complained, "I've been waiting for you."

"Yes, I know. But I met someone from back home on the bus, whom I hadn't seen for ages, and he was telling me about Malanje. We stopped for a beer. He'd just come back from there. I'm sorry, but I just had to hear some news."

He might be telling the truth, Sara thought to herself. With Malongo, you never knew where the lying or the joking started. Vítor immediately probed him about what he had just said. "So there's war around Malanje?" Maybe he was trying to deflect the conversation.

"Well, he left before the fighting started. He left in February.

There were loads of people being put in prison in Malanje and in Luanda. Riquito, a friend of mine, was arrested in Malanje. Before that, Baixa de Cassanje was bombed from the air. Lots of people were killed. He says people in Luanda are alarmed: the whites because of the Blacks, and the Blacks because of the whites. Whites are dismissing their Black servants because they're scared they might poison them."

"And what about UPA?" Sara asked.

"He knows as much as we do. He only heard about it here."

"So who carried out the attacks in Luanda in February? Wasn't he there then?"

"He doesn't know anything. Some priest was rumoured to be the leader. But everyone was scared, no one said anything. It's all very hush-hush ... It looks as if Sporting Luanda are going to win the championship. They've got a young player there who's a rising star."

"Let's stop talking about soccer and go eat," said Sara.

They crossed the road and went into the Casa dos Estudantes. The canteen was on the first floor. They made their way through the tables, greeting those who were already sitting. Aníbal waved to them from a table at the back. They sat down with him. Malongo immediately asked him, "In Lisbon at this hour, Aníbal? Have you deserted or what?"

"I managed to get two days' leave. I've got a couple of things to see to."

Aníbal, who would later be known as Wisdom, was a trainee junior officer. He had finished his degree in the history of philosophy the year before and had gone off to do his obligatory military service. After presenting himself at the Mafra recruitment office, he was assigned to an infantry unit near Lisbon. Every week, he would drop in at the Casa to see his friends. As always, he was in civilian clothes. Uniform was only for the barracks, he would say, uneasy in his role as a soldier.

Sara asked for news from home.

"I don't know much. Only that there are more and more ships leaving, loaded with soldiers. A bunch of officers who were recruited at the same time as me have already gone, and others are being mobilized. Entire units are on their way."

"So what about you?" Malongo asked. "Are you going too?"

"My unit hasn't been mobilized yet."

"And if it is? Are you going as well?"

"That's not the type of question you should ask, Malongo," he answered curtly. "In the barracks, there's talk of a counter-offensive to win back control of the whole north. They are concentrating troops in Luanda ready to advance on the Dembos, which is where the situation is really ugly. But it's still going to take a bit of time. You can't gather enough troops in just a couple of days to take back the entire north, which is two or three times the size of Portugal. And those forests . . . I had an uncle in Nambuangongo; I used to spend my holidays with him sometimes. It's just one forest after another. A well-organized group of guerrillas could hold out there forever."

"Any news of your uncle?" Sara asked.

"My parents haven't heard anything. In fact, it doesn't look like anyone in Luanda knows a thing. He had a small coffee plantation, just a tiny patch that was always under threat from his neighbours, Portuguese planters who kept trying to grab his bit of land. We know that UPA is attacking those working for white planters, most of whom are from Huambo, where our friend Vítor here comes from. But I don't know whether they're also attacking local Black planters."

"He may have joined UPA," Vítor said.

"Who knows?" said Aníbal. "But tell me, Malongo. Your Benfica are going to get trounced up in Porto, aren't they?"

"Get off it! Benfica are at the top of their game. Even though I can't even get on the subs' bench. That's what I can't understand.

I'm always training, I'm in great shape. But they just stick me in the reserves. I must be cursed."

The conversation drifted off into soccer, fed by Aníbal and Malongo. Sara understood: Aníbal didn't want to talk about serious matters with the others. As far as he was concerned, Malongo was just a soccer player, with not much in the way of ideas in his head. He had told her this bluntly one day, when she had started going out with the boy from Malanje. I don't understand, Sara, what you, almost a doctor, see in that guy. Okay, he's nice enough, and maybe even good looking, but he's so empty-headed... Sara had known Aníbal ever since she had arrived in Lisbon. At one point, she even thought their relationship might go beyond mere friendship. But he never tried anything with her, and as the tradition was that the male had to take the initiative, they remained as they were. Lots of talk, trips to the movies, nothing more. With regard to Vítor, for Aníbal he was just a kid with an unformed character; he could explain a few things to him, but he didn't venture into more intimate matters. He only opened up with her. Sara withdrew from the conversation about soccer, which didn't interest her in the slightest, and sat contemplating the dining room.

All the tables were now occupied by groups of four. Most were Angolans, white, Black, and mixed race—these latter the most numerous—mingling together. The Cape Verdeans, who consorted freely with the Angolans, were almost exclusively mixed race. There were fewer Guineans and São Toméans, and they were Black. The Mozambicans were all white. And they tended to stick together. A table made up only of whites was immediately assumed to be from Mozambique. The British colony, as the Angolans would ironically refer to it. Of course, there were exceptions, such as that table at which Belmiro, a Black Guinean, sat with three white Mozambicans. But that was because Belmiro had arrived late, and the only place left was at that table. If he could choose, he would have gone to another, if only because the conversation on the Mozambican table became more inhibited than usual. The Angolans didn't have such problems, in spite of recent events. At the same time, she felt, a barrier was beginning to make itself felt ever so subtly; something hard to define was driving people apart, tending to push some white Angolans toward the groups of Mozambicans. Was race beginning to count more than geographical origin? Oh, I'm starting to imagine things. Had she herself not noticed, when she approached some groups of Angolans, expressions becoming more guarded, conversations falling silent? Yes, it was true. It was inevitable. Angola was fast heading toward a racial war, where there was selective repression. And this provoked repercussions in Lisbon.

With lunch over, the four of them went to the Rialva. Malongo ordered three coffees for the others and a yogurt for himself. An athlete wasn't supposed to drink coffee or wine. He was sticking to these principles because he wanted to be a star player for Benfica. But the club didn't know about his smoking; he just couldn't kick the habit. When Sara made clear the inconsistency of such behaviour, he laughed. You smoke, so I've got to as well, otherwise it'd be horrible when I kiss you because I'd be able to smell the smoke on your breath. And he would have a few glasses of beer. That doesn't do any harm; beer is low in alcohol.

Not long afterwards, Vítor said goodbye, I've got to study, and Malongo took the opportunity to leave with him, after arranging to meet Sara at six, as he didn't have training that afternoon. She agreed, and he kissed her. The two of them left. After a short silence, Aníbal asked her how things were going with Malongo.

"They're going okay. Well . . . One's always on tenterhooks with him. He comes and goes, doesn't turn up, he's always got something mysterious going on. But he's sweet, and he's trying hard to be a proper professional."

"Yes, he seems to take his soccer seriously. I'm no expert, but I'm surprised he hasn't broken into the first team."

"He's really serious about it. Soccer is his life. And music. He bought a guitar and he's now learning to play it on the quiet. It's quite possible that the reason why he's so busy now is that he's got to go and practise his guitar. The other day, the same thing happened. I phoned him at home to confirm our date. And the landlady said he was in his room because she could hear the sound of his guitar. When I ask him, he says, Oh I'm just learning one or two little things. He'll only come out and tell us when he's learned how to play properly."

Aníbal then invited her to go for a stroll with him downtown. She was supposed to be working on her final dissertation, which she would be examined on in July, but she agreed. One afternoon wasn't going to cause serious delay. They caught a bus and contemplated the busy movement of the avenues in silence. There were a lot of people wandering around, taking advantage of the afternoon sun. They got off on the Avenida da Liberdade, so as to walk to the downtown Baixa area.

He took the initiative. "I wanted to talk to you alone."

"I thought as much," she said with a laugh.

"The situation is really serious. A complete crackdown, the PIDE going crazy. They're bound to be closely monitoring the Casa in their investigations. It'll be their main target at this point. It's a good idea to avoid talking about more serious matters in both the Casa and the Rialva. Did you notice that guy with the hat sitting next to us in the café? He doesn't fool anybody. Back at the barracks, I get the feeling I'm being watched. There's always someone hanging around, and the other day, my bookshelf had been messed with. My books were all neatly arranged, but not in the same order I always leave them."

"So, did you have any dangerous books there?"

"With those guys, you never know what's suspect when it comes to books. I've got *Autopsy of the United States* by Matthias there, for example. Sartre's *Dirty Hands*. Philosophy and history books of all inclinations. Zamora's *Historical Process*, that one's Marxist. But would they even be aware?"

"But don't start looking behind you all the time to see who's following you . . ."

"I may be paranoid. But they certainly rifled through my books, of that I'm sure. Just as I'm almost certain there must be PIDE informers at the Casa. And I'll throw myself under a train if that guy with the hat isn't a police snoop."

"Yes, we need to be careful. They'll have their eye on us, that's inevitable."

"There's an atmosphere of suspicion in the army. Every day, there are long patriotic speeches, lectures directed at the conscript officers, et cetera. They know the vast majority of non-career officers, all university people, are against the war. Some more progressive than others, but all of them against it. But which are the officers who are going to be sent to war? It'll be the conscripts, because there's almost no one else. That explains why they're giving us such tender loving care, with talks, speeches, and PIDE spooks to keep an eye on us all."

"Is that why you asked for leave, without waiting for the weekend?"

"Yes, it was partly because of that. You need to warn people to take care. But I also got a letter from abroad, don't ask me who from. There's talk of another party out there."

He looked over his shoulder and then either side. The sidewalk down the avenue was very wide and there were few people around; they could talk without any concern.

"It's led by Mário de Andrade and Viriato da Cruz, at least outside the country. It's said it was they who organized the attacks on the prisons in Luanda. It's called the Popular Movement for the Liberation of Angola, the MPLA."

"What a devil of a name! M-P-L-A. UPA sounds better and is easier."

"Forget the name. That doesn't matter. It's the program that's important."

"So what is it?"

"They're going to send it to me. But he told me in his letter I should warn people about UPA, which is a northern tribal movement, and racist to boot. Nothing good will come of it. Mário and Viriato are already well-known, two major thinkers, and they offer far greater guarantees of substance."

"Of course. Wow! I feel relieved. You can't imagine how relieved I feel!"

"That's what I felt, too, which is why I came to warn you. Having to choose between colonialism and UPA, really . . . Well, I suppose UPA is the lesser of two evils."

They both laughed. Sara especially. She hadn't laughed so hard for a long time. It was the sun, the presence of her friend, the news he had brought. Her worries vanished; a weight was lifted from her mind. She looked at Aníbal, who was happy at her joy, and she laughed again. He joined in, albeit more soberly. They were approaching the Praça dos Restauradores, and there were more people, even on the central sidewalk. She put her arm through his, so that they could talk quietly.

"Isn't it risky for you to get letters through the mail? They inspect everything and you've been on their watch list for ages."

"The letters reach me by a safe route."

Aníbal was short and lean, not much taller than her. He had deep-set eyes and thin lips and nose. To those who didn't know him, he gave an impression of frailty. However, she knew he was the opposite; he possessed a huge reservoir of inner strength. He had managed to complete his degree, paid for by a grant from a Protestant church, had achieved outstanding results, often defending ideas that were the complete opposite of those of his teachers.

He had gained fame in the university community, and many people, even from other programs, would come and attend his public viva voce exams, sensing that they would be polemical. The audience was rarely disappointed. Faced with the strength of his arguments, teachers had no choice but to award him the highest marks, despite his progressive positions. His final dissertation was an apparent provocation, an analysis of nineteenth-century colonial policy, in which he demonstrated that the Portuguese state had destroyed the Angolan bourgeoisie, which had been developing an awareness of its difference and evolving toward an aspiration to autonomy inspired by the principles of the French Revolution.

He was, of course, summoned on various occasions by the PIDE. As they were unaware of his involvement in political activities, they limited themselves to intimidation, and they waited to pounce at the first opportunity. Aníbal was extremely careful, but Sara suspected that he had links with a clandestine organization, probably the Portuguese Communist Party. She had never asked him, for during the course of her twenty-four years, she had learned that there were secrets one should not pursue.

"Even so, you're worried," Sara said.

At this stage, after having given his main piece of news, he would normally have embarked on some harmless, though always interesting, subject. If he felt they needed to be discreet, they would have turned round and walked back up the Avenida da Liberdade. Not so today. He walked on in silence. This was a sign that he was worried.

"Can't I hide anything from you?"

"Look, I know you. Can't you tell me? If you can't, just say no, and we'll go and see a movie."

After some hesitation, he said, "Of course I can. Yes, I'm worried." He lowered his voice. "Sooner or later my unit is going to be mobilized. As for me, what am I going to do? It's not a question of me, and what's better or worse for me, but for our homeland."

"I don't understand."

"One option is to go with the unit and work as a sapper. Sabotage, do you understand? This could help mobilize Angolans in the struggle against colonialism and help stop Portuguese civilians massacring Blacks. But I ask myself whether a Black officer would have such freedom to act, because I'm bound to be closely watched. The other option . . ."

By now, they were passing crowds of people in the Rossio, and any word uttered a little too loudly might be heard and interpreted by some informer or other. All the more so because the couple stood out: it wasn't common to see a Black man and a white woman walking arm in arm in the streets of Lisbon. That was why he whispered in her ear. "Desert, run away. Cross over to the other side. I'd probably be of greater use."

"Is that possible?"

"Maybe. But I'd need time. And I've got to decide now in order to prepare things. If it's possible . . ."

"How much notice will you get of your departure?"

"A week at the most. Which doesn't leave much time."

They fell silent, avoiding running into people hurrying along the Rossio to catch the Metro or a bus, or women with children busy shopping.

"Can I buy you a ginjinha?" he asked her suddenly. "I'm rich. For someone who studied on a scholarship, an officer's pay gives me money to burn."

"That would be nice," she said.

They went into a tavern that was well-known for its cherry liqueur. It was a narrow drinking den that could scarcely accommodate ten people. He ordered two glasses.

"With or without the fruit?" asked the barman.

"With, with," replied Sara, laughing.

They drank, standing at the bar, like all the customers. They fished the cherries out with a toothpick and spat the stones onto the floor, which was all part of the ritual. Just as it was part of the ritual in the Amazonas Bar on the Arco do Cego to drop the skins of the lupin beans onto the floor, so that by the end of the night it was carpeted with them. They left the bar and walked round the Rossio in silence.

When they reached Restauradores, he said, "I've just remembered something. Have I already told you that when I was a kid, I went to your part of the country? Yes, I must have done. I went to spend my holidays at an uncle's house in Benguela."

"Like a good native of Luanda, you've got uncles in all corners of Angola."

"Luandans get around. To civilize the barbarians . . . I've also got relatives in Lubango, but I've never been there. But when I was in Benguela, I got taken to a beach to the south of the city. Caota."

"I know it. They catch a lot of fish there."

"That's it. What you may not know is Caotinha, a little cove next to it, on the other side of the hill. It's hard to get to. You can only reach it on foot or by jeep.

"I've heard people talk about it. They say it's incredible."

"It's fabulous," he said. "The water's clear but cold. Just hills and the sea. Sand and boulders, a small bay, and full of fish. Wonderful. Anyway, I went diving there. You've got to believe me. I came face to face with a gigantic octopus when I was down below exploring the depths. I got the biggest fright of my life. I don't know how I got ashore, I don't remember a thing. The only thing that stuck with me was the image of that terrifying octopus, with all its tentacles turned toward me. Even now, when I have nightmares, that octopus appears. Some people dream they're in free fall, others dream of the dead, I dream of that creature. Anyway, I swore that one day I'd go back there, properly equipped, and kill the octopus."

"Maybe it wasn't as big as you thought."

"It might have been a child's imagination. It might not have been Jules Verne's *Nautilus*. But it was certainly huge."

They had returned to the Avenida da Liberdade, where they could talk again more freely.

"Yesterday, I dreamed of that octopus."

"And so?"

"Nothing. It just means I'm worried. What do you advise me to do?"

"You're asking me? All I can do is help you think things through."

"That would be a great help. I might not follow your advice, of course. And I'll ask others. But I'd like your opinion."

It wasn't a problem she had ever had to face, not least because women weren't called up for military service, not even women doctors. But one idea appalled her, and she expressed it carefully, choosing her words.

"I don't see you disembarking in Luanda and parading down the Marginal at the head of your company. What will people say? 'That fellow Aníbal used to preach out loud, but in the end, here he is, ready to kill his Black brothers.' That's what people will think."

"That's just histrionics. It doesn't matter what people think of me. I'll be making myself useful, operating undercover, organizing groups, maybe stealing weapons for those who are fighting. I can't yet tell what I'll be able to do, but when I'm there, I'll know."

"Well then, you've made up your mind to go . . ."

"Nonsense! It's just one possibility, that's all."

"It's the easier of the two. I find the other more to my taste."

"It may be the easier of the two now. But once I'm there, it'll be the hardest. The other option, to run away, is the most difficult now, because it involves considerable organization. Afterwards, it'll be easier, because I'll be able to fight for my country directly. In the meantime, what can I do outside the country? Just stay put and watch things happen?"

"There will always be things to do. Others out there have already done things, according to what you told me a little while ago. Why not you? You've got military training. That might be useful. And you've got ideas, which is even more important."

"You may be right, I don't know. I need to ask a few other people..."

"I wouldn't think twice. I'd desert right away. There are ways and means of getting to France, everyone knows that. It may not be easy, but the means exist."

He remained silent, in the throes of his dilemma.

After a little while, Sara asked, "What are you going to do?"

"I don't know yet."

"But you've got to decide fast, you said so yourself."

They continued to stroll along, without returning to the subject. It was a glorious afternoon, and she was determined to enjoy the sun and the company. What else mattered? Her misgivings about Malongo were far from her thoughts, even more so her worries about her finals. And as for the situation in Angola, there was now a tiny glimmer of hope. She had a right to draw a deep breath and enjoy the friendship of Aníbal, who always gave her a sense of security even though he seemed so fragile and insecure, especially today. Sara savoured the fresh air voluptuously and pressed up more closely against her companion.

2

Training had gone well. In the last session, they had made him play in the first team, slotted in with Benfica's star players. It was a pity he'd missed that goal due to his nerves. But apart from that, his performance had been satisfactory, and at the end, the coach had told him, "We've got a grown man here, Malongo, we've got a man." Did that mean they would play him on Sunday? There was still going to be one more training session together, so they hadn't reached a decision yet. At least he might be promoted to the substitutes' bench, waiting for his chance when a teammate pulled up injured or had an off day. If they'd only give him a chance, he'd show them what he was worth on the field. He was at the stop, waiting for his bus, when Arsénio drove by from training in his new car. Arsénio stopped and offered him a lift. Malongo accepted and got in.

"If you're passing the Alameda, you can drop me there."

Arsénio was also an Angolan and an established favourite after two years in the first team. He occasionally turned up at the Casa dos Estudantes, though he led a very unassuming life devoted to his family. He was always calm and was a respected voice among the students because of his advice, despite his lack of schooling. His wife affectionately called him a quiet old pussycat, because he very rarely showed his claws. And he was like a cat, too, on the field in the way he deftly juggled the ball.

"The coach was happy with you. I think you'll be in the first team on Sunday."

"Have you heard anything?"

"No, he never says anything out loud. But I think you'll make your first start if you train tomorrow like you did today. We're playing at home, the opposition isn't much good, and it's a great opportunity for him to give you a run out."

"I just want him to give me a chance."

They were silent for a while. Arsénio turned on the radio and concentrated on the traffic. Malongo mulled over every word he had said. The other guy was an experienced club player and wasn't going to talk just for the sake of it. He might even influence the coach in that gentle way of his, during an idle moment of conversation. His chance was coming up, and he mustn't let it get away.

"Could you put in a word for me, maybe?" said Malongo.

"Don't you think I already have? More than once. But Otto Glória has got his ideas. He's always watching his players and doesn't let himself be influenced. If he doesn't play someone, it doesn't mean that player isn't as good as the others. It's just that his style of play may not fit in with his particular game plan. Then, all of a sudden, he'll bring someone into the first team. And that's it, he either makes a success of it or goes to the dogs."

Malongo didn't say anything. This is a nice car. This guy Arsénio must be rolling in money. A flash of envy put an end to his good mood from training. Not to worry, I'll buy a Mercedes yet. And then I'll be able to drive around with a car full of girls, treating them to snacks in the best patisseries. With his name hitting the sports headlines, "Malongo Beats Sporting All by Himself" or "Malongo Makes All the Difference to Benfica." He sat back in the car seat, watching the billboards drift by.

"The training session tomorrow will be the clincher," Arsénio said. "Just focus on that. Don't worry about anything, and get an early night. No parties, no beer."

Malongo lit a cigarette. His companion pulled a face.

"And none of that."

He threw the cigarette out the window in an automatic gesture of obedience. Arsénio smiled. That's it, good lad. They had reached the Alameda, now bedecked in its spring colours.

"Wouldn't you rather I left you at the Casa? It's all the same to me."

"No, here's fine. Thanks for the lift."

"Focus on the training. Take good care, and no parties."

Malongo got out of the car. Why was he going on so much about parties? Otto Glória had once told him a soccer player should lead a regular life. Could it be the club's view that he thought too much about partying? Was that why he was stuck in the reserves until he came to his senses? One of the directors had also given him a lecture. Without being specific, he had nevertheless given him to understand that they didn't much like his propensity for late nights. If that's the case, they're being unfair, Malongo thought. All right, he never missed a dance at the Casa and would dance until morning. He was a regular at the bashes thrown by the Maritime Club, originally founded by African sailors in Lisbon. But never before a soccer match. The reserves played their games on Saturdays, and it was only afterwards that he would go to a party. All right, once or twice a game had been played on a Sunday morning, and he had gone dancing the night before. His legs had quit on him, and he'd had to be substituted before the first half had even ended. But that had only happened on a couple of occasions. And he didn't overdo the beer, just a few to keep himself hydrated. He never drank wine. Hell! A player isn't made of stone; he needs to have a bit of fun.

He went into the Pão de Açúcar, a café popular with students, where he knew he would find Denise. He walked over to her table with the coolest swagger he could muster. The blond laughed and pointed to a chair.

"How did the training go?"

She was French and in Lisbon to perfect her Portuguese, which she spoke reasonably well. She lived in a room nearby and spent her time studying in the Pão de Açúcar.

Malongo had been obliged to revise the idea he had of French girls. They went to the movies together sometimes, and one day he went back to her room but they didn't get beyond kissing and petting. When he took her to bed, she allowed him to fondle her breasts and touch her private parts, but she refused to get undressed. Weren't French girls supposed to be free and easy? On a second occasion, it had been in his room. Vítor went for a walk to leave them alone, and he was more persistent, and she eventually stripped as far as her panties. But Denise would only allow him to rub his penis against her pudenda outside her panties. I'm not ready for this, please try and understand. They had been doing this for a month. And he was ever more anxious and insistent.

"Shall we go to a movie this afternoon?"

"I've got classes. Shall we go to the six-thirty show?"

They arranged to meet there a little while before, and he went off to have lunch at the Casa. He had once again missed his meeting with Sara. And today of all days, when he had some good news to give her. She'd be happy to hear he would probably be making his debut in the first team next Sunday. He felt a few pangs of remorse, which he brushed aside. Denise was twenty and a real babe for heaven's sake; he couldn't throw away the chance of screwing a French girl. Sara would understand. Not his intentions with regard to Denise, but his not having turned up. She would go looking for him, and he would come up with an excuse. Sara was a few months older and a bit motherly, which was why she had to accept these faults of his. But if she found out about Denise . . . That was why he kept his little adventures on the side well under wraps. He never took the French girl to the Casa, even though she had asked him to a number of times, out of curiosity, so she said, to see the beating heart of the African revolution in Lisbon. And the meetings in the café were quick and almost formal, for there were members of the Casa who also frequented the Pão de Açúcar and might talk. Vítor was the only one who knew, and he helped him cover things up. He was a good friend, old Vítor, in spite of the fact that he was from Huambo. He took after his father, a Kimbundu from Golungo, who had been exiled to Huambo as a nurse.

It had also been difficult with Sara. They had gone out together for months before she had allowed things to get more serious. But eventually it happened, and he slept in her room twice a week. This was luxury accommodation for a student. A large room with its own separate entrance and a private bathroom, which was very rare in Lisbon. Of course, she paid a lot for it. She was the daughter of a wealthy trader, had a generous monthly allowance, and she could afford certain luxuries. Including that of putting her landlady in her place when she complained one day upon seeing Malongo leave her room early in the morning. Now, relations between the two women were limited to the bare minimum. The Portuguese woman was deeply shocked that Sara, a doctor, could be sleeping with a Black man. And under her roof. But it wasn't easy to find someone who could pay for such an expensive room. She swallowed her scruples and turned a blind eye. But she no longer asked Sara how her parents were or whether her studies at university were going well. Only when she was suffering from some ache or pain did she come and ask for advice. And she often had pains, for she was elderly and her joints hurt her. That was another advantage of having Sara in her house.

Malongo went straight to the Casa, sat down at an empty table, and began eating. Later, Vítor turned up. No, Sara hadn't come looking for him. On the one hand, that was better, he had some free time. But deep down, he didn't like it. Before others sat down at the same table, he was able to confide in Vítor. "Today I'm taking Denise to a movie, and it's now or never."

"You should be more careful about Sara. It's starting to rile."

He didn't answer because at that point Horácio arrived. He was a mulato who had published some poems in the Casa's *Bulletin*, which were considered quite good for a novice, with the result that he now never missed an opportunity to monopolize debates about literature. Malongo listened to Horácio's theories about the influence of Brazilian writers on young Angolan literati. He wasn't paying much attention, but that didn't matter because Horácio didn't discuss things; he just talked to himself. Vítor also seemed to have his mind on other things, eating slowly, without looking up from his plate. Then Furtado turned up. He was white and from Uíje, and desperate for news from his parents, coffee planters in the north—a region engulfed by the March rebellion. Before, Furtado used to openly talk about the need for Angolan independence. He had even had problems with the PIDE for speaking out. But now that the struggle for independence had affected his family directly, he had become more moderate. Horácio stopped his literary monologue to ask whether he had received any news about his parents.

"No, nothing. They must have been faced with a whole bunch of problems, for sure. If they had managed to flee to Luanda, they would have written by now. They must still be on the plantation, alive or dead."

"Or in town," said Vítor. "Is the plantation far from town?"

"It's twenty kilometres from Negaje."

"They must have escaped to Negaje," said Vítor. "And it can't be easy to send letters from there. The place must be completely cut off."

"Yes, maybe. But all that was more than a month ago. You're probably right, Vítor. I hope so anyway."

"Negaje has come under attack," Horácio said, rubbing salt in the wound. "Only yesterday, the papers were talking about the attacks on Negaje, which have so far been unsuccessful. But defence is almost entirely in the hands of the settlers, because there are practically no soldiers. The town must be completely isolated and could fall at any moment—"

"Stop it," Malongo interrupted. "We need to think positively. They're in Negaje, and they're safe. In a few days, you'll get news from them, Furtado. It's no good letting things get to you."

Horácio didn't like being contradicted, but he realized that this was not a good topic of conversation. He returned to literature, advising the others to read Carlos Drummond de Andrade, as far as he was concerned, the best poet in the Portuguese language of all time. To hell with Camões, to hell with Pessoa; Drummond was the man, it was all there in his work. Even the situation in Angola could be inferred from his poetry. "This is why I'm telling you people, the Portuguese spend their time inculcating us with their poetry, we have to study it at school, and they hide the Brazilians from us, our brothers, sublime poets and writers of prose, who depict problems we can identify with and in an idiom that is much more familiar to us than the language we speak in the cities. Whoever hasn't read Drummond is an ignoramus."

The others went on eating, occasionally exchanging conspiratorial glances. Until Malongo and Vítor finished their lunch. Malongo got up and took his leave. "This ignoramus hails you." Vítor and Furtado laughed; Horácio pretended he hadn't heard. He grabbed Furtado's arm and went on regaling him with Drummond's verses along with his own, dedicated to the great Brazilian.

"He's a brainbox," Malongo said once they were outside. "He can talk for two hours about literature and still not get tired."

"He's a pain in the butt, that's what he is," Vítor said.

And they went home, without dropping in at the café. Vítor

tried to do some studying while Malongo, reclining on his bed, practised his guitar. Sara phoned at five o'clock, and Malongo made his excuses. He had remembered an important matter that had to be seen to without delay, which meant that they would only be able to meet up the next day. At six, he set off in his best clothes to meet Denise. Vítor shook his head in silent disapproval. Up yours, pal, I'm not going to turn down a French chick like that. Today's my big day: great in training and it'll be great in bed.

Denise was waiting for him. She was wearing a white summer dress, in response to the fine weather. Her blond hair cascaded in locks, and her short dress showed off her shapely legs. It's got to be today, Malongo thought, as he crossed the road toward her, his eyes taking in every detail of the body he lusted after.

He chose seats in the back row so that they would feel at ease. Only when the lights went down did he take her hand. And only when the feature film began did he start caressing her, first her arms, then her legs. There were few people in the theatre, and the back rows were completely empty. As they kissed, they forgot the film. And in the face of his persistence, she gradually opened her legs, allowing his hand to caress her inner thighs. When he touched her most intimate parts, she groaned and slid down in her seat until she was almost lying down. Her legs parted more widely as she offered herself up. He began to stroke her vulva with two fingers, through her panties, while at the same time kissing her. Until her first gasps began, silent because their mouths were glued to each other. She tried to react, but he kept rubbing her gently. Her orgasm was long and juddering. She lay shaking in her seat, her teeth biting his thick lips. When Denise calmed down and he drew his mouth away from hers, she murmured, "Si bon, si bon." Her hand felt for his penis, which was trying to burst through his trousers. But he brushed her hand away. "I don't get off like that. I want to make love to you."

Denise sat up straight and watched the film in silence. A

little while later, she whispered, "It's not fair. I came so hard . . . I want you to come too."

"I don't get my kicks like that. I'm old school: it's the real thing or nothing."

The film was an American love story. They watched it for a while, and then she said all right, let's go back to my room.

They left the auditorium in the darkness, him holding her close so as to guide her to the corridor. Once in the street, they walked quickly, hand in hand, oblivious to whoever might see them. They almost charged up the stairs of her building. And she was so out of breath she could hardly fit the key in the lock. At last, she got the door open. I knew today was my day, thought Malongo, as he went in, holding her close for the rest of the night.

3

The protest march was set to start at Arroios. From there, it would proceed downtown to the Baixa area, where it would join up with others from elsewhere in the city. Sara had been busy at the Casa beforehand, organizing fellow marchers. Malongo refused to join. "I don't get involved in that kind of thing. I'm neither a student nor a worker." Vítor was more explicit: "That's a problem for the Portuguese, it's nothing to do with us." She tried to argue that May 1 was a day for all those who were against capitalism, and this year was especially important given the recent events in Angola. But neither would budge. There were probably going to be PIDE spooks, and she should be careful. She began to discreetly query close friends. Furtado was hesitant at first, before agreeing to come. As did Laurindo, a youngster from Gabela in his first year in Portugal, who was curious to witness a demonstration. So now, there were three of them, in the midst of two hundred students and workers, shouting "Long live May first" and "Down with fascism," carrying no flags or banners, marching along the streets leading to the Rossio. Sara was between the other two, all three with their arms linked. This gave them greater self-confidence in the face of the likely police charge. For the time being, the police limited themselves to guarding crossroads without any heavy equipment.

Sara remarked, "Are the people from the Casa backing out? It's just us three."

"Maybe they're in other groups," Furtado said. "We'll only find out when we get down to the Baixa."

Most of the demonstrators were young people. At the front were one or two older men who looked like workers, leading the protest chants. People opened their windows to peer out, but few left their houses to join the crowd. Some thirty young people emerged from a side street and joined them. Among them was a white Mozambican who came over and marched alongside the three Angolans.

"What about the others?" asked Sara.

"No idea. I don't think they're coming. They're scared."

"It's not that," said Furtado. "With the war in Angola, views have radicalized. The people from Angola, at least, don't want to get mixed up in side issues."

"He's right," Laurindo agreed. "They told me they had no reason to join in. May Day was a white problem. I said I was coming because I wanted to see what was happening. They told me I was just a kid. If I wanted to get beaten up by the police, then go ahead. 'Round here, we just get beaten up and nothing changes. When the police see you, they'll make sure you're the one on the receiving end. Our fight is back home, it's not here.'"

Laurindo was the only mixed-race person they could see on the march. On previous occasions, there had always been quite a few involved in the confrontations between students and the forces of the regime. Sara agreed with Furtado: nationalism was leading to radicalization. But she also understood the attitude of the non-whites, who were easily identifiable and attracted the attention of the police.

As they entered the Rossio, where there were already hundreds more demonstrators, someone shouted, "Down with the colonial war! Independence for the colonies!" Few people joined in, and soon word went around that it's a provocateur, it's a provocateur. Sara and Laurindo had responded to the lead by joining in the chant. Why was this a provocation? Shouting "Down with fascism" wasn't a provocation, but "Independence for the colonies" was? Wasn't it all part of the same struggle? Were the people at the Casa right? Could it be that it wasn't any longer? In her anxiety to know what was going to happen, Sara had no time to dwell on the matter, but she did sense something troubling her. It didn't last long. The serried ranks of police at the back of the Rossio looked menacing, and their attention was focused on them. The people in bars and cafés rushed into the square to watch. Many left their offices or shops and crowded together next to the buildings. Soon, the Rossio was packed and it was impossible to distinguish between the demonstrators and those drawn there out of curiosity.

"I don't think the police will baton charge," Furtado said. "We're all mixed up; they'll beat up whoever is just watching."

The tone of the chanting increased and hit its rhythm. "Down with fascism, long live May first, democracy." At an order relayed from the front, they veered right and began to advance uphill toward the Chiado. The police let them through.

"That's silly," said Furtado. "Once we get to the Chiado, they'll charge us."

"They want to pass by the offices of *A República*," Sara said.

The *A República* newspaper had assumed an anti-Salazar stance and, in spite of censorship, adopted a position that was favourable to the students and to democracy. The street where the offices of the newspaper were situated was a traditional focal point for demonstrations supporting it. But it was a more enclosed space, which favoured police charges—Furtado was right. Meanwhile, even more demonstrators had packed into the Rossio. Behind them, there were people who looked as if they might be civil servants or office clerks, walking with them in silence. More out of curiosity than conviction. They reached the newspaper offices, and the chanting grew more raucous.

The journalists leaned out of the windows, and the photographers took pictures from up above. Then suddenly the front line turned around and became the tail end of the march. The demonstration started moving back down toward the Rossio. It was at this point that the National Guard made its appearance on horseback, emerging from the Carmo barracks. The police had blocked access to the Rossio. And the cavalry charged.

"Didn't I tell you?" Furtado shouted. "Every man for himself. That's what we're supposed to do now."

In the confusion, the three let go of each other, because running arm in arm just wasn't possible in the circumstances. "Let's head up to the Bairro Alto," Sara shouted to Laurindo.

The National Guard began to deal out baton blows from their horses, and the demonstrators dispersed in confusion, all trying to run up alleyways or into the doorways of buildings along the Chiado. Sara and Laurindo passed very near the guards and managed to sneak off up a steep street where the horses wouldn't venture. A door opened and a woman's voice said, "Come in." The door shut behind them.

"You'd better come through to the lounge," the woman said.

There, they saw three men and five women sitting. You didn't need to be a genius to figure out what kind of establishment this was. Sara did her best to stifle her instinctive urge to leave. Petit bourgeois prejudices: they're just women, like the rest of us. And they helped us. She smiled at the one who had opened the door, a middle-aged woman with crooked teeth.

"Thank you."

"If the cops turn up, hide in one of the rooms. Feel free. At this hour, they're all empty; business only begins later. These gentlemen have also taken refuge from the demonstration."

The men had grown visibly embarrassed at Sara's arrival, for she was clearly not a whore. But they soon all laughed together in solidarity. One of the men, the oldest and dressed in worker's overalls, said, "I didn't know this establishment. But as they've been such a great bunch of girls, I might just become a regular, that is if my old lady lets me . . ."

The other men laughed. The woman who had opened the door to them sat down next to him. She took his hand.

"Do you have to get your old lady's permission, sweetheart?"

"She's the one who controls the money. And she's a penny-pinching old Semite . . ."

They laughed again. Sara noticed the bigotry in the man's comment. She herself was of Jewish background and for that reason was particularly sensitive. I'm being silly; it's a term that's entered common parlance and there's no malice intended. He probably doesn't even know what it means, except that it's attached to someone who holds onto their money. I'm the one who was prejudiced when I realized where I was. In a society full of prejudices, who's got the right to cast the first stone? A weak light filtered through the half-open window, leaving the room in shadow. There wasn't much clattering of horses' hooves or shouting coming from the direction of the Chiado. Either the violence had shifted back down into the Rossio, or it was all over. They could hear the ever more frequent sound of police sirens. They must be making plenty of arrests.

Sara spoke to the middle-aged woman, "Why did you help us?"

"Well, sweetheart, you were running away from the cops, and we don't like the cops. They're always giving us a hard time, putting us in the slammer for a few days. Just to annoy us. You'd think even Salazar didn't need us either."

"He doesn't need you, that's for sure," said the man sitting beside her. "They say he was born without a thingy."

"That's why he's got that bishop's air about him, poor wee fellow," said the woman, laughing.

She went and opened the window and leaned out. She turned and faced them.

"It's all quiet. Whoever wants to can leave, the danger's passed . . . You, lady, will want to go, of course. And you, my handsome little darkie, wouldn't you like to stay?"

Laurindo, who had been ill at ease from the start, peering at the women surreptitiously, blushed through his coffee-coloured skin. Sara laughed because she knew that it was because of her presence that this boy of eighteen felt so intimidated.

"No, no thank you, we'll be off now."

They left, thanking the women for their help. The street was quiet, and the echoes of the sirens were only coming from down the hill. They hurried to the first tram stop and got on a streetcar without even noticing where it was going. All they cared about was getting away from the area of greatest risk. They got off at the Marquês de Pombal, still keeping quiet. They walked in the direction of the Casa, although it was still some distance away. Without even consulting each other, they each knew the other wanted to walk.

Laurindo broke the silence. "I'm wondering what the use of all that was. There's a bit of shouting, the police turn up, throw their weight around, everyone scatters. And nothing changes."

"In a country where censorship exists, where one can get no information from the press or radio, it's useful for people to see that there are forces at work against the regime. It's important. And it helps the left to organize more effectively."

"I don't know, but it seemed like a bit of a game in which all sides agreed on the outcome."

"Don't be unfair, Laurindo. You didn't see the bloodstained heads, because we got away quickly. Nor did you see how many were arrested. A game?"

"That was just a way of putting it. But it doesn't achieve any results."

"It's a first phase. There will be other ways of carrying on the struggle later."

It was clear to Sara that Laurindo was adopting the attitude of other Angolans, for whom the stage of peaceful demonstrations had passed. They didn't seem to realize that before anything else, there had to be both organization and common purpose for a mass struggle. Where had she read that? It must have been in *Avante*, the Communist Party's newspaper, which she sometimes got hold of.

"And another thing," he continued, "why did they avoid the reference to the independence of the colonies? They called the guy a provocateur."

"Yes, that surprised me too. I'd like to give it a bit more thought. Maybe it's because people are very sensitive at the moment and consider what's happening in Angola acts of terrorism. Mention of it would keep people away."

"That's what folks say. The Portuguese, even those on the left, are reacting as whites. As far as they're concerned, the nationalists in the colonies are terrorists. Of course, UPA didn't help the cause with those bloody attacks. But . . ."

"That doesn't mean the cause of independence isn't justified. I agree with you. I was also taken aback."

"What do you think, Sara, do you think Furtado was also taken aback?"

"I don't know, but he didn't join in the chanting in support of the provocateur. I noticed it was only us two shouting."

"I noticed that too. And the Mozambican slunk off straightaway. I didn't see him again."

"Furtado must be all mixed up by what happened to his parents. He's got news from them now. They're safe in Luanda, but the plantation was burnt and completely destroyed. Yes, he must be completely baffled."

They walked on in silence, mulling over their thoughts. The streets were very busy, and it was quite possible they were being watched. They didn't take any precautions apart from keeping their voices down. Laurindo said, "When I first arrived here, we used to talk a lot. Perhaps because we were both born in the coffee area. It was in fact he who taught me these ideas of ours about independence, gave me literature on the subject, and so on. But when February fourth happened, he didn't rejoice. Of course, it was a topsy-turvy situation and was no cause for any great celebration. But for the first time, something was happening to show that people there wanted change; it was extremely important. He was strangely silent. From that moment on, we gradually grew further apart."

"That may well be the case. The whites are in a difficult position. If they back liberation, they have to go against their original class, against their society, and, most importantly of all, against their parents. That's what complicates things. They know they're going to have to forfeit their privileges, and some accept that. But they can't accept that their parents should be made to suffer. It's only human."

"So what about you?"

"Not a day goes by when I don't ask myself that. I've been pro-independence for a long time now, and I know that sooner or later, it will happen. I can fight for it, and in my own way, I do what I can. But I also wouldn't want my parents to be killed just because they're white. Or expelled."

"But what if there was no other option and you were faced with having to choose between independence and your family's lives?"

"I would find that terribly hard, of course. But I have no doubt that I would choose independence. Although it almost certainly wouldn't be the kind of independence I would have wished for."

"You're very special, Sara."

"No, there are others. My parents would pay for crimes committed by others. Oh, my father isn't a saint, of course. In that place, no one gets rich by doing acts of charity . . . But he hasn't committed any crimes. I hope it'll be an independence that enables us to distinguish between the actions of people and allows us to have justice."

"That will happen. You'll see."

"Not with UPA."

"No, there are other forces at play."

Sara fell silent. Laurindo was already aware of the existence of other organizations. And he was a kid, as yet scarcely involved in the Casa and its secrets. Meanwhile, she, a long-established member, had only been told about this by Aníbal some two weeks ago; no one else had mentioned it, not even Malongo. Strange barriers were being raised. Malongo was different, maybe no one had kept him in the loop. But Vítor was certainly better informed than Laurindo, and besides, they were friends. In other words, everyone knew about the MPLA, and they must have been organizing themselves, while she was left out in the cold. It could only be because she was white. That hurt. It's normal to be wary at this stage, she reasoned. But even so, it still hurt.

They continued walking. The day was coming to an end, and people were leaving work. The traffic was increasingly heavy. It was a radiant early evening, on a day that had been hot and dry for the time of year. That sky, the colour of that sky, Sara thought. Really only in Lubango, after the rain, would one see a sky with that shade of blue and the same clear air.

"In Gabela, the people are being massacred," Laurindo said, all of a sudden. "There wasn't exactly a revolt there, although there was a lot of talk. The settlers took advantage of the situation and organized themselves into armed militias. The victims are mainly small coffee plantation owners. So that they can seize their lands for themselves."

"It's the same old story. That has always happened in the coffee-growing areas. And your family?"

"I got a letter. My father is very cautious and says very little. But they are well, in the city. They left the foremen in charge of the farm. But apart from a couple of incidents, there hasn't been an uprising there as there was in the north. Of course, he's now scared that his lands will be seized, as his neighbour is a major white planter who was always trying to buy a hill off him, which produces good coffee. That guy is the leader of the militias, and he may well use force to annex the hill."

"But isn't your father white?"

"No, my grandfather was. When he died, the land was divided up between my father and his brother and sister. Those two sold their land to the big white planter and went to Luanda. My father was left with a third of the plantation and the house. He earned enough to live well, but now I'm no longer sure. My father must feel he's stuck in the middle. On the one hand, there are the whites who want to take advantage of the situation to expand, and are accusing the Angolans of terrorism to achieve their ends. On the other, there are the Blacks who may rise up at any moment and who say the mulatos are just like their white fathers. When the sea crashes over the rock, it's the mussels that bear the brunt. A mulato is like a mussel. That's why I can understand what you said a little while ago. It's not just progressive whites who are in a difficult situation."

"Of course," said Sara. "The same goes for Blacks who studied or who've got reasonable jobs, even if it's true that there are only a handful of them. But they are almost certainly also viewed with suspicion by their racial brethren, because they climbed socially in the world of the whites. And by whites, who consider them terrorists."

"Quite. That's what colonialism is all about."

"But here, among our own group, there are no differences between Blacks and mixed-race people; everyone is united."

"Don't delude yourself," Laurindo replied. "There are some groups of Blacks who don't want anything to do with mulatos. Not many, but they exist. They say that the Angolan elite is largely made up of mulatos, and that they can't dominate them. That this elite helped colonial rule to take root and benefitted from it. They end up supporting UPA, deep down and very secretly."

The boy enjoyed talking, and Sara liked his honesty. But she didn't want to use her influence to get confidential information out of him. Discretion was needed; it was so easy to get labelled a PIDE informer. She was curious to know things, now that she realized she had been sidelined and kept at arm's length. It was all very different from earlier times, when they had talked about everything in front of her. It was important to her that she should know more about the environment in which she was living, but that should never be done by cleverly extracting the crucial elements from a still naive young boy, as the police did. That was why she didn't ask him any questions.

"I read Aníbal's thesis, which I expect you know," Sara said. "He used similar terms to describe that nineteenth-century elite, which consisted of mixed-race people, as well as Blacks and whites. Yet Aníbal would never support UPA."

"I know. I've never read the thesis, but I've heard about it. He was even going to do a presentation on it at the Casa. But then it became clear it would be dangerous, and now it doesn't even bear thinking about."

"Yes, absolutely, it would have a whiff of provocation about it. Aníbal mentioned the idea to me. He agreed to speak, but it would have been silly. As you can see, one can acknowledge the positive or negative historical role of a particular social group without taking a radical political position regarding the descendants of that group."

"The elders say the son of a snake is a snake. That's true in nature, but not in human society."

"That's a good way of putting it, Laurindo. I like it."

They fell silent once more. They were nearing the Arco do Cego. Sara had decided to go and look for Malongo, either at the

Rialva or at home. And Laurindo was sure to be making for the Rialva, so as to discuss his impressions with his friends. When they were almost there, Sara couldn't resist firing a question at him. "So what do you think of relations between the whites and mixed-race people?"

He replied swiftly and candidly: "Look, I don't understand much about this kind of thing. But I get the feeling that mulatos, not all of them of course, are moving away from the whites. Precisely because of the criticism levelled at them by the pro-UPA Blacks. As they are charged with having played the white game, they now want to show that they have nothing to do with whites, only with Blacks. Many of them have forgotten their white father, and only talk about their Black mother."

"That's opportunism."

"Yes, of course. But it's happening. Whites aren't much help when they behave like Furtado. As long as it was all talk, he was in the front line. When action is needed, he steps back. That's when mulatos say the Blacks have a point; it's a strong argument. So they push aside the whites, even when they're friends. They can no longer be introduced as friends, only acquaintances."

"This is all very sad. But maybe it's just a passing phenomenon."

Then they entered the Rialva, on much more familiar terms than when they had set out on the march. In fact, Sara hardly knew Laurindo. But he knew her. The soon-to-be doctor enjoyed great prestige in some quarters, and no one could accuse her of inconsistency. But she now felt that all their antennae were tuned to her, that a number of eyes were watching her every move, waiting for any signs of hesitation. And they weren't the eyes of secret policemen either.

Malongo was in the café with Vítor Ramos. Furtado was also there, but at another table. He shot them a questioning look: Everything all right? Sara answered with a signal, all okay. And they sat down at Malongo's table. Vítor scarcely waited for them to sit down before asking with undisguised anxiety, "So, how did it go?"

Laurindo was about to answer, but Sara stopped him with her hand. She looked around. At the next table sat the now familiar fellow with the hat who had caught Aníbal's attention a couple of weeks before. Senhor Evaristo came over, and Sara ordered a beer. As Laurindo hesitated, she told him she would stand him one. "You must be thirsty." He smiled and was happy to accept.

Malongo was sprawled in his chair and asked her with a knowing look, "Are you having dinner with us?"

She said yes. His question contained an unspoken proposal that they should go back to her house together afterwards. She immediately understood the allusion her boyfriend was making, even though he had been very elusive of late. They carried on with small talk until dinnertime. As it was still early, they managed to get an empty table at the Casa and sat down, the four of them together. There, they were able to explain to the others how the demonstration had gone. Malongo was in stitches when he found out they had taken refuge in a brothel. "That's what happens when a doctor gets into a punch-up with the police." They told them the old workingman's jokes and laughed. Everyone was looking at them, for the sound of Malongo's laughter was loud enough to be heard even in the street. From various tables came requests: Hey, tell us what happened too. Laurindo even felt like jumping up on a table and giving the whole dining room an account of what had gone on. But Sara had warned him that it was not the right time to broadcast to all and sundry that they had been at a demonstration, for the ears of the PIDE even extended to the Casa.

When they had stopped laughing, Vítor said, "It's like I said. There's no point in us getting involved in Portuguese affairs. And they shouldn't interfere in ours."

Sara was on the point of replying but thought better of it. Was it worth it? Even she was no longer so sure of the positions she had held before.

Laurindo agreed with Vítor. "That's exactly what Sara and I were discussing on our way here. As far as I'm concerned, that was my first and last demonstration. Nothing will come of it."

"What did you expect us to do?" she replied, horrified. "Storm the ministries on the Terreiro do Paço and then get scattered by gunfire?"

"Well, at least it would make more noise," said Laurindo.

"Let's call it a day at this point," Malongo cut in. "It was great when you were telling us how things went. Don't spoil everything with an argument that just gives us all a headache and doesn't lead anywhere. By the way, while we're on the subject, what's the address of the brothel? I must drop by there and thank them for the help they gave you people."

"You rat!" Sara said, laughing.

Once again, there were new bursts of laughter and this jolly atmosphere prevailed until dinner was over. Then they went back to the Rialva, this time for coffee. The man with the hat was still there, with the same empty cup in front of him. He was reading a paper. Fifteen minutes later, after talking trivia among themselves, Sara and Malongo took their leave of the others, who had decided to go to a movie. They went back to her house. Malongo hugged her the moment the door to her room was closed. She kissed him but then stepped back.

"We've got to have a talk first, little boy."

"We've got all night to talk."

"Bullshit! After we make love, all you do is mumble and then fall asleep."

He sat down obediently on the sofa next to the window. He couldn't conceal a certain despondency. He had always been a man in a hurry, greedy for sex, thought Sara. Prejudiced people would define him as a typical African. She didn't know whether he was typical or not; he was the only man she had ever known. She sat on the bed and lit a cigarette.

"There are one or two matters I need to discuss with you. First of all, you've been very elusive of late. I've hardly seen you. You don't show up when we arrange to meet, and then you don't even appear at all. What's going on?"

"Well, I've been in low spirits."

"Because they didn't play you on Sunday?"

"I trained well with the first team, and then I didn't even make it onto the subs' bench. It's enough to piss a guy off."

"At times like that, you usually come looking for me to give you some encouragement. This time, you go missing. And last week, too, you made yourself scarce."

"It really is this pressure over soccer, believe me. And as I've been a bit depressed, I haven't come looking for you much so as not to let my low mood contaminate you as you've got so much on now, what with your internship and the report."

"Thanks for your consideration, but I'm afraid I don't buy that. I don't recall ever having made demands on you, and I'm very understanding. Be honest, is there another woman?"

He jumped up suddenly. "Stop talking nonsense." He stepped across the room and went to take her in his arms. Kissing her on the neck, he said, "Where did you get such a crazy idea? Honestly, Sara." They remained like this for some time, in each other's arms, as he caressed her persistently. She wasn't about to let herself be undressed. "Wait, I haven't finished speaking yet, or finished my cigarette." Despite this, her blouse already lay over the back of a chair. Sara sat down again on the bed and made him do the same.

"Secondly, a political matter. Have you heard talk of the existence of a party called the MPLA, which was founded abroad?"

"Vítor mentioned something to me, but I didn't pay much attention."

Sara got to her feet. She stubbed her cigarette out in the ashtray. She tried to control her anger. Was he making fun of her? Could he really be so irresponsible that he failed to show interest in such an important piece of news? Sometimes, she couldn't decide whether he was an inveterate liar, or just an occasional one. Her first suspicion seemed unfounded: he had been sincere, he hadn't come looking for her because he was bothered about his soccer. But it was hard to believe that he could be so uninterested in politics at a time like this.

"What do you mean by 'didn't pay much attention'? You're lying."

He raised his arms upwards and rolled his eyes in the direction of the ceiling.

"I was more worried about other things, and he didn't go on about it. He said he'd received some documents from this MPLA, which sounds phenomenal. He didn't show me any document and we didn't talk about it anymore. I don't know what you're trying to find out."

"I'm not trying to find out anything. I already knew about it. I wasn't waiting for you to tell me, because otherwise I would have remained in the dark forever. But what I want to know is why I'm being kept in the dark. That's the nub of the problem."

"I haven't understood anything you've been saying. I may not be very smart, but you're talking in such a way that not even Einstein would understand you."

"What I'm saying is that I'm starting to get sick of being used as somewhere you deposit your sperm whenever you feel like it."

"Damn it, Sara, there's no need to overreact."

"Oh yes, there is. You could tell me things that concern me, because I'm living through this time just like you and the others."

"You know very well that politics isn't my forte. I've never been interested."

"Politics! It's your life, your family's life. That's what this is all about. Don't come to me with stories about all this being of no interest to you, that it's only about soccer. There comes a moment in life when people have to forget trivialities, to worry about the really serious things that affect them. And the same goes for you."

"Of course I'm interested to know what's happening back home. But that's all. I'm not going to get involved in organizations. I've got no idea which one is better than the other. And I didn't remember to talk to you about it because I think we've got more important things to do together."

"Making love, for example. That's all I'm good for."

He hugged her again. He stroked her hair. Sara felt like crying. Not because of the argument and her disappointments, but merely because he was caressing her tenderly. I'm not going to be weak, she thought. And she pushed him away. She lit another cigarette to help her keep her distance.

"Don't you find it strange that neither you nor Vítor or anyone else spoke to me about this new organization, knowing that I was worried? It would have been natural to tell me about it. But you shut yourselves away; you must have had secret conversations, all of you. It seems I no longer deserve to know about some things. Why, because I'm white?"

"So are you the one who's got complexes now? Leave the complexes to us, who've got a reason for them. All right, it was my fault. I should have told you what Vítor told me. But it wasn't out of malice; I just didn't think that it was important. I was more worried about why the coach keeps hanging me out to dry. I could start thinking I'm not getting a game because I'm Black. But I don't think like that. The club has always treated me well; they just don't play me. Am I going to start calling the coach a racist?"

"But are you or aren't you involved in political discussions?"

"The others are. As for Vítor, he's now discovered he's only interested in politics. He doesn't study anymore; he just reads banned books. And he pissed me off, telling me I'm apolitical, that I've got to join in. Join in what? He hasn't told me what. He tells me the same old story as you do, the one you always have. But I don't give a shit. I just want to play and make the first team."

Sara had to acknowledge that Malongo was being sincere. Either that or he was some ultra-clandestine cadre, with foolproof camouflage, enabling him to play a double role. That couldn't be the case; he didn't have the staying power for that. She took another puff of her cigarette. She had calmed down.

She spoke in a sad tone, but no longer with any aggression. "I believe you. But the others ... Before, they always used to come to me to discuss problems, whatever they might be. Now, they stop their conversation when I turn up. These aren't complexes. They're things that really happen."

"Yes, maybe. People are very suspicious at the moment. They say the PIDE is tightening the noose on the Casa."

"That's true."

"It's not right, but they're starting to blame the whites for everything bad that happens. Even those whites who have always been openly critical of colonialism. They say they'll defend their parents against us. Yes, I sometimes hear things like that. But not many talk even to me about these things. Either because I'm a soccer player and earn more than the others. Or because I'm going around with you, who knows?"

"You see you're now talking seriously about politics? Do you think they also sideline you from their conversations?"

"Some do, yes. Not Vítor, of course. But some of the others."

"Maybe that's because of me. Because you're my boyfriend, they may think you're a traitor. That you tell me secrets."

"What secrets? Fortunately, I don't have any secrets, I can sleep peacefully ... But there are one or two characters who look away. You know what I'm like—I don't give a damn about these things—but I've already noticed that one or two won't look me straight in the eye. And they stop talking when I arrive on the scene. Even your great friend, Aníbal . . . The last time he was here, he avoided talking about politics in my presence and changed the subject to soccer. Do you think I didn't notice? I'm not that naive, you know. Sometimes I just pretend. I bet he talked to you about politics afterwards, but I'm not even going to ask what he said, because I'm not interested."

Sara extinguished her half-smoked cigarette. There was no doubt about it: he was no fool. Well, I already knew that, I wasn't going to fall in love with an idiot just because he's good-looking and spends his life running after a ball.

"Aníbal has reasons of his own, and they don't involve side-lining you. You're apolitical, and he thinks these things bore you. But the others, well, yes, that's bad . . . There are lots of fault lines beginning to appear, and they're destroying old friendships, which is very sad."

He pulled her toward the bed. She undressed. There wasn't much left to say. At least love blew the night mists away. And Malongo exuded enough heat to cause any mist to evaporate. For her, each time was like the first in the wonder of new discovery.

4

There had been a lot of work to do that morning in the hospital. Her teachers viewed her as a qualified doctor; all she needed to do now was to present the final report on her internship, which was equivalent to a graduate dissertation. So they allowed her to treat a growing number of cases on her own. Occasionally, she doubted her diagnosis and asked a teacher. But this happened ever more rarely. She had no time to worry about her own problems as she was continually having to confront those of others. But whenever she was alone for a moment, she asked herself, How many days over am I? She never managed to focus on an answer, as a new patient inevitably appeared, and her instincts as a doctor kicked in. She had been afflicted by this idea ever since arriving at the hospital. How long was it since she had had a period? Certainly longer than usual, as she was not always very regular. But how long?

She only managed to work things out after she left the hospital and, in spite of her tiredness, decided to walk for a bit. She wasn't expecting the sunlight that awaited her, the first real sign of the approaching summer. She knew Malongo wouldn't be meeting her, he had told her the previous evening. That was why she walked on, trying to recall the dates. This was difficult because she never kept a record of her periods. She more or less followed the rhythm method, the only really safe way available if one wanted to avoid the frustrating condom. But she didn't do this with any great rigour. Unforgiveable considering she was a doctor, she admitted. Before, when she'd studied the subject, she began to use a written record, with the days of her period on it. She did this for a year. She noticed that she was rather irregular. But at that time, she didn't have a man, and she was still a virgin. Just a few casual boyfriends, relationships that didn't go beyond kissing and cuddling. Then Malongo appeared on the scene. She hesitated for a long time before agreeing to go to bed with him. Plenty of time to take precautions. But she didn't and he never asked. She remembered on one occasion, she spoke to him about the possibility of using a condom. Stop that, he'd said. Are you saying you'd rather eat a sweet with the wrapping on? She never raised the issue again. And now, almost a year later, she was having misgivings. Of course, she interrupted their relations during the week she thought ovulation would occur. But when did she ovulate exactly, if she was always so irregular?

She tried to remember with precision the date of her last period. Yes, it was before she had last seen Aníbal, when they went for a walk in the Baixa. Some days before that, she was menstruating, because she had told Malongo that he wouldn't be able to sleep over at her place. He'd been annoyed. "One of these days, I'll have to field a substitute. That's why the elders back at home are never happy with just one woman: polygamy has its advantages." Yes, that bitter observation was two or three days before Aníbal appeared. And she hadn't seen Aníbal for over a month. Only a week ago, they had been talking about how he hadn't resurfaced; he must have been mobilized and didn't even have time to let them know. Some of them had replied that was impossible, he would always find a way of letting them know. So, her last period had been more or less forty days ago. That was too long; her cycle had never been that long. The idea didn't scare her. Deep down, if she had never taken many precautions, it was because she didn't mind becoming pregnant.

She took a deep breath. *I must accept that it may really have happened. Tomorrow, I'll make use of the privilege of working in a hospital and get a test done. And until I get the result, I'm not going to panic.*

In the meantime, she couldn't stop thinking about it. To have a child? Was that good or bad? It had always been the greatest fear among her female student friends, because it meant they would have to interrupt their courses and often forfeit their scholarships. She didn't have to face that problem as she was at the end of her course. Okay, so she might find it harder to embark on her career, but that wasn't the worst thing that could happen. And of course, she dreamed of having Malongo's child. It would be a beautiful little girl. Girl? Yes, without a doubt, it could only be a beautiful little mulata. Born in Benguela in keeping with tradition. Wasn't the city of acacias known to be the cradle of the most beautiful mixed-race women in Angola? Well, then! That was settled, it would be good to have this child. Especially a dark-skinned little girl with huge eyes like the father. Her mother's nose, just slightly retroussé despite her already mixed-up Jewish origins, average lips, dark hair, like both her parents, but slightly curly just as it should be. Of course it would be good, in spite of all the problems the world might throw at her.

Were there problems? Yes, of course there were. First of all, Malongo. Would he accept paternity? When she was sure about it, she would be perfectly open with him. Malongo had no obligation whatsoever if he didn't want it. There would be no hurried marriage or anything like that. Heaven forbid, she hadn't adopted progressive ideas on a whim. And she could perfectly well shoulder responsibility for her daughter on her own, if it came to it. But he should at least give her his name, so that she wouldn't be the daughter of an unknown father. Malongo would agree to that, she had no doubt. Their relationship had always been free; they had never made plans for the future, nor had they tried to shackle each other. It wouldn't be any great problem for Malongo to recognize his daughter for reasons of bureaucracy.

But what about her parents? Ah, yes, there would be problems there. Pregnancy outside marriage would be a family disgrace. And all the more so with an uneducated Black soccer player.

Her father was very proud of his ancestors who had arrived from the lands of Israel many centuries ago. He would tell the story to whoever was willing to listen. They had settled in Portugal in the thirteenth century, having fled from other parts of Europe. Due to religious persecution, three hundred years after having settled in Évora, they had converted to Catholicism and changed their family name to Pereira. Almost all the New Christians, the term by which converted Jews were known, chose the names of trees. What she didn't know was whether they were given a choice or were forced to accept them. But even so, discrimination didn't end. Her grandfather tried better luck in Angola at the beginning of the century, and her father was born in Benguela. In spite of hanging onto the residues of certain aspects of his original culture, her grandfather had no religion whatsoever, and in Angola he married a lady without any Jewish forebears. That was why her father was only partially Jewish. But he behaved as if he were entirely so, except in his religious practice. He knew the Bible better than he did the Talmud, which he was, in any case, incapable of reading, given his ignorance of the language. At heart, what linked him to the Jews was merely the memory of persecution, which made them seem like the world's martyrs, exacerbated by the Nazi extermination camps of the Second World War. He hated all Germans without exception for being racists. He'd not once agreed to a business deal with a German, no matter how profitable it might be. And there were quite a few in the region, either those fleeing Nazism or, after the war, Nazi refugees. But he lumped them all together and refused to have any contact whatsoever with them. The racial persecution suffered by his ancestors over centuries, if not millennia, should have made him more tolerant toward other races. Such consideration, however, was anathema to his views. Perhaps because he had managed to increase the fortune built up by his father in trading activities, and he had a lot to lose. And so Senhor Ismael Pereira would proclaim in a loud voice that he was against racism, that it had only provoked bloodshed throughout history, but at the same time, no Black person ever entered his house unless as a servant.

Her mother's background was different. Her family had been in Angola since the eighteenth century, exiled on the order of one of Portugal's most serene majesties, who, by doing so, was trying to purge the country of impure blood. They had first settled on the banks of the Kwanza. Some generations later, they were in Benguela, already mixed with other blood. And Sara was sure that her maternal great-grandmother was a mulata. Her mother, Dona Judite, doesn't deny it, what does it matter? When Sara asked her about their origins, Dona Judite pointed to her veins. "There's everything in here, except maybe Chinese. There's even Boer blood, but don't remind your father, because for him, Boers and Germans are all the same."

Of one thing Sara was sure: her family would not welcome the idea of a mixed-race grandchild at all. And worse still, outside marriage, not even a registry office one. Especially in this time of racial hatred stoked by recent events. Her father's letters were symptomatic. He had forgotten the pogroms suffered by the Jews in Europe twenty years before. And he was advocating the theories of Salazar, he who, like almost all the electors in Benguela, had voted systematically for the liberal opposition to the "Jesuit dictator." Dona Judite would eventually accept it, but at the cost of how many hidden tears? And David, her younger brother, who was doing his military service in Huambo, disposed to defend the faltering dreams of empire by force of arms, certainly would not support her.

It mattered little; it was her life, and her choice as well. She had always assumed she would graduate and then immediately return to Angola. That was her fate. But now she wasn't sure. To appear with a mixed-race baby in her arms and open a practice in Benguela? Her social milieu would reject her. Perhaps not for that reason alone, because Benguela was the land of mestiços. It had been, it was once. Would it still be? A small society, where people knew everyone else's business and gave running commentaries, either in the big townhouses where families met for lunch on Saturdays and Sundays or at the sidewalk cafés. She would probably get few patients. Well, they could go to hell! She could always get a job in a hospital. People would gradually forget, even if only because this intolerance would pass when the country became independent. It wasn't as if she had ever conceived of opening a private surgery, which only served the rich. She preferred the idea of working in the poorer health centres on the periphery, where those who really needed her lived. How she would do this, she didn't yet know. But she had always advocated for preventative medicine and working with the most vulnerable communities. These people didn't give a damn about racial prejudice. They mingled together at their whim, and they would now be more unprotected than ever. It wasn't long now before she would complete her medical degree, and she had to decide on her course of action, once back home. Her father had enough money to establish a luxury practice for her in the richest part of town, he had often promised her that. But would he agree to invest his money in a people's clinic in Camunda or Massangarala, without any prospect of profit to boot? And all that after she had turned up with a little mulata baby in her arms, saying "Let me introduce you to your granddaughter"? A clinic in a poor area with free or almost free consultations, that's a communist project and my money isn't going into communist schemes—that would be his only answer. Yes, she would initially have to work in a hospital and then find out how she could get into the peripheral areas. Without any support from the State, because it only helped the rich. And without any support from the rich because they only helped themselves. Life certainly wasn't easy, no, certainly not. Only when the country became independent.

She caught a bus halfway home, because she was already tired of walking. At home, she prepared a quick meal and immediately got down to working on her dissertation. She didn't make much progress because her thoughts prevented her from concentrating. Should she start preparing her parents for the news, by telling them, for example, that she had met the man of her life? And in another more detailed letter, should she tell them Malongo's life story? Nonsense. The less they knew, the better. She shuffled through the notes made during her internship, looking for a piece of information. Then she would consult a textbook in order to back up a theory. Then again, would her test be positive? She ended up not achieving much. Recently, she had been wasting too much time, and what had looked easy in the beginning, given that she had been a good student with some practical experience, was now starting to worry her. She had less than two months to present her report. The examiners would then have four weeks to study it, after which she would have her viva on it in July. Time was short, and she didn't want to limit herself to merely producing a report; she wanted to write a proper scientific thesis. And she wanted to get the highest mark possible, otherwise she would feel all her efforts over the last six years had been wasted.

She was counting down the days on a calendar full of crosses in red ink, when there was a knock on the door. Malongo at this hour? Strange, but one never knew with Malongo. She went to open it. It was Aníbal.

"It's so good to see you. We were wondering what could have happened to you. You never showed up again."

He came in quickly, kissed her on the cheek, and sat down in the only armchair. He was in civilian clothes, as he always was when he came to Lisbon, but he was carrying what looked like a heavy, fully packed overnight bag.

"I've come to Lisbon a few times, but never with enough time to make an appearance. I was always busy with things to see to. And the less I appeared at the Casa, the better."

"We thought you really had left for Angola. But then we'd say no, he'd let us know."

"It's tomorrow. We were told today that we would be leaving tomorrow. They gave us some time off this afternoon to say our farewells and do some shopping, that sort of thing . . ."

"Oh no! So sudden?"

"They used to give people more warning. But now it's like this, so people won't get any ideas. And we've been three days on manoeuvres, almost without any sleep. But the bastards never told us what the manoeuvres were for, as if they were just part of the routine. The manoeuvres come to an end, and they tell us we're leaving."

Aníbal looked tired. Three days of manoeuvres and then this devastating news, no wonder he had such a face. Sara felt like giving him a hug, but she held back. He lit a cigarette; she followed suit. The question was on the tip of her tongue and it burst out without her being able to stop herself. "Are you going?"

"No."

She took a deep breath. She was afraid for him, but at the same time, she was happy. Aníbal wouldn't be seen by the people as a cheap turncoat. He was deserting, providing an example to many others who sooner or later would find themselves in the same situation. Tears came to her eyes, and she murmured thank you. She hugged him, crying, repeating thank you, thank you. He pushed her gently away.

"Why are you thanking me? You're under absolutely no obligation to do that."

"Yes, I am. Because you didn't disappoint me. That's the image I want to keep of you, forever. That of the most coherent man I have ever known."

He waved away the idea with both hands. He smiled, despite the clear tension. He spoke very quietly, but as they were very close, she heard every word:

"I don't deserve anything at all. Or almost anything. I still think it would be harder to leave and carry out clandestine work there. That certainly would be a difficult tactic to adopt. But I'm not going to hide anything at all from you. I received orders from abroad to desert and get out of the country. Or rather, not orders because it was never about that, but a suggestion. The people outside the country think I can be of use with my military experience. Which is what they need."

"So how are you going to do it?"

"I'm here to ask a big favour of you. If you can't help, don't give it another thought. I know it's going to cause you problems, and if there were any other solution, I wouldn't ask. But I don't have any alternative right now."

"Don't be so evasive ... Tell me what you need."

"I don't have anywhere to stay tonight. Our leave lasts until midnight. If I turn up at two or three in the morning, no one is going to be bothered. But by six o'clock, I'll be a deserter. Tonight, I need to sleep here. Meantime, I'll find somewhere else to stay until I can get across the border."

"So much beating about the bush just for that. Of course you can stay here. What's the problem?"

"You've got your life, and I may get in the way. And if the PIDE find out, they can pester you."

"They can't pester me much. All I need to say is that I didn't know you had deserted. You asked to sleep here, that's all. That's no big deal. Make yourself at home."

"What about Malongo...?"

She laughed. Aníbal hadn't changed at all, as sensitive as ever, avoiding subjects that might offend her. He knew she was sleeping with Malongo, but he was incapable of mentioning that directly. It wasn't the kind of conversation one had with a woman, even if she were a great friend.

"I'll tell him he can't come over today. Relax, you won't cause any trouble. The only thing is that you'll have to sleep on the sofa."

"Of course. Good grief, I'm a soldier. I even slept on the ground the last few days. The sofa will be marvellous."

"And do you want to have dinner here or out?"

"I've got to go and meet someone for dinner . . . The fellow who was going to fix things. He should be able to find me a safe haven until I can get across the border."

Aníbal said he would be back at about eleven and left his overnight bag behind, slipping out of the room as quietly as he could. Was he already training for secrecy, whispered words and furtive glances on street corners? Poor Aníbal, thought Sara, he will need a lot of support to get away. I hope everything is resolved at this dinner.

She tried to do some work, but now it was even harder. To her own problems were now added those of her friend. She could already imagine him crossing frontiers. The one between Portugal and Spain shouldn't be that complicated. But to get to France, he would have to cross the fearsome Pyrenees. Wasn't it the Carthaginian general, Hannibal, who crossed the Pyrenees with elephants in order to attack Rome, in one of the most incredible feats in history? Yes, she was sure the Carthaginians had a general called Hannibal. But was that really his name? The great themes of history were now distant in her memory because of the need to remember those of medicine. She would have to ask Aníbal; he was the specialist. If the other had got across with elephants, it would be much easier for him to cross alone. Even the coincidence in the name helped, a favourable omen. But this did nothing to calm her down. No matter how well she knew him, the first impression was one of frailty. A soldier was used to such adventures, but Sara never viewed him as a soldier or an adventurer. Short, skinny, always clutching at his books and his ideas, he wasn't exactly the image one had of a hero. And she nurtured feelings for him that were almost maternal. She told herself she was being silly, but she feared for him. She couldn't help it.

She gave up trying to work and prepared something to eat. In the corner of the room, there was a little stove where she cooked, especially at night. She boiled two eggs, ate them, and had a glass of milk. Then she made a coffee. And she went and sat down at her desk again. She remembered Malongo; she must warn him not to come. She opened the door that gave her access to the rest of the house and asked the landlady for permission to use the phone. The phone was in the hall, but she always had to tell her landlady, so that she could jot it down in a little notebook and charge for phone calls at the end of the month. Any extra, such as a phone call, had to be paid for. But when the landlady was suffering her aches and pains, Sara didn't charge for her consultation. That's right, she ought to charge her too, she thought, knowing full well she would never have the courage. Malongo wasn't at home, nor was he at the Rialva. Nor at the canteen in the Casa. She managed to leave a message with Vítor: she was going out this evening, and there was no point in Malongo coming looking for her.

Now more relaxed, she sat down again at her desk, determined to get some work done before Aníbal arrived. But she didn't have much to show for it. She had hardly made any progress when she heard a light tap on the door leading to the stairway. Aníbal came in looking still more tired and seemingly discouraged because of bad news. He sat in the armchair, leaned forward and muttered, "They're preparing my escape, but it won't happen within the next two weeks. I was prepared for that. But they don't have anywhere to hide me, at least for the time being."

"You had a month to prepare things, ever since that time we talked about it. Did you take long to decide?"

"No. I reached a decision straightaway. Everyone I consulted said the same as you. And I warned those whom I had to warn to prepare the operation. The problem was that I had no departure date, and other more urgent things must have cropped up. Only now are they starting to move. And as I'm not Portuguese, I haven't got first priority in the clandestine network. At least that's what I assume is the case."

"Is it Portuguese who are in charge of this?"

"Who did you think it would be?"

"Communists?"

Aníbal looked at her in silence. Sara sensed that she shouldn't have asked him that question, but it was too late. She apologized. "Hell, it's none of my business."

He smiled. "It doesn't matter. I can understand your curiosity. But the less you know, the less dangerous it is for you. That's one thing. On the other hand, it's unfair not to tell you. There are things you should know, even if only because you will have to confront them and be prepared."

He sat back in the armchair and lit a cigarette. Sara lit one, too, straight afterwards.

In his own unique way of talking, which would one day earn him the nom de guerre of Wisdom, he said, "The Communists are the only ones who are organized effectively. They dominate the student movement, and you can be sure that the students don't do anything without their support, or at least their approval. Even in the Casa. Without us all being aware, they are very influential. The anticolonial movements that have begun to emerge, even independently, have always more or less benefitted from their tacit encouragement. On the basis of a united struggle, the important thing was to bring down fascism in Portugal, and the problem of the colonies would be automatically resolved. There were always those who wanted to do things differently, but they ended up accepting this influence of theirs, because it's one thing to talk as we do and it's another to organize and really take on the PIDE and all the other pillars of fascism.

"I had links with them. I liaised between them and more politically aware groups of students from the colonies who were coming together to debate problems and even to envisage carrying out certain actions. But I was never one of their cadres. Why? Because I felt Angolan and thought each one should work in their own sector, albeit through coordinated actions. But then the situation in Angola erupted and Angolan nationalism asserted itself. In a very muddled way, but it asserted itself. Now there are two positions. The communists think one should work inside the regime and destroy it from within. And the Angolan nationalists, ever more radical, think that Angolans should fight inside Angola, completely independently and without having to listen to the big daddies of the Portuguese left. We are fighting for the independence of the country, and for that reason, we should have entirely independent political movements. It is we, with the war in Angola, who are going to bring down fascism. That's what the argument is about."

"But what has all this got to do with your situation?"

"The Communists are sending their militants and sympathizers to Angola, to fight from within the regime. They don't agree with desertion unless the circumstances are exceptional. They didn't say as much, but I think they had other plans for me. I frustrated them because I decided to desert. They understand, or at least say they do, but they are not including me in the high-priority category to escape from Portugal. They'll do it, but without compromising their clandestine operations. In any other situation, they would pull out all the stops. But in my case, no.

Besides, they foresee that many will want to escape, and there are a lot of Angolan nationalists here. Their support systems would be overwhelmed if they helped everyone. And sooner or later, they would fall into the traps set by the PIDE. Also, they don't have much confidence in our degree of militancy, and they know that the student milieu has been infiltrated by PIDE agents. As you can see, the game isn't an easy one, and they have to take care to defend themselves. It's our fault, with our traditional inability to organize ourselves. A lot of talk, plenty of arrogance, but not much skill in strategic planning. To the extent that if you were now to kick me out, I wouldn't have anywhere to go. The students can't accommodate me; their rooms are full and they're easily watched. Only the Portuguese left has the capacity to hide someone. But it's always a risk, and not everybody is willing."

"You can stay here."

"Today, yes. But tomorrow and after that? They were very specific. Within the next two weeks, they'll get me into France. But until then, where shall I stay? And I can't walk down the street and sleep in the Metro. With my colour, they'll identify me straightaway."

"We've got to find a way. But for now, you're staying here."

Aníbal patted her hand. He took a deep drag on his cigarette.

"Sara, Sara, you've got a big heart. But now we've just got to use our heads and no more. It's obvious I can't stay here. By tomorrow, the whole of the PIDE will have my photograph and start their searches. Where will they look? They'll start with the lodgings used by the people from the Casa. In a few days, they'll ask your landlady if she's ever seen me. And it'll be impossible for me to hide from her. She'll sense that there's a man in the house. And then they come and tidy your room, or is it you who does it?"

"It's a cleaning woman who comes three times a week. I just make my bed."

"Isn't it obvious then? They'll discover me."

"You can be out in the morning, because she always comes then. We'll hide your things. And before you leave, check to make sure there's nothing here that might betray your presence. If they sense that a man has slept here, it's not a problem . . . They're used to it. I'm an independent adult."

"The problem is that I can't wander the streets, even in disguise. There's always a neighbour who'll think it strange: a Black man leaving that apartment every morning? The PIDE has a long reach. And at that point, you won't have a leg to stand on. You'll go straight to jail because of me. How do you think I can accept that?"

Sara remained silent, trying to think. There was a solution, there must be. They'd find one if they kept their cool. And she wasn't afraid to help her friend. Either he got across the Pyrenees or they'd both go to jail. That much she had decided. A decision she didn't need to make, because it was so crystal clear.

"You don't have to accept anything. You're already here. And you're only leaving when we find a safer place. If we stay calm, we'll find something."

"I've always been proud of my race, although it is so despised by others. Ever since I was a kid, I had this pride of mine. For many, it's different; they'd give anything to be white. And today, they're racists in relation to whites. I never had those problems, maybe because of the environment in which I grew up, I don't know. But right now, I curse my race. If it was winter, I could hide my hands inside gloves, and my face with a scarf and a hood, along with some dark glasses. But in this hot weather, I'd attract even more attention. For a Black man to go unnoticed in Europe really does require a superhuman effort."

"Stay here as long as you need to. Go out quickly first thing in the morning, find somewhere to hide yourself . . ."

"Movie houses don't open in the morning."

"Yes, that would be the perfect place. A garden. That's somewhere you wouldn't be noticed, someone sitting on a park bench reading the paper or a book. Never the same garden, of course. Or a library, there's one near here."

"It might work for a day or two. But what then?"

"By that time, we'll have found somewhere else. Come back home at midday, because the woman will have cleaned the room. Take my key, come up the stairs as carefully as you can and don't make any noise. As for food, don't worry, I'll see to that."

Aníbal seemed to accept things. Of course, he had no other choice. But even so, he returned to the matter in hand: "Do you know what you're risking, Sara, and why?"

"Yes. Firstly, you're my friend. And even if you weren't . . . you're a nationalist who is going to fight for his country. This is my way of helping Angola."

"And what about Malongo, have you thought about him? He mustn't know anything. Let's be clear, I don't mistrust him at all. It's just that, sorry, he seems a bit irresponsible to me. He might talk just for the sake of talking. You can't conceal my presence here for long. He's going to want to visit you."

"Yes, that's a problem. But it's my problem, and you don't have to worry about it."

"Apart from anything else, that's all the more reason for yours truly here to have misgivings. I may unintentionally cause problems between you two."

"Oh yes. His macho pride won't accept that I'm sleeping in the same room as another man. But that's all. And even then, I'm not sure. He might even take things better. But as I've already told you, Malongo's my problem, and no one else's."

They needed to get some sleep. Sara took the initiative and made up the sofa as comfortably as she could. Then she went to the bathroom. She made use of the moment Aníbal took his turn to go there to take off her clothes and get into bed. When he returned to the room, she turned away so that he could change and get into bed. They were friends but weren't used to such intimacies.

Sara slept very badly. She spent the whole night trying to think of a way to hide Aníbal for a few days. She went through all her friends or acquaintances, whether Angolan or Portuguese, who didn't live in a rented room and who therefore had a greater degree of independence to shelter him. None of them were any use. Those with larger houses didn't offer any political guarantee, which was the case of some relatives of hers who lived a little way outside Lisbon, in a huge detached villa, an ideal spot, but they were far too reactionary. They would either refuse outright to put up a future terrorist or they would call the police afterwards. The more modest had such small homes that she didn't have the heart to ask them to make this sacrifice. And if they had children, the risk of some involuntary denunciation increased. There were also people who had the means and were open-minded, but their houses were permanently under surveillance by the PIDE and therefore could not be considered. There had to be a solution. She kept repeating the thought to herself by way of comfort, but it didn't resolve anything. She went back to her search.

Aníbal was asleep. His steady breathing should have calmed her. But it didn't. Aníbal was asleep, not because he was confident but because he was exhausted from his military manoeuvres. A strange feeling sometimes took possession of her. She wanted to go over to the sofa and hug him. Not out of any sexual desire, but merely to protect him. And she recalled, with tenderness, a comment he had made when he found out she was slightly short-sighted but only wore glasses to read. It wasn't for reasons of aesthetics. "Without glasses, my vision is slightly blurred. So, for example, people seem better looking because I can't see their blackheads, their warts, or hairs in places they shouldn't be, which make them uglier." "That's so typical of you, Sara," he had said. "You always find a way of seeing people from an angle that favours them. You're generous, but you're not a realist." "Liking people gives me pleasure," she had said. He'd smiled and squeezed her hand. That was all. Now it was she who wanted to hug him. Just to transmit tenderness and a feeling of safety. Would she make love to Aníbal? Oh, yes, without a doubt. Naturally, without questioning herself or him. Something as natural and easy as breathing. She had never done it, because the opportunity never presented itself and because he never seemed interested. Would she do so now, in spite of Malongo? The idea troubled her. It was different, one thing didn't invalidate the other. With Malongo, it was a torrent, to use a rather trite term, passion, sexual attraction. Aníbal inspired in her a sense of communion. She would make love with him in order to fuse, or to commune, with him. She fell asleep, recognizing that there was something religious in this idea, which stemmed perhaps from the mystic beliefs of her ancestors.

5

They tidied the room together, barely exchanging a word. They hid Aníbal's bag in the bottom of the wardrobe and had a quick bite to eat. Aníbal left, taking the keys with him and carrying a book. Sara walked around the room again to make sure there were no traces of his presence. Then she followed him out, slamming the door behind her.

Once in the street, she looked up angrily at the radiant sun. For the first time in her life. Aníbal was right, winter would help him camouflage himself. But this sunlight was an enemy. She eventually smiled at the incoherence of her sudden hatred of the thing that she had always adored, and whose absence made her weep with yearning for her luminous homeland. On the bus, she tried to order her thoughts. First, she would have to do the pregnancy test, although she hardly considered it necessary. And she needed to find a solution for her friend's problem. It would be very dangerous for him to stay with her for more than a couple of days. Even without her attracting anyone's attention, it was likely that the PIDE would suspect her and make a routine visit to the apartment. They would search high and low for him throughout the country. At this very moment, they would have been informed of his absence from the barracks. The hunt had already begun. And there were probably few deserters. If there were a lot, the PIDE agents would be overburdened with the task of finding them all. But now they only had one hare to hunt. And there were so many hounds ... An uneven contest, as in the Steinbeck novel she had just read in the original English, furtively lent her by a colleague, Marta. Marta! The idea almost made her jump. Was that a possibility?

Like Sara, Marta was also coming to the end of her course. They had been friends for a long time, both with similar preoccupations. Only a few days before, they had exchanged views on the May Day demonstration. Marta hadn't gone because she was unwell. And she felt guilty. She was the daughter of wealthy farmers in the Alentejo, but she was progressive. She didn't join student or political organizations, she said it was a waste of time, that politicians start by being politicians and all end up as thieves. The very concept of an organization made her suspicious, nurtured as she was by her readings of nineteenth-century anarchists. The only selfless aristocrats of political life, she called them. As for Angola, she had immediately approved of armed insurrection. The Angolans are showing these left-leaning politicians, who only plan their revolutions sitting at café tables, how things are resolved. That's the only way to do it, kick some ass. She never got involved in group politics but never missed a march. "And if I were a man, I'd pick a fight with the police, just to see whether they're not scared as well." The previous night, Sara had dismissed Marta from her thoughts, because her apartment was very small. Now she seemed to think it might offer a solution. The apartment only had one room, kitchen and bathroom. But it belonged to her, a present from her father when she passed her exams to enter her fifth year. She had no landlady to answer to. And she wasn't being watched by the PIDE, because her father had influential friends in the Salazar government. Marta had told her what she had said to the minister of justice over lunch on her parents' farm in the Alentejo. The minister remained serenely blue, her father had turned puce with fury, and her mother had left the table, red with shame. A festival of colours, you'd have to be there to believe it. "It's her age, she'll get over it," the minister had said once the lunch was over, in order to placate her father. No, when it came to Marta, they didn't interfere with her.

She arrived at the hospital and went straight to the laboratory to do her test. She would get the result the next day. Her professor was already in his office, and she began work, doing the rounds of the patients. Marta was on another ward. Halfway through the morning, she took a quick break and went to look for her. She was tall, much taller than Sara, and she walked like a man, swinging her arms energetically. Sara had already planned her strategy: she was just going to put out feelers. She would have to get Aníbal's agreement in order to put the matter to her clearly. She asked her if she felt like a cigarette. Marta left what she was doing, and together they went to the staff lounge, where they could smoke.

"How's your love life?" Marta asked.

"Just the same. And yours?"

The other woman burst out laughing and slapped her on the thigh. Sara thought this was a typically male gesture. And it was, her friend imitated men unconsciously. No, it wasn't a question of imitating them; it was a spontaneous act for her, a natural way of expressing her independence.

"Haven't I told you yet? I sent António packing... António the engineer, you met him. He started giving me that crap about how women shouldn't work. As far as I was concerned, he considered me an exception, but the rest should stay at home and look after their children. And all this came with a kind of marriage proposal. Just imagine. Me getting married to a macho pig like that. I told him, look, sunshine, this has gone on for as long as it was good, and neither of us got on each other's nerves. Now, you're getting on my nerves, and so bye-bye, go and get on with your own life. He phoned me yesterday full of sweet talk, and asking whether we could meet. See you in hell. And I hung up. Piss off, son of a bitch!"

Sara laughed. António, who was new to her, followed on from

Germano, Álvaro, Fonseca, and ... she had lost count. Marta's love affairs didn't last long; she would find an excuse to break free of them as soon as the novelty had worn off. Maybe Sara's laugh had been too brief, because the other woman noticed. "What's wrong? You're not looking yourself."

"Don't worry, one or two problems."

"With your man?"

"No. At least he only gets on my nerves because he hasn't broken into Benfica's first team. Apart from that, all's well."

"I've never had a soccer player. It must be cool, says the person who doesn't understand a thing about soccer."

"I had to learn."

Marta gave her another slap on the thigh. She looked straight at her, as only she knew how. Then she said, seriously, "You've got some problem, it's obvious. Something to do with the situation in Angola?"

"No, no ... Well, yes, in a way."

"Tell me. It'll do you good to get it off your chest."

"It's just one or two problems. Why should I trouble you with them?"

"Oh, is that so? I tell you everything, except for how many times a night I fuck because I know you don't like that kind of talk. And you shut up like a clam. Is that how friends are supposed to behave toward one another?"

Sara lit another cigarette from the stub of her previous one. She'd managed to arouse Marta's curiosity in the matter, not that that was hard. But she had to proceed with caution, because the situation was precarious.

"It's not my problem, but a friend's, a good friend. He's in a difficult position and I don't know how to help him. That's why I'm worried, that's all."

"And aren't we allowed to know what the problem is with this friend of yours?"

"I don't know whether I have the right to tell you. You understand, it's his problem."

"Look stop beating about the bush. Tell me what the problem is and then let's go and see to our patients, because it doesn't look as if there are too many today."

"He needs somewhere to stay for a few days. A safe place, where he won't be noticed. And I just don't see where such a place can be found. He's a great friend, and I can't help him. Do you see why I'm worried?"

"But can't he go to a guesthouse?"

"That would be crazy. It's crucial no one notices him, don't you see?"

Marta suddenly slapped her hand on her forehead. She became more serious and lowered her voice, which was normally very loud.

"I've got it, the boy's in hiding. Politics?"

"Of course. He must have every PIDE agent on his tail as we speak."

"I should have known. Your problems always turn out to be political. When are you going to ditch those things?"

"It's a problem linked to a friendship. It's only by chance that it's political."

"Do I know this friend of yours?"

"No."

She was lying, but she needed to. She had already introduced Aníbal to Marta, and they had even got on well. They had kept up a long theoretical debate on a trip to Cascais. They had irreconcilable views: he defended the need for organizational planning in order to carry out any revolution, while Marta maintained that politicians are merely candidates for corruption in waiting. That had been two years ago, and they hadn't met again since, even though she would occasionally ask her what had become of Aníbal, that revolutionary friend of hers. They got on well, even though the debate had been a fiery one. It would inevitably be like that whenever they met.

"Is he Angolan?"

"Yes. And he's Black, if you want to know. Which makes things harder, because it's not that easy for a Black person to hide among whites."

"Do you want him to stay at my place?"

The direct question was typical of Marta. Sara blamed herself for not having foreseen this. With her friend, it was very hard to prevaricate, to make veiled suggestions. If Marta was interested in a man, she would ask him openly when they were going to bed, today or tomorrow? All the more so in this case.

"Well, I don't know ... You asked me to tell you my problem and I told you, that's all."

Marta got up. Abruptly, as was her habit. Except that this time it was too abrupt, and she almost knocked the white chair over.

"Fuck you, don't be a hypocrite. You know I hate hypocrisy. If you want it, fine, tell me it to my face. And I'll tell you, that's all right, he can stay there. I'll do you this favour, but it's for you, not him, nor for any party or whatever. I want to make that very clear."

Sara felt a huge sense of relief and at the same time felt somewhat ashamed. Her friend had shown up her subterfuge and called it hypocrisy. She was right. Marta couldn't understand that certain delicate situations obliged people to be prudent, to tread warily. In a word, to act politically. She tried to correct any ill feeling, convinced from the outset that she would fail.

"You're right. But you must understand that it was a request that was loaded with risks. If they find out, not even your father will save you. I thought of you in fact, but it was my duty to be cautious. And to tell you that it's very dangerous. If you refuse, I won't think badly of you."

"There you go with your waffle ... How long?"

"About two weeks."

"Shit, having to put up with a guy for so long! And what's worse, he might be a bit of an idiot, like your man."

"He's the most intelligent man I know."

Marta sat down again and slowly lit a cigarette. She looked her in the eyes. She muttered, her eyes gleaming maliciously, "You're not hiding something from me, are you?"

"Yes . . . You've guessed, it's Aníbal."

They both laughed. Sara thought, With Marta, precautions are pointless. She either trusted her and blurted it all out, or she remained silent. Their many years of friendship should have taught her that.

"Is he at your place?"

"He slept there last night. He left home early because the cleaning woman is coming to tidy the room. He's probably sitting in a garden trying not to be noticed. He can't stay on at my place for long; sooner or later, the landlady will find out. And the PIDE know we're friends and are bound to turn up."

"Of course. There'll be no problem at my place. As long as he doesn't stick his nose outside. The only worry is that I never know whether some relative is going to visit me. Alentejans have huge families; they're like Africans, you know. But we'll find a way."

"As for his food, I'll see to that."

"Go to hell. He's my guest and you're going to cook him food? So what's the point of having him as my guest? There's just one thing I can't understand. Why you didn't shack up with him, instead of choosing that soccer player. He's got much more to him, despite his size."

"Tastes aren't up for discussion."

Marta got up. She looked at her watch and sighed. "We've got to go back to work. What time will you be bringing him along?"

"Not so fast. Before anything else, I should have a word with him. It's even possible he's found some other solution. I'll phone to tell you I'll be delivering the letter."

"You love these little secret codes in covert politics. Okay, let me know when you're delivering your little letter. And what a weighty little letter!"

Marta gave her a further slap on the thigh, stubbed out her cigarette, and went back to her patients. Sara remained sitting there, breathing deeply. This girl Marta is a wild horse, a buffalo. I pity the poor gentleman who tries to throw a saddle on her. Unless he's a Tarzan. Aníbal is going to have to stock up on his patience, or else their discussions are going to be heard right along the block and they'll have the police on their doorstep. I've got to warn him about her personality, her little ways.

Malongo was waiting for her at the door of the hospital. Sara had been running late with some last-minute things to do, and his patience was wearing thin. These days it was rare for him to come and meet her, which was why she found this odd. There must be a problem, she thought when she saw him sitting on the steps up to the entrance. But no, Malongo kissed her naturally and complained calmly, "I thought you were never coming. I was on the point of leaving. Many dead?"

"I haven't killed anyone." She laughed. "So how did your training go?"

"Same as always. They put me in the reserves. I scored a beautiful goal. That may count for something. But I'm not hopeful anymore."

She put her arm through his. She was happy Malongo had come looking for her. That must mean something. She nestled up against him. The midday sun shone down on her face and she was grateful, getting over her unfair thoughts of earlier that morning. She had to give Malongo some time, as he had come to her for some moral support.

"You've got to believe in yourself. If you begin to lose hope, how are you going to convince others of your talent?"

Malongo didn't answer. He just squeezed her tighter. They

walked as far as the bus stop. There was a long queue, and people gave them surreptitious looks. Sara saw disapproval in the eyes of the women. I'm just becoming paranoid. They're simply looking at us out of curiosity. She was irresistibly drawn to do something she generally avoided, as it wasn't a common sight in Lisbon. She kissed Malongo quickly on the mouth. He was caught by surprise but responded. It was a fleeting kiss, a mere brushing of the lips. Was it just her impression or was there some movement of rejection among those waiting in line? An old man was now openly looking at the two of them; he seemed about to say something. Sara was convinced, no, it wasn't paranoia on her part. The old man couldn't conceal his silent reproach. A fossil, leaning on a closed umbrella. A black umbrella, as convention required, even in the summer. She pulled Malongo out of the queue. "Let's walk for a bit. Get away from this bunch of reactionaries."

"Ah, did you notice? I no longer care. But your kiss really did provoke them. You were lucky no one said anything."

"Are you sure you're not too tired to walk?"

"I'll soon get my strength back. I could even play another ninety minutes. But Sara, you've got to get used to racism."

"The incredible thing is that all these people are the product of a long process of racial mixing. Two hundred years ago, more than fifteen percent of the population of southern Portugal was Black. Slaves brought to work in domestic service, cleaning the city streets, and in agriculture in the Alentejo. And in Lisbon, the percentage was even higher. Those Blacks blended in; they weren't killed or expelled. They went around making children. And before them, there were the Arabs, who once made up the majority of the population. And Jews, and goodness knows who else. There was never such a thing as a pure Portuguese. They always were mixed. And now, screw them, they start being racist."

"I never felt it before. Either I was really naive or things were different. They might look at me in the street, they might even make a comment they wouldn't make to a white. But there was no malice in it. It was obvious that I was accepted without any fuss. Now it's different. There's hostility."

They walked in silence for a while. As they strolled along, Sara watched the people who passed them. There was no doubt: they were at least the cause for curiosity, they didn't pass unnoticed. And people looked her up and down: Look at that white woman clinging to a Black man. Would it reach the stage when they threw stones at her in the street? No, that would be too much for the passive Portuguese personality. Who knows? Who can tell how a crowd will react once they've been whipped into a frenzy?

"I've been wondering lately," Malongo said. "My not making the first team—is it because I'm Black?"

"Nonsense. What the club wants is to win. They're not interested in the colour of their players. Their biggest stars are Black or mixed race."

"Yes, but maybe one more is too many. It may be that they've put two and two together, and have come to the opinion that one more might provoke a backlash."

"Well, they'd cancel your contract. They wouldn't pay you your wages just to wallow in the reserves."

"If they cancel my contract, I'll go to another club. A rival. They're paying me so as not to let me go and strengthen one of their rivals. That sort of thing happens, didn't you know?"

Sara understood little about soccer, much less the inner workings of a club. But she instinctively rejected the idea. There must be other reasons for their not playing Malongo. Benfica could not, in its regulations, contract foreign players. This was why it recruited the best players in the colonies, who were legally Portuguese and cost them less. No, the explanation must lie elsewhere. One day, she would have to try to find out. Maybe they would tell her what they were hiding from Malongo. When she was less taken up with other worries. All of a sudden, she got the feeling she wasn't doing all she could for Malongo. His future should be an important concern of hers. At the same time, whether because of some prejudice against soccer or for some other reason, she undervalued her boyfriend's frustration. Was it lack of love? Did she just feel physically attracted to him, not caring about the rest? She rejected the idea. She even wanted a baby with him. But the doubt kept reverberating in her mind in a troubling manner. She leaned into him, feeling the warmth of his powerful body, indifferent to the looks they were attracting.

"So, the young lady went out on the town last night? I got a message from Vítor just as I was about to head over to your place."

"Yes, I had something that needed doing."

"What was that?"

It wasn't going to be as easy as she had imagined. Malongo could call off meetings or even just not turn up. He would give an excuse and that would be it, it wasn't mentioned again. But she had to explain every little thing, and this had become a habit. A bad habit. The relationship was not one between equals. It was her fault, no doubt.

"Look, Malongo, there's something going on that I can't tell you about. One day, I'll tell you, I promise, and as soon as possible. But for the time being, you're just going to have to trust me. It's nothing for you to feel ashamed about. It's just that I can't tell you."

"I don't like you doing things I can't know about."

"I know, but this time, that's how it's got to be. Please, don't insist. It's nothing bad, quite the opposite."

Malongo got offended and stopped talking. Every time Sara tried to engage him in conversation, he muttered a few monosyllables. Soon he said, "I'm tired, let's catch the bus." At the bus stop, he kept quiet, even though they had to wait some time. He continued to feel sorry for himself during the journey. They got off at the Praça do Saldanha, where they would normally part, as she would be going home and he would go for lunch.

"I'll phone you later," Sara said.

"I'll come home with you. I don't feel like having lunch at the canteen. We can buy something on the way and eat at your place."

This is what they sometimes did. But why today when he was upset? Was it only because he wanted to make peace, or did he suspect something? And why fall over backwards to try to make peace, when he was the one who had got annoyed? Sara took a deep breath. She felt a spat brewing on the horizon.

"That won't be possible for the reason I just told you. You can't come home with me. I'm sorry, but that's how it's got to be. Please understand."

They had stopped on the sidewalk and his glare was becoming increasingly angry.

"What are you hiding from me?"

"I can't tell you, you know that already."

"Very well, if that's what you want," and he turned away angrily. He didn't even say goodbye and crossed the road. She stood there, her arm outstretched in a helpless gesture to hold him back, torn, unhappy. She watched him walk quickly away toward the Casa dos Estudantes, without a backwards glance. And she walked slowly away in the opposite direction, wanting to cry. Then she came to her senses. She wasn't going to cry like a little girl just because of her boyfriend's show of macho displeasure. Her tears obeyed her. It was a short-lived victory that gave her no great comfort.

In a grocer's near her home, she bought some things for lunch. This helped her calm down and return to the reality of her duties. As she left the grocer's with her bag of purchases, she looked attentively up and down the street. She took particular note of people leaning against the walls of buildings who looked as if they might be spies. If someone had noticed Aníbal's presence or had recognized him that morning, the house might already be under surveillance. But there was no man pretending to read a paper or walking up and down in front of the door to the building. Nor were there any cafés where a PIDE agent could hide. Fortunately, the entrance door was open. It was only at this point that she realized they had made a mistake. If the door were closed, which was often the case, she would have to ring the landlady's bell. She would say she had forgotten to take her keys with her, but she would have to enter her room through the communicating door to the rest of the apartment. Aníbal would already have locked it to avoid a sudden surprise visit by the landlady. So how would she explain that the door between her room and the landlady's apartment was locked from the inside if she had left it open for the cleaning lady? She would be giving away the presence of a stranger in her room. She climbed the two floors nervously and lightly tapped the door to her room which had direct access to the stairs.

Aníbal opened the door and smiled. She breathed a sigh of relief and fell into his arms.

"Hey, calm down, you're shaking and you're as white as a sheet," he murmured.

She told him her fears. And then, as they prepared lunch, she explained her conversation with Marta and the advantages of moving to her place. Aníbal agreed. "It's not ideal, but it's better than here." He only had a few misgivings regarding Marta. "That anarchist friend of yours is capable of setting fire to Lisbon just to burn a few right-wing and left-wing politicians."

Sara defended her friend. "Sometimes it takes some snipers to solve problems." That was the case now, when organizations were proving too cumbersome to improvise. Marta would claim, she thought without voicing it, that organizations only act to protect their interests, bound by their own logic of self-protection and scorning individual problems. And society was made up of individuals, whom they deliberately forgot. But that was a matter for Aníbal and Marta to debate face to face; she would leave it to them.

They arranged to only leave the apartment in the early evening, when it was getting dark. At that time, there were more people in the street and he would be able to pass unnoticed. She would leave first with the overnight bag, and Aníbal would then go and meet her at the nearest taxi stand. This was a subject of much discussion. Taxis were dangerous: the PIDE might have distributed his photo or a physical description of him to taxi drivers, who were in the habit of collaborating with the police. They wouldn't get out right in front of Marta's building, but the whole area would be under suspicion. And the greatest risk was to Sara, who might be recognized if seen in his company. In the end, it was Aníbal who made the decision. He would be the first to leave, without his bag, which might look suspicious. He would catch a taxi by himself and get out on the Largo do Rato, which was a very busy square. From there, he would continue on foot for fifteen minutes until he reached Marta's house. Sara would leave later with the bag and take a taxi directly to Marta's. She would arrive before Aníbal and wait for him down below. They wouldn't be seen together, which meant that Sara's safety would be assured. And the walk from the Rato to the apartment was sufficiently long to considerably widen the search area for the police, in the event of his being reported by the taxi driver. It also had an advantage because he knew the area well and he would be able to make sure that he wasn't being followed, or he would be able to throw his followers off the scent if it became necessary. He took a note of Marta's phone number, just in case he had to arrive late. Everything was fixed and they had lunch, talking about other things.

Sara didn't mention her scene with Malongo, for it would only make Aníbal feel guilty. And she didn't want to try to make herself a martyr for a cause for some trivial reason, in the face of someone who was risking everything for the same cause. Above all, they talked about Marta, Sara explaining her friend's ways.

"It really is annoying," Aníbal said. "I'm going to alter the daily life of someone I hardly know. For two weeks, she's going to live a life of uncertainty and have to follow another routine. I'll try not to be too much of a burden, but even so ..."

"The basic rule is that you never leave the house nor open the door to anyone, if you are alone. And shut yourself in the bathroom if she's at home and someone turns up. Of course, she'll immediately say she's on her way out on an urgent matter. And she'll drag the visitor out with her. But you'll fix all that between yourselves. And you'll see, she's got an answer for everything, and she's very quick to get out of sticky situations. What worries me is that you may get into political discussions, and at that point she'll lose her head and start talking louder than a commentator at a soccer game."

"Doesn't she have a boyfriend? In these things, boyfriends can cause problems."

"No, she's free. She broke up with the one she had. And if she gets herself another one, she certainly won't give him her address. Now, one more thing ... If she goes out, whatever the time, never ask her where she's going. She guards her independence far too jealously, and she'll tell you to get lost."

"Oh don't worry. I'd already worked that out."

"I'll visit you every day to see whether you need anything and bring you newspapers. That won't raise any suspicions, because I often go to her place."

"No. That wouldn't be prudent. Just imagine if they start following all the people who might be linked to me. And they discover that you're going to a particular house every day. Don't you think they're going to want to know what's going on there? You'll get news from me via Marta, whom you see every day at the hospital."

Sara nodded. Sadly. Would she not see Aníbal again before he left the country?

"Of course, you can go there from time to time. As often as you usually do. It's important that you don't modify your habits. Any change may look suspicious."

After lunch, she tried to work. But Aníbal's presence and her problems with Malongo didn't let her. He sat in the armchair, reading and making as little noise as possible. But she would often get up from her desk and think of something to say. The afternoon progressed without her dissertation advancing even a millimetre. As they were tidying things away in order to leave, Aníbal suddenly remembered, "I'm going to spend my whole time reading. Has your friend only got books by Kropotkin or on medicine?"

"No, she's got lots of others. But choose any from here you haven't read."

"My bag's full. If I need any more, I'll ask her to ask you. I'll just take this one I've got in my hand."

And he showed her Sartre's *Nausea*. In his situation, it's not a book I would have chosen, thought Sara. But she just smiled. Aníbal had a strong character, he didn't need romantic novels to keep his spirit up. She was always forgetting that.

6

Denise's stay was coming to an end, and she was due to leave in three days' time. The university ran holiday programs for foreigners, but she wanted to spend the summer in France and her Portuguese was now so advanced that she no longer needed to attend another course. Malongo was trying to persuade her to stay on for a while, as he hadn't yet had enough of her. Their relationship had become much more public ever since Sara had turned so secretive a week earlier, to the point of even refusing to have lunch with him at her place. He took Denise to the Rialva and to the Casa dos Estudantes. She was a real hit. All his friends eyed the blond and came over to try to engage her in conversation. They slapped Malongo on the back, whispering to him, "Yes sir, you're eating well these days." He was proud of the covetous looks directed at Denise.

And her popularity was even greater when, after lunch, they went through to the lounge of the Casa to talk. Many of the students skipped their usual coffee to chat to the French girl. She revealed that she was a supporter of the Algerian FLN and had even been active in a group that supported Algerian independence. For the first time, students were able to hear the nationalist version of that war, which had brought such hope to Africa. Denise took delight in being able to explain the origins and main features of the struggle in Algeria and how some French were supporting their Arab comrades. The Portuguese press only reported the colonialist French version of events. And they openly argued for the theories of the French far right, which was organizing itself under the banner of the OAS. And so it was refreshing to be able to discover that the Algerian "terrorists" had great leaders such as Krim Belkacem, Ben Bella, Aït Ahmed, Ben Khedda, Boudiaf, some of them in jail but soon to be released, others preparing to negotiate with the de Gaulle government in order to achieve independence. They listened to her talking about the battle of Algiers, Kabylia, and Aurès, names reported in the press but now described in completely different terms, wrapped in an aura of heroism. The audience grew bigger, and the beautiful Denise was ever more coveted. Malongo listened absent-mindedly; he had already heard her talk about these things, though only in dribs and drabs, because he kept interrupting her for more important matters, such as lovemaking, for instance.

When, at four in the afternoon, they left, Denise was invited to return more often, preferably every day, for she still had so many things to teach them. Someone even proposed she give a talk on the subject, but the others replied, "You must be crazy; in the situation we're in here, that would just be an excuse to close down the Casa once and for all."

"And even this conversation," Furtado murmured to Laurindo, "is going straight into the PIDE files, and the beautiful Denise will never get another visa to return to Portugal." Laurindo agreed, inconsolable for having to admit that his former friend was right.

Malongo only allowed the others to think he might be in a relationship with Denise; he never confirmed it. He was annoyed with Sara, but Denise was leaving and Sara was staying. The day after she had refused to have lunch, Sara phoned him, saying, "Come over to my place tonight, the situation has changed, and in a few days' time I'll be able to explain everything." He made an excuse, he already had a commitment, and he went and slept with Denise, something he was doing with increasing frequency. Then when Sara turned up at the Casa looking for him, he was cold toward her and refused to talk things over. Two days later, she tried again and he maintained his frostiness, so as you should know I'm not a doll, he said. And yesterday when Sara sought him out for the third time and asked him whether their relationship was over, just "so we know where things stand," he stammered, "I'm angry and I want a complete explanation."

"But I can't give you one yet, trust me and wait a while."

"Well, when you can give me an explanation, then come and see me, but not before." And he went off to meet Denise for a final few rounds.

The current situation suited him, he thought as he made for the Rialva, where he was going to meet Vítor. He had plenty of free time to spend these last few days with Denise. And even a ready-made excuse, in the event Sara heard something about this relationship of his. Of course, I was angry with you, the French girl arrived on the scene, and I had to find something to distract me. It never would have happened if you hadn't started hiding things from me. And so, he had to maintain the facade of hurt pride, at least until Denise had left. But he didn't take her back to the Casa. Once was enough. He had risen in the esteem of his companions, who now treated him with greater deference. But it wasn't a good idea to overdo these conversations about politics, which Denise adored. Firstly, they made him want to nod off. Then she became all excited and wouldn't stop talking, even when they'd taken off all their clothes. Quite frankly, when a man penetrates a woman, his concentration needs to be focused solely on that, he can't get distracted by speeches. Music is the only thing that should accompany sex; music even helps, it improves one's rhythm. Plus the police were now becoming very watchful, and they might even start pestering him because of the French girl's big mouth.

By now the situation was getting really serious. Even Vítor was becoming more and more careful and conspiratorial, particularly when they weren't at home. Here, of course, he would speak his mind. About politics naturally. Yesterday he said, "Be careful with what you say, the PIDE boys are watching us like never before, especially since Aníbal disappeared." Some days before, news of this had exploded in the Casa like a bomb. The officer disappeared just as he was supposed to be leaving for Angola. He had even said goodbye to one or two people, "I'm going to fulfill my duty." People had remarked, "Just look at the guy, so he's going to fulfill his duty by killing Blacks." Then a few days later, the truth had come to light. Aníbal hadn't gone to Angola; he'd vanished into thin air. There were stifled laughs, happy glances, victory signs. Aníbal was cool, and it was just that he didn't go around shouting to all and sundry what was going on inside his head, nor what his duty was. The hiss of conversation became more animated; his friends wore more joyful expressions, despite the times. But it didn't last long. Strangers appeared in the Rialva, people who went to the Casa without even being members, student hostels were kept under surveillance, halls of residence as well. Malongo hadn't noticed anything, but Vítor pointed to a man who was always standing in front of the building on the Rua Praia da Vitória. They were keeping an eye on every possible nook and cranny in their search for Aníbal. Or for other things.

For the first time, he remembered his military situation. He had done military service at the age of twenty-one, but only as a conscript. Benfica had found a way of getting him exempted after six months. Could it be that he was now going to be called up because of the war in Angola? He had been away from active service for the last two years, but he wasn't free from being conscripted again, especially if there was a shortage of military personnel. It was the same for students who could get postponements until the time they completed their courses, provided they didn't fail their exams. There was talk that this might come to an end, and that all men aged twenty or twenty-one, whether or not they passed their year, would be mobilized. Fuck, they'll catch me, and this time Benfica won't be able to save me. So what shall I do? Am I going to wage war, me whose only love is soccer? Aníbal's solution might be attractive for romantic young girls, but it was the action of a politician. Of course, Sara must be happy; she adored that weedy little intellectual and she agreed with everything he thought. But he wasn't so easily charmed by someone who only read and loved philosophy. He'd have to have a word with Vítor. He wasn't at all happy with the situation.

His friend was sitting at a table with Laurindo. They were going to see a film after dinner. Malongo turned down an invitation to join them. "I've got a lot to do." The others laughed, since he never had anything to do. Vítor shot back, "You're going to meet Denise." Malongo nodded and Laurindo stopped smiling. "What's wrong with this guy—does he want to screw the French woman as well? The kid's already dreaming big." But Malongo pretended he hadn't heard and changed the subject to the matter that concerned him.

"Is it true they're going to call up students and not allow them to defer anymore?"

"There's talk of it," said Vítor. "It's a real war zone back home, and the whole of the north is in the hands of the terrorists."

As Vítor spoke, he looked at the next table, where a fellow wearing a grey hat had visibly stiffened behind his newspaper when Malongo had asked his question. Vítor used the word *terrorist* on purpose, as that was the official term. In this way, he didn't run any risks. And his friends understood that they should choose their words carefully. Vítor is becoming a true undercover agitator, Malongo thought. Another politician in the making, he concluded with distaste.

They went for dinner. The atmosphere was gloomy; people spoke discreetly, looking around them as they did so. The ears of the PIDE were listening nearby. Malongo had a safe subject for conversation: soccer. But even provoked by Laurindo and Vítor, he didn't show much interest. He wanted to talk about his military situation, but he didn't dare. Vítor was the right age for military service, and he had failed his exams the previous year. He could be called up at any moment. So he should have had an interest in talking about this, but not there, where one couldn't talk with any ease. For Laurindo, it wasn't a pressing matter, because he was still too young. He would only get called up in two years' time; he could relax, so much could happen in two years. Malongo answered his friends' questions quickly, while trying to figure out how he could have a private word with Vítor, who was going to see a movie while he, Malongo, would only return home the following morning. It was too late. As with everything else, Malongo couldn't wait.

He went and met Denise, anxious with worry. "You're different," she told him when they were alone. "Has your day gone badly?" He should have started undressing her. But he sat on the bed and looked at her. She took off her summer dress and bra. She no longer had any inhibitions, and even wanted to provoke him, for she, too, wanted to make the most of their last few nights together. As Malongo didn't react, she sat on his lap and kissed him.

"I'm worried. They may call me up for military service, and I don't want to fight in a war. It looks as if they're going to mobilize all those who've managed to avoid it up until now."

"That's what happened to the Algerians and the French as well. You've got to escape."

"Escape, me?"

"Of course. Go to France. No one can come and get you there. And I'll help you. You can get a job and take things from there."

"And stop playing soccer?"

"I don't know how easy it is to play there. But there are certainly good teams. The important thing is to get away in order to bring about the revolution. Soccer's a secondary thing."

"For me, it's the main thing."

Denise became thoughtful. He couldn't make up his mind whether to caress her. She couldn't feel Malongo responding physically to the heat of her body. She stopped moving around sensuously on top of him, seeking a reaction. She said, "Are you going to get called up soon?"

"I don't know. But it won't necessarily be tomorrow."

"As soon as I get to France, I'll try to find out whether it's easy for an African to get into a soccer team. And I'll write and tell you what I come up with. Of course, I'll be careful, because I know letters get read before they're delivered."

"I don't speak French. I learned some grammar, but I don't speak it."

"You'll soon be speaking it. You studied French for five years at school, right?"

"But I was a very bad student."

Denise deployed all her skill to make him forget his concerns. Her caresses and kisses caused him to get an erection. Nature came back to the surface and Malongo forgot soldiers and wars. He suddenly took off his clothes and involved himself in another kind of combat, one for which he was far better qualified.

7

Sara got a message from Marta that Aníbal wanted to see her. A week had passed since his desertion. It would be normal for her to visit her friend; it couldn't cause any suspicion. She had noticed one or two strange goings-on in front of her house, but only two days after Aníbal had already left. Individuals leaning against doorposts on the other side of the street, one or two who would catch the same bus as her. She got on with her usual routines, except for meeting Malongo, who was giving her the cold shoulder. She didn't worry too much about police surveillance, because she was sure it had only started after Aníbal had moved to the other house. They were probably doing this with all of Aníbal's possible contacts. Laurindo had told her that the people at the Casa were being almost brazenly watched. But they seemed to have stopped hounding her since the previous day. She got into the habit of remembering the faces of those who got on the bus with her and of those who got off. She would walk for a bit and look back, while adjusting her shoe or pretending to look in a shop window. She made a note of those standing around in front of her house. And ever since yesterday, she hadn't seen anything suspicious. They had given up; they couldn't monitor everyone all the time.

However, when she accompanied Marta back from the hospital, directly to her friend's home, she paid attention to everything around her. In the middle of a banal conversation, she whispered, "Have you taken care you're not being followed?"

Marta laughed. She squeezed her arm. Trying to keep her voice as low as she could, her Alentejan colleague said, "I'm a perfect undercover operative. I notice everything. And you know I've got the memory of an elephant. I can guarantee you, they don't suspect anything. Aníbal helps, too. He hasn't set foot outside the house, and if he's alone, he doesn't open the door to anyone. He's like a cat: he doesn't make a noise even when he's moving around. If the windows are open, he never goes near them. I don't think he's looked out into the street since he arrived. They can't possibly suspect anything."

Even so, Sara remained alert. They bought whatever they needed for lunch and went up to Marta's apartment. There was nothing suspicious in the street, Sara was sure.

Aníbal looked thinner. She commented on this, and Marta intervened in mock horror, "If you think I'm treating him badly, you're mistaken."

Aníbal smiled and spoke. "I've never eaten better in my life. It's just your impression, nothing more."

"The food's good, that I know," Marta said. "It's just that this guy doesn't eat much. He must get his energy from somewhere else."

Marta went to the kitchen. The two friends sat down near each other. Sara told him the little she knew of the siege to which the Angolans were being subjected. And of the reactions caused in the Casa by the news of his desertion. Aníbal smiled. "Others will follow." He said he was well stocked with literature. Marta, after all, had an abundant library. And the discussions between them weren't as heated as he had imagined they would be. "In short, she's great." Sara told him how she had been spied on, but that it now looked as if it was over.

"That's normal," he said. "After a few days, they don't find anything and give up. But don't drop your guard, your sixth sense must be kept alert. They may come back at any moment."

They chatted about the political situation, the news in the papers, which they had to learn how to interpret. And then, out of the blue, Sara said, "I'm pregnant. I'm going to have a little girl."

"How do you know it's a girl?"

"Intuition."

"How did Malongo react?"

"He doesn't know yet. You're the first person I've told. And don't say anything to Marta."

"You should tell Malongo."

"Yes, one of these days."

Sara didn't tell him they had practically broken up. Why cause Aníbal any more worries? She would have had to tell him the quarrel was because of him. Aníbal would declare that Malongo wasn't worth it, might even suggest she get an abortion. And the problem was hers and hers alone; she didn't even want to discuss it. At the same time, she found it strange that she had felt the need to confide in Aníbal. Even if her relationship with Malongo hadn't hit the rocks, she would have told her friend first.

"Look, Sara, I asked you to come over to do me another favour. Of course, I wanted to see you and have a chat. But I also have another favour to ask. As I've always told you, you can refuse, and I'll find another way. But it would be best if I didn't have to go out."

"Don't worry, I'll do whatever's needed."

"There's an element of risk, but only slight, as long as you take care. You'll recall, when I turned up at your house, that I had dinner with a comrade who was going to get things ready for my escape. Since I moved here, he doesn't have my contact details. I need to get in touch with him. I know of a way to meet him, but it would be better if I didn't leave the house. Can you contact the fellow?"

"Yes, of course."

"We had arranged a meeting in a garden tomorrow at four in the afternoon. If I couldn't go, you would. He's got your description. But wear your glasses. I told him you wore glasses and now I've remembered you often don't wear them, so that you can see the world more beautiful than it really is."

They both laughed, and Sara was astonished at how Aníbal managed to be so calm and even to remember apparently insignificant details. Was this due to his experience of difficult situations or merely moral strength? That strength given him by an unshakeable faith in a cause he considered just. Or perhaps it was only a desire to demonstrate confidence so that others might feel it as well. In any event, it required courage.

"Take Marta's phone number jotted on a scrap of paper. Go up to him and say you've come on behalf of Joaquim. I chose the most Portuguese name there is! Ask him if he has any news for Joaquim. When you leave, shake hands and discreetly give him the slip of paper with the number. Before that, tell him he should only phone at night, when Marta is at home, because I don't answer it when she isn't there. And he should ask to speak to Joaquim. In the meantime, I'll tell Marta that I'm Joaquim."

"How will I recognize him?"

"He'll be reading a newspaper and sitting on a bench next to the statue of Diana. He's middle-aged with black hair, and he'll be wearing a check shirt. We agreed on that just in case I was unable to go. If the bench next to the statue is already occupied, he'll be on the nearest one to it. There aren't many, and it'll be easy to identify him. After that, give me a call. From a public pay phone, not from home. Don't come here. Phone."

"Shall I speak to Marta or to you?"

"Tell Marta you want to speak to her friend and don't mention names. And don't say yours. Marta recognizes your voice. Then speak to me, only to tell me everything has gone to plan and whatever news you have. Briefly and indirectly. It can be the journey is on such and such a date or something like that. Okay?"

"Yes, that's clear. You just haven't told me which garden it is."

He told her the name of a little garden not far from where she lived. She had often walked through it but had never noticed the statue of Diana. She told Aníbal this and thought she'd better go and familiarize herself with the place.

"No. Only go tomorrow at the exact time. There won't be a problem; it's the only statue there is. If you go there today and then again tomorrow, that's not your usual routine, and it might attract attention. And make sure you're not being followed. You know the usual tricks, don't you?"

"I've read lots of crime novels, don't worry."

"Yes, they have their uses sometimes. I've never had the time to read many. I've had other concerns."

"The prejudices of an intellectual, who only has time for great literature."

"No, there are some great whodunnit novels. I never had time. I was always engaged in other things. But I've read one here at Marta's."

Their friend said the food was nearly ready, and Sara went and laid the table. The three of them chatted, and Sara noticed that the other two seemed to get on well, even when it came to political matters. They had different opinions: Aníbal defended Marxist theories, Marta argued against them. But each one listened to the other's arguments, and no one got excited or tried to dismantle them. It was a civilized conversation. Sara noticed there was some sort of special degree of affection in the way they spoke to each other, although they were extremely discreet. That's it, two intelligent people always understand each other, even when they have different ideas, she thought. And apart from anything else, they had a lot in common, a hatred of the Salazar dictatorship and a belief in the independence of the colonies. They were opposed in their preferred methods and in their way of seeing how society should develop in the future. A society in which the State would abolish classes, according to

Aníbal; a society without a State, for this would only serve as a cover for new classes to come into existence, according to Marta.

Sara went home, not knowing whether she would see Aníbal again. She hid the sadness this idea caused and said goodbye quickly. He did the same. But the kiss he placed on her cheek lingered longer than usual. A farewell? Maybe for the rest of their lives.

She managed to do a little work, although she couldn't stop thinking about the next day's meeting. Recently, and so as to forget Malongo's behaviour and everything that was happening, she had tried to work late at night. And she had made some progress on her dissertation. She was learning to live with her preoccupations, and this was a source of some pride and self-assurance. She slept badly, which was becoming a habit. And the following morning at hospital, she kept looking at her wristwatch. There was still plenty of time, but she couldn't afford to arrive late. She knew that in these things, every minute counted and the comrades were very strict. From the hospital, she went straight home; she didn't even try to contact Malongo. In fact, she made an effort not to think about him too much and to regard their separation as stupid but irreversible. She was going to have to get used to the idea of having a daughter with no father. It wouldn't be good for the child, but everything in life had a solution. The important thing was that she should be born. Sara felt herself capable of being both a mother and father at the same time. And what was more, she sensed that she was against the idea of a traditional family.

She left home at three in the afternoon, glancing discreetly all around.

She hailed a passing taxi and asked to be dropped at the Parque Eduardo VII. The speed with which she had caught her taxi was enough to throw any follower off the scent. Nevertheless, she constantly watched her back. She got out of the taxi and went into the Metro station. She caught the first train, alert to everything happening around her. She got off three stations later and caught one going in the opposite direction. She was sure she wasn't being followed. She got off after five stations and caught another taxi. By now she was calmer, but she continued to keep an eye on the cars behind her. The taxi dropped her near the garden, but it was still only a quarter to four. She went into a café and ordered a bica. She felt a pain in her stomach, as if she were about to go into an important examination. When she was younger, she used to throw up before exams, despite being the best student throughout her school years. She left at five to four and went into the garden, constantly keeping her eye on the time and watching her back. She reached the statue of Diana at four o'clock on the dot, and there was a man sitting reading a paper. And wearing a checked shirt.

"I'm here on behalf of Joaquim," she said, almost in a whisper.

He put down his paper to reveal a pair of vivid eyes closely scrutinizing this woman in front of him and the whole area around them. Sara was experiencing her first encounter in the flesh with a living myth, the undercover militant operative. Maybe it was this that had given her a pain in the stomach, and not her fear as such. He gestured to her gracefully, and she sat down next to him.

"Do you have any news for him?"

"He'll have to wait for at least a week. But everything is running according to plan."

"He's had to move house. I've the phone number on a slip of paper, which I'll give you when I leave. Phone at night, a woman will answer and ask to speak to Joaquim."

"That's okay. Stay here for five minutes and then leave."

The man got up, shook her hand, receiving at the same time the paper with the phone number on it. He walked nonchalantly away, breathing in the fresh air and looking, enthralled, at the flowers in the flowerbeds. Sara sat observing the garden. There was only a pair of lovebirds sitting on a bench at the back of the garden, totally oblivious to the world. She let five minutes pass, apparently resting, but focusing on the boy and girl and on what else might be going on. She walked out of the garden, then back along the street skirting it, saw the boy and girl in the same position, and took a deep breath. She could now go to the nearest public phone and call, mission accomplished.

She felt lighthearted and almost joyful. She had already distributed leaflets, been a member of the student committee for demonstrations against the government on Student Day, signed petitions demanding free elections, given a talk condemning colonialism at the Casa, and participated in other less important activities. She had almost certainly had contact with members of the political underground, without knowing it. This was the first time she had spoken to someone in the full knowledge of who he was. Prudence demanded that she immediately forget the face and manner of this communist. But she couldn't. Those lively eyes, the warmth of his speech, his affable, almost affectionate air remained etched on her memory. These were the anonymous heroes who risked their lives every day in order to fight the dictatorship. In order to create another far worse world, Malongo would say. Marta too.

She had often talked with Aníbal about questions of ideology. And with Furtado as well, in the days when he was a keen proponent of world revolution. She had read the odd book, not much, because Marxist literature only entered Portugal secretly and was very difficult to get hold of. Once, Aníbal told her of Khrushchev's report on the crimes of Stalinism. He hadn't read the text itself, only a summary from secondary sources. But he was perturbed; one couldn't construct a fair society on the basis of crimes and persecution. Furtado, on the contrary, called Khrushchev a fat cat who was betraying communism. She didn't have any fixed position; she didn't feel sufficiently well informed.

She believed in a fair society, built on values of equality. She admired the courage of the Communists, who were in prison and saw their network destroyed but who rose again and continued the struggle. At the same time, she sensed a growing reserve in Aníbal toward these mythical beings. Long before the events in Angola. She instinctively assimilated Aníbal's reservations into her own. And now he, her compass, was about to disappear for good. She had to have an honest conversation with him before that; her friend couldn't leave her adrift.

She phoned. She left the message. Then she asked, "Aníbal, before you go I need to talk to you. For me, it's vitally important." He agreed. "Don't worry."

She was unable to work. She needed to see people, to get out and about. And so she headed for the Rialva. It was too early for Malongo to be there, which suited her. She didn't want to feel humiliated today. She needed to run into someone nice, pleasant, with whom she might exchange ideas, even if it was only on the state of the weather. And at one of the tables she found the poet, Horácio, giving Laurindo a literature lesson. She sat down with them, even though she found the pretentious poet abhorrent. He didn't even stop what he was saying to greet her; he waved to her and went on with his discourse, declaring that the latest poems published by the Casa dos Estudantes were concrete proof of the influence of Brazilian modernism on Angolan writers.

"Just look at that book by Viriato da Cruz. He heralds a definitive rupture with Portuguese literature. He uses the voice of the people, in the language spoken by the people of Luanda. This no longer bears any relation to what came before, and especially not to the Portuguese. From now on, literature will express the popular sentiment of difference. The Brazilians did this thirty years ago."

Laurindo was looking anxiously around him. He couldn't hide his desire for an excuse to escape. Sara noticed this and gave him a way out.

"Sorry, Horácio, but Laurindo's got to come with me. This conversation is so interesting, but I've come to fetch him."

She got up; Laurindo hurriedly put away the book pointlessly open in front of him, said goodbye to Horácio, and followed her. Once outside, he said, "Thanks, Sara, you turned up in the nick of time. He hadn't let me do any work for the last two hours. And to cap it all, talking about Viriato. Doesn't he realize that name is banned, even if he is only a poet?"

"When he talks about literature, he forgets about everything else. He's right that Viriato heralds a definitive rupture. In poetry and now in everything else. There may even be the influence of the Brazilians, I don't know. But to say that out loud in the Rialva is worse than spouting a political tract."

"Does he do it unconsciously?"

"Not really," said Sara. "The feeling I get is that he wants to be persecuted, even jailed. The poet arrested because he's a revolutionary. And writing poetry in jail. The romantic hero. A need to affirm himself, a need to suffer in order to feel a man. And to be admired by others. Maybe I'm being malicious, very unfair ... Poor Horácio, the PIDE don't take him seriously and won't give him the glory of a prison sentence."

They laughed. Sara felt relaxed in Laurindo's company, a complicity that had established itself during the demonstration. He was very young and immature, but he was willing to learn and had quickly become integrated in the student community. He didn't seem to her like the usual young man, dazzled by new freedoms far from his family, wasting his scholarship at the beginning of every month on trivia, and relying on loans to get by for the rest of the time. And he was open, which had become a major virtue in these untrustworthy times.

"Where are we going?" he asked.

"Wherever you feel like. I can stand you tea in a posh patisserie on the Avenida da República? Or shall we go to a movie?"

"The posh patisserie sounds good. I've never been in one. But let's go Dutch."

"Don't even think of it. I'm the one who invited you."

Laurindo didn't answer. There were those who would accept a woman's invitation but protested at the form it took, while expecting her to pay nevertheless. And there were those who would cadge an invitation, without any scruples at all. He was neither. Nor was he the type to ask her to pass him the money under the table in order for him to appear to be the one paying.

They had tea with toast. The patisserie really was a posh one. It was frequented by elderly or middle-aged women, showing off jewellery and expensive dresses. There were one or two men dotted around the tables, wearing suits and ties bought at the best outfitters, who looked as if they were in the liberal professions and well off. They contrasted with his student's appearance. And what was more, Laurindo was mixed race. But they didn't feel awkward sitting there at a table away from the others. They could talk about anything, without the uncomfortable presence of a man in a hat, forever reading the same page of a newspaper. Their conversation eventually turned to the situation in Angola and Aníbal's escape.

"People are now worried about the possibility of mass mobilization by the army. There's a lot of talk about that. And no one says it out loud, not even to their best friend, but everyone is thinking of following Aníbal's example."

"There's no other solution," Sara said.

"Personally, I don't have that problem yet. But I've already decided, I'm not going to fight. At least, not for this side. Do you think Aníbal's in France yet?"

"Yes, he must be. He must have fixed everything beforehand."

"That's good. I only knew him by sight. But he's held in high esteem by us all. I hope he goes and joins Mário and Viriato, not UPA."

"You can be sure of that. I know him well enough to swear to it."

"Vítor told me you were good friends."

"Yes. But lately we haven't seen much of each other, because he was called up and was stationed outside Lisbon."

She had to lie. To hide the truth. She didn't like to have to do so with Laurindo, an honest guy, but was there any other way? It's funny, I never had any problems of conscience when I hid things from Malongo, and yet he is, or at least was, my man. What a devil of a relationship did I get myself into with Malongo? And I no longer get offended if I hear barely concealed warnings from all and sundry about his lack of serious commitment.

"This atmosphere is getting harder and harder to bear," Laurindo said. "It's literally stifling. We fear our own shadow. We see PIDE men everywhere. The news from Angola is only about those who've been imprisoned, including intellectuals. Even whites. At any point, we may get caught in the net, even just for talking about things."

"Yes. Have you suffered a lot of racism here?"

"People look away more than they did before. I ask myself whether I'm imagining things, sometimes I'm not so sure. But what I can say is that no one has ever insulted me. Maybe there's more abruptness in a queue, maybe a show of impatience if I can't decide whether to buy something in a shop, maybe . . ."

"Be in no doubt, there has been an increase in racism. Recent events have produced a wave of patriotic fervour. They can well say, 'We are all Portuguese, and we have a multiracial society.' But coloured people are seen as undesirable foreigners. Worse, they're dangerous! Nationalism has provoked this."

"Even Angolan nationalism, Sara?"

"Isn't it also provocative?"

"Do you mean that any nationalism provokes racism or xenophobia, even ours, which we are fighting for?"

"In our case, or in Africa generally, nationalism is a necessary stage and it's worth fighting for. I don't have any doubts about that. But it also encourages unfair exclusions. And if it gets out of hand, it causes societies to shut themselves off, and not take advantage of the progress undergone by other peoples."

"A marriage between nationalism and internationalism, is that it?"

"You've defined it very well. A harmonious marriage between two antagonistic opposites."

"But that's Marxist terminology."

"Indeed. All that remains to be seen is whether this utopia can be achieved. Some people say they have already achieved it, with communism."

Laurindo shook his head, more in wonder than in shock. And with barely concealed fear, she noticed. Official propaganda was getting results. Even for the most earnest people, communism was a frightening spectre. Not only for the bourgeoisie, as Marx thought.

"Do you think our people outside the country believe in this utopia?" he queried.

"I have no idea."

"I've read a few tracts, but they don't talk about it. Have you read any?"

"No, no one's shown me any," she replied bitterly.

"I had to read them very quickly. If I ever get hold of them again, even if only for a few hours, I'll pass them on to you. Can I go to your house or phone you?"

"Any time you like. And thanks for your thoughtfulness. It's not nice to feel excluded."

They left the patisserie and said goodbye nearby. Sara went home, to spend another night alone. Would she do some work? She was going to try; she didn't have anything else to do. That and to think about her situation. The conversation with Laurindo had reminded her of something she always tended to forget, maybe as a form of psychological defence. What really was her position? People were beginning to think that the paradise of freedom was to be found abroad. One didn't need to talk to them in order to understand what was going on inside their heads. France was Eden, the benevolent haven for all the persecuted, the land of tolerance and of honey. Paris, known only through the movies, was the Babel, the place of convergence for all the world's rebels, the humiliated of every generation. The Angolans looked to Paris, without even daring to say it. And she? Was she going to finish her course and put herself in the lion's mouth of colonialism and racial hatred? Or stay here in this ambiguous society, her mouth tightly shut by the same fascist regime, fearing at every turn some anonymous denunciation? She still had to include Malongo in this equation with so many different variants, so many that she got lost in all the calculations. Beyond a doubt, only Aníbal could shed some light for her. Sara arrived home, the euphoria of her meeting in the garden long gone, with the sensation of being stuck in a boat without any oars, blindfolded, being swept along some powerful river like the Cunene, toward a waterfall.

8

The elders had asked him to do something for them. And Vítor had been very proud, because for the first time, they were inviting him to take part in something. It was very straightforward and apparently of little importance. However, he was already sufficiently familiar with the atmosphere in the Casa to know that behind something banal lay hidden something more important. The elders were students who were reaching the end of their course, or who had even finished it, and who would meet at each other's homes to discuss matters relating to their homeland. There was often a little bit of guitar playing mixed in with this. It didn't seem a particularly well-organized group to him, but they might well have links to what was going on abroad. In fact, they would occasionally share a secret document with him or a more serious account of events. And they would also pass along fresh news from back home. They operated in the background at the Casa dos Estudantes; some of them were on the board of directors and were decisive in influencing elections at the General Assembly. But this all happened without any apparent prior organization.

So off Vítor went on the train to Cascais, to fulfill his mission of inviting Elias to a dance at the Casa. He had met him in Huambo one holiday, for Elias was from Bié. He was some six years older. They had both studied at the high school in Lubango but at different times. By the time Vítor went to Lubango, Elias had already left. Later, they had a chance encounter in Lisbon.

They recognized each other and arranged to meet again, which they continued to do from time to time. They weren't the closest of friends, if only because they lived so far from one another, and they seldom met. Elias lived with three or four other students from Bié and Huambo in a hostel belonging to a Protestant church in the outskirts of Lisbon. These students never went to the Casa or even to the cafés frequented by their peers. Perhaps because they lived outside Lisbon, or maybe because they were Protestants.

Vítor got off at a station along the line and looked for the address. It was a villa, set back from the road on a quiet street, without anything that indicated its religious affiliation. Although they weren't banned, Protestants suffered many restrictions in Portugal, where the official religion was Catholicism. Elias was in the hostel and invited him to his room, which he shared with another student, who wasn't at home. Vítor explained the reason for his visit. The invitation was extended to the other Angolans, naturally. Elias smiled, as he cleaned his thick glasses. He had a calm, quiet way of talking.

"They should know that I don't go to dances. Neither do my companions."

"They're probably aware of that, of course, but this is more than likely a pretext for a meeting. I can't be absolutely sure, because they only asked me to deliver the invitation."

It was a modest room, typical for a student. Two iron bedsteads, two desks, a wardrobe, a small sofa, and some shelves for books. It was painted white and spotlessly clean. Sitting on the sofa, Vítor tried to decipher the titles of the books on the shelves. There were some textbooks, a good proportion of them in English. Another on Angola, probably by missionaries who had been there.

Elias noticed his interest and said, "There are various anthropological books about Africa and some about Angola. They're not mine, but belong to the hostel. That's why I can't lend them to you."

"And what's more, in English . . ."

"It's an all-important language. There are also a few in French. By Frantz Fanon. Have you heard of him?"

The name was completely new to Vítor. He felt ashamed to admit that he hadn't, because this would demonstrate his ignorance. Elias smiled, as he understood the other's awkwardness.

"It's natural, he's practically unknown here and, of course, completely banned. His is the most violent criticism of the colonial process. But rest assured, his work is really going to give people something to talk about. Reading Fanon is absolutely indispensable if you want to understand the present and future of our countries. He is West Indian, a doctor, but he's joined the Algerians in their fight for independence. He says, for instance, that it is only through violence that the colonized will overcome the inferiority complex inculcated in him by the colonizer. The colonized will only be able to assume the personality of a free man through the exercise of violence. Any violence is justified in this way. Like the son who kills his father, at least in his dreams, in order to become an adult."

"Following this theory, the violence of UPA can be justified."

"Precisely. It's the violence of the oppressed in order to overcome the traumas caused by the violence of the oppressors."

"I don't agree. UPA kills people from my area and yours, the contract workers who go and work on the coffee plantations in the north . . ."

"It's a necessary phase. So that they may gain consciousness of their colonized state. There's no reason for them to go to the north in order to allow the planters to grow fat. They are collaborating with colonialism, albeit unconsciously. In this first phase, terror is necessary to create consciousness. Afterwards, it will end. And there will be a process of integration in an independent country."

"I didn't know you upheld UPA's theories."

Elias went back to cleaning his glasses. He looked at him fixedly with his myopic eyes. He didn't smile. He had the face of a priest, and if he wasn't a Protestant, he could certainly be in a Catholic seminary, Vítor thought.

"Listen, Vítor, it's the only theory that has been successful in mobilizing whole populations to fight with sticks and machetes against colonial power. Do you know a better way?"

"Yes. The one that says all Angolans must fight together against colonialism, without massacring civilians, whoever they may be. And that even includes mixed-race Angolans."

"That's utopia! It doesn't work in practice. I know, those are ideas doing the rounds in the Casa dos Estudantes. But the Casa is dominated by the children of colonials, whether they are white or mixed. Deep down, all they want is a more effective integration into multiracial Portugal. They all talk about independence, but it's not the same idea. It's to change so that everything can remain the same, with the Portuguese lording it over the Black. You align yourself with these utopias because your father isn't a peasant. Mine is. And the only chance I had to study was by accepting a scholarship from my church. The peasant can only be mobilized for the struggle by means of a very concrete message that he can understand—for example, his hatred of the white man or the distribution of white-owned lands. Go and talk about the struggle against colonialism as a system, without mentioning the planters and the traders. No one will support you except for the urban intellectuals. And they don't count in a struggle like this one."

Vítor felt intimidated. He had begun to read one or two things, to debate things with the elders, but he acknowledged his ignorance. How could one argue with someone who spent their life reading and discussing the theories of people he had never even heard of? And what was more, without raising his voice, patiently, like a teacher or a priest explaining something to a child.

"You should read Fanon. Unfortunately I can't lend you his book. Just imagine if I did, even without the knowledge of the directors of the hostel, and the book was seized and its origin discovered. It would create huge problems for the church. Even now, as things stand, we are accused of fomenting 'terrorism' and they are persecuting Protestants in Bié, Huambo, and Benguela, just because we're Protestants. I'm sorry, but you should read him. Many of your utopias would crumble into dust."

"Don't you honestly believe we can all live together one day in Angola, without injustices or inequalities?"

"Not with whites and mulatos. They will always have a propensity to dominate us."

"And yet the missionaries who educated and helped you are white."

"Americans or Brazilians, not Portuguese. And much less Portuguese born in Angola, who believe they have rights over the land because they were born there. Those are the worst, even if they had a Black mother or grandmother. A mother or grandmother who was no more than a white man's servant. They carry within them from birth the supremacy of their white side over their Black."

"They would have to kill their father in order to liberate their mother."

"Exactly."

Vítor had used the words somewhat ironically, but Elias didn't notice or didn't let it worry him. In previous conversations, Vítor had been impressed by the thoughtful manner in which his Protestant friend approached problems. There was something amenable about him, which was immediately captivating. That was before the events in Angola. He was still the same, still affable, but now a barrier had been created between the two of them, one of those barriers in which it is impossible to define the contours. Without anything else to say, he insisted once more.

"You could go to the dance. It's always good to chat with people from back home."

"A dance is a futile excuse. I won't refuse to talk; I'm always ready. But not at dances, nor at that Casa. Whoever feels like talking can come here. You can give them the address. Don't get me wrong, Vítor. Individually, I'm incapable of harming anyone: all human beings are worthy of my greatest respect. But we're dealing with an entire people, and here, there's no room for sentimentality."

"I have mixed-race friends who are as nationalist as I am. Even one or two whites, who have helped me understand things."

"And who, at this moment, are getting ready to go and defend their parents and properties."

"Not all of them. Though some will, of course."

"Let's concede that there may be one or two fair-minded ones. They are no justification for us to alter our strategy, the only one to guarantee victory. They will be left as the great victims, not of us, but of colonization. It wasn't we who summoned their parents to settle there. It's not our responsibility, so why waste time dwelling on such thoughts?"

"A people never forgives massacres, even if they take place in the name of liberty."

"History has taught me that people have short memories. One generation is sacrificed, but the next one becomes integrated, and that's it. All powers are established on the basis of violence, at a particular moment. After the necessary phase of violence has passed, then one can become democratic. And the people pride themselves on their freedoms. But only once they have acquired a free, autonomous personality."

Vítor felt an urge to leave. He didn't linger. He said goodbye to Elias, who gazed at him ironically as he showed him out. The Protestant raised his arm to wave and called affably, "You've got to abandon sentimentality, Vítor."

He walked back to the train station without a backwards glance. Was he going to take advantage of his free day to go for a walk on the beach? There were already swimmers, even though the water was icy for an African. He turned away from the station and headed for the beach. The air was warm, anticipating summer. But the waves that crashed against the rocks gave him a glacial feeling. Like the words of Elias contrasting with the warmth of his myopic eyes. He had never thought that an Ovimbundu like him could support UPA, which had butchered Bailundos, as all the contract workers from the Central Highlands who went to work in the north were called. Elias couldn't be the only one. The other residents in the hostel must certainly think the same. At least they all had the same desire to distance themselves in relation to the Casa, and he now understood why. He sat down on the sand and watched the sea crashing against the rocks.

He sat there for a long time, enjoying the sun and contemplating the sea that he always found hostile, for he had been born in the interior of Huambo. Ancient familial echoes reverberated, associating sea with death, echoes coming from the slave caravans which, when they reached the sea, came upon the port that would witness their departure for exile in the plantations and mines of Brazil. Or, more recently, for forced labour in São Tomé. His family had not been affected, but they were still receptive to these distant echoes now etched on collective memory. Though, who knows, perhaps his own renegade ancestors had done the dirty work of going into the interior to capture people and force them into the caravans. Many people made a living out of this, and it wasn't only the Portuguese. His father was from Golungo, in the north, and had been able to study nursing. Was this a privilege rooted in slave-trading families? And his mother's family, from Huambo, with a direct link to the chiefs? If there were secrets, these were well hidden.

He noticed a dark-skinned woman at the end of the beach, lying on the sand. There weren't many people in between them, but the distance didn't allow him a clear view of her. He got up and walked toward the woman. He sat down some three metres away. She seemed to be asleep. He could see she was a mulata, and she had a shapely body. Eventually she turned and saw him. Vítor felt his chest burst: she was such a beautiful girl. He didn't know her; he didn't think he had ever seen her before. She looked at him intensely, as if searching her memory. Then she lost interest and turned toward the sea, by this time sitting up. But Vítor felt impelled by some force that made him overcome his timidity. He had nothing to lose. "Forgive me, but are you from Angola?"

She looked at him again, with a hint of curiosity. She nodded.

Vítor seized the opportunity and moved closer. "I'm from Huambo," he said.

"And I'm from Lubango."

"I went there for my final year at high school. It's a beautiful place. I came from there three years ago. I'm studying veterinary science. And how about you? I don't remember seeing you before."

She laughed and displayed an even row of gleaming white teeth. Every bit of her was pretty, the most beautiful woman Vítor had ever set eyes on, of that he was sure. Her swimming costume revealed her perfect, youthful curves. Her skin colour was dark, and yet her black hair was almost straight. The effects of racial mixing. Her eyes were another mystery, because sometimes they seemed light brown, and sometimes they seemed to be green, depending on how the sunlight was reflected in them. Vítor forgot his troubling conversation with Elias. All the racists in the world could go fuck themselves. Faced with such a girl, even a neo-Nazi would surrender before the superiority of race mixture.

"I came last year to study nursing. Now I remember you. You were older, which was why you didn't notice me. Weren't you after Esmeralda?"

Vítor winced involuntarily. It brought back sad memories. His crush on Esmeralda, a white classmate from Moçâmedes who played basketball and never paid him any attention whatsoever. His ardour wasn't reciprocated, which made him the butt of jokes. Out of racism? Probably. It was certainly true that he had never had the courage to declare his love openly, but Esmeralda knew, as did their classmates. Lubango was like Huambo: a Black boy who looked at a white girl got noticed. Nothing more might come of it, but it was still the reason for snide jokes. A cousin of Esmeralda had even come looking for him to say, "You're playing with fire, everyone knows you can't take your eyes off my cousin." It was then that he realized that his love was public. And certainly impossible. His departure for Portugal was a liberation, for at least he would forget the basketball player. And now here was this beauty to remind him of his frustrations, his humiliations.

"Bad memories, a young boy's problems. But I see you've got a good memory."

"Oh, it wasn't that long ago. And it got a lot of people talking."

"I can imagine."

"I was just a girl, in the first years of high school. And I would stand on the first-floor balcony with my classmates and look down. You boys would be in the yard, where there were bamboo trees, during break time, smoking and talking. And you unable to keep your eyes off Esmeralda, who was on the ground-floor veranda, in the corner, next to the laboratories. Isn't that how it was?"

"If you say so," he said uncomfortably.

"We all knew she was doing it on purpose. She planted herself there so you could admire her. She would twirl around on her heels and draw attention to herself. And her girlfriends would laugh, because you hung on her every gesture."

He sat without speaking, looking at the sea. He had suddenly discovered that his most private thoughts had shone in the sunlight. The sun's rays always uncover the hidden sides of the diamond, even when it is buried in the sand. All one needs is to know how to use one's eyes. And people are malevolent enough to know how to use them. For two years, he had been a figure of ridicule, when he thought he was being platonically discreet.

"Now, I think she has shown her true character. It all ended badly."

"I never heard about her again," said Vítor.

"She had an affair with a married man, a teacher at the high school, and that caused one hell of a scandal. Then she got herself another man. Then another. Nowadays, she's in a nightclub in Lobito. A prostitute more or less. So you can see, even then she was cheap ..."

She chose her term carefully, but there was no need, Vítor understood. It was no consolation for him to know that Esmeralda had fallen so far. He never wanted revenge, merely to forget. And today it made no difference to him whether Esmeralda was a princess or a whore; it was all the same. Society was still racist and still thought it absurd that a Black man should fall in love with a white woman. And if their paths ever crossed again, he famous and in a position of power, she a whore standing on a street corner, Esmeralda would still be able to tell him, "I had you eating out of my hand. I could have done what I wanted with you, you filthy Black." She could go to bed with him, but because of his money or his power. Yes, this young girl was right, Esmeralda was no good. And society likewise. "But what is your name?"

"Fernanda."

"Have you been in the water yet?"

"You must be joking! I just came to get some sun. But I'll go and dip my toe in. My toe will hurt, I know, but I've got to do it."

Fernanda got up and went down to the water's edge. Vítor hadn't been mistaken when he had seen her lying there. Her body was perfect. She walked across the wet sand, then skipped daintily back. She sat down on her towel, laughing.

"Didn't I tell you? I'll never get in the water here. Not even at the height of summer."

"I've never been in either. In fact, I'm not a great one for the beach. To be honest, I've never, literally never, bathed in the sea. In Angola, I always lived in the interior, and this is the first time I've ever been to a beach."

"Do you know how to swim at least?"

"I can just about keep afloat. I learned in the river. But very badly."

She laughed. Her laughter was like the sunset over the mountains of Huambo after the rain, when all the rainbows blend in with the pinkish purple and blue of the clouds, brushing the black rocks at the top of the green escarpments. Or else it was the crystal-clear water falling from the top of the Unguéria Falls mingling with the strange sounds of the pale violet-brown Namib Desert. Oh, I won't even try and describe her laughter, he thought. I'll leave poetry to Horácio.

"I love swimming. I learned at the Senhora do Monte pool, and in the holidays I would go to the beach at Moçâmedes or Benguela. But here, I've come to the conclusion I can only swim in a swimming pool."

They chatted and time passed. He had nothing pressing to do; he had already given up on the idea of sitting his exams. He was going to fail again, but his studies and his future career seemed so remote to him, of such secondary importance, that he no longer felt any remorse for uselessly spending the money his father, at great self-sacrifice, sent him every month. He wanted to stop the course of time, just like in the Brazilian song that had been such a hit in the dance halls of his childhood. Even the sea had shed its hostile air; it purred against the rocks, casting spray into the air. He was enjoying a moment of long-lost peace. Just like when he was a child and he would go down to the river at Kahala with his friends, and they would forget the world in order to focus their thoughts solely on the joy of play. Life had killed off that sensation of freedom. Fernanda's presence had caused it to be reborn.

But nothing lasts forever, and she was the first to notice the time. "I've got to go." Her words brought back the icy chill of the sea and life's torments. It was no use him saying stay a moment longer, no use trying to grab hold of time with both hands. She was already putting her clothes on. Vítor made one final effort.

"Are you going to Lisbon? We can take the train together."

She agreed and they walked slowly to the station, still chatting away about everyday matters that might bring them together. She lived in a hostel run by nuns. Vítor delayed their parting for as long as he could, until he dropped her at the door of her hostel. Now, there was nothing that could prevent their separation, and he made a proposal: "On Saturday, there's a dance at the Casa dos Estudantes. I'd like to invite you along."

"But that Casa you're talking about has a bad reputation. Are you a member?"

"Yes, of course I am. It's where all the African students come together. I don't know why it has a bad reputation."

"They're all communists. That's what people say."

"Nonsense. Is that what the nuns say?"

"Not only them. My friends do as well. And I got a letter from my father warning me not to go there. They organize political activities against the government. And I don't understand a thing about politics, nor do I want to."

Vítor felt his nationalist sentiments rise to the surface. Throughout the afternoon they had spent together, he had steered clear of such matters, because he had understood, from one or two things she had said, that Fernanda was still raw in terms of political awareness. All she wanted was to complete her nursing degree, and she lived in a universe that didn't favour her education in any other matters. And what was more, she lived with nuns. But now everything was converging, the collective interests and his own personal ones.

"The Casa is an association which makes life easier for students from the African provinces." He avoided the term *colony* so as not to shock her. "We have a canteen where one can eat cheaper than anywhere else. And a clinic. And there are many cultural and leisure activities. Is that bad?"

"If it was just that! They say it's just a cover for other things."

"Come along to the Casa, you'll meet the people, see what it's like. And you'll find out for yourself that you're being deceived by being made to avoid the place."

"I'm late. I've got to go in."

"Will you come to the dance?"

"Give me a call beforehand. I'm not at all sure, and I'm an obedient daughter. Besides, the nuns seldom let us to go out on weekends. And of course, never to a dance."

"Well, in that case, let's meet up tomorrow or the day after. We can talk things over calmly, and find a way."

"Okay. Wait for me tomorrow at four, outside the nursing school."

She tossed him the most radiant smile he had ever received and went into the hostel. Vítor stayed rooted for a few moments, enjoying the memory of that smile.

They met up the following day, and the next one as well. Vítor was extremely careful as they discussed the thorniest of subjects, and he agreed with her when she condemned the violence in the north, although he didn't discuss events further. Her father was a settler from Madeira who had gone to Lubango to work in farming and had achieved a stable position. He married a Black woman, and their wedding even took place in a church, which was a rare thing in that part of the world. They had four children, and all were studying. Fernanda, the eldest, had come to Lisbon; the others would follow. Her father was terrified, even though nothing like what had happened in the north had occurred in Lubango. Was he scared of being killed or of losing his small farm? Both, for sure. His letters revealed a pessimism that left her scared. Vítor listened, happy to know everything about her, and carefully tried to make clear to her that society was sick. He argued that there was racism in Lubango, and she agreed here, for she had also experienced it because of her Black mother. But Vítor raised these matters with utmost caution, out of fear that he'd lose her by being branded a communist, the worst of all evils, only comparable to having made a pact with the devil himself, the self-same Beelzebub who was the terror of Fernanda's childhood dreams.

After two meetings, she wanted to go to the dance. She had, after all, been severed from the social environment in which she had grown up. In the hostel, there was only one other African girl, from Guinea, but she was very reserved, and they had never really become friends. She wanted to be among people from her homeland, to dance to the rhythms of Angola, Brazil, or the Caribbean, all of which coursed through her veins. But it was impossible. The nuns would never let her go out. Unless someone completely above suspicion were to go in person and ask them to let her spend the weekend at the home of a thoroughly respectable person.

Vítor said goodbye, with a promise to meet her again, as long as she wanted to, when she came out of school. But the dance seemed out of the question. He'd have to come up with a solution and he only had two days. But how? Who, among his acquaintances, had a sufficiently respectable air to be able

137

to convince the nuns to let Fernanda spend a weekend in their home? They were occasionally allowed out to go to a movie on a Saturday. But they had to be back by midnight. That would be when the party would just be getting underway. That was why it would have to be a really trustworthy request, for her to spend the night away, with all the guarantees of decorum. It was obvious he didn't know anyone capable of convincing the nuns. There was Dr. Arménio, but Vítor wasn't sufficiently confident to ask him. No, it didn't bear thinking about.

However, as he was walking into the lounge, he noticed Sara sitting on a sofa chatting with Laurindo, and the idea struck him. Sara was respectable, a doctor, and, what was more, white. She was capable of doing a friend a favour. But he dismissed the idea immediately. How could he possibly frame such a request to Sara, especially now when she had just been jilted by Malongo? He sat down next to them at a signal from Laurindo. They were in the middle of a quiet chat about cinema, but he was too worried about other things to join in; he just listened. If Sara were on good terms with Malongo, everything would be easier. But she might have included him in the resentment she must feel toward Malongo. In fact, Vítor felt a little guilty for what had happened between the two of them, and he had once warned Malongo that he was not behaving well by always getting involved with other women. But his friend didn't care; he said Sara was his wife, the others his mistresses. And don't let anyone lecture him, there wasn't an Angolan who didn't have mistresses; it was part of Angola's national identity. In matters such as these, Malongo always played the philosopher. Except that this time, things had gone too far, and they were scarcely speaking to each other. It was serious, because Malongo didn't want to talk about the matter. Was Denise the problem or some other woman? Malongo glowered and didn't answer.

Laurindo was called downstairs, and the two of them were

left alone. They had to talk to each other, but he only responded to her questions in monosyllables. On his studies, news of his family, that kind of thing. He made an effort to be a little more expansive, in case Sara thought he was being defensive over Malongo and might be taken aback.

"I've got a load of problems right now."

He let it all out spontaneously, as a way of atoning for his lack of cordiality. But then he immediately realized that he had embarked on a subject that would be difficult to abandon. She responded immediately, "What's the matter?" He smiled. Timidly. Sadly. Sara's expression shifted to one of concern. "Is it as serious as that?" He had to admit that it wasn't that serious. If he told her the truth, he would once again be cutting a ridiculous figure over a question of love. No, to hell with it. She was a woman; she could understand that sort of thing better than anyone. He suddenly forgot his sad experience with Esmeralda and his subsequent frustrations, which he had always hidden from others. He needed to open up and confide in someone.

"I'm in love. I know, you'll laugh. But it's not a laughing matter."

"Laugh because you're in love? Was that ever a laughing matter?"

"It's just that I may appear ridiculous. I've been ridiculous various times before."

"To those who don't know what love is, a person in love can appear ridiculous. I've often asked myself whether I don't seem ridiculous."

As if by magic, Sara had put him at ease. Of course, she couldn't fail to understand him; she had similar problems. Vítor felt a deep sense of gratitude for the doctor, even if she were unable to help him.

"Her name is Fernanda, and she's from Lubango. The prettiest creature I've ever set eyes on. We're not an item yet. I haven't plucked up the courage. But I wanted to invite her to the dance, and then things might get started. But she lives in a hostel run by nuns, and of course they won't let her go. And to make matters worse, the Casa has a very bad reputation in those circles. Only if some respectable person were to ask them to allow her to spend Saturday night in their house. Someone who could claim to be an old family friend. I don't know anyone who could do this. Then when I saw you with Laurindo, I thought you might be able to help. But I can see I'm asking a lot."

Sara laughed, not in a teasing way but out of sympathy. "Is that the big problem then?" She patted his hand affectionately. "Are your feelings really serious, or are you just after a bit of fun?"

"If it was just a bit of fun, I'd switch off and that'd be it. Apart from my personal interest, there are all the other things. She needs to be politicized. She's got a head full of cobwebs."

"How old is she?"

"Eighteen."

Sara observed him, smiling. Vítor tried to guess what was going on inside her head. She was probably weighing up both sides of the problem, so there was hope.

"Do you think the nuns would consider me a respectable person, as you claimed?"

"Oh yes. A doctor. You studied in Lubango, so you might well have known her family. And now you've discovered she's here. You'd like to take her out to see a film and have a chat, but then it would be too late for her to go back to the hostel. So you'd deliver Fernanda back on Sunday morning without fail, in time for ten o'clock mass. You've got a way about you, a way of introducing yourself that gives people confidence, they'll agree."

He avoided mentioning her skin colour; there were things one mentioned only when absolutely necessary, for the sake of decency. And it wasn't necessary. Sara understood.

"Look, Vítor, I'll go along with it. On one condition. I'm also coming to the dance. I was initially in two minds, but I've now decided to go with my friend Fernanda. And you're going to behave decently toward her. I can just imagine the situation, a very young girl from a nuns' hostel, innocent, defenceless. You can dance and talk together as much as you want, that's not my business. But no indecent proposals or groping—"

"Honestly, Sara!"

"Oh I know you men, you don't waste any time. She and I will go home at six in the morning. Alone. Afterwards, I'll take her back to the hostel. And another thing. If possible, I'll ask whether I can return her in the afternoon, so that we can get some sleep. If the nuns insist she must attend ten o'clock mass, then so be it, we won't sleep, and she'll go back at that hour. Now you've got to promise you accept these conditions and that you'll be on your best behaviour with her."

"Do you want me to swear an oath?"

"That's not necessary."

"When you see her, you'll also see why I'm in the state I am. It's serious. Sara, can I kiss your hands? You're a saint."

"Just a friend. And save your kisses for Fernanda's hands."

Malongo came into the room, saw them sitting on the sofa, scowled, and left. He was going to have dinner for sure. Vítor was embarrassed and avoided looking at Sara. Yes, she certainly had a problem. And was he helping? Not a bit, he was selfish. But then how could he help? Would it help if he told her the truth about Malongo and Denise? He who interferes in marital strife only makes things worse. Denise had left yesterday, so maybe things would resolve themselves. Selfishness? Perhaps. But she wasn't asking him for help, and she didn't even mention the matter.

"Will you come and have dinner with me, Sara?"

"No, no. I was about to leave."

They arranged to meet the next day with Fernanda, so that they could get to know each other and plan what was going to be said to the nuns. And then Sara left, without passing the canteen, where Malongo would almost certainly be. Vítor remained sitting on the sofa, trying to order his thoughts, gazing distractedly at two colleagues playing ping-pong. He was overcome with delight, in spite of his desire to control himself.

9

Fernanda was indeed an attractive woman. Sara could understand why Vítor was so smitten, although she feared that his attraction was solely caused by the girl's physical beauty. But when she met her, she became aware of other things. She did have a lot of cobwebs in her head, as Vítor had said, but these might be swept away with a little patience. Would he be up to the task? She had to assume so.

The three of them were in her room, eating. She hadn't had any guests for a long time and she had insisted on preparing a special dinner, worthy of the occasion. After all, it was the first meal Fernanda and Vítor were having together. The conversation with the nuns had been easier than she had thought it would be. For this, she had put on the best dress she had that was both sober and tasteful. And she adopted the responsible composure of a doctor. At first, the director of the hostel had wanted Fernanda home by midnight. Sara didn't dismiss this but merely showed how this would complicate her life. But if there was no alternative … She eventually won the argument, but she would have to be at the door at nine o'clock in the morning. She herself went to fetch Fernanda at four o'clock on Saturday afternoon, and they hung out together until Vítor appeared. That gave them some time to talk, obviously starting with their studies in Lubango. Little by little, Sara became aware that the other woman was sensitive to social issues. She talked to her about preventative medicine, the social character of their two professions (after all, wasn't Fernanda studying nursing?), and the girl readily agreed with her ideas. It was only a matter of time before that pretty little head would begin to work properly.

And so they were having dinner when the phone in the hallway rang and the landlady knocked on the connecting door. Sara went to take the call and it was Marta, saying that her friend wanted to see her. She had to think on her feet. She couldn't leave the two of them alone in her room; they would feel awkward and Fernanda might even think it was all part of some indecent plot. She arranged a meeting for after ten, and Marta told her she had until midnight.

Vítor behaved like a perfect gentleman, attentive, hanging on Fernanda's every word and look. Fernanda was more reserved but couldn't conceal a certain interest in him. It was pleasant to watch the pair, probing each other, gently finding common ground. The eternal but always unfamiliar game, Sara mused. Then they both went and did the washing up. They left for the Casa at about ten. There were already a lot of people going in, and loud music could be heard from down below. She watched them climb the stairs; she told them, "I won't be long," and went and caught a taxi.

Marta wasn't at home; she had gone to a movie so that they could talk at ease. Aníbal didn't wait for her to sit down but told her straightaway, "I'll be leaving tonight, in the early hours. As you asked to speak to me before I left, I asked Marta to call you the moment I was told the date. And even if you hadn't asked, I would have done so anyway. You've been a friend and a comrade, and I had to thank you."

"You didn't need to. Yes, I wanted to talk to you. I'm a bit confused. I feel brushed aside by my friends, and to be honest, I don't know who to ask for an opinion. At first, I thought I should go straight home after finishing my studies. But now I just don't feel I can live in that colonial society, with all its racism. The others seem to be on the go, I see them discussing things, but they never say anything to me. I'd like to join some collective project and not have to make an individual decision about my life. Do you understand what I'm saying? I don't need to desert, because I'm not going to get called up by the army. But deep down, I have to make exactly the same decision."

"I understand perfectly. And if some people hadn't thrown up barriers, you would know what's going on and understand as well. The Movement outside the country is calling students. They need cadres for the struggle. Although I've been isolated from the world these last two weeks, I know this. And in a way, I'm responding to this call. Don't ask me how, but there are all sorts of ways. So, we need you all. We need you as a doctor."

"I'm not one yet."

"You'll have your diploma very soon. And if you don't have your diploma, it hardly matters; you have the knowledge and that's what counts. You've got to focus on one thing, Sara. Leave Portugal and join the ranks of our fighters. You don't have a choice. You'd blame yourself for the rest of your life for not having done so."

"You've been more open about what I would like to do than I myself could have been. At the same time, there are problems…"

"Malongo? The child?"

"Malongo has become a secondary problem. The child is, of course, more serious. But that's not all. What guarantees do I have that I'll be of any use? If I'm already being sidelined here, won't it be even worse outside the country?"

"It's a risk. And I have a duty to be brutally honest with you. I can't guarantee you a single thing. Racism on one side has provoked racism on the other. Nowadays, the white nationalist is viewed with suspicion by Black nationalists. Colour counts more than ideas, than actions. It's sad, but it's true. It may last, or it may be quickly overcome. Who knows?"

They sat looking at each other. Sara was thinking that perhaps she would never see her friend again. For a start, crossing two borders was a risk. And after that, what did a life of struggle have in store for each of them? They would always be friends, this she knew. But would they be able to meet again?

Aníbal continued, "I don't have much specific information. But as far as I am aware, the Movement seeks the collaboration of all Angolans, Angolan being understood to mean all those who want to join in the struggle for the creation of an independent country. But is that merely my subjective interpretation, what I want it to mean? It may be that the Movement doesn't see things the same way. But come what may, I can guarantee that if I manage to reach them, this is what I shall fight for. But I can't promise I'll win that battle. I don't know the circumstances."

"If the Movement doesn't have the same vision you have, then it's not mine either. And what will I do there? Work in a hospital in a foreign country? Until when? Because I can't then come back here."

"You can always come back. You can request a passport and go legally. You're going to celebrate the completion of your studies. What better excuse? Then you can stay there if you feel it's worth it. Or you come back."

"I'm on a file at the PIDE. What if they don't give me a passport?"

"Then you explore other options. This is top secret, and I'm going to tell you it in absolute confidence. Once there, I'm going to help people here escape, those who can't get a passport. That's going to go on for quite a while. If you apply for a passport now, you'll know in a month's time whether you can travel legally or not. If they turn you down, then you can make use of this other route."

"I'll think about it. No. I'm going to do it. I have no other choice."

He smiled. He shot her a look of admiration. Were there tears in Aníbal's eyes? No, it must be her short-sightedness deceiving her. But there were other things she had to ask; she didn't have time to worry about such sentimental details.

"If I do go, how will I then contact people, the organization? I'm not going to put an advertisement in the newspaper."

"Can you remember an address in Paris, without ever writing it down or repeating it to anyone, anyone at all?"

"Of course. Have you forgotten I learned the anatomy handbook off by heart?"

"I'm a historian, and I was never able to learn dates. Listen carefully then."

He spelled out the address, and she repeated it. She was sure she would never forget it. If necessary, she would dream about it.

"And if I can't go legally? Will the people here keep me in the picture?"

"I'll fight for that, I promise. And as soon as I get to Paris, I'll send you a postcard signed Joaquim. You'll know I've arrived safely."

Their time was coming to an end. She still had so much to say and hear. But she had to go. Aníbal needed to rest and prepare for his journey. It might seem silly, but she felt that she shouldn't stay any longer. Maybe because that strange urge to embrace him was beginning to grip her, to say goodbye for good in another way, not just as a friend. It seemed like anything might happen between them at that moment, and this made her scared. A fear of what would come afterwards.

"Is there anything you need?" she asked, trying to remain cool.

"No, everything's ready."

"I'm going. There's a dance at the Casa."

They gave each other a hug in silence. There was no longer any place for words. She left quickly, with the feeling like it would be a very long time before she'd see Aníbal again. Perhaps a whole lifetime.

She left on foot, making sure she wasn't being followed. Then she caught a taxi back to the Casa. She was only going to the dance because of Vítor and Fernanda, although they didn't need her for anything. But she had promised to perform the boring role of a chaperone. Before, the prospect of a dance at the Casa always excited her. Those were other times. She would have to see Malongo scorning her, dancing with other women, playing ruler of the roost. He wouldn't let the opportunity slip. And the damned fellow was a fine dancer, especially when it came to the merengue. When they were still seeing each other, he would say, "I'm not dancing a merengue with you; you're too stiff. I'll find a Black girl." She didn't mind; she preferred to watch him put on a dancing spectacle, and what a spectacle it was! He would be covered in beads of sweat, but he never stopped. Other couples would often pause to watch him. Today, she imagined, Malongo would put on an even bigger show, just in order to provoke her. See? I don't need you was the message each of his sambas would convey. She approached the dance as if she were heading for the scaffold.

The atmosphere was very lively, but it hadn't yet reached its peak. That would only happen after midnight. There were perhaps a hundred people in the hall, half of whom were dancing. She walked past the groups leaning against the wall or on the balconies, greeting people here and there. Old friends she hadn't seen for a long time, others who had come from Coimbra or Porto. The dance was an excuse for people to meet up, renew friendships. At the same time, there were more closed groups and there were various fissures down national or racial lines, which were becoming more evident. Vítor was dancing with Fernanda. When the music stopped, she went over to them. At that point, she saw Malongo, sitting on a chair. Normally, only the women would be sitting down; the men always stood, dancing or talking. Malongo was on his own, which was strange.

"All the better that you've come at last," said Fernanda. "The atmosphere here is insane. And to think I didn't want to come…"

Fernanda was invited back onto the dance floor and she couldn't finish what she was saying. Vítor said, "It's been like this since we arrived. They won't leave her alone, everyone's after her."

"You were dancing with her just now, because I saw you."

"I'd like every single dance with her. I should have put a notice on her, 'Private property, trespassers will be shot.'"

Sara squeezed his arm. "Careful with these reactionary ideas about women as property, that's when it all starts going downhill." He laughed. He said Fernanda was enjoying the party, and that was what was important. "She even came across friends she hadn't seen since she left home."

Malongo got up and came over to them. He invited Sara to dance. She accepted, surprised. It was a bolero, and they danced for a while without exchanging a word. Then, after a while, he said, "Are you still keeping your secrets?"

"I've already explained a thousand times. Something happened I couldn't tell you about at the time. And I still can't. But it had nothing to do with either of us."

He didn't say any more. When the music stopped, he accompanied her back to her place. He thanked her politely and stood next to her, but in silence. Fernanda couldn't stop praising the party and greeting people. A group was already preparing to come over and take her away, but Vítor got in first. "The next one's with me." Fernanda laughed and looked at Sara, who gave her a wink. No sooner did the first notes strike up than Vítor put his arm round Fernanda.

"Vítor's got a real fight on his hands," Malongo commented. "They all want to dance with her. He's completely besotted. I've never seen him like this."

Horácio, the poet, joined them. But he was already talking, completely unfazed by the loud noise of the music that was drowning his words: "...which nevertheless still represents the vitality of an intrinsic culture. The truth of the matter is that influences are considered a disadvantage, when in fact ..."

Sara didn't catch any more of what he was saying because Malongo pulled her back onto the dance floor. Horácio continued his discourse, now directed at the neighbouring group. He never missed a dance but only in order to drink beer and talk, most of the time to the smoke that hung over the party. Malongo danced the rest of the number without talking. Then he stayed silently next to her. Sara was perturbed. It was obvious he was trying to make peace, but that maybe he didn't know how to while maintaining his dignity. But it was more than that: he was really sad. Vítor knew nothing, or didn't seem to care, absorbed as he was in his all-out war to keep Fernanda with him at all times. Who could explain things to her? Yes, Arsénio, his Benfica teammate, was there. If the problem was soccer-related, Arsénio might know something. There was no point in asking Malongo, he would deny everything. "I'm great, never felt better ..." It was time for her to worry a little more about Malongo and herself, Sara decided.

She excused herself—"I shan't be a minute"—and she went over to see Arsénio, who was with a group of people but immediately moved away with her to one of the balconies.

"I'm sorry to pull you aside like this, but I needed to talk," she said. "It's about Malongo. Could you tell me, in all honesty, whether he's got a problem with Benfica? I promise I won't tell him or anyone, if that's the case."

"Oh, it's no secret. I'm not sure of the exact root of the problem. But I'm certain that Benfica are ready to let him go."

"Let him go? Show him the door?"

"More or less. They could loan him to another club, one in the second division, for example. He'd get much lower wages, possibly nothing at all. Or they could quite simply show him the door."

"But what's happened then?"

Arsénio looked to one side, to where Malongo was standing next to Vítor. Sara had also noticed Malongo wasn't taking his eyes off them, no doubt imagining they were talking about him.

"I'm speculating, Sara, I don't know whether the club is going to let him go. What I do know, for sure, is that Malongo threw away the chance of a lifetime. He was all set to do one more training session with the first team and he would have played the following Sunday. That really was beyond doubt. He turned up at that final session as if he'd spent the night clubbing. He was unable to control the ball, he was shattered. What do you want a coach to do? Now he can't even get into the reserves. He does some work in the gym and that's it. The coach has forgotten him. That means his days are numbered at Benfica. I warned him, I really warned him. That's why I'm relaxed about it. If he asks, you can tell him that I spoke to you myself. A soccer player can't go around partying."

"I'm even surprised to see you here."

"That's because you're not interested in soccer. If you were, you'd know that there are no league games tomorrow. That's why I came. But my wife's got her eye on the clock, and at two in the morning, she's taking me off to bed. That's what you should have done with Malongo: kept him on a leash . . ."

What a nerve! Now she was being accused of not reining him in. As if she even held the reins.

"You forget I'm not his wife, Arsénio."

"As far as I'm concerned, it's as if you were. And it's your responsibility to turn him into a serious guy. If you don't, nobody will."

"The problem is that he doesn't consider me his wife, nor will he accept that I should control him. And to be honest, I don't know how to either."

"It pains me, you know? He's got huge talent, he could have been a great player."

"You're already talking about him in the past tense. He's only twenty-four years old."

"Yes, there might still be time. But . . . He doesn't have the strength to get over being let go by Benfica, to start all over again at another club, get a grip on things . . . For all that, one needs willpower; one needs to be a fighter. And he isn't, Sara. He can't resist some nice music, and he goes on a bender. Only if you get a grip on him."

"It's not my style. Thank you for your honesty. At least I now know what is torturing him."

She went back to the group. For the third time in a row, Vítor was not dancing with Fernanda. The two friends were downcast, each in their own way. Sara got the feeling that once again, she was going to have to be a crutch, she thought sadly. So often a crutch is thrown away when another more attractive one becomes available. She shook these thoughts away and made an effort to behave naturally.

"So, Vítor, still fighting?"

"As you can see. The problem is I don't have the right to tell her, 'Okay, the fun and games are over, now you only dance with me.'"

"It would be a mistake. Let her have fun. Go and dance with other girls as well. With me, for example, since I seem to be such a wallflower. If you stand around moping like a beaten dog, she may lose respect for you."

Vítor agreed and they danced. Malongo stood watching them. It was a merengue, and he didn't even bother to seek out a partner. Then Laurindo walked up and said something to him. Sara was dancing but kept an eye on Malongo. She had to help him, but how? It was obvious he was leading a double life. Even before the decisive training session, he went partying, as Arsénio had said. It could have been her fault as well, for keeping him away at a crucial moment. No, she didn't keep him away. She had counted on his understanding and good faith, but he had shown himself to be inverterately macho. She couldn't feel any remorse; her attitude had been the only possible one in such circumstances. If Malongo were serious about his profession, there wouldn't have been a decisive training session. He would already be holding down his yearned-for place in the team. Before being called up, he was very young and played in the juniors' first team, where he was considered to have great promise. He got into the reserves, which was a stepping stone to further progress. He went and did his military service, and that interrupted his career for a time. But despite that, he was selected for the military team, which was no doubt a major endorsement. Benfica pulled a few strings and got him out of military service. In other words, the club was sure of his potential. He then had two years to make a name for himself. Two years during which they had been seeing each other. Sara did everything she could to support him, but he didn't make use of those two years, and he never got out of the reserves. Something was wrong with him, and it wasn't her fault.

After dancing, she returned to her spot alongside Malongo, her mind set on not taking the blame. She had enough to worry about. She could help him if he wanted, but not as some form of expiation. She wasn't a doormat either. Malongo immediately invited her to dance, even though Laurindo had made a sign to her just before. And Vítor managed to grab Fernanda.

"Was Arsénio talking about me?"

"Yes."

"I thought so. And I bet he was defending the coach, saying he was right not to play me. I haven't even been included in the reserve team for tomorrow. That guy Arsénio is useless. I thought he was my friend, but he's hand in glove with the club. Instead of defending me, he just stands and watches."

"You're surely being unfair. Don't blame others for what happens to you."

"Oh, I've got the message. They hung me out to dry. They've

got too many coloured people. I was the one chosen to make way for a white."

"Maybe that white player turns up at his best for training, without looking as if he's been out on the town."

"Is that what he told you? Did the jerk tell you that?"

"And he went even further. He said you might be released by the club. He's not certain, but he suspects that may be the case. And you only have yourself to blame."

Malongo fell silent. He was dancing mechanically. His body was there, but his head was somewhere else. He didn't indulge in any of his usual improvised steps, which always won the admiration of those watching and which always confused Sara, who had never got used to responding to his inventions. Today, dancing with Malongo was easy; he never strayed from routine. Much easier but much less attractive. When the dance finished, he suggested they go to the canteen and have a beer.

There were various groups sitting around. Nearly all men. They were taking the opportunity to have a drink and rest their legs a bit, as they had been obliged to stand around all night. There was no room at the tables, so they sat on the stairs, each holding their beer. It wasn't very comfortable, because there was a constant stream of people going up and down, squeezing past them.

Malongo went on the attack again. "It's as I said. Yes, they may well sack me, but it's because of race."

"We've already talked about this once. And I'll repeat what I said then: I don't believe it. Of course, this society is full of racism, but that's not the case here. Don't seize on baseless excuses. It's not going to help. Face up to the truth, dammit."

"So what is the truth then?"

"A lack of any real commitment. You didn't fulfill what the club required of you. You go partying instead of resting before training and matches. What this partying involves, I don't know.

But it's clear to the coach and to the directors of the club. I don't know whether there's still time, but change your attitude, take things seriously. Stop the parties."

"Fuck parties! That's their excuse."

"There have always been a few secrets in your life, that's true. I've been aware of them. I didn't think they were important and that your passion for soccer was stronger than anything else. Now I'm no longer so sure. If they send you packing, you've only got yourself to blame."

"It's impossible to talk to you. You don't know what's happening, and now you start parroting Arsénio."

"Arsénio is an honest guy. And he advised you to be sensible."

"Did he tell you that too?"

"He did, but he didn't need to. I remember very well him once saying that to my face. At the time, I didn't take it very seriously, I thought, of course, you'd act like a professional. But then . . ."

Malongo put his head in his hands. He remained like this for a while. Then he said in a despairing tone, "If you abandon me as well . . . If you don't believe in me . . ."

"I want to help you. But I can only do that if you want to help yourself. And you're not going to help yourself by inventing justifications based on race."

"So what should I do, doctor?"

Sara preferred to ignore the implicit sarcasm in his question. It wouldn't help by seizing on details, for that was a tactic of the vanquished. And Malongo was the one vanquished, even though he didn't want to accept it. All she could do was to ignore insults, if there were any, and give him her hand. She had done this from the beginning, despite Marta accusing her of playing the good Samaritan. Vítor had also told her, "You're a saint." Dammit, do you want to see me end up on an altar?

"Take your training and your life seriously. Stop all your party-ing, all of it. And if the club still lets you go, then go to a smaller one, and train and play seriously. After a year, Benfica will bring you back again and play you in their first team."

"That would be fine. Except that if Benfica let me go, I'll get called up to complete my military service, and I'll end up fighting in the war. There'll be no other way."

Sara felt her heart miss a beat. He was raising a matter of genuine concern. Yes, he was right. No one could save him from the years of military service he hadn't done. Especially now when they needed people. She took his hand and by doing so acknowledged all his despair. She forgot her resentment and the suspicions created by Arsénio; nothing else mattered, only her boyfriend. Was that the right word—was he still her boyfriend? It mattered little now. They sat for quite some time, hand in hand, leaning against each other, without talking. People came and left, climbing the stairs, beer in hand, from time to time, someone more the worse for wear would bump into them. But they didn't seem to notice. Until she spoke.

"But they haven't sacked you yet, have they? Maybe they'll give you one more chance. Grab it with both hands. Come on, let's dance and forget our gloomy thoughts."

They went back upstairs to the dance hall, where the party was at its height. Furtado, who had already had one too many drinks, was trying to prove to an uninterested Vítor that the Angolan rebellion was destined to fail, with the counteroffensive being prepared by the colonial army. "These things have got to be done well, such as in the Russian Revolution, for example, really well-organized peasant uprisings have always ended in failure." Laurindo was listening with an air of tedium and some anger. Sara put an end to Furtado's banter. "You're on the wrong floor, political discussions are in the canteen today. It's dancing only here." Then Fernanda rushed up, breathless. "I've never danced so much in my life, I'm exhausted." And Laurindo seized the moment to say, "Before you cool off, it's my turn now." The two stepped onto the dance floor, but Vítor smiled at Sara.

They left the dance at six in the morning, just as the sun was coming up over Lisbon. Malongo and Vítor accompanied the two women back to Sara's house. As they said goodbye, Malongo said, "Shall we go to a movie later?" And he kissed her on the mouth lingeringly, like in the old days. Vítor, timid and nervous, just gave Fernanda a peck on the cheek. They arranged to meet on Monday. The two women went up to the flat, to wait until it was time for mass at the nuns' hostel. They had a lot to talk about, and the time would pass quickly.

10

In the end, Benfica let him go after all. He was summoned by one of the directors, who told him their decision. He had one month to decide. Either he consented to Benfica loaning him to a second-division team, or he could take his chances and look for a team to employ him at his own risk. For the next month, he would receive his wages. The club where they were thinking of sending him was one of their feeder teams in the north. He would have to leave Lisbon and live in a small town out in the sticks. If he proved himself, he might be called back the following year. The director was crystal clear: "We gave you plenty of opportunities, you didn't make use of them. While you were in the military, you must have developed a weakness for whores because you weren't like this before. Let's see if you come to your senses now."

He certainly wasn't going north. Out in the sticks was for the fat and ugly, the provinces were always mocked by Angolans, and he wasn't going to debase himself by going to live there. Denise had written to him: "There may be a few openings here, I spoke to some guys." But she didn't have any influence, nor did she know anyone with connections to the world of French soccer; these were just speculations. And Malongo wouldn't get a passport to leave Portugal, with his military service interrupted. If Sara, a future doctor, hadn't even been able to get a passport . . . She'd been notified the day before after an interview at City Hall. She'd said they'd showered her with questions. They wanted to know all about her activities at the Casa dos Estudantes. They even asked her about Aníbal. At the end, they'd said, "We are very sorry, but you can't leave the country." Sara had received a card from Aníbal some weeks ago: he had arrived safe and sound in France. That was when she had told Malongo what had happened, why she hadn't let him go to her place when she was hiding Aníbal. "As you can see, I couldn't tell you anything until now." Malongo was irritated by her lack of trust, but she told him everything patiently and said, "In this business of clandestine politics, there are no friends or even lovers, because above everything else, a secret has to be kept." He eventually swallowed it, although it upset him to think of that know-it-all Aníbal spending a night on the sofa in her room. Against his base instinct, he ended up justifying Sara's action: she had to keep the secret to herself. And he didn't even insist on knowing where he had spent the rest of his days while on the run. It wasn't his business. The fact was that if not even Sara had managed to get a passport, how would they give him one, for he hadn't even finished his military service? If he went and applied for one, they would call him up for the army on the spot. And then he wouldn't escape the war.

But he couldn't accept being relegated to playing for a second-division team, which wouldn't have sufficient clout to get him out of military service. He had to get away. Sara had already touched on the subject in a cautious manner: "If you have to go to war, do what Aníbal did." In a conversation with Vítor, he himself had made the same suggestion. Vítor was feeling suffocated by the lack of freedom and the omnipresence of the PIDE watching over their every move. He was buoyant over his romance with Fernanda, which he had finally managed to get off the ground. But he said that Portugal was no longer a place for them to live; they had to fight for independence. Malongo was beginning to agree with him. At the end of the day, politics was something that affected everyone, even those who didn't want anything to do with it. It wasn't any use saying, "I don't give a hoot about politics." It was interfering with his present and his future, without so much as a by your leave. Yes, he had to get away and seek asylum in France. He, too, was a political refugee, like the opponents of Franco who had sought refuge in that country and so many others before them. Wasn't Benfica's getting rid of him a form of political persecution?

Sara heard the news without any great surprise. So they were already counting on her, Arsénio had made it quite clear. Malongo said straightaway that he was turning down a move north and would never leave her alone in Lisbon. And the people of the north of Portugal were a bunch of savages, always about two centuries behind the capital.

"What are you going to do?"

"We've already talked about it. I'm going to escape to France. I've got to find a way."

Sara didn't say anything. France now seemed to all of them like some promised land of absolute freedom. Not only Vítor, but the other day, even Laurindo, a mere kid, had sighed when they talked about Paris. And other friends too. No one said, "Let's escape," but they were all thinking about it. He understood everything now that he was aware of the atmosphere in which people were living. Sara also yearned to get away, which was why she had applied for a passport. It was like a wave that affected all of them.

"Look, Malongo, you won't succeed on your own. You don't have contacts with the underground, nor would they trust you enough to take the risk of getting you out of the country. After all, you were always apolitical. But I know that preparations are underway for a mass exodus of Angolans from Portugal. Take the opportunity to go with them. I want to go too. The problem is that no one talks to me about this, and I don't know how things are being organized. The most likely thing is that they'll forget about me because of my colour."

"Do you think Vítor may be involved? He was talking about this the other day."

"I think he is. Or he will be when the time comes for it."

"I'll go and talk to him. Dammit, we were friends after all, we live together. He'll tell me if he knows anything."

Sara nodded. They were sitting, hand in hand, on a bench in a garden. He had learned with her that gardens are the best place to talk about these things. Even her room was not very safe; the PIDE had places bugged so they could listen to conversations. And ever since she had requested a passport, they must have been spying on her left, right, and centre. Relations between them were at their best, but when he visited her to spend the night, they talked of trivial matters, for fear of hidden microphones. Sara said, "Let's change the subject. I've got some news for you. I've been keeping it for over a month. As we had that spat, I didn't say anything, as you might have taken it as some kind of pressure tactic. But now I've got to tell you."

She paused, and he sat waiting. He looked around to see whether they were being watched, but in the end, it wasn't any untoward movement that had caused Sara to stop. It must be something she found difficult to say, some serious confession. Malongo had a funny feeling in the pit of his stomach.

"I'm pregnant."

Malongo looked at the abundant mass of flowers in front of them. He thought there might be a microphone hidden there. Stupid! Pregnant. By whom? Surely! Was that a question he should ask? Every time they made love, he fucked her good and hard, to cite his usual turn of phrase. Given the intensity and frequency of their relations, the child could only be his. Hell! It wasn't as if Sara was the type of woman to have other affairs. Of course it was his, and to ask might offend her.

"I'm about three months gone. I did a test and everything. I want this child and am going to keep it. But you are under no obligation whatsoever, I want to reassure you right now. If you don't want it, I'll assume responsibility alone."

What was she talking about? Malongo hardly even understood the meaning of what she was saying. He was going to have a son, shit, he was going to have a son, and he'd teach him to play soccer and to be the most successful of all Angolan womanizers. He'd also teach him to play the guitar, so that he could compose music like the Ngola Ritmos and Mestre Liceu. Together, they would form the Duo Malongo, a good name for a musical combo. He could no longer contain himself, and he jumped to his feet, shouting. He gave a few leaps, much to the astonishment of the people who happened to be in the garden. He hugged Sara and kissed her. One or two old men gave them disapproving looks. Malongo turned toward them and exclaimed, "We're going to have a son. We're going to have a son."

Sara looked at the old men and laughed, but their expression became even more closed behind their lined faces. They muttered something to each other, but Malongo didn't even notice, so busy was he kissing and caressing Sara. He looked at her belly and placed his hand gently on it.

"It doesn't show yet," she said.

"We've got to celebrate this. Let's throw a party."

"Are you mad? Wait for her to be born."

"Her no. Him. It's a boy."

Sara didn't argue. They kissed again. One of the old men got up and walked off. The other shook his head, disgusted. But a courting couple toward the back of the garden smiled and waved at them. Sara said, "Let's go, we're making an exhibition of our-selves. Soon, the police will be along to find out what's going on."

"To hell with them all! I'm happy—can't I show it?"

But she got up, and he followed. They walked arm in arm as far as the Rialva, where Malongo wanted to announce the good news. Sara convinced him not to. "No noise, let's tell our friends as if it were the most natural thing in the world." He didn't agree: "It's not a natural thing, it's a phenomenal thing, but fair enough, if that's what you want, we'll be discreet." As they walked along the street, he was making plans and told Sara about his idea of forming the Duo Malongo. She laughed, happy. "But if it's a girl, you can still form the Duo all the same." It wasn't the same, he thought, but there wouldn't be a problem because they'd produce a boy next time round. Because he wanted lots of children. He had never thought about the matter, nor had his relationship with Sara ever caused him to ponder that particular problem. Now it was out in the open, he wanted a large brood. When he grew old, he would give his advice to numerous children and grandchildren, he would be a respected elder, a patriarch. And he would assemble his family council every Saturday for a traditional funje, seated at the head of a long table under the mango tree in the garden.

They ended up not going to the Rialva but back to Sara's. She had already submitted her dissertation and was now awaiting the viva examination. But she had to study in order to prepare for her discussion with the examiners the following week. Naturally, she didn't do much studying; Malongo wouldn't let her. He was all excited and even went and gave Sara's landlady the news. She screwed up her sallow face but made no comment.

Sara had to go to dinner with him at the Casa, because he wanted to give the people there the good news in her presence. Afterwards, they would go and celebrate at the Bar Amazonas, with plenty of beer and lupin beans to nibble. He forgot he'd been kicked out of the club and only had one more month's wages. He was going to be a father, and this made him euphoric. After having to endure so many defeats, this, at long last, was his only victory.

Things went as Sara wanted. All right, she was the one who called the shots today, she'd given him a nice present. They told their friends without too many cheers or hugs. There was no speech, much less any noisy rejoicing. Everything was done with maximum discretion; after all, Sara might feel some shame. Malongo guessed this might be the case, so didn't exaggerate in his celebrations. But he did drag one or two friends off to the Amazonas; he had to down a few beers. And that little bore Laurindo was going along, too, as Sara's special guest. He said no, not that kid, but she put her foot down. She was getting on so well with the brat, who was so busy playing the politician, while still smelling of his piss-soiled diapers.

Malongo couldn't forgive Laurindo for his honesty when Denise was in Lisbon. One day, he called him to one side and told him he had no right to treat Sara like that, forever two-timing her. There had been a time when he'd even suspected the boy had his eye on Denise, when he was in fact annoyed over Sara. Of course, he'd told him to beat it: "Mind your own business or I'll smash your face." Why, not even Vítor, who was a friend of his, spoke to him like that . . . Now, Sara had invited Laurindo along and it was he, Malongo, who was paying for the drinks. Oh well, today, he could forget everything. But the kid had better not try any funny business, otherwise he'd give him a thrashing right there in the bar. Dammit, he would soon be a family man, and he wasn't going to put up with any lack of respect, much less from a guy who knew nothing about adult life.

There were ten in the group. There were large glasses of beer, with dishes of lupin beans and olives. Soon, the conversation veered toward politics. Malongo tried to change the subject, but to no avail. It was as if there were no other subject. Sara didn't say anything, maybe because she suspected they might be overheard by someone in the bar, or maybe because she was thinking about her baby. The most irritating of them all was Furtado, now a convert to pacifism, when before he had been a firebrand. Vítor and Laurindo engaged with him, providing counterarguments, trying to prove that societies never change without major convulsions. What a boring conversation, Malongo thought. Trust those two to spoil a good party.

Fortunately, Horácio turned up and improvised a poem for the occasion, about babies born in difficult times, destined to live in idyllic futures, when all men were equal. The poem was endless, because he kept correcting it. "How was it I put it in the beginning? No, that won't do." He would give it a new tone, and it would always turn out the same. But at least he changed the topic of conversation. Wherever Horácio was, no one else could get a word in. And he made people laugh, because he wove together all the delicacy of flowers with workers surrounded by engine grease and purple sunsets with generations of pregnant women dragging along their bellies full of revolutionaries. Malongo wanted to go and get his guitar to accompany the poem, but Sara managed to persuade him not to. "It doesn't matter. Horácio, tomorrow we'll compose one or two things together, with your poem and my music." And that was how everyone discovered that Malongo was learning the guitar, a secret he had religiously concealed, and that not even Sara or Vítor had mentioned to anyone.

This revelation of Malongo's musical tendencies served to revive the discussion. Tito, a native of Golungo Alto who was a member of the Ngola Kizomba, a band from the Casa dos Estudantes, invited him to rehearse with them one day. Malongo radiated joy at his success, for he had managed, at least once, to steal the limelight from Horácio, the lord and master of all conversations.

11

S ara had finally completed her degree. The viva for her dissertation had gone well, and the examiners passed her with distinction. Marta also got a high mark, albeit without distinction. They went up together to receive their diplomas and decided to celebrate with tea and toast in a patisserie. They still talked about their studies and their new status as doctors. Sara knew that they would inevitably talk about their prospects for the future, and she feared this because she would have to conceal her plans, which were now fairly advanced. Malongo had told her that preparations for the exodus of a large number of Angolans were almost ready, and that it could happen at any moment. Vítor was keeping him up to date with the essentials; he just didn't know who was organizing it. His friend mentioned some elders, without naming names. Malongo was on the list now circulating secretly. "And what about me?" Sara had asked. "Obviously yes, we're going together." It seemed too good to be true, and Sara wasn't sure she would be included. She thought, I must stop being paranoid, but her doubts persisted.

"That friend of ours, the one who stayed over at my place, has dropped me," Marta said. "I got a card, like you. And then a letter without an address. As you know, I've got a passport from when I went to Italy. I'd told him I'd go and visit him straight after finishing my studies. In his very tender, charming letter, he told me to forget him. And then he doesn't put his address on it.

Even if I go there, I've got no way of contacting him. Bastard!"

"He's got other things to do. He might even be somewhere far away by now."

"The letter's got a Paris postmark. I wasn't expecting that. The first guy I didn't dump ... went off and left me."

Sara couldn't quite understand her friend's disappointment. Of course, Aníbal had a mission to carry out and couldn't commit himself to having visitors, even friends who had helped him. Unless ... she was beset by doubt and asked, "What type of a relationship developed between you?"

"Come on, don't be naive! The one that develops between a man and a woman who live in the same room together for two weeks. Fucking hell! All the others got on my nerves after a while, but with Aníbal it was different. When things couldn't get any better, off he went. All right, he had to go, but now he's quite simply dropped me. That'll teach me a lesson."

Sara was shocked. The revelation that they had been intimate hurt. Heavens! What did I expect? She had always viewed Aníbal as some kind of a priest, dedicated to ideas. She had never suspected he had other interests, nor had she heard him allude to any previous women. She hadn't found this strange before, because she'd placed him behind some glass partition where she kept unblemished friendship. But was it a blemish? He had merely proved he was human; she was the one being stupid.

"You never told me."

"Yes, I don't know why. As a rule, I tell you about all my affairs. They're not secret and no one has anything to do with them. But this time it was different, it was serious, I really fell in love, and here I am suffering more than a cow that's lost its calf."

Sara was confused. Marta drank her tea sadly, while she took a moment to try to think straight. It was hard. No matter how hard she tried, she felt disappointed. Aníbal was a man, and what was natural had happened. She could tell herself this a thousand times over, but deep down she couldn't accept it. Did she feel jealous? That seemed a hugely loaded term to her. Then, she admitted, does a sister feel jealous when a brother has another relationship? Does she feel it? Or only if there is something incestuous in her feelings? Incest? What a joke. She told herself, I love another man and am pregnant by him. There is no ambiguity in me. To be in love with two men at the same time, that just happens in movies.

"Did he promise you something?"

"No, never. That's the thing. He was as gentle as anything. When I talked about travelling to see him when he was abroad, he just laughed. He was quite clear in what he said: let's leave things as they are."

"So what are you complaining about?"

"Fuck, don't you understand? It was so powerful, so good, that I allowed myself to dream. Once abroad, he would yearn for me. Things couldn't just end like that! And I don't even know where to look for him, it's such a huge old world out there . . ."

Sara had his Paris address. It was information she had the power to divulge. But she wasn't going to give her the address. Aníbal had told her not to reveal it to anyone, and only to remember it when she was out of the country. Maybe he was thinking of Marta when he swore her to secrecy. She wouldn't give her the address, out of complicity with Aníbal and so as to respect the rules of clandestine politics. She got a bit of a kick out of this. Can I be such a sadist? She drank the rest of her tea, which now seemed to her strangely bitter.

"You're like this because it wasn't you who broke off the relationship. This is all about pride."

"No. I'm like this because the relationship hadn't come to an end. Everything must come to an end when it starts to smell putrid. There always comes a moment when it needs to be buried, like a corpse. At that point, there's no reason for disillusion, nostalgia. But our relationship was smelling ever sweeter. And it was precisely then that it was interrupted. It hurts, it leaves you feeling even thirstier."

She ought to console her friend. But she didn't know how. Words of encouragement are as useless as good intentions. She could only console her with an action, by giving her his address. All the rest would be to conform to conventions both women shunned. She couldn't fall into the trap of meaningless formality, which, apart from anything else, she would find hypocritical. Marta had benefitted from the secret love of Aníbal, which she had sensed a thousand times and had, after all, profoundly desired. If she were a true friend to Marta, she would do anything to help her in her need, but on this occasion, she was wounded, she had to acknowledge this fact. As if the other woman had committed sacrilege. Who am I, in the final analysis? she asked herself. She was exasperated. She sensed that she was losing the high esteem in which she held herself, which was the worst thing that could happen to someone. Malongo was on the verge of this, when he was rescued by the news that he was going to be a father. She held on to the memory of Malongo, who was now so affectionate, so serious, to the point of even agreeing to take part in discussions about politics.

"I have to go, Marta. You must understand Aníbal's gesture; he freed you because he has nothing to give you. Have you forgotten he has a revolution ahead of him?"

"I know all about that. But how the devil am I going to forget someone like that, such an extraordinary character? And do you know something else? It also hurts me to know that he's wrong, that he's going to destroy himself."

"How do you mean?"

"If he doesn't die, which fits in better with his way of life, he's going to become disillusioned. The so-called revolution ahead of him isn't going to be what he imagined. No revolution ever matches the dreams of its dreamers. He's a dreamer, despite all his rigorous communist language. In the end, he's got more libertarian ideas than I have, and I'm the one he calls an anarchist. Revolutions are to free people, and they do so when they're successful. But only for one fleeting moment. The next moment, they wear out. And they become rotting corpses that the so-called revolutionaries have to carry around on their backs for the rest of their lives."

"Is that what you told him?"

"Of course. He laughed in that patronizing way of the enlightened, those who have a monopoly on the truth. As if I were some cute little child. I wasn't offended, nothing about him offended me. But we argued a lot. I told him the French Revolution ended in terror and Napoleon, and that the Bolshevik Revolution ended in Stalinism, even before Stalin became the boss. He tried to counterattack; he's very strong on historical arguments. But deep down, I could see that he'd been shaken. Because a dreamer is a utopian. Worse than I am. He either dies or becomes disillusioned, there's no other alternative."

"In Angola, it will be different."

"You're talking like him. The enlightened always say that their revolution won't get derailed like all the others. They don't dare proclaim it openly either because they are or want to appear modest, but this is what they're really thinking: if I believe in this, why shouldn't it work out as I imagine it will? And they are always betrayed, always . . . In fact, that's all they're cut out for: to be betrayed."

Sara got up. She was already familiar with Marta's ideas on the inevitability of political processes becoming bureaucratic and ending up in an oppressive system which they, the revolutionaries, have themselves created. She didn't share this pessimism, nor did Aníbal. But she didn't want to argue today. She was too confused by the ambiguous feelings that she had discovered in herself. She paid the bill. Marta didn't want to go with her; she remained seated at the table and waved her hand tiredly by way of a goodbye.

She almost ran to meet Malongo, as if she were seeking a refuge. She always knew exactly where to find him now: he led a life of routine, from home to the Rialva, then from there to the Casa dos Estudantes, and from there back to her room. His one month's notice from Benfica was almost up and his last wages were almost gone. He was waiting to escape. He played his guitar, chatted, and made love to her. And he thought about France. He was more open than ever, and this gave Sara confidence.

Sure enough, there was Malongo at a table in the Rialva. He couldn't hide his nervousness—why was she so late? As she went in, she looked at the clock on the wall. Six in the evening. She wasn't late, but Malongo had grown impatient. That much was obvious. There were few people in the Rialva; Senhor Evaristo was nodding off behind the counter. Malongo got up the moment he saw her. "Let's go for a walk." She was puzzled, it wasn't like him, but she turned around and they left together. Senhor Evaristo didn't even wake up. Once in the street, Malongo whispered to her, "It's tonight."

"What?"

"Come on! You know very well. Vítor will go to your room tonight, along with Laurindo. They're going to pick us up from there at ten. I was waiting here to warn you. Pack a small bag with the things you need. You can't take a suitcase, only a bag."

Sara was walking robotically, almost propelled along by Malongo's powerful arm. She gradually absorbed everything he was saying. She had always hoped she would get more warning, so many things would not get done. To hell with it all, the important thing was to leave, the rest didn't matter.

"If you can, prepare something to eat on the journey, we're going to be travelling all night by car and on foot. Assume there'll be four of us. I don't know why they included bloody Laurindo in our group, that kid makes my flesh creep. But there was no time to argue. We're going in groups of four and we'll meet up at the border. Some are going by train, others by bus, so I've been told. Maybe thanks to you, we are going by car. Vítor should have more details; he's the leader of our group. I'm going home to pack my bag and then I'll head over to your place. The first one to arrive will be Laurindo, at seven o'clock. It was Vítor who decided, I can't think why. The last one will be me, at eight. Vítor at seven thirty. It's important we don't all show up at the same time, because that could draw attention."

Malongo walked off, on his way to the Rua Praia da Vitória. And she thought, with their bags, they're going to draw attention to themselves, even if they arrive separately. And all of them getting in the same car at ten, each one with a bag . . . Fortunately the house wasn't under surveillance, she was sure of that. By the time the PIDE noticed, they would already be over the border. Oh, to hell with it, to hell with it, let's go, let's leave this godforsaken country where one can hardly breathe. She tried to remember a poem by Éluard that had been secretly circulating, about freedom, but she had only retained the first verses. She headed home, trying to make a mental list of all the things she should take. Then the hardest decision was what to leave behind.

Laurindo arrived at seven on the dot. He was, naturally, very excited. Her room was turned upside down, her clothes spread around across the bed and over chairs, cases open on the floor, books and papers in a disorder that defied description. She had already chosen the bag she would take but had so far only packed items of personal hygiene. She looked at her worldly goods in despair, without knowing where to start.

"Can I help?" Laurindo offered.

"I don't even know. Look, put the books and all those papers in that brown suitcase. I've got to think about what I should take."

She put some underclothes in the bag, the best ones she had. In France, it was also summer, so she should leave her heavier clothes behind. She would take just one coat, because of the Pyrenees. Laurindo carefully started to tidy the books. The case was full, and there were still books left over. She told him to put the rest in the other case, the larger one. "Aren't you taking any?" "No, they're very heavy." But she remembered her diploma and the certificates attesting to her having completed her course in medicine. She put these in the bag, on the side, so that they wouldn't get crushed. That was really important. Suddenly, she remembered she still had to cook, so she decided to do something simple. She had some eggs and meat. Rice to go with it. She'd do that after seeing to the problem of the bag.

Laurindo spoke, without pausing from what he was doing. "Did Malongo tell you about how hard he fought for you?"

"No, he didn't say anything. Did he have to fight?"

"That's one way of putting it. Strange he didn't tell you anything. I had to give it to him. Honestly, I had to give it to him. He was like a lion."

Sara stopped thinking about her bag. She turned toward the boy. What was all this about now? Yet another secret. But Laurindo didn't give her time to ask a question.

"They weren't going to let you come. Malongo said he wasn't going without you. He said you were pregnant and you were going to get married in France. He fought and argued so hard that they gave in. I think Vítor helped as well."

"But who didn't want me to go?"

"I don't know. The elders. I found out about it more or less by chance. And I don't know who exactly is in charge of this whole thing, all they say is that it's the elders. I was surprised that Malongo made this type of demand. No one ever took him very seriously, and we expected they would say, 'Well, you're not going either, and that's it.' But he managed to persuade them. When it comes down to it, they want as many Angolans as possible to escape."

She didn't say anything. On the one hand, she was grateful to Malongo for his loyalty. On the other, she was irritated because, once again, they wanted to cast her aside. She angrily threw some clothes into her bag. It was full; it would be hard to close it. She chose the longest, warmest coat she had, and the others she put in the large suitcase into which Laurindo had just finished packing her books. She tried hard to focus on what she had to do. What was she to do with the cases? She would leave them all nice and tidy in her room, with a note to her landlady. She had already paid her monthly rent, so she didn't owe her anything. In her note, she would just ask her to give the cases to Marta, who would call for them. And she would phone Marta and ask her to pick up her bits and pieces the following day and dispatch them to relatives of hers in the country. She might get them back one day. She would only write to her parents from Paris. They would be shocked, as they were expecting her back in Benguela within the next few months, but she didn't want to think about that now.

She went and phoned Marta. On her way, she told her land-lady not to worry about the noise. "There are one or two friends coming over to eat, but by ten o'clock, all will be quiet." The landlady didn't say anything, the attitude she had adopted ever since she had heard she was pregnant by a good-for-nothing Black. Marta was at home, she asked for details, but she couldn't give them to her. "Just come over here tomorrow and grab one or two things I have here, and then I'll explain everything, it's urgent." Marta promised, imagining she must be involved in some other business similar to that of a few months ago, when she'd presented her with Aníbal. And wasn't it the same kind of thing? Later, she'd write from Paris apologizing for all the secrecy, but the situation required her to make use of friends without beating around the bush. There would be a lot of swearing from Marta, but she would end up laughing.

There were still a few things to put in the last suitcase. They managed to cram them in somehow. They closed both cases and placed them in the corner of the room. There were still some items of kitchen equipment, but she would give these to the landlady. She sat down at the desk and wrote her a curt note, saying that she had to leave for Porto at short notice, after receiving a message from her family, and that she hadn't wanted to wake her because the message had come at a very late hour. She should give her suitcases to Marta, who was already known to the landlady. The room was free; she had already paid her to the end of the month. She placed the note on top of the last case.

"Let's think about dinner now."

It was then that Vítor arrived. With a large, heavy-looking bag.

He sat down on the sofa next to Laurindo, gasping with the effort of having lugged his bag up the stairs. Sara was waiting for the water to boil in the saucepan, so that she could cook the rice. She would do the steaks and eggs later. She took advantage of the pause to say to Vítor, "You must know what's going on. So they didn't want me to go?"

Vítor glanced at Laurindo. He seemed to be accusing him of revealing a highly confidential secret. Laurindo looked down, acknowledging his mistake.

"There were some problems. You must understand, it's not an easy situation. But everything has been resolved and it's over and done with, forget it."

"Am I the only white person going?"

"Why do you put things like that? There are others. Three or four women married to Angolans. But they are Portuguese or from other colonies. Yes, it looks as if you're the only Angolan woman."

"And men?"

"I don't know. Don't ask me, you'll see later when we all meet up. There are very few people who know everything that's going on. Those are the rules."

Laurindo fidgeted on the sofa. He refrained from speaking, possibly because Vítor was older and had been around longer and was leading the group, which indicated some measure of responsibility on his part. But eventually he blurted it all out.

"The funny thing is that there was no problem for the Portuguese women. But for Sara, there certainly was. Because she's Angolan. Or was it because the others are the elders' wives?"

"If you're asking me for my opinion, I don't know. I imagine there are a lot of conflicting views outside the country. The Portuguese women didn't represent any difficulty, they'll always be foreigners, they are not a risk. But white Angolans are not accepted by many, because they may come and claim the land, which is also theirs. And, well, I shouldn't say this, but what the hell, I'm going to! If you think this got resolved because Malongo and I pushed back, then forget it. Sara is coming because an outside order was received indicating that she should be included. Though there were those who, in spite of this, didn't want to obey the order."

Aníbal, thought Sara. He'd had her back out there and pushed it through. He, who was no last-minute nationalist jumping on the bandwagon, at least fulfilled his promise. It wasn't a coincidence that a demanding, freedom-loving girl like Marta had fallen in love with him, the extraordinary one, as she had called him. By an association of ideas, she remembered Fernanda.

"Vítor, as we're all ignoring the rules of secrecy here, talking about what we're not supposed to be talking about, and in a house that shouldn't even be used for this meeting because it might be under surveillance ever since they refused me a passport ... I'm going to break one more rule. What about Fernanda?"

He grew suddenly sad. During the previous conversation, he

was tense, his brow furrowed, almost angry. Now he was like a deflating balloon. It took a visible effort for him to respond, and even before he did, Sara already regretted bringing the subject up.

"She didn't want to come."

"There probably wasn't enough time to persuade her. When did you speak to her about the possibility of escape?"

"Some days ago, when I realized we were going to have to. There was no way she could be persuaded. We argued a lot, oh, we didn't talk about anything else. You're right, there was very little time. She's very attached to her family. Flight would be a betrayal of all the hopes her parents had invested in her ... And she's scared of what's going to happen next."

"Yes, there was so little time," said Sara. "And then who knows how our lives will turn out? We are more mature, and many are balking, that's for sure. All the more so, a young girl who only began to discover a few days ago that the ideas imposed on her by her family and her school aren't true. Maybe she'll join you later."

"Maybe. But I don't think so. I'll write to her. I'll try and maintain contact. But I don't hold out much hope. She's in an environment that isn't going to help her gain an awareness."

"Love counts for a lot, Vítor. Don't lose hope."

He didn't answer. But he had the air of someone who didn't have much belief in the power of her love. Maybe he was right, Sara thought. There had always been much more interest on his part. Fernanda accepted him as a boyfriend, but that could have been just to break out of her routine at the nuns' hostel. And when she was faced with having to take a leap in the dark, placing her trust in him alone, she froze and stood back from the brink. To be honest, there wasn't much proof of love there.

Malongo arrived, with a bag and his guitar. Sara went and prepared dinner. Vítor forgot his disappointments in love and assumed the role of group leader.

"I told you it was only one bag. The guitar will have to stay here."

"Don't mess with me. It won't get in anyone's way. It's my problem, I'm the one carrying it."

"It takes up space in the car."

"It'll go on my lap, it won't take up any space. And you'll see, I'll still have to help you carry that heavy bag of yours. Have you forgotten I'm an athlete? Weight isn't a problem for me. And all the others will have guitars; it's not something one leaves behind. A guitar or a woman."

Vítor shrugged and gave up. Laurindo went and helped Sara, while Malongo strummed his guitar until dinner was ready. They ate hurriedly, constantly checking their watches. Sara looked around the room, opened and closed drawers, in case she had forgotten something important. Everything seemed to be in order, money in her pocket, diploma in her bag, her heart where?

As ten o'clock drew near, Vítor got up and stood by the window, peering out. No one had said a word for quite some time, inhibited by their nervous tension. And what if the car didn't show up? What if the whole plan had foundered, and they hadn't let them know? Questions came and went in Sara's head. Judging by the faces of the others, even Malongo who had stopped playing or telling jokes, the same questions were tormenting them.

Finally, Vítor spoke, almost out loud, "There's the car, it's that one there. Let's hurry."

Each one grabbed their bag and went down the stairs. Sara was the last. She took a last look around the room where she had lived for six years, saw her suitcases piled there with all her worldly goods, switched off the light and closed the door, sensing as she did so that she was also closing a chapter in her life.

Epilogue

The group of fugitives were stopped on the border between Spain and France by the authorities of General Franco. Immediately informed of this, the Salazar government requested their extradition to Portugal. Prison and torture awaited them.

A humanitarian organisation, Cimade, which had planned their flight, alerted Western governments to the desperate plight of Angolans. Some embassies in Madrid put pressure on the Spanish government. Finally, Franco allowed them to continue their journey to Paris, the city of light and hope.

The group split up. Many went to study in countries in Western and Eastern Europe, or to the United States. Others immediately joined the two liberation movements. Sara and Malongo remained in Paris. Aníbal was no longer there.

THE
SAVANNAH
(1972)

Still the desert.

Now, grass has sprung from the desert and the desert has become savannah, has become chana. But under the grass, there is sand. And what is sand if not the desert's blanket?

No, that's not true.

The savannah isn't a desert, it has nothing in common with a desert. The sand is a mere detail, it isn't the soul of the desert. The desert is a closed world. The savannah is various closed worlds, which cross each other. The complexity of the savannah lies in its very definition. For some, the optimists maybe, the savannah is a terrain covered in grass surrounded by a forest; for others, the pessimists, the savannah is a terrain without trees that surrounds a forest. When we think about it, why distinguish between optimists and pessimists? Isn't the forest, in the second case, a mere island, a kind of Mussolo where coconut trees born from the sand seek to caress the clouds with their crowns? Or could it be that the savannah, more prosaically, is merely a treeless terrain, which we need to cross in order to reach the yearned-for forest?

And upon deeper reflection, isn't it fruitless to define the savannah?

(From a page torn by the wind out of Wisdom's notebook.)

I

The man is the tiniest dot on the savannah. The sun has just risen and lost its bloody hue, preserved for a few moments after it had violated the night. The man has already left behind him a long stretch of terrain, covered only in grass. The woodland, abandoned when he had noticed the first glimmer of daylight that pointed him eastward, was now far away, and it assumed the bluish haze of distance. He cannot make out anything before him, except for an ocean of knee-high grass. But he knows that where the savannah ends, there will be trees and shade. At the end of a savannah, there are always trees, just as there are to the right, to the left, or far behind; the savannah is an internal sea, the only uncertainty residing in the time needed to reach its far shore.

The rising sun has shown him the way and warmed him up after the night's chill. The man greets the warmth on his face as if it is a very special caress. He knows that soon the caress will become uncomfortable, and later, torture. But for the moment, the sun is merely the being that has chased away the night chills and fears, it is still benign, but it will later be cursed and then, after it disappears again, desired. The fate of any ruler . . .

The man has a weapon, a Kalashnikov of Soviet manufacture, propped over his left shoulder. A green beret hides his abundant crinkly hair. His full beard ends in two points on his chin. The large whites of his eyes are thrown into relief by the evidence of a night's fitful sleep. He is dressed in camouflage fatigues and clad in military boots. From his belt hangs a cartridge case for his spare magazines, on his right-hand side. On his back, he carries a coil of rope. On his left, his canteen and a dagger, adapted for use as a weapon. Stuck into the front of his beret is an oval-shaped emblem featuring a torch brandished by a Black hand: the man is a guerrilla fighter.

He is moving steadily toward the east, his restless eyes taking in the whole of the savannah. From time to time, he pauses suddenly and moves his head, or cocks it in order to listen. Then he sets off again, ever more quickly. His uniform, his boots, and his beard are dirty with accumulated dust. The dry season is coming to an end, but the rains haven't started yet. The savannahs are bone-dry and covered in dust. The new grass has already sprouted and contrasts with the yellow of the previous season. In the places affected by fires lit by hunters, the scorched blackness has already succumbed to the potent green penetrating the topsoil. In three months' time, the entire savannah will be waterlogged; stagnant water will be the breeding ground for tadpoles, leeches, and mosquitoes, in constant copulation. By that time, any forced march through it will involve the torment of dragging one's legs through knee-high water, frequently falling due to hidden holes, with the constant buzz of mosquitoes around one's head.

For now, the savannah is still dry, and the man marches rapidly toward the safe haven of the border.

2

His group was made up of eleven fighters. They had been on the move for nearly a month, from Bié toward the Zambian border. They had crossed the highlands where honey is king, rivers and streams, marshes, savannahs, but above all woodland. In some places, they would rest for two or three days, wherever food was abundant and the people welcoming, which became rarer as they got nearer to the border. Then they would set off again, ever more tired but all the quicker, as the woodlands of Moxico were left behind and Zambia seemed to be approaching. The man had been summoned back across the border by the Movement's directorate, and the guerrillas were going to fetch ammunition. To avoid delay, he refused the company of people who were asking to join the group, and he set up camp away from the fires of the women, old people, and children who were retreating toward the border, fleeing the war.

From the remotest stretches of the Kembo, Cuanavale, or the headwaters of the Kwanza came columns of desperate, naked people. Old women with wizened stomachs dragged with them children with distended bellies and gaping eyes. The elderly and the men and women, their hips wrapped in ragged cloth, carried on their backs balls of beeswax and baskets with the last stores of their manioc flour. The menfolk were still equipped with a little axe, with which they harvested honey in the forest. Women carried the ever-more-useless cooking pots. The beeswax was their only asset, the capital to be traded with the first merchant they encountered on the border, in order to survive their months of hunger.

Enemy offensives had depopulated their villages. Helicopters spewed out bombs, machine gun fire, and men trained to kill. Fields of corn and millet, plots of manioc, vegetable gardens—all had been devastated, either by defoliants launched from planes or by rabid men who tore plants from the soil with the same rage as others before them had smashed children's heads against tree trunks in the north. If someone was captured, they had no choice: either he showed them the way to the guerrilla base or he was immediately killed. The offensives took place simultaneously and were accompanied by propaganda, leaflets, communiqués, agents who infiltrated into the villages, special radio programs: "You out there in the bush, suffer and die, while the terrorist chiefs live like princes abroad...You out there in the bush live like wild animals, but those who are with us are well treated. They live as Portuguese citizens...Don't follow the bandits, who are exploiting your suffering...The soldiers are your friends..." And then the helicopters came, and the airplanes, followed by the commandos, the GE special auxiliaries, the police Flechas, all of them armed, an eerie glint in their eyes, to tear up the manioc and corn, in the name of friendship. And then the ultra-Christian crosses of Christ, painted red on the fuselage of the bombers, came and scythed the Black bellies of children with blood-red gashes.

The people lost faith in the guerrillas and created a vacuum around them, retreating in their thousands toward Zambia. Around the campfires, during the cold nights of their endless trek, the lips of the elderly whispered the same despair as could be seen in the eyes of the children, heralded the same horrific visions as the withered pudenda of the womenfolk: hunger, cold, death. We can do nothing about it; the enemy is too strong; our sons, fathers, and husbands dared to defy them; they stoked up the slumbering ashes of the bad spirits and cast a curse on us all. That which is at peace should not be stirred. Let us flee, flee, flee to Zambia. And their legs moved on, cut by the thorns of all those weeks, obeying their terror.

When they caught sight of a group of guerrillas, the people would come and beg them: Let us go with you, we need the protection of your weapons. He paid no heed. He told the group to advance more quickly.

"Don't abandon us. You are our guerrilla fighters. You, who are a chief, let us join your group. We won't delay you. We'll ask our legs for added strength so as not to inconvenience you. You are a muata, a man of responsibility, you should listen to the people ..."

He did not answer. The lines of people had no food, they scavenged for it among dried sticks, they were a useless burden. And worse still, he would have to share with them the last grains of salt lost in the linings of their pockets. That was why he gave them a wide berth, camping far from them, making a detour if he caught sight of some ahead. He felt no remorse; this was a struggle for survival. He had long ceased to question himself, as he did before when he considered himself an intellectual.

On the banks of the Kuando, they heard helicopters flying over the river. They pressed forward anxiously. Only the day before, they had seen what remained of a group of country people who had crossed the Kuando and had fallen into an enemy ambush on the left bank: the bodies of two women abandoned in the undergrowth and the bloody traces of those who had been dragged to the helicopters. When he had sensed the constant presence of helicopters, he said we should only journey at night, because they may have left soldiers on the ground ahead. The guerrilla fighters refused to travel at night, invoking all manner of excuses. They never mentioned the real cause: their fear of the chieye, the will-o'-the-wisp which emanates from the phosphorus of decomposing bodies. He insisted, but in vain. As their leader, he could force them. But that would be even worse, because the guerrillas would invent a reason to stop after an hour's march. Only when he is out on the savannah, and the enemy is on the prowl, does a guerrilla fighter agree to travel through the night; only his fear of an enemy presence is stronger than his fear of the night and its phantoms. He knew he was heading for disaster. But the villages were deserted or inhabited by old people who declared they had nothing to eat. It was probably true. However, they did come across a lone villager, an old man who was almost as thin as a stick, and who gave them some makolo liquor. "It's the last drop I have, there's no more fruit left to make liquor. The still was there, about to be abandoned, so drink the rest with me, and afterwards I'll go and lie down over there and die." Drinking the liquor and looking at the old man preparing the place where he was going to die, he decided, We've got to hurry, and even travel through the day.

So that was how they advanced during the day and fell into the expected ambush. The first salvo killed the guerrilla at the front. He and two other fighters responded to enemy fire and then retreated. He got separated from the others in the confusion of retreat deep into the woods, with bazooka shells exploding next to him and bullets becoming encrusted in trees or smashing branches right overhead. He ran, leaping over trunks, crawled, somersaulted, continued on all fours, without fear, unconsciously, with no feeling of pain, but with only one aim: I've got to get out of here. He stopped when his lungs were bursting and his throat was on fire. He had lost any notion of time or the distance he'd covered. The gunfire had stopped by now and he no longer knew from which direction he had come. The sun above told him it was noon and was no use as a compass. He was lost.

He walked around in circles for the rest of the day, looking for paths or traces of his comrades. He wasn't even aware he was walking in circles; he didn't try to orientate himself but only looked at the ground, yearning for the print of a boot. But all he could find were his own prints. He didn't become too alarmed at this. They were more or less level with the Ninda military post, on the right, when they were caught by surprise. The border couldn't be more than three days' march, and he would be able to pick up the direction the following morning, when the sun came up. The worst thing was that he no longer had his backpack, which had been carried by one of his fighters, in order to give him some respite on the trek.

When it grew cold at night, he had to acknowledge that Wisdom was right in never allowing anyone else to carry his backpack. Wisdom said, One day I'll lose the others and be left without a blanket. That was why Wisdom, the little weakling, always carried his own. Somewhat unwillingly, he had to admit that Wisdom was the more prudent of the two. As far as he was concerned, the problem had always presented itself as follows: carrying one's own backpack was undoubtedly safer because one never knows what lies around the next corner; however, apart from being spared the torture caused by the weight on one's back, it also gave him some prestige in the eyes of the people, because it is a symbol of one's importance to have a porter carrying the leader's backpack. Wisdom didn't care about this, but in the end, when they arrived in a new village, they always gave the best seat to him. And never to Wisdom, because he carried his own pack like any other guerrilla fighter. He always got his own back on Wisdom by accepting the seat while leaving the other sitting on an uncomfortable little stool or even on the ground. So as to keep up appearances.

The enemy was so close that he didn't dare light a fire. He didn't sleep, as he shivered with cold and acknowledged ever more angrily that Wisdom had been right, Wisdom who, even there, was managing to humiliate him. And he remained lost in his thoughts and recollections, while he waited for morning.

3

Two years earlier, Wisdom had told him:

I watched an interesting xinjanguila at the village. I'm not going to describe it to you, because you've already seen one, but I think it's worth pointing out one or two details you may not have thought mattered.

The secret of the dance lies in the interaction between the activity of the group and that of the individual. Twosomes can be danced by only two people. All that's needed is music, a man and a woman, or two women, or two men. The absolute limit is just one dancer. But in the xinjanguila, the basis lies in collective action, not only for the rhythm maintained by the hands and feet of the others, but by the different configurations that are formed when four or five people leap from the periphery of the ring into the middle where they meet, in order to return to the periphery to invite the person on their right, who in turn leaps into the middle. In this way, the movement is one of four or five broken lines in a zigzag, moving from left to right, while also intermingling. All this in combination with movements of shoulders, hips, arms, and legs.

But what about the single individual initiative? That comes in the brief moment when the person on the left, returning from the middle, invites you in with a stamping of the feet or the nudge of a hip, or a wriggling of the belly in front of you to mimic the act of sex. It also comes in your taking to the middle, where you will meet others, and when you return to invite the person on your right. It's really a constant balance between the customary purpose of a ring dance and the particular aim of a twosome. The pleasure derived is not in feeling your partner's body vibrating to the music and to contact with yours. Here, pleasure comes from feeling the collective joy of rhythm and feeling the other person's body come alive and vibrant as it comes toward your own, but without ever touching.

I was between Maria and Mussole. You don't know them. Maria must be about seventeen or eighteen, Mussole maybe a bit younger. Maria is taller, a little fuller. Mussole is as flexible as a blade of grass. In the beginning, Maria was on my left and so she invited me. Then we swapped places and Mussole was on my left. Maria is a torrent: she's the strong wind that makes the woodlands howl. Her dance is made of wide curves, her arms embrace the world, her tongue between her teeth, her frenzied belly a volcano. Mussole, on the other hand, is a deep upheaval discernible only in the static waters; she is the teeming life of the savannah. Her arms crossed over her breasts, her head cocked to the right, her hips rolling gently, profoundly. Everything happens within her, as if she were enjoying her own body. Maria throws herself into the dance, the rhythm. Mussole absorbs the rhythm into her; she is the female in charge of the action, not through the visible movements of her body, but by the deeper contractions of her vaginal muscles. Maria is what is commonly called a hot woman, the dominator, who can take the initiative with a man. But Mussole is the true dominator, because the heat of her promise is only transmitted in what one thinks one perceives in her. She is far more sensory, subtle.

If I didn't describe them to you like this, would you prefer Maria from the outset? That's what happened to me, as happens with all short-sighted people. I preferred Maria. I went into the woods with her, and I made love to her to the rhythm of the xinjanguila, which we could hear from there. Afterwards, we returned to the dance.

And Mussole was now on my left. There was a bewilderingly full moon that threw into relief the faintest line on her little nose puckered up in the cheekiest of laughs. Then Mussole came toward me, without so much as a care for me, all of her focused on the pleasure of the rhythm which she absorbed from the air, the moon, the savannah. And it was then that I understood the power behind Mussole's pleasure. I stopped paying attention to the dance, to my body, to the light emanating from the moon, to the dust kicked up from the ground, in order to surrender to the trepidation which preceded Mussole's approach. I began to advance a little more, so that our bodies touched for a split second. And everything else faded to nothing. Pleasure was the expectation of that one instant and its occasional recurrence. Until she became sensitive to the expectation rather than the actual touch of my body. Or maybe she only became aware of it then, I don't know. The truth is that she integrated my body into her pleasure, her steps changed, and in the split second she came toward me, her doe-like eyes not only examined what was going on within her but the body that was going to meet her as well. How much time this went on, I have no idea. The source of the pleasure kept changing; it switched from the pleasure felt in the vibrations of her belly rubbing up against my sexual organ to that of the promise of Mussole's deep, silent orgasm, resulting from the rhythmic copulation against my stiffened mast.

Everything comes to an end. Including the dance. We were left helpless, face to face, painfully absent from the others who were taking their leave of each other. The interruption had been brutally abrupt, and I felt the bitter taste of something incomplete. At the same time, it was hard to escape from the feeling of failure, in which the eyes were kissing, given that the bodies no longer had the excuse to do so in front of all the others. And it was she who decided, as always, through the hidden game of intuition. I understood her silent invitation by the kind of cramped tic that rippled gently across her belly, the convulsion of two thighs squeezing under the cloth of her dress. Only I was capable of capturing that discreet message, because I had succeeded in entering into the secret contained within that budding adolescent body. I took her by the hand and led her into the bush. She lay down on the sand without saying a word. She made no gesture to help me undress her. She made no gesture to help me enter her. She remained silent practically the whole night. But it was an illusory silence. Her pleasure could be felt in the long, uninterrupted convulsions born in her uterus and which spread, dying in the muscles of her vagina, in regular waves, each one savoured as if unique.

Mussole taught me the secret of life that night: the pleasure of living lies in enjoying the pleasure of an instant, as if it were unique. Spaced out so that the recollection of the previous one is linked to the expectation of the one to come. But sufficiently frequent so that the moment of stillness isn't rendered painful through yearning. I had to leave the next day to come here, and I brought with me the tiredness of an unforgettable night and an unbearable yearning for Mussole. To put it in a nutshell, I'm in love . . . But it's not the end of the world.

That is what Aníbal, Wisdom, told him two years ago when they had met again. Wisdom was not a man to hide anything; he liked to talk, making use of everything to impart a lesson. Maybe to humiliate others . . .

4

The sun is getting hot. His eyes are fixed on the horizon, on the shade which doesn't seem to get any closer. Behind, the same pale shadow of the trees he left behind.

Suddenly, the man halts, holding his breath. A distant, indefinable noise. The wind or a plane? He turns this way and that, looking for a bush. The nearest one is on his right, some three hundred metres away. He listens again. It could be a helicopter. He makes a dash for the bush, his heart beating in time with his steps. As he runs, he seems to think the noise is getting fainter, but that could be the effect of his physical exertion. He reaches the bush, which isn't more than a metre wide and is almost bare. As he gets his breath, squatting in the middle of the bush, he realizes that he can no longer hear anything. He waits there for ten minutes, resting. Nothing.

He has been walking for five hours at too fast a rhythm. The final dash has worn him out. His legs hurt, his spleen hurts, his breathing is irregular. There is the effect of hunger as well: two days without food. And he remembers he's thirsty. The heat is whiplashing him. He must move forward so as to reach the woods.

The sun is almost directly overhead. He looks back in the direction of the forest which he abandoned, but he is unsure. His headlong rush has left him disoriented. He has an idea of the direction he must take, but it is vague. He starts to retrace his footsteps but ends up losing them, for he crossed a section of hard terrain. Panic begins to rear its head. He is in the midst of a vast expanse of savannah, whose distant edges can barely be made out, and the sun isn't any help at all. He turns back and tries to cut across to where he had heard the noise. It's a dip in the savannah, where there is bound to be water, which is why the terrain doesn't show his footprints. He kneels down and pulls out his dagger. He digs for a bit, and muddy water bubbles up. He must wait for the muddy sediment to settle, leaving clear water. But his tongue seems to have swollen in his mouth and he doesn't wait. He drinks it as it is. He fills his water bottle and goes back to trying to retrace his steps. If he were an experienced guerrilla fighter, he would easily find a blade of flattened grass or some other clue. But he was always someone in a position of responsibility. He always had someone to guide him, who studied the terrain for him. He had other concerns. His eyes didn't exercise themselves and now they are as if devoid of sight. He searches, his vision obstinately nailed to the ground, and now he has moved away from the bush. When he tries to find it again, so as to resume his journey in the direction that he vaguely knew in the beginning, he is unable to distinguish it from the others situated within a range of five hundred metres.

I'm completely lost, I really am. It's a conclusion rather than a cry of despair. At the same time, his panic is more acute. What can he do? He hammers a stake into the ground. It's not yet noon, and so its shadow will point to the west. He knows that's not quite true, for at that time of year, the sun doesn't cast its light perpendicularly. He tries to think. The sun should be perpendicular to the Tropic of Cancer, so . . . So nothing at all! I don't know what I'm talking about anymore. Yes, Tropic of Cancer, it's summer in Europe. So what? What help is it to know it's summer in Europe? They're at the beach at this very moment, the women only thinking about getting a tan. Or about the guys who are going to take them to the nightclub. And here I am on this beach without a sea. What's the use of thinking about the Tropic? Tropical is the name of a movie theatre in Luanda. Just as Tropic is the name of a shop in Brazzaville. And Tropicana, a cabaret in Bucharest or Berlin, or who knows where...I couldn't give a fuck about the *Tropic of Cancer.* Cancer. *Cancer Ward.* Who knows, maybe me as well? Marilu didn't read it, she said Solzhenitsyn was a reactionary and she didn't waste her time on crap. Marilu with her obtuse prejudices: where was she now, where were her prejudices? Marilu wouldn't join a revolutionary political party, not out of prejudice—she was made for such a party precisely because she was incapable of living without prejudices—but her personal behaviour prevented her: she had created the prejudice of total freedom in her private life, and that is the only prejudice that no party can accept. Marilu ... Shit, I don't give a fuck about Marilu. What I want to know is which direction to take. How I could do with a map with all directions marked, like the ones for the Metro in Europe. There I am thinking about Europe, in the middle of this godforsaken Africa. As woebegone as I am.

He decides to press forward in the opposite direction to the shadow shown by the stake. That's what he does. His steps are painful and automatic. He is thirsty again. The most annoying thing is that it wasn't a helicopter after all and there was I, shitting myself, running around like a headless chicken. It must have been the wind howling across the grasslands, the anhara. Here, they call it the chana, a word that also has two *a*'s. Or savannah, which means the same thing as well. It's no coincidence. The repetition of the sound is a sign of sameness, drabness, and frustration. *Chana* isn't a regionalism, as politicians would immediately label it, but the word *anhara* sounds better. *Anhara arachnid.* A giant spider, Marilu. Psychological webs that entangle you, then she sucks her victim, sucks anything of use out of him, and then she discards the dried-up shell. That's what she had done to him, but he had managed to drag his shell, by an effort of will or pride, and in time, he had grown back fully again, like a worm. Am I a worm? It looks like it at least, judging by the slowness of my progress. I need to try harder. And to think about something other than the vampire sexual appetite of Marilu. She was no more than a pair of hot thighs, hotter still the further one's hand ascended them, an animal lovemaking machine. She wanted to be a boa constrictor, but she hadn't got beyond being a spider. A failed boa constrictor, at the end of the day. Poor Marilu. Her prejudice as a boa made her proclaim to the four winds: 'I'm free, I devour life. Her tactic was that of a spider, physical or intellectual attraction projected toward anyone within her range. But in the end, all she did was to suck out life; she never swallowed it all. That's why I left her. A pair of thighs . . . Four years? Yes, four years, in Europe. In the end, the only image he still had of her was of a spider disguised as a boa constrictor, sucking on a worm. It wasn't a very flattering image of him, he had to acknowledge. But there is grandeur in the recognition of one's insignificance, he consoled himself.

It's two in the afternoon, and he's been walking for eight hours. The woodland is nearer, but the man senses that he has deviated from his route. The sun is beating down on his back, and he is following his shadow. A worm swallowing its own shadow.

Hunger, heat, and exhaustion have all given him a headache. Sometimes, the forest seems just a short way ahead, but then, as if on a whim, it recedes. He no longer feels his legs, his feet, or his back. The pains from all over his body are now concentrated in his head. He is also tormented by thirst. He knows he won't find water in the forest. So he keeps what he has in his water bottle, because there's nothing worse than sleeping when you're thirsty. When he gets to Zambia, he'll make a cool squash from orange or maboque. He'll squeeze the orange, then he'll add water, but without forgetting to take the pips out. There's nothing more tiresome than drinking an orange squash with the pips floating around on top. He won't add sugar; what he wants is to be able to taste the natural flavour of the juice. Just as he did in Europe, when he was a student. In Paris ... he liked to drink a citron pressé in Montparnasse, in a quiet café frequented by artists. At a time when there were still artists' cafés in Paris, at the beginning of the 1960s. He would put a lot of sugar in because lemon is sour. But with orange, you don't have to. He would wander along the banks of the Seine at two in the morning, alone, when the city was dying and the river flowed for him alone. The tramps, sleeping under the bridges, didn't move as he passed. He would pee into the river, right next to Notre Dame, which gave him a special frisson of pleasure. Afterwards, he would end up in a bar on the Left Bank, have a nice cool beer, and find himself a woman who didn't charge too much. But Paris was only during the holidays. He was studying in Cologne. In fact, folk said he had studied Cologne aplenty, but ignored his course of study. He got to know every corner of the city and all the angles of shade produced by the cathedral; he lived at the expense of an old lady who wanted a Black man among her collection of exotica; he tried to forget Fernanda, who had refused to leave Portugal; he lost his scholarship after failing in two successive years; he met Marilu, lost in the jungle of the great city; he lived by working as a researcher for an advertising agency, until he was fired for filling in the questionnaires himself at home because he couldn't be bothered to interview people; and he returned, summoned by the Movement because he hadn't completed his studies. So unfair, for others in the same situation had stayed in Europe.

But he had agreed to join the fighting without putting up much resistance. He was sick of discussing revolutions in cafés with Africans and Latin Americans, revolutions that were doomed to failure from the very beginning. He was sick of European committees supporting the struggles in the Third

World, more revolutionary than the people they were supporting, who demanded a moral purity worthy of seminarians and were shocked at the free and easy mores of the Africans. Just like the European priests in Africa, the same kind of people, except that they were scruffier and dirtier. Despite his progressive discourse, he eventually fell out with the guys on the committees, above all because of the old lady. They reprimanded him for prostituting himself. It was nothing of the sort, merely mutual assistance. The lady wanted a bit of exoticism, and he wanted the good life she could provide. It was a transaction like anything else. The committee members also criticized him for the little effort he made to share in the work of putting out the never-changing information bulletins, inventing victories in the Third World, which were tangible proof that world revolution was just around the corner. They wanted to involve him in their own ideological struggles, by providing the moral impetus of a true son of Africa to their squabbles over the trivial details of some political program. He had debated an endless list of intolerances with those who were pro-Chinese, pro-Soviet, pro-Guevaristas, Trotskyites, Situationists, pro-Albanian revolutionaries. Tito-cooperativists, anarchists, anti-everythingists, poseurists, utopian socialists, African socialists, Euro-communists. He was sick of having his movements and the company he kept watched, so that they could confront him with lessons on revolutionary ethics. He was sick of listening to the same discussions about this or that text by Marx or Lenin, the sacred canon which they were required to know and interpret at the drop of a hat. That was why he joined the armed struggle. He undertook some basic military training and was sent to the front, first as a political educator, then as a zonal commander.

And now he's lost out on the savannah, his eyes fixed on a forest which refuses to advance toward him. At the same time, the forest is clearly nearer, as he can now distinguish the trees. He will rest when he gets to the forest. Then he'll continue through the night, taking advantage of the cool air. It's three in the afternoon, and the heat hasn't abated. He could really do with a cool drink of pineapple juice. The Portuguese soldiers carry it in their ration pack; he sometimes sees empty cans lying along the woodland trails. Once, in Zambia, he bought a pineapple and ate it all by himself. He'd never had a whole pineapple to himself. He hadn't cleaned it properly, and afterwards, his tongue stung because of the prickles. Pineapple punishes people for their impatience, it's like a military operation. He tries to remember the taste of pineapple; he goes beyond the taste and reaches the bitter end, with his troubled taste buds. The pineapple has a personality of its own, like the passion fruit or the monkey orange. Some fruit has no personality at all, like pears, apples, or figs. Here I am discovering that fruit have personalities! Oh, how I could murder some grapes right now ... Wine! The idea gave him a jolt. A nice cool white wine, an Algerian la Trappe, for example. It's years since he had a nice cool glass of wine. Francine used to get tipsy regularly on red wine, especially a Bordeaux as she was from that region. Intoxication made her say silly, gross things, and she ended up playing the role of a cheap whore. When she was sober, she was great company. Her weakness was getting drunk on red wine. Helga got drunk on whiskey, no expense barred. She was possibly even more vulgar than Francine; one day she had walked down the corridor of the university residence stark naked, hugging everyone she passed and rubbing up against their crotch. Or Erika who, at a party, had drunk too much beer and champagne and had suggested an orgy and he'd had sex with her, a once-timid young virgin. He had so often attempted to conquer Erika, and she had always refused, either out of fear or shyness. But at this party, she was deflowered in front of them all by a disgusting, fat industrialist who said he was a left winger and who was hosting the party. The appetite awakened by the drink in Erika had then been satiated by five men, him included. The members of the committee were astounded. Erika was one of their latest, most competent recruits. But Helga and Erika had an excuse, for they never got drunk on red wine. Francine had no excuse; she had never understood the refinement of a chilled white wine. Francine justified herself, saying it was due to her proletarian background. She would brandish her red wine like some aristocratic coat of arms.

He had noticed this in certain European intellectuals who, because of their lack of any lived experience or action that might prove their proletarian sympathies, sought succour in their real or imagined origins, now that it no longer constituted a risk or was a source of shame. Like some mestiços who, during the triumphant phase of nationalism, turned their backs on their white fathers and declared themselves solely the offspring of their Black mothers. And they were completely unabashed by their newfound virgin birth. Or the next one along, the cabrito, of even vaguer contours, who in the absence of a Black mother, ran and clung to his grandmother, using her name as his nom de guerre. As if this could hide the paleness of his complexion. I am proud of being Black, but I really am Black. And those years are over when being Black was a humiliation, synonymous with being a slave or uncouth. Nowadays, being Black is to be armed and to combat the colonizer, whether he's white or not. Many Africans in other countries are astonished: "But do you really have the courage to fight the whites?" The complex of the colonized so common throughout Africa. But we are not like that at all here. The white man is the master of technical knowledge and political power, but he is not a god. And today, the white woman desires the Black man, just as in the old days, Black women desired white men, by virtue of having to accept them. The Black man is now a symbol. The woman has always desired the man who beats her husband, the woman desires the overlord who gets revenge on her previous overlord. Let the feminists swallow that, for they had it coming. The Black man today is becoming a symbol of dominion, because he dared rebel against his master. He is a sexual symbol: the phallus of power is Black! He grins clumsily, satisfied with his discovery.

The forest is now less than five hundred metres away. The man stops. His thoughts have distracted him. He needs to be careful as he enters the forest, as it's a good place for an ambush. If the noise he heard in the morning was in fact a helicopter, it may have left soldiers in the forest. The soldiers may have caught sight of him some time ago and prepared a trap. He scrutinizes each tree, trying to discover a hidden presence. His heart thumps in his chest.

The same sensation he had last year while crossing the River Cuando ...

They had used two dugouts for the crossing. He climbed into the smaller, swifter of the two, which belonged to a fisherman. There were eight guerrillas in the other one. His was much faster than the other during the three-hour journey. He left it behind, for there was an enemy offensive and there was no shelter against helicopters out on the river or in the marshes. He regretted reaching the other side. The "harbour" was completely exposed and a dugout could be seen from far away. The stretch of savannah along the river, where there was normally tall grass that would conceal the arrival of a dugout, had been burnt either out of carelessness or by the enemy. The forest lay in an arc, four hundred metres away. The fisherman left him on the riverbank and set off back to the other side. He thought about forcing him to stay but then decided against it. He wouldn't be any help because he wasn't armed. And he wasn't going to ask him for any help so that he could hide in the bulrushes on the riverbank, because that would be shameful for him to be seen as a cowardly commander. He remained alone on the bank, wondering what to do.

In the middle of the savannah, there was a spindly monkey orange tree. He decided to press forward as far as there, his finger on the trigger, his eyes watching the forest. The day before, he had heard explosions, and the Tugas might have set up camp there. Today is my day, today is today! His chest was aching due to the strain on his nerves and the crazy galloping of his heart. He thought he was never going to reach the tree. But he did. He threw himself to the ground next to it, seeking the protection of its fragile trunk, his gun aimed at the woods. The wind was causing shadows to move, creating physical shapes. A feeling that the enemy was there . . . He decided to stay by the tree. The soldiers were waiting for him to reach the forest so they could take him alive. Well then, if they wanted him alive, they were going to have to come and get him, advancing across the open terrain. He would take out a few and the gunfire would warn his comrades, who would get away. This was the only possible course of action. Half an hour passed. The enemy couldn't make up their minds to appear. But he could make out a lot of moving shapes. His taut nerves were on edge and making him grind his teeth. After a further fifteen minutes, the second dugout reached the riverbank. He thought the enemy would now start to fire because he was no longer alone, and it would be hard to capture him alive. The guerrillas advanced nonchalantly, and he waved at them to warn them of danger. They crouched down and proceeded with caution. When they reached him, his fear vanished: he was no longer alone. Even so, he sent two fighters on ahead to reconnoitre; the others remained lying flat under cover. The scouts reached the woods and signalled the others to advance. There were no enemies. The wind and his imagination had conjured up human forms in the forest. He felt obliged to give them an explanation about the necessary measures for their security, more to justify himself than to instruct his comrades. The guerrillas reacted with irony, in their mocking rustic silence.

He pretended not to notice, and it still riles him today when he recalls it.

Do I move forward or not? Now, he doesn't have a group of fighters behind him; he's alone, truly alone. Everything he does will depend on him and will be geared to his own survival. The only insignificant advantage is that he doesn't need to hide his fear. He takes a few steps forward, his gun at the ready, his index finger brushing the trigger. He is three hundred metres away. The sun is beating down on the leaves of the forest, creating a whole range of differing tones, from greenish yellow to brown. The trees where the foliage has died have already renewed their vestments, and their green curtain looks impenetrable. The man stops. He goes down on one knee to hide himself among the grass. He stays in this position for fifteen minutes, resting and watching. If the enemy is there, he must have been seen long ago and the ambush is waiting. If that's the case, they must have spread out on his left, on the edge of the forest that forms an arc, with one group straight in front to open fire. The group on the left then advances across the savannah in order to take him alive. That must be their plan. To the right, the savannah stretches away. Perpendicular to his direction of travel, on the left, the forest is about one kilometre away. I must set off quickly in that direction. I'll force them to lift their ambush and advance along the edge of the forest to cut me off. Their policy now is not to kill, but to take captives. It's much more demoralizing for a guerrilla fighter to hear their captured commanders spouting repentance over the radio. They call it "psycho-social operations" ... I've got to take advantage of this psycho-social operation. I've got a chance to enter the forest before them and see who can run faster. In spite of his fear, he feels pride in his level-headedness and sang-froid. It's not by chance that one comes from chiefly stock, whatever they say.

The image he has conjured up of himself gives him courage. He dashes off to the left at a gallop. After a while, he slows down to keep up a steady pace. Fatigue and hunger make him feel dizzy. He watches the forest on his right while he moves along, but he doesn't see anything suspicious. He starts to veer off toward it, trying at the same time to catch his breath. And when he's a hundred metres from the edge, he sets off at a sprint once more. The rhythm of his steps doesn't allow him to feel any fear, but he imagines the sound of the first shot. Should he go on running or throw himself flat? It's best to run, take a risk, they'll fire into the air. He reaches the trees and nothing happens. He keeps up his march and looks around, astonished. Then he lets out a nervous laugh, punctuated with sobs. There's no other human presence in the woods.

He sits back against a tree and stays like this until the sun goes down and the night chill surreptitiously takes over. He gets no relief from his giddiness, and his hunger becomes unbearable. He tries to keep his water until he lies down to sleep. But he's going to walk as far as he can tonight. He wouldn't be able to sleep with the cold anyway. He'll wait for the Southern Cross to rise above the canopy of the trees to guide him. It would be good to be walking across the savannah now; it would be easier to get his bearings. But unfortunately, he's in the forest. Everything is the opposite of what it should be. It's like this damn war. When someone is counting on the enemy to turn up and devises good defence tactics, the enemy doesn't appear. And then he surprises us when we least expect. Damn war! Those who started it have abandoned it, let the rest look after themselves ... Damn it! I'm talking like the people. But shit, it's true. No one had forced him, he was taking part because he wanted to. No, stop it, I know very well what this business of being a volunteer involves: a person is pressed into it. What will my friends say? What will the future be like? A forced volunteer! And this obligation we call political consciousness, a handy term with which to delude us. For a few people, it's to delude themselves; they are the idealists. For some, it's to delude others; they are the clever ones. It's all a con. Here am I, cold and hungry, knowing only that my salvation lies to the east. And what for? A few people outside the country use my sacrifice and that of so many others in order to turn up in friendly countries and receive money. Of this money, half goes into their own pockets and those of their family and friends. The other half is used to sustain the war. The part destined for the war is the capital invested in demonstrating success to their friends so that they can receive yet more money. It's not because they're interested in liberating the country.

I've been stupid. I've believed in the sincerity of all. Now they don't fool me anymore. I'm not coming out here to fight again. If they think I'm going to return to the front, they're completely mistaken. Let them go. They're the ones who control this war. Let them come and see if they can fight like this, without supplies, without a popular following, and with guerrilla fighters who run away when the first shot is fired. Of course, they'll say, if the fighters lack courage, it's because their commanders don't fire them up morally. But how are you going to spur a man on with fire in his belly when he understands how unjust everything is? They'll say it's the influence of enemy propaganda, the petit bourgeois who've infiltrated the guerrilla movement...What are we, all of us, if not petit bourgeois? If it's enemy propaganda, it contains a grain of truth. Or does the enemy always lie?

Night has already fallen over everything. He'll soon have to resume his march. He can't be far from the border, only one more day of hardship perhaps. Unless he's lost his way . . . He dismisses the thought.

He'll get to Zambia, of course he'll get there. And he'll say exactly what he thinks and propose radical changes in the Movement. The situation can still be saved, but honest, determined men are needed to lead things. They've got to get rid of all the special favours dispensed, along with the inept and the thieves.

They've got to end the supremacy of northerners, who have proven to be failures in the way this war has been waged. Like any organism, the Movement depends on the replacement of the old by the new, by the constant renewal of cells. The curious thing is that all parties of the left accept this dialectical principle; they spend their time preaching it. And yet they never apply it to themselves, and the older an individual is, the better leader he will be. The old never give up power. They have to be forced out. But new blood is always needed, one generation replacing the previous one, renewed vigour originating in the cadres. Only by doing this will they succeeded in regaining territory. The enemy is like someone in a state of paralysis: he is underdeveloped both materially and morally, an obscurantist. If he remains where he is, it is because we don't know how to act. Look at me, surrounded by enemies, am I not outwitting them? I pass right through them in the middle of an offensive, and the poor wretches aren't even aware I'm there. All it takes is courage and intelligence. They're peasants from Portugal, or peasants from Angola. Can you forge an efficient army out of people like that? And it's the same for us, either we promote the young cadres, or it's game over . . .

He gets up, encouraged by these thoughts. He returns to the savannah and picks out the Southern Cross. The constellation had always seemed ugly to him, ungainly, but now it looks positively beautiful. He should advance eastward with it on his right at all times. He enters the forest, trying to maintain his coordinates. He loses sight of the Cross, which is hidden by the tops of the trees. He has to rely solely on his sense of direction. After half an hour, he reaches the end of the forest, having tripped on roots and fallen over three times. He looks for the Cross and spots it behind him: he has been marching north. He crosses the savannah, now in the right direction. It doesn't last long because once again, he's in the forest. He keeps on going, stumbling, falling, crashing against fallen branches, trembling with cold, his legs bleeding from smashing against trees, his sole concern being to keep heading east. He can never see the Cross when he's in the middle of the forest. He walks on like this for two hours until he emerges once again onto the savannah. The Cross is now on his left. He's been walking westward all this time. He lies down in the middle of the savannah, exhausted, in despair. His night march served no purpose at all, quite the opposite. He decides to rest right there. But he cannot bear the cold. After five minutes, he gets up. Then he hears the noise of the river coming from the north. He walks toward it. At least he'll have water to drink.

As he approaches it, he begins to make out the contours of the riverbank. What river could it be? Not the Cuando. They had left it a long time ago on the right and it then turns south. The Tundombe? If it's the Tundombe, he's on the right route and has only deviated slightly. The Kapui? No, he must have passed that one on his right. Yes, it can only be the Tundombe. He's safe.

He reaches the shore and his illusion is shattered. It's a large river. The Tundombe, at this time of year, is dry—why didn't I think of that? Which river is it? It can't be the Cuando. He's on the right bank of the river, and if it was the Cuando, he'd have to be on the left. Besides, it doesn't look like the Cuando, which flows through marshlands. He is overcome by an anguished foreboding: the Ninda? Yes, it can only be the Ninda. There isn't another river, and it's quite possible if he has been marching northward. His feeling of panic now becomes impossible to control. If it is the Ninda, he's going to have to cross a trail and a highway, avoid the military post . . . and it will still take him a good two days to get to the border. I'll never make it, I'll never do it. He drops to his knees and remains paralyzed, unable to decide what to do. After a long time, he decides to drink some water. He fills his water bottle and then heads to the woods. There, he lies down, without daring to light a fire.

It's midnight. There's only one thing for it: get ahead right now. He's got to cross the Chiume highway and the Tundombe trail tonight. By day, it's too dangerous, because the area is patrolled by soldiers, especially near the military post. He's got to skirt this latter, but he can really only do so at night. He musters what remains of his strength, tries to forget his bodily pains, and sets off again toward the east. He goes along the edge of the forest, next to the savannah which extends down to the river, so that he can benefit from the guidance provided by the Southern Cross and the river. When he reaches the post, he'll make a detour to the right. He can no longer order his ideas and recollections properly. Only fear propels him along the edge of the forest. He prepares himself mentally to be surprised by the searchlights from the post, but it seems as if he'll never reach them. And it's already three in the morning.

He lies down next to a tree, wondering whether he will be able to get up. He is no longer hungry; he has passed that stage. At last, his tiredness is pleasant, because it no longer allows him to feel the cold and plunges him into an almost dreamlike torpor. Images cross his brain as if he had witnessed what he had never seen. But Wisdom had recounted things with such feeling and colour that he could see Mussole, her lithe body dancing for him, her broken body bleeding for him. Tears streaming from Wisdom's eyes as he leaned over her. Yes, it was he who had loved Mussole, it was he who had experienced ecstasy from her caresses, it was he who had died with her on that April day last year, when the savannahs sang aloud with bright flowers and the rivers combed themselves with large round leaves. On that April day last year, made for love, on that day when he had returned to Kembo to meet Mussole for the fourth time. It was on that April day when he was rushing to Mussole's village, after three months of separation since the two weeks he had spent with her during their third encounter. Yes, on that April day when he was coming to fetch her, to pay her parents the bride price, to buy the warmth of her body with a cover and the promise of other gifts he didn't have. And he ran through the savannah on the banks of the Kembo, anxious to plunge into the silent secrets of Mussole's affection, Mussole, a gazelle who was swifter than the giant sable, an antelope with eyes that were sweeter than the honey dripping from his lips as he chewed the nectar, gold like her skin when it stole the sun's reflections, she, his Black duiker, source of all his love. Yes, it was on that April day full of treacherous rains that he arrived at her village. It was in April last year, he doesn't know the day, Wisdom didn't say, but it was when the thunder served as backdrop to the lightning's whiplashes, that he saw the charred, still smouldering village. It was on that day in April last year (why was April such a fateful month, with the death of the Hero, his breakup with Marilu?), it was in that tragic April that he visualized Mussole's violated, butchered body. It was on that April day that he sobbed until he no longer had a voice, rocking the young girl made for life, princess of hidden tenderness, whose doe eyes remained open for him alone. Yes, it was on that April day that he shut his heart, like a book that had been read and reread and no longer wishes to be abused, and he filled his brain with cold hatred for those who had robbed him of his life's source. Yes, that April when the savannahs were covered in pale violet flowers, he dug Mussole's grave and vowed to fight until he was shot down, even if he were the only fighter left, no longer out of some conviction but for the pure pleasure of vengeance, now that their collective decline was irreversible. And did Wisdom now want to usurp his right to weep for Mussole? Mussole was his; it was he who yearned for her as it had been he who yearned for her body, as it had also been he who had later acknowledged her loss, Mussole, Mussole, Marilu . . . Fernanda.

He wipes away his tears with the back of his dirty hand and remembers that he has to advance until he sees the post. It's four in the morning, and he must cross the highway under cover of darkness. He gets up unconsciously, leaning against the tree so as not to fall, for his legs are trembling and all he can see are red flashes in front of him. He's surprised that he can still walk, and he's conscious that it's not because of some miracle but the effects of fear. And so he sets off, dragging his feet, until he senses the first patches of daylight in front of him. He won't get to the highway in time to cross it. At that point, the searchlights sweep away the dying night over the trees. The Ninda military post. He draws a little closer, penetrating the forest. All of a sudden, he sees the highway and the bridge on his left. Morning finally emerges triumphant.

The man retreats to the forest. He'll have to spend the day in hiding, cross the highway at night, the Tundombe trail, and advance along the river as far as the border. Will he be able to endure it? He begins to lose count of the days of hunger and sleeplessness. He knows he won't be able to get any sleep during the day, for fear of being discovered, so near the post. How long can a man's resistance last?

5

Two days before his departure, Wisdom had said to him, "How many have died in this war? How many abandoned homes, how many refugees in neighbouring countries, how many separated families? What for? When I think of all the different causes of accumulated suffering, of the individual hopes shattered, the ruined futures, the blood, I feel enraged, an impotent rage, but what is the target exactly? It's no longer just the enemy. The enemy fulfills his role as colonizer. The colonialist is a colonialist, and that's it. One cannot hope for anything from him. But what about us? The people expected everything from us: we promised them paradise on earth, freedom, a peaceful tomorrow. We always spoke of tomorrow. Yesterday was the dark night of colonialism, today is the suffering of war, but tomorrow will be paradise. A tomorrow that never comes, a today without end. So endless that the people forget the past and say that yesterday was better than today."

"It's a long war," he replied cautiously.

"True. But it wasn't planned properly. We promised a future just around the corner, in three months' time, just be patient. You'll see, there'll be cloth, salt, technical experts will come, they're already on their way. The people were full of hope. The cloth never crossed the border, it was spent on drink; the salt just turns the rivers of Zambia into brine; the experts are living comfortably in Europe. And the people, stripped bare, cultivating crops for the guerrillas, with no compensation except for an occasional bombing raid or an enemy incursion. A people gets tired if all it hears is lies. Nothing was organized, and I'm no longer saying for the better, but at the very minimum to maintain the standard of living of the population. Nothing, or very little. And what do you see today? Moxico depopulated, Cuando Cubango depopulated, Eastern Bié depopulated, Lunda, the same. The only population there is, is either in Zambia or in the enemy outposts. Here in the forests, few villages remain, but even these are ready to be abandoned. The words of their songs are limited to 'Let us flee, let us go to Zambia.' Who betrayed them? Was it the people? No, the people were heroic, resisting for so many years. But all resistance ends if there is a lack of perspective."

"The northerners did a lot of damage."

"You're caving in to regionalism, Worldly," Wisdom said, biting on a blade of grass. "You blame the northerners. Yes, the first commanders came from the north. They had experience of war up there, which is why they were usually the commanders. There were good ones, and there were bad. The majority were good patriots, ready for any sacrifice. And they fought hard. But they encountered a population that was at another stage of development, not integrated into the colonial-capitalist system, and as a consequence less prone to violent resentment against the occupier. The population accepted the supremacy of those who came with arms and the technical apparatus of war, which is always a source of respect and cowering admiration. A people with different customs, who didn't dare rebel against the settler but who were awoken by those who came and gave them support."

"And the northerners instituted their own form of colonization. They recruited local guerrilla fighters, but they ensured that they remained in command. They took charge of the planning and got themselves women with the spoils that accrued from war. But no one could touch their women, not even to shake their hand. Deny that if you can! And what about the executions? A fighter who committed a somewhat serious mistake would be shot. There were traitors, of course, but all of them? Whoever had a pretty woman risked being shot in combat, except that he was shot in the back, and the commander kept his woman for himself. Let's see you deny that!"

"That was never proved. I admit that cases like that might have occurred, but they weren't common. And there were guys from the north who were shot. That happens in all wars. People get tired, cross over to the other side, or commit crimes that need to be punished. People exaggerate nowadays when talking about these things."

"The funny thing is that they were generally poor fellows from the east."

"You react like a man from the south, Worldly. I would say that's quite natural if you knew no better. If you had always lived in the bush and your understanding of the world was constrained by the limits of your village, that reaction would be perfectly normal. But you studied, you lived in Europe; you were born in Huambo, but you lived in cities. You should be less passionate in your reflections. And apart from that, Huambo isn't in the east or even the south. I'm from the north, but I've never ordered anyone to be shot, you know that only too well. I've never treated a man of the people with disrespect, just because he's from the east. I've never behaved like a colonialist. I've never sought any privileges. Deny that if you can."

"It's true. But you are different."

"And yet when comrades get excited, they call me a Kamundongo, as if that were an original sin."

"Because they don't know you. They're used to being lorded over by Kamundongos."

"No," said Wisdom. "They know me. I've been living among them for years. Before, they never used to call me this. They might have thought it, but they didn't have the courage to say it out loud. The commanders, whether they were from the north or the south, wouldn't allow it. But nowadays, they talk like that. In one way, it may be better, because at least people are showing outwardly what they used to hold back inside. But why was I a comrade yesterday, while today I'm looked upon as an enemy? I've been living in these forests for five years; I speak the language of the region; I loved a woman from the east in all good faith, a woman whose death almost killed me. Am I really from the north? I never saw myself as that. I'm just an Angolan. So why are they turning against me now? Why is all that I say false, when before it was considered gospel?"

"There were too many crimes committed by Kamundongos, so now they don't accept any Kamundongo at all. You must understand."

"It's not just that. It wasn't only the Kamundongos who made mistakes. Didn't you yourself execute men from here? I can remember one instance, Vítor..."

"I was obeying the orders of the Kamundongos," Worldly replied.

"Didn't you send Panga on a mission merely so you could take advantage of his woman? And you're not a Kamundongo, even though your father is. Why do you now consider me a murderer, I who always fought against this type of thing, who accused you, men from the east and the south, of mistreating your own people? Did my name Wisdom merely come from the fact that I had a university degree? I may have one, but who's to know that? They gave me this name because I taught them many a moral lesson. I always spoke about defending the people. No, that's not the only problem. Now, it's the commanders in the east who are stirring up the guerrilla fighters against the Kamundongos. It's the lower cadres who scream accusations— some of them true, most of them false—so as to eliminate the northerners and thus gain promotion within the organization. For the opportunist, any tool is useful, even the most blatant lie. The masses will support them, demagoguery is king, so why not take advantage of it to sully the names of others, even those who were once friends, in order to get a position, preferably a civilian one, because those are the ones that give you access to material assets? And the guerrilla fighters, when they see that happening, knowing that they can never climb because they lack the minimum qualifications to compete with the eastern cadres, start demanding money to fight. Even the people demand money to return to the field."

"All right, Wisdom. We're the ones who tainted the war effort; we're the opportunists. You didn't make any mistakes. You were the good guys who came and taught us how to wage war and eat with a spoon. But we learned and we wanted your positions in order to get a radio and a watch. And so we began to stir up regional troubles. That's it, isn't it?"

"Quit the sarcasm. And stop talking like a regionalist. Why do you say 'you' and 'we'? Are you standing on the other side of the barrier as well? You're just digging a trench between us, an unnecessary trench."

"I'm not digging one. The trench already exists, haven't you noticed?"

"Have I contributed to it?" Wisdom said.

"And have I contributed to it?"

"I don't know. I no longer know. Before, it would never have crossed my mind. But I see you talking about 'you' and 'we,' and you've been even more reserved ever since those letters from across the border arrived. You talked about them among yourselves, making sure I didn't hear. You never talked to me about them, you never gave me any news, but you kept clinging to them, reading them to the others in a low voice. If that trench already exists, who dug it?"

"The crimes, the mistakes ... committed by the northerners. Not by you, I know. But your kinsmen wrecked everything."

"You're sticking to your position, aren't you? If there's a regional division, everything's finished, and the enemy is the one who'll take advantage. We're already weak. Division will leave us annihilated. Think of those women and children who still look to us for hope. We were the saviours, the redeemers. How will we fulfill that if we fight among ourselves?"

"I'm not fighting you, Wisdom. I'm not dividing anything. I'm only saying that such a division exists and that the militants and the population at large don't trust the Kamundongos. If there were men from the east who made mistakes, which is true, they still learned them from the northerners. Who educated the men from here? Wasn't it the examples they gave rather than the beautiful words they spoke? People can tell me twenty times a day that we are all equal, but practice proves only some get all the privileges. And who are the privileged ones? Those from the north. A few from the east? Yes, one or two turncoats within their orbit, who accept everything in return for a few crumbs from the cake. Dammit, isn't it obvious? Over the course of time, the people from here learned. It took a while, but they learned. And now they've put their foot down. Whose fault is that, Aníbal? Why did they teach us about equality if they didn't practise it themselves?"

Wisdom was on the point of interrupting, but Worldly waved him aside and continued. "Let me finish. How many commanders eliminated their subalterns from the east, just for fear of being unseated? Not through forced physical elimination, but by political means. They would lay a trap, the one from the east would commit an error, and hey presto, they'd be demoted, a black mark on their curriculum. You know this as well as I do; we've already talked about a number of cases. Who began this power struggle? Wasn't it the ones who wrecked the war? At the very moment when the people gave their support, they were taken advantage of. When they decided to join the guerrilla fighters, they were mistreated, humiliated. 'You're a bunch of monkeys, we are the ones who are men, bearers of a superior culture, we speak Portuguese or French, we know how to read. You will just be the fighters, and your women will work for us.' It's true this region was more backward, but what was done to develop it, to educate its menfolk? Hardly anything. And today, there are still more cadres from the north than there are from the east, after six years of this war front. And there were thousands and thousands of guerrilla fighters. So where are the cadres?"

"You are right there, Worldly, more should have been done. But why don't you blame the Movement, its leaders? Why only blame northerners?"

"Who are the leaders? Aren't they from the north?"

Wisdom threw more wood on the fire. A group of guerrilla fighters was sitting by a fire twenty metres away, watching them. The barrels of their guns, reflecting the light of the flames, cast metallic flashes into the night. The weapons are tired, they no longer shine, Worldly thought.

Then he said, "When people talk about the Kamundongos, they're talking about a group of middle-ranking commanders who dominate the Movement. They're not all from the north. But they are the majority. Even the mixed-race people are called Kamundongos, although not all of them are. There are mixed-race members from the south, and many of them have got good ideas. But they enter the dominant group, if you like, they form part of the ruling class. The term *Kamundongo* nowadays means privileged."

"And yet there are privileged people from the east and the south, like you . . . Between us two, who takes more perks? Be honest. I never send anyone over the border to buy me cigarettes or sugar or coffee. I don't even have enough money for that. But each caravan that arrives always brings stuff you've ordered. I never keep the cotton fabric that comes for the high command to give to their women..."

"Well, that's because you always refuse your share. You have a right to it."

"No, I don't think I have a right to it. I think it's fairer to distribute the cloth among the people, who have no clothes. The awful thing is that you people are now opposed to the northerners not in order to correct their mistakes but to take advantage of those mistakes. I would agree with you if you were to say that the Movement doesn't care about the people; all the cloth should be distributed so that people can have clothes to wear; let's abolish the privileges enjoyed by the commanders; get rid of traditional power structures. But no. You say we have a right to keep a share, a right that was put in place by the first commanders, which the Movement tolerated. But to have that right, one needs to be a commander. And that's why we get rid of anyone else so that we can enjoy that right. You're not thinking about improving things, of correcting all the mistakes that caused the struggle to slide backwards. Like the others, you only think of using the current situation for your own benefit. That has a name, and it's called opportunism."

"It's just impossible to argue with you. All you do is resort to insults."

"I'm not insulting you, I'm telling the truth. And I'm telling you because you're my friend. I wouldn't dare say it to anyone else because I'd risk being shot in the back."

"Don't dramatize things. You've always said we're a peace-loving people, and if we wage war, it's because we're forced to. Why would we settle scores by resorting to guns?"

"One never knows, Worldly. Killing and watching people die encourages some to value human life less. Even when there's a political justification for every enemy killed. And when there's no educational training, it's easy to forget the meaning of combat and to then kill simply for the pleasure of killing. The smell of blood becomes overwhelming, and when there's a quarrel, arms can burst into song. It happens in all wars. So why not ours, in which there are so many who no longer know what they're fighting for?"

"But from there to actually shooting you, who haven't done anyone any harm ..."

"Well, it's unpredictable. A bit too much honey wine and they start calling me a Kamundongo to my face. If I then tell them one or two truths, it's easy to imagine what might happen. That's why I spoke to you, but I won't say anything to the others."

They sat watching the flames of the fire. Pallid flames that lit up the twenty huts arranged in two semicircles surrounded by trenches.

"We've known each other ever since Lisbon and the Casa dos Estudantes. How many years is that, Aníbal? Twelve, thirteen, I'm damned if I know. And we've been three years together, more or less, on this front. In Cuando, Kembo, Cuanavale, here. We've always been part of the same command unit. After all this time, you should know me ... I've always regarded you as a friend. Do you think I'm an opportunist?"

"I don't know, men change. Before, I used to think you were a bit shallow, inconsistent, but honest. Not always courageous. I'm not referring to physical courage—you always behaved like a man of courage who knew how to conceal his fear—but to moral courage. Nowadays, I'm no longer so sure. Circumstances cause a man to change. Before, you used your position as a commander to get privileges, though not that many, I hasten to add. But it was understandable: it was institutionalized, you'd had an easy life in Europe, you'd gotten used to certain things. But in any case, you abandoned all that comfort to come here, which is laudable. You were young, you could perfect yourself, act in accordance with your political ideals. But then all of a sudden, you changed. I noticed it when I returned from the latest mission. In my absence, you had changed. And you were a different person; all it took was three months. And when the letters arrived, you became almost hostile toward me. The only thing you said was that you'd been summoned back across the border. And you avoided speaking to me. Today, perhaps because you're leaving, you've come over to talk. Remorse for leaving me on my own?"

"Why remorse? They've summoned me . . . And sometimes one just doesn't feel like talking."

"And yet you spent hours in discussions with the others. There's nothing else to do here. There's only fighting when the enemy attacks. We live hidden away in the forest like animals. We spend the whole day in the base. There are no books. Only honey wine and talk. There's no point in denying it: you were avoiding me. Have I committed some error, done anything to you? I don't think it's that. We're used to talking frankly with each other. It can only have something to do with the letters and the regionalism that now prevails here."

"It's no use, Wisdom. You're a pessimist, and you see ghosts where there are none. Is there never a moment when you just don't feel like talking to someone?"

"It doesn't matter. Everything will become clear sooner or later."

"But it does matter. The opinion you have of me. Am I an opportunist, then?"

"You're adopting the attitudes of an opportunist. That's not quite the same thing."

"Thank you for being so condescending. You could call me an opportunist without beating about the bush."

"I'm not being condescending. Would it be simpler for you if I were to call you an opportunist? That would give you a good excuse to cut yourself off completely from me."

"Fucking hell! This has now become a persecution complex."

"Maybe. Who isn't driven crazy by this absurd war?"

"See what you're like, Wisdom? You even say this war is absurd now. You're completely demoralized. And do you know why? Because you don't want to admit to your mistakes. How can you put things right if you don't accept your mistakes? It's time for some honest talk so that this war can mean something again."

"Deep down, we're both saying the same thing. I'm not saying that the fight against colonialism is absurd, but the direction the war has taken most certainly is. Look at our fighters. Today, they are a bunch of outlaws, almost mercenaries. There's nothing of the revolutionary combatants about them, absolutely nothing. What is their main worry in life? The wife who went and slept with another man, the young girl who's coming of age and who they're all fighting over, the honey wine that isn't ready to drink yet, and that guy over there who's eaten more meat than I have. And when there's any problem, the excuse is always tribalism, regionalism. Because the guy over there is Umbundu or Mbunda or Kangala. Or else, the worst sin of all, because he's Kamundongo. Isn't it all ridiculous?"

"It needs to change."

"How? Placing only men from the east in all positions? Is that how you're thinking of changing the situation?"

"No, it's not that. But more positions should be allotted to men from the east."

"Even if they're worse than others?"

"Even if they're worse than others. Positions have to be shared more equitably."

"Do competence, honesty, revolutionary discipline not count for anything? Is the rule about proportionality all that matters?"

"That was always the deciding factor, Wisdom. Competence, honesty, and what was the other thing you mentioned? That never counted. What did count was whether you were from the north or not."

"You're exaggerating. Didn't you progress within the organization? You were never just a guerrilla fighter. You went straight into a position with responsibilities."

"I was better as well! I'm one of the few. I wonder whether the fact that my father was Kimbundu from Golungo didn't have some bearing. But I'm not interested in my case, I'm interested in those who are still in the same position as before. If I was speaking for myself, yes, that might be opportunism. But it's not about me."

"How many commanders from the east are there? Just one? Even illiterates rose to become commanders because they were good fighters. That's fair."

"So why weren't they taught to read and write? Why weren't they properly educated? They could be platoon commanders, but they can't rise above that because they're illiterate."

"You're correct to point out the error. But one or two were educated, let's not exaggerate. And they were promoted in any case."

"Of course, that's because there were no longer any others available. The northerners didn't want to fight; they were all across the border. They needed commanders. Great, promote any illiterate who is a good combatant. But will that guy gain a voice anytime soon? Never, because he's illiterate, he's hampered. Little has been done to educate the men from here. If I got a bit of an education, let's say, if I studied, it was at my father's expense and not because of the Movement."

"You had a scholarship in Germany. You didn't make use of it. You used to admit that you didn't do much studying."

"And how many northerners are there who take ten years to finish their degrees, just because they're from the north and have got friends to protect them?"

"Be frank. You know perfectly well what happens. They refuse to come to fight, the Movement cuts their scholarship, and they manage to get another one by themselves, what with all the aid organizations there are in Europe. They say they're preparing for national reconstruction! You chose to come when you were called, and no one can take the credit away from you."

"We weren't talking about me."

"You're the one who brought up your case. When it's in your interests, you always cite yourself as an example . . . But on the subject of the illiterate commanders, I've always said that the Movement should have done more to train cadres. It was an admirable aspiration that was even used as propaganda, but in practice . . . Other more immediate priorities cropped up. It may be only unintentional, but the human factor has always been overlooked. This comes down to an absence of sensitivity, which is linked to society's own lack of development. But it's not because they're from the north or from the east. I just don't see things like that."

"You can't see it! That's the difference between us. You're from the north, and you unconsciously defend your people. It's a cultural issue."

"We always come back to the same problem. Except that now I'm the one favouring my own region."

"Yes, at heart, that's it. Look, Wisdom. Even with the slogan 'down with tribalism,' one can actually uphold tribalism. All you have to do is spout the slogan every time our positions are attacked. They're accusing me of making a mistake because I'm from such-and-such tribe, so they're being tribalist. And sometimes it's just because I've made a single mistake. But when the slogan gets trotted out, everyone gets scared and refrains from going on the attack. No one wants to be accused of something they were taught was the gravest of all crimes. It was you who once drew my attention to this."

"I remember. And I took that position in order to defend a guerrilla fighter from the east who was being unfairly accused of tribalism, because he criticized a northern commander, for which he was completely justified, because that commander was a rascal."

"Well then? The tribalist shouting 'down with tribalism' in order to save his skin ... At this precise moment you're defending those who made mistakes for sentimental reasons. Isn't that adopting a narrow regional stance, albeit totally unconsciously? Think about it."

"Okay, when we get to this point, there's just no arguing with you."

"As I already told you, there's a trench. Wherever there's such a trench, we tread ever so carefully, but we always fall in. Wisdom! You've got to leap over the trench, but you don't understand this."

"By forfeiting my ideas and proclaiming to all and sundry that the Kamundongos sabotaged the war? I blame the Movement or, to be more precise, its leadership."

"Trained by northerners ..."

"Not only them. There's a bit of everything among the leadership. And among the northerners, there are intellectuals who agree with us in our criticism. They've gone beyond such things, Worldly, as you know only too well."

"Have they really gone beyond such things? Have you yourself gone beyond them? You've given so many examples, oh yes, you certainly have ... And yet, when it comes to the crunch, you refuse to leap over the trench, out of some strange loyalty."

"Listen, Worldly, this discussion isn't going anywhere. To be quite honest, the best we can do is to look at what can be done to salvage the situation."

"That's what I'm trying to do. So what do you propose, Wisdom?"

The group of fighters turned in for the night. The two sentinels stationed at either end of the base gathered around the fire to get warm. Their posts were left unguarded, but there was little danger of an attack during the night. After some time warming their hands over the embers, the guards glanced reluctantly at the two commanders and returned to their positions.

Wisdom said, "We've already talked about this on many occasions. The creation of a revolutionary party within the Movement is now more urgent than ever. This should form the nucleus directing the Movement, which in practice would become a broad front. The membership of this party would be handpicked, and only those militants without blemish would be admitted."

"Yes, we've already talked about that. I no longer believe in such a possibility. Who would handpick these members? And who would judge their value?"

"A commission, I don't know, a group."

"Don't you see the problem, Wisdom? This would obviously have to be public. A conference would decide to create this party and the commission to go with it. Or do you think it would all happen in secrecy? That would be very risky."

The other limited himself to shaking his head.

Worldly continued, "Even if such an idea were agreed to, problems would arise when it came to selecting the commission. There would be a northern majority, and the people wouldn't accept it. Or worse still, it wouldn't say anything, and this party would be sidelined from the outset. Don't you see? At that point, we would prevent the northerners from judging our militant credentials."

"What do you suggest then?"

"What I've already told you. An equal number of leaders. From the north and the east. It's a first step but a necessary one. Afterwards, the most able, competent, and honest can progress, as you say. If the people see that leaders from the east are also capable of retreating from the struggle, then they'll only accept the best as their leaders."

"What do you mean precisely by *afterwards*, Worldly? When everything is over and done with? If the struggle falls even further back, then it's all over. We'll have arms but no men. We're already on the brink of disaster..."

"In the first stage, the guerrillas and the people will be reassured, and they'll all return to their posts. If, later, the struggle stalls, then everything will be as it is now, or maybe better. But it will be much clearer to everyone."

"Utopian dreams! The people won't want anything more to do with us, and they'll give themselves up to the Tugas. That's quite simply suicide. If the leadership isn't good now, it'll be even worse afterwards."

"Why worse? We slash all the worst elements from the leadership and replace them with the best from the east. It won't be any worse."

"And how will the choice be made? If everything is motivated nowadays by regionalism, demagoguery, what guarantee will there be that the best northerners remain in positions of leadership, and not the worst? And how do we ensure the same is the case for those from the east?"

"It's a risk. But anyway, your formula won't work, Wisdom."

"Because you don't want it to. And yours is suicide."

"How little you trust the masses and the eastern cadres."

"I know them, and that's enough. And stop including yourself in the eastern cadres. Of course, being from the east is to say you oppose the north in everything. Apart from anything else, I refuse to see you as someone from the centre or the south or the east. We are merely Angolans, that's all."

"The people don't see us that way, Wisdom."

"The people...the poor people, always pulped. Pulped tomatoes! Manipulated by everyone. As always throughout history."

"I had many friends from every region," Worldly said. "In Germany, for instance, I was the only student from the east or, as you say, not from the north. Among ourselves, we never noticed the difference, sometimes we would joke when we compared the cities we came from, but no one ever took it seriously. Who was going to say that Kahala was more of a city than Luanda? So, I don't consider myself as being from the east or any other region. I certainly feel more at home in any city than out in the bush in Moxico or Huambo. I'm a city man. And preferably a large city. Only Luanda, which I barely know, can give me a pale idea of my dream city. What I really like is Paris or Cologne or Hamburg. A regionalist, me?"

"I'd like to believe you, but today I just can't. Sincerely. Your argument, your behaviour don't leave me feeling very confident."

"I defend what seems fair to me. Maybe I'm more sensitive to these problems because I was born in Huambo. But I would think the same if I were from Cabinda or Uíje."

"I'm not so sure, Vítor. But it's late, and we've got to get some sleep."

6

It's midday. The man is still lying in the forest, his gun between his knees. From time to time, he dozes off, warmed by the rays of the sun filtering timidly through the leaves. But he wakes up immediately, his nerves flayed by the sound of a branch falling or the screech of a bird. Then he returns to his memories, the ghosts of his past. These are ever-present, clinging to him, like his fear.

Malongo abandoned Sara and their daughter, Judite. He met them in Paris, on his way to Algeria, summoned there by the Movement. They were living in the same apartment he stayed in every year, during his holidays. Now, there were just two of them. Malongo had gone to Amsterdam on the trail of a Dutch woman; he was playing and singing in a cabaret but never sent any news. Sara was working as a doctor in a hospital, and during the five years since she had fled from Lisbon, she had been her family's sole breadwinner. She bore Malongo's frequent disappearances, invariably because of women, with resignation. He would turn up again after a while, promising that it wouldn't happen again. Sara pretended to believe him, merely hoping that the Movement would call her to the front. But it never did, and then Malongo would disappear once more. This time it was different, he had gone and hadn't come back.

"If he does return, he'll find the door shut, it's over, I'm fed up," Sara said. He told her she was right. His friend was impossible. He was even worse now than in Lisbon, and any hope of reviving his soccer career had been squandered. He played his guitar in third-rate nightclubs and during the summers he busked in the Latin Quarter, playing to tourists. The money he earned was enough to cover his wine, but he never offered to help with household expenses. This made him embittered, and Sara and Judite paid for his bad moods. Until he fled once and for all, saying, "I'm going to make my fortune in Holland." Worldly stayed at Sara's home in Paris for two days before catching his flight to Algeria. He would undergo military training, he didn't know where, and then he would go off to the war.

"If you come across Aníbal, tell him friends are supposed to answer letters, no matter how busy they may be. I never saw him again, and I wrote to him a number of times. I only ever got one letter from him, and it didn't say much. You can also tell the Movement that I'm waiting for a response to the dozens of letters I've sent them suggesting I should go to one of the border zones, although it appears they don't seem to need any doctors in their rearguard. Judite's no problem, she'll go with me. And she'll put up with what the other children have to put up with. A lifetime in exile is much worse than anything I might have to endure on the war front. Laurindo always wrote to me during the time he was in Cabinda. Then he was transferred goodness knows where, and I got no more news from him. As for Horácio, he's still in Prague and sometimes sends me a poem; he's hoping to join the guerrillas once he finishes his degree, which won't be long now. Get ready to have to put up with him if you find yourself in the same sector. I never heard from Fernanda again—did you get any news?" He had to tell her he had long lost hope of meeting her again; she had probably returned to Angola. Or she had married some white in Portugal. He said it jokingly, but the very idea caused his stomach to churn. Yet another frustrated love. He really didn't have much luck with women.

These were the conversations he had with Sara, who fixed

him up with a first-aid bag containing all he needed, not forget-ting anti-malaria and anti-diarrhea medication, and even some tranquilizers for the stresses and strains of war. He hadn't been able to say goodbye to Malongo and had lost all contact with him. And he was his great friend; he was sorry. Sara said a sad goodbye. "Speak to Aníbal, don't forget, tell him to write from wherever he is, I need to hear from him." And he hugged Judite, a pretty little five-year-old, who reminded him of another mulata he had met on a beach in Portugal in a former life.

Sara never stopped thinking about Aníbal, with whom he had a final conversation before leaving the battle front for the border. "I've come to the conclusion that it would be better if you left the country with me." Wisdom rejected the proposal. "I haven't been summoned. I've got no urgent business to attend to over the border, and besides, I detest the atmosphere of political conspiracy one experiences there. My place is here with the fighters." Worldly did his best to persuade him. He spoke of the danger he'd face if there was some sort of disciplinary problem and found himself having to admonish one of the combatants, which might provoke an uprising, given the current climate of revolt against the Kamundongos. Wisdom had always been stubborn. "Didn't everyone know him? So you regret leaving me after all ..." Rubbish, that was just to offend him and to put a stop to the conversation. He gave up. Let him go to hell, it was his problem. If he continued the conversation, they would get to the point they had reached two days before, but with an even more conclusive rupture. And they were friends in spite of it all.

He remembered Sara and told him to write. He would post the letter once he was across the border. She was still in Paris and waiting for news; anything, even just a note, was a palliative for ten or eleven years of exile. "So what am I going to say, that she should wait and keep the faith, one day she'll be called, like the just who await the grace of God? No, Worldly, I stopped promising paradise long ago, when I lost sight of it myself. I don't know how to lie. Let her think that it's marvellous here, that we are fighting heroically and generously for the future of the land. The truth will destroy her. At least she's got a job there and living without hardship, and her daughter's studying. She doesn't really have any grasp of what we're doing here. She should be allowed, at least, to maintain her illusions as some form of compensation."

Worldly said, "Until the next time we're together. I'll send you coffee and sugar from across the border. Do you need anything else?" Wisdom needed a pair of socks; the pair he had were full of holes that could no longer be darned, so often had they been sewn and sewn again. They embraced, Worldly assured him it was the first thing he'd do when he got there, and he set off for the border.

7

The day is coming to an end. Soon another night of cold, fatigue, and terror will arrive. Abandon everything. Seek the warmth of a house, even a prison cell; a human presence, even an executioner; food, even a crust of stale, mouldy bread. Abandon everything. And it's so easy. The Ninda military post is less than a kilometre away. He heard the noise of cars, voices, dogs barking all day long. What will they do to him if he surrenders? Little or nothing. He sometimes hears announcements on the radio that those who surrender will be well received. There are rumours among the people that such-and-such a guerrilla who surrendered today is now a commander of the "irregulars"; another is leader of the Flechas. Is all enemy propaganda false? If it were, it would have no credibility among the population. The colonialists are no longer as stupid as they had been at first, when everything they spouted was ridiculous. Today, they have learned to leaven their overall lies with one or two narrowly focused truths.

Jaguar was a great fighter. He received citations on a number of occasions for his heroism. But his leg had been badly injured and then had to be amputated to avoid gangrene. They say he now lives in a camp over the border, suffering cold and hunger like the others and dragging himself around. What kind of Movement is it that doesn't even care about its mutilated war veterans?

At the military post, they'll interrogate him. They'll make him talk over the radio, appealing to his comrades to follow his example and surrender. Angola in Combat, the Movement's radio station, will label him a traitor. And after that, he'll be free. He'll be able to return to his native Huambo and his parents, whom he hasn't seen for fourteen years. Isn't it worth it? Put an end to hunger, the pointless exhaustion, the cold, the fear, in exchange for being tarnished a traitor by an organization that no longer has any importance and will never achieve power. Along with his uniform and his gun, he will abandon the sobriquet Worldly and reassume his real name, Vítor Ramos, profession: student. In Nova Lisboa, he can study veterinary science; he'll graduate by the age of thirty-five, it's still not too late. It's out here that he's not going to achieve anything. Even if he doesn't die, or if he's captured, what will become of him when the Movement collapses? It'll certainly go into decline. It might survive for a bit longer, but it'll be defeated. What will become of him and the others? They'll be refugees in Zambia and treated as such. He'll have to surrender to the colonialists in far worse conditions, because he will be surrendering to the acknowledged victors. At that point in time, they may still welcome him because they can make use of him. Then he'd become a busted flush, worth nothing. He's got to choose the right time, and now is the right time. Afterwards, it will be too late.

Kapangombe had the most beautiful wife in his zone. The commander, a Kamundongo, lusted after the woman. She spurned him, claiming she loved her husband. Kapangombe was a brave, disciplined fighter; everyone respected him. During an ambush in favourable terrain, Kapangombe was killed. No one could understand why. The enemy had barely returned fire. During the ambush, Kapangombe had been placed next to the commander. A month after Kapangombe's death, his wife moved in with the commander. That was when everyone understood why Kapangombe had died, though no one dared to say anything.

In everything there's a risk, Worldly thought. When you go to war or court a woman, when you look for a job, there is a bunch of factors in competition with each other: the target you're after and the disastrous outcome. Your skill lies in being able to analyze the contradiction thoroughly and to choose the strongest side. Today, the Movement only has any strength overseas. Dialectics always tell us that it is the internal factor that has primacy. So who doubts that the Portuguese will win? Only lunatics like Wisdom. For him, it's no longer even the need to believe in order to keep the faith in something; it's not even the mystique of revolution. Today, for him, the only thing that counts is revenge. I'll accept the risk but when there's a chance of winning. To take risks when our side holds no cards whatsoever is just stupid. The time for romanticism is over.

As old Samalanga used to tell him in confidence as they sat by the fire at night, "The struggle started and we were very grateful. Now, many days have passed and I don't know when the war reached Muié. Before, we heard rumours, and the first ones to arrive were the UNITA fighters. We were told they were in Chikolui. We asked, 'What weapons have you brought for the struggle?' Walking sticks. Are you going to chase away the Tuga with a walking stick? And we scorned them. Are we going to abandon our homes just like that? They were sowing confusion and we said when you turn up here, we're going to complain to the Tugas. Are you bringing us that smash-and-grab war, like in the old days of the slaves? They went away and never came back. Then the district administrator turned up, all rattled; he was threatened out on the Kalimbue trail, so much so that when he got back to his post, he couldn't talk. We watched. What could this be all about? Scarcely a week had gone by, and those who had family out in the bush had already gone. Then a column of personnel carriers full of soldiers turned up and told us that the place where our chief was threatened, they're going to clean it up right away. And off they went. When they got back, we couldn't ask them what was going on. They brought Xinjana with them, a true Angolan. Xinjana died because of the food he grew. The commander of the Movement turned up and went straight to where Xinjana grew his crops. Xinjana said, 'I've seen how you people really want to fight the Tugas, so take whatever food you want.' When he was caught by the Tugas, Xinjana was tortured right in front of us, and they chopped his balls off. They said whoever gives the terrorists food is going to be treated like Xinjana. No one slept that night. Not even taxes hurt as much as the harm they did to Xinjana that day. That's when we began to want to abandon all our riches and join the Movement so as to expel the colonial murderers. We went off into the woods. Others, who were on this side of Muié, said they were still going to wait and see. The soldiers forced them to move inside the barbed wire compound and seized their cattle. So they said hey, those others took off into the woods, they were right. And off they went too. The guys in the Movement began to mobilize us because we're all comrades.

"But in the end, it was just a lie. All they did was come and eat the food belonging to the people. Many young lads agreed to fight, some of them were punished for no reason, and that wasn't fair. I thought to myself, That fellow Chapuile's from my tribe, I can talk to him. I asked him, 'How is it you're fighting but not getting anywhere? And punishing people just like that. We're not happy.' Chapuile said he took orders from that elder, the Kamundongo... After that I was caught by the soldiers, and they took me off behind the wire. I worked as a builder for the commander of the PIDE. In the month of December 1970, columns came up from Luso, some on their way to Gago Coutinho, others to Cangamba. The Cangamba ones hit a mine, and the ones going to Gago did as well, and Muié and Cangombe too. The Tugas went bananas. The vexation at those brand-new personnel carriers blown into the air, dammit. The prisoners they took in the woods, they started machine-gunning them in front of us. That's when I fell to the ground. I thought, I'm getting out of here again, this isn't working. I said to the wife let's go. The PIDE got wind of it. They'd pay me a hundred escudos a day as I was a good builder, but I didn't take any notice. I came back to the woods. But is this the war you wanted to bring us, just so the people would die? It'd be better to get it over and done with now."

That's how the people talked. How could he, an interpreter of the people's aspirations, force the masses to support a war they no longer wanted?

Wisdom had said one day, "War is an excuse, either for the weak to convince themselves they have power or for criminals to legally commit acts of sadism, or if not legally, then justifiably. Or for the strong to risk their own image, like the boxing champion who invites others to challenge him for his title for the love of a risk. Or a kind of intrinsic justice in seeing the king stripped bare, showing up his weak points, if not to everyone, then at least to his own circle or his queen."

Soon afterwards, he had added, "No, this is a religious notion of war. It's waged by mystics, each one according to his ability and manner, but when seen in its totality, it ceases to be mystical."

"The poor devil who is sent to war against his will, is he a mystic?" Worldly had asked.

"He could refuse to go. He follows the mystique of fear of disobeying the established order, that which comes from above, the law. What is that if not mysticism? Superstition has become ingrained in everything, my old friend. It is a residue from a time when man lived in caves and saw a terrifying god in every flash of lightning. Tyrants will confirm this to you, or the overlords of the church who have always known how to make excellent use of it, as if by miracle."

He gets up as night falls. He starts to make for the highway. When they hear him on the radio, his comrades won't believe it;

they'll think he was captured. That's what they always think of those who pass over to the enemy. What will they say about him? I couldn't care a fig. Sooner or later, they'll all follow me. And what about Wisdom? No, not him, he'll have to be hunted down and shot. Wisdom will say, 'I'd already noticed some changes in him, he was demoralized, his morale undermined. That's why he didn't resist their torture.' Wisdom will humiliate him once more with his haughty condescension. He wasn't a bad boy, but he didn't have much courage, moral courage, that is. Fuck Wisdom. Won't the Tugas make him show them where Wisdom's base camp is? Won't they put him in a helicopter to witness the destruction of the base, maybe even participate? No, not that, he'll refuse. And if they torture me, will I resist?

Almost unconsciously, he starts veering to the right, avoiding the military post. No. He'll have to put up with hunger and exhaustion; his salvation doesn't lie at this post, but in Zambia. Salvation doesn't come from having a full belly, but in forever knowing that he was responsible for Mussole not being avenged. The justice maker may die before justice is done. That is inevitable and isn't in his hands. But he cannot be the agent of the inevitable.

8

The highway is a wide, clear serpent in the darkness. He remains there for ten minutes watching each side before deciding. In the end, he runs out of the forest, climbs the slope, crosses the road, and jumps into the forest on the other side. And he lets himself flop to the ground, exhausted.

How can a man endure hunger, exhaustion, lack of sleep, cold, fear? What is man made of? What more can they demand of me? I'm not superhuman. Why avoid the military post if at least all this would end there? Hunger, hunger, the number one concern of this war, the dream and nightmare of the guerrilla fighter, central topic of his conversation. He had never really felt true hunger. How many books describe the famines of India, sub-Saharan Africa, or the northeast of Brazil? How many films had he seen? But he had never known what it's like to look at a squirrel jumping from one tree to the next and to see it not as a long-tailed creature but as a plump piece of meat roasting over the fire. Only now does he know what hunger is like.

The good bourgeois of the First World, as he settles down at his table in a restaurant, doesn't even think that he is doing so in order to satisfy some primordial need, but as pleasure, entertainment. What fraction of the day's length does he dedicate to thinking about what he should eat? Only if he wants to go on a diet in order to slim down. The richer a society becomes, the less it thinks about the basics. How unfair. How can there not be rebellions? The true class struggle is the contradiction which pits those who spend the day thinking of the stomach they have to fill against those who, when they think of their stomach at all, do so only to try to empty it. And don't come at me with your theories; this is the only truth there is.

He gets up again, surprised that he is still able to do so. He drags himself forward, seeing on his left the searchlight from the military post periodically sweeping across the canopy of the trees.

Some hours later, the Tundombe trail appears. He pauses. Maybe it's better to follow the trail and try to reach the guerrilla base he once knew. But maybe it's already moved, and the trail may be mined. He decides to approach the river, now that the military post has been left far behind, and follow it all the way to Zambia. That's the wisest thing to do. He marches for the rest of the night, trying to keep going northeast. He doesn't get as far as the river. Morning returns. Another one. The same as all the others, cloudless. The sun appears at his back, which means he has deviated to the west. He may still be near the military post, he has no idea. This Ninda forest is famous: two attacks on the post had already failed because the guerrillas got lost in it at night. He considers this without any emotion. He lies down and tries to sleep, enjoying the abating cold. What does it matter whether or not he's near the post? He is now indifferent to everything. He tries to think in order to stay awake. But the accumulated fatigue of the past few days overcomes him once and for all.

He wakes up with the midday sun above. He has at last slept. He tries to get up but fails. Sleep has sharpened the pains all over his body. And his thirst. I've got to drag myself as far as the river. He leans against a tree, his gun in his left hand serving as a staff, and pulls himself up. He staggers forward a couple of paces and falls flat on his face. That's it, I can't move, he thinks. All that will remain for him to do is to contemplate the leaves, the sky, and to calmly take his leave of life. So near his goal! He crawls over to a tree and tries once again. He manages to get up. He steadies his legs, leans slightly forward, and falls over, some ten metres ahead. He repeats the operation once more. After ten falls, he realizes that he is reaching the end of the forest. He falls another three times and emerges from the trees. He sees a manioc plot. He looks around in every direction. No one. He gets to the first plant and pulls it up by its root. The tuber is edible. He tears up another couple of plants and crawls back into the forest. With his dagger, he peels the tubers and wolfs them down almost without chewing. The manioc is good; it's the sweet kind. If it was the other type, the least he would get is a bout of diarrhea that would eventually kill him. But he was lucky, very lucky. He sits resting for a long time. He gradually begins to regain his strength, heralded by his quickening pulse. He crawls back to the plot and pulls up more plants, stuffing his pockets full of tubers. I've got to get away from here. If the owner of the plot turns up, he'll follow his tracks so as to demand compensation for the robbery. And if he's not linked to the Movement, he'll denounce him to the Tugas. He gets up and moves forward, falling less often now. He's already got food for the night; he must now find water. If he hasn't got lost again, he'll reach the border tomorrow. And at night, he'll be able to light a fire, once he's sure he's well away from the military post.

It's two in the afternoon. He glimpses the savannah through the trees. He has marched almost without anything to guide him but trying to keep going northeast, in order to reach the River Ninda. He calculates that he is near the old military post of Monteiro, abandoned by the enemy some time before because it was vulnerable. On reaching the savannah, he sees the river ahead. At last! I must have gone round and round in circles to have strayed so far from the river like this. He approaches it and falls to his knees on the sand, his face in the cool water. After he has drunk, he gets up and looks to his left. And his heart misses a beat as all he can see in front of him are red flashes: he's right next to the Ninda military post.

He plunges into the bulrushes on the riverbank. How is that possible? He cautiously raises his head and sees the houses, the barracks on top of the hill, the huts of the local population near the river, the tin roofs reflecting the sunlight, the smoke coming from the chimneys. It's less than a kilometre away. He can even make out the sentry in his little watchtower. And it's only then that he hears the noises coming from the post, people shouting, dogs barking, which he hadn't noticed before because he was so tired and thirsty. It's finished, it's all over. The locals and the soldiers will come and fetch water from the river; someone might come a bit further downstream and find him. Damned war, damned war. Who told me to set off on adventures? Wasn't the adventure of life enough? Calm down, calm down, you've been in worse spots. Stop it! I'm never going to be able to get away from this bloody post; it's like a magnet. The manioc plot belongs to people from the post, so he'll be found. No, it's too late for them to go there. Only tomorrow morning. I'll be far away by then.

There's only one thing for it: to lie low among the rushes until nightfall, pray that no one has seen him, and follow the current of the river. He'll reach the border in the end. He looks at his watch, two thirty. He's still got four hours of affliction ahead. What will he do if some soldier appears? Open fire and run away. If he can. He can't go to the woods now. There are too many risks of him being found. Hasn't the sentry seen me? He may have. If he has, he may think I'm a soldier. He'll never think a guerrilla fighter would dare to come so near in the middle of the day. He remains with his eyes stubbornly fixed on the houses and the river. A truck turns into the post. He can hear cries of joy. It must be bringing food and wine. The bastards, they get the best food and drink, waging war is easy that way. Then a doubt strikes him: a lone vehicle has come from Gago Coutinho? That means the guerrillas no longer control the highway, before those guys only travelled in convoys of ten or more trucks. This war is all fucked up.

At four, a group of soldiers leave the post and head down to the river in single file. They're armed, so it must be a patrol. The soldiers reach the bank and start following the course of the river. Toward him. I'm done for. There are ten soldiers. They're coming down the Monteiro trail, parallel to the river. They're five hundred metres away now. If he runs into the forest, they'll see him and become suspicious. The chase will be on. He won't stand a chance, weak as he is. Nor do the rushes provide enough cover. Is he going to wait for them to get near and open fire? He'll only hit one or two with his first salvo, and the others will return fire. He'll be holed up between the woods and the river; he'll be easy prey. He looks around wildly for another hiding place. His despair seizes hold of him and wipes away the dreamy torpor that had descended over him ever since he ate the manioc. The soldiers are now four hundred metres away. There's only one thing for it and that is to get into the cold water. He crawls the couple of metres that separate him from the river and enters the water, leaving the tip of the barrel of his gun above the water line in a firing position. If they're not expecting anything, they won't notice his head emerging in the middle of the bulrushes. He can no longer see the soldiers, but he can hear their feet on the sand. It may just be a routine patrol. If so, they'll just pass by and not notice.

He can hear their footsteps ever more clearly. And he picks up the first words: "It must just be a rumour." A few more steps crunching the sand and a few more words. "Those guys are screwed, they're not planning any attack, Sergeant." "You never know" came a voice with a Portuguese accent. "They attacked

Chiume." Again, the first voice: "Sergeant, the people get scared at the slightest thing. There's not much point in believing them."

Before long, the soldiers will be level with him. It's strange, he thinks, how years of existence can be decided in a split second. The so-called love of life and danger, the moment of truth that adventure seekers talk about. Love of life, my ass, it just leaves you with a pain in the pit of your stomach. What can Laurindo have thought when they caught him and his column of fighters in a river up in Lunda? Did he have time to be scared, or did he die in the first volley of bullets? His body was never found, the Portuguese army communiqués didn't mention it, and those of the Movement simply ignored it. Was he killed by a bullet, or did he drown? Drown, surely not. I hope he didn't. A quick death with a bullet's a thousand times better, a shot in the head or the heart. Laurindo was an excellent commander; that mulato from Gabela was a great guy, from the Central Highlands like him. Up in Lunda, did they also consider him a Kamundongo? That would be unfair. Laurindo was a really cool fellow.

"They were Turra footprints," the same Portuguese voice spoke. "All the same kind of sneaker prints heading in all directions. That's because there's a group of them nearby."

"Let's go back. Those who've just arrived will have news from Gago Coutinho. And beer . . ."

He suddenly remembers and the memory almost makes him faint: his boot prints in the sand. *His boot prints in the sand.* They're bound to see them. They'll follow them down to the river. He's caught. Now it really is all over. And from what he's heard, it's not just a routine patrol. When he crossed the trail to drink water, he didn't worry about leaving traces. He thought he was far from the military base, he didn't even look to his left. I've signed my death sentence. No, not death sentence. I can surrender straightaway. I can say I was going to give myself up but was waiting for nightfall, because I was afraid they might open fire when they saw me. If they apprehend him, it won't be for long.

The soldiers arc in front of him. It's now or never. He's going to get up and call them. Goodbye war, goodbye Movement, I'm going for peace.

"Look, Sergeant! Over there in the woods."

The shout stops Worldly as he's on the point of waving, and he remains lying in the water, paralyzed by fear.

"Something moved over there."

At first, he shuts his eyes, trying to avoid seeing the inevitable. Then he opens them again and looks in the direction of the enemy. The soldiers have stopped in front of him, their backs turned, and are scrutinizing the woods. It wasn't because of him. He makes an effort to think, to cling to his stroke of luck. He has a perfect view of them, because he has raised himself a little. He could open fire and kill a fair number. But what for? And the others? The war has finished, everything has finished, all he has to do is give himself up. He no longer feels able to cling to his elusive stroke of luck.

"A person?" asks the sergeant.

"It looked like it."

"He's seeing ghosts, Sergeant," the other voice says. "Surely you know Simão by now? He's always like that."

Simão! Worldly remembers him now. A former guerrilla fighter who went over to the enemy and is now a guide for the soldiers. An infallible tracker, he'll find his footprints, there's no doubt about that. I'd better surrender right away.

"He sees ghosts, but he always finds his prey. Are you really sure, Simão?"

"It looked like it, Sergeant."

"Hey! You people over there!" comes a voice suddenly from the direction of the army post.

The soldiers turn. The sergeant signals the approaching person to be quiet, but he doesn't seem concerned, because he continues to shout. "What's up? What are you doing?"

Worldly no longer understands what's going on, and he doesn't have the strength to understand. Only one idea dominates him: surrender. To raise his weapon above his head and shout to them. It's so easy. But the same distant voice continues. "Didn't you hear me call you?"

"This guy's crazy," the sergeant moans. "These little student officers are the ones wrecking this war. Yes, we've heard, Lieutenant. We're on patrol."

"Come away from there. There's going to be a parade. Major Calado is arriving."

The soldiers look at the sergeant in silence.

"All right," says the sergeant. "Let's go then, lads." A parade! Leave your ghost alone, Simão, the lieutenant isn't interested in that kind of thing. And it'd serve them right if it was a reconnaissance group, and they attacked the garrison and killed Major Calado and the little lieutenants and all the other motherfuckers. Bastards! Maybe they'd learn you don't play at organizing parades when there's a war.

And before Worldly's astonished eyes, the soldiers turn round and march back to the base. As Simão moves, he keeps glancing anxiously at the woods on his left. He knows that he risks everything every single day, that he is a traitor and there will be no pardon for him if the guerrillas by any chance take the post.

Gradually, without yet fully believing the miracle, Worldly's heart begins to beat again.

9

He has left the water and is lying on the sand. The sun will soon disappear, and he'll be able to get away from this goddamned place. He feels cold, his uniform is soaked. He hasn't quite grasped what happened; he only knows he hasn't been caught. But his brain starts functioning again, albeit hesitantly. Apparently, the soldiers had heard rumours from the locals that there were guerrillas in the vicinity. It must have been his footprints that had been discovered, because he had been prowling around there for days. I don't know though, because they kept talking about sneaker prints, like the ones used by guerrilla fighters, and I've got boots like those worn by the Tuga army. It doesn't matter. The group had come on patrol and had been interrupted by this Major Calado guy. And they were some ten metres from the marks made by his boots. The boots that had belonged to a dead Tuga soldier, salvaged from some fight, and which he, as the commander, had decided to make use of. I've been more than lucky, Worldly thinks. What distracted them? Some furtive shadow in the woods. But what shadow? A worm swallowing its own shadow. Not even Simão himself was sure.

One thing's strange: if they had found his footprints, why did they come out on patrol on the eastern side of the post rather than the west or south, where he had been? It was the first time he had approached the post from this side. Is that really true? I don't know. I no longer know where I've been. I get lost as soon as I enter the forest. No, there's just no way of understanding it. I only know I did very well not to stand up, otherwise they might have fired. But maybe they wouldn't have. But they would find his excuse suspicious. Excuses, Marilu, excuses, it won't happen again. If he had surrendered right here, they would have said you saw there was no escape and you gave yourself up. That's not the same thing as turning up at the military post and surrendering. They would think, of course, he was part of the reported reconnaissance group. He would bend under torture and tell them the whole truth and nothing but the truth. The truth they wanted to hear because they would never believe his own. And they still say some people have no luck! He had been lucky his whole life through, because he knew how to play the game.

No, you're lying to yourself, Worldly. This time, you took no risks. You weren't your own master, your sovereign self, as you like to say. The master of his own self, as you understand it, is proud, maybe haughty, trying to surpass himself. He conquers his luck, and he triumphs over himself when his luck is bad. You are not a master of yourself, you were vanquished by your bad luck, you didn't try to turn it around. You made use of your luck; you didn't conquer it. You didn't master yourself, you didn't turn your nerves into the strings of a guitar, you shied away from victory before the game even started, and now you're being a cheat. It's the effect of exhaustion, despair at this absurd war. That's his excuse. No, Worldly, acknowledge it. The master of himself, when he cheats, is impelled by the pleasure of deceiving, belittling, dominating; he is a cruel cheat. But you, you're a mean-spirited cheat, because you seek to justify yourself. It's no longer any use to you. Abandon this myth of being master of yourself. Fuck morality! Who am I to judge myself? I'm sounding like Wisdom now. I'd like to see others in the same situation. What I'd better do right now is think how I'm going to get out of here. What should I care about opinions people may have about me or my actions? Does Marilu care? Did Mussole care? She didn't make any effort to get to know me. Oh! How I wish I could sleep, sleep, and not think about what will happen if they catch me.

The cold of his damp clothes makes his teeth chatter. At least, that's what he tells himself. Or is it fear? It must be his fear that is now abating, which is why it's making its presence more readily felt. A short while ago, it had been too intense for me to be aware of it. When it comes down to it, you're a coward. Yes, I am, so what? I shit myself. Marilu knew it, she always knew it, and that's why she despised me. Mussole died before she could find me out. I shit myself, but that's nobody's business. Your beautiful self-sufficiency when in danger was a mask...So, who doesn't wear a mask? Who is the same on the inside and on the outside, on his head and on his tail? Oh, if only I could get this over with once and for all. Why didn't they catch me? They'd beat him, torture him, and then it would all be over and done with, and they'd leave him alone in a cell so that he could sleep in peace, because there would no longer be any hope. It's like when you have a tooth pulled out. I was always terribly afraid of the dentist. And he would tell me it was better to be brave, it would hurt a bit, but then it would all be over. But I was never able to make a decision, and it was only when the pain drove him to the edge of despair that he would throw all caution to the wind. Later, he would say he had spent days on end in pointless suffering when, after all, it was so easy. You're a chickenshit, that's what you are. I'm thinking clearly, I acknowledge my cowardice, and I don't care anymore.

But now he needed to think what to do. When night hid him from the lookout post, he would advance along the trail beside the river, always keeping to the river. Later, he would leave the trail, which must be mined. And continue along the banks of the river. Like that, he'll no doubt reach Zambia tomorrow or the day after.

So is he going to spend the night in his damp uniform? Stumble along for another day or three? With a few lousy manioc tubers? Given that luck has favoured him, it would be better to take advantage of it and keep his aces in the hole. He'll go and surrender once the sun has set, that's what he'll do, so he doesn't have to put up with the frightful cold that he knows is coming. Why not now? No, they're on parade, they may get nervous and overreact. When it gets dark, he'll make his approach. He'll shout to warn them that he's going to surrender. It would be stupid to be hit by a bullet just as he decides to go to the dentist. It's the other way round, Worldly. You're putting off having your tooth pulled out. Stop getting on my nerves. What you're saying is true, but let me be a weakling just one last time. Then I'll be another man. A traitor, a renegade, I'll go and show them where Wisdom's base is. I'll give them every single detail about the organization, explain how they should exploit the existing tribal rivalries, how to isolate the Kamundongos even more. I'll talk about their crimes over the radio. I'll do everything they ask me to do. I'll be a different man. I won't be a weakling anymore. But let me live the anguish of the last minute once more, the anguish of still having to decide. After that, I'll no longer have to decide, they'll decide for me, and I'll just follow them loyally. Like that, I'll be able to rest.

It's icy. The sun is hidden behind the trees, and darkness will soon fall. The temperature drops at night at this time of the year almost down to freezing. In Europe, that's nothing; it may even make them sweat. But for us ... and to make matters worse, wet! He lies on his back. The sky is still lit up, cloudless, while the land and the river and the military post take on the dun colour of death. A feeling of peace overtakes him. I'll eat some manioc, enjoy its sweet juice, and then drink some water. Then I'll smoke, have a bath, they'll give me clean clothes, I'll lie down in a bed and rest. With peace and quiet so near, why did I take so many years to see it? Yes, it was nice in Europe, in the good times before and during the time he knew Marilu. He was admired, he belonged to a country that was fighting for its freedom, he was a rare creature, a novelty. And he never missed an opportunity to give those young imbeciles who dreamed of world revolution a lecture on politics. He became an authority in student circles, and all that before 1968. Now he will be again. An ex-terrorist! Everyone will want to know him, to see what a leader of the Movement looks like in the flesh. How easy life is, in the final analysis, when you know how to live it.

Night has now fallen. He pulls himself to his feet and walks toward the trail. He's not going to follow it, because they may see him in the distance. First, he'll go into the forest, then he'll turn back toward the post. Before he reaches the barbed wire, he'll shout out that he's going to surrender. Poor Wisdom, he won't avenge Mussole. He's going to stop him. That'll be a fine turn of events. What right did Wisdom have to take his place, he who should be the one to avenge Mussole. But it's stupid to avenge her, what is Mussole except for a backward creature from these forests? Pretty? And how many pretty women have not been avenged? Why should it be this woman more than any other? Wisdom always was an idiot and now he's going to learn his lesson. He enters the woods.

"Halt!"

He stops, once again horrified. His surprise leaves him paralyzed.

"Yove ya, who are you?" he is asked in Mbunda.

I've been foolishly caught. Fuck! At least it's all over. Two shadows emerge from his left, their guns trained on him. A sudden flash of lucidity runs through him. And he blurts out, trusting his luck, "I'm from the Movement, comrades."

One of those pocket flashlights that looks like a pen, and that can barely be seen in the forest, focuses on his eyes and gun.

"Where were you going?" they ask him, once again in Mbunda.

He's not sure and that's the cruel truth. He can't make out

the details of their uniforms, only their faces. His intuition tells him they're guerrilla fighters. If they were soldiers, they wouldn't be so careful. By now, he is trusting his luck.

"I'm Comrade Worldly. I got separated from the others and found myself near the post. I've been trying to get away from the area for two days, but I keep getting lost and find myself back where I started. This Ninda forest. Don't you recognize me, comrades?"

"No," one of them replies. "Come."

One walks in front, the other takes up the rear. They go further into the forest. Worldly's brain now goes into overdrive. They're guerrilla fighters, and once again, he has escaped by the skin of his teeth. Just a few more metres, and he was going to turn round and head for the post. And so, as they intercepted him in time, they really must believe him when he says he was walking away from the post and into the forest. If they suspected him, they would have taken his gun from him. They walk for about ten minutes and then the one in front signals them to stop. He whistles faintly. The answer comes from the distance. They advance once more. Until they come to where there are five men sitting.

"Here's the comrade we were watching this afternoon," says the man in front.

One of them gets to his feet. They saw me this afternoon, Worldly thinks. I've got to tell the whole truth, except for what was going on inside my head.

"I'm Strong Blood, head of section," he says in Mbunda. "What's your name?"

"Worldly. Commander of F Zone."

"Ah yes, I remember. At the time, I was just a simple guerrilla fighter."

He shines the flashlight into his own smiling face. He is trying to see if he recognizes him.

"It rings a bell," Worldly says. "But I've been away from there so long."

"How did you end up here, comrade?"

Worldly lets himself fall to the ground. He summarizes the journey, the ambush he fell into, the solitary march, the approach to the military post, and his fruitless attempts to get away from it. Later, he would give a more detailed account, but for the time being, he is so exhausted; he just can't take it anymore.

"You're very tired and hungry, comrade. You'd better have something to eat. Mukindo, open a tin of meat, quick. We're reconnoitring the post for an immediate attack.

"They already know you're here," says Worldly.

"Is that so?"

"Yes. When I was in the river, a group of soldiers came out from the post and stopped right next to where I was. I heard what they were saying. The locals had told them about sneaker prints, loads of them. I thought they were mine. Then they saw something in the woods . . ."

"And then another soldier came and called them. It was our guy Culatra who didn't hide himself in time. We saw you crossing the savannah, comrade, on your way to the river. At first, we thought you were a Tuga. But then we saw your gun, an AKA. We were surprised. What was a comrade doing so near the post?"

"I didn't see the post at all. I thought I was far away. All I could think of was getting some water to drink."

"Yes, you were a long time without anything to drink. Mukindo, is the tin ready? Eat, comrade, and I'll go on talking. Can you drink cold milk? We can't light a fire here. It's just for you to gather a bit of strength. We've got to walk for a bit. But it's near. It's not far. Then you'll be able to eat as much as you want and sleep by a fire. Mukindo, open a tin of milk. Culatra, bring your canteen, prepare the milk. Do you want some manioc as well? Heavens, so many days without food . . . This war is hard."

Worldly nods in agreement, while he devours the tinned meat and manioc.

"Back there, we've got meat and we can make cassava pap," Strong Blood says. "We're not going to continue our reconnaissance. We're returning to base. Did they really see us?"

"Their guide, Simão, do you know him? Simão saw a shape, but then the officer appeared and they went away. They may come back. Tomorrow."

"Don't talk, comrade. Eat. We'll talk later round the fire. Our fighters saw you go to the river and thought it strange. We got a bit nearer. Then the soldiers appeared. We hid in the woods, but that fellow Culatra took his time. When the soldiers went away, we retreated, but I left two fighters to keep an eye on you, comrade."

"You thought they might seize me, right?"

"Well, to tell you the truth, I thought they were going to meet you, comrade. To get information from you. You might be an infiltrator in the Movement."

"Yes, that's true," Worldly says. Luckily, the darkness stops them from seeing his uneasiness. "Comrade Strong Blood is very observant. You were completely justified. But I was just trying to escape ... I was very lucky."

He hadn't seen a soul for days on end. He had been lost in total solitude. Suddenly he has discovered that the world is crowded. Everyone appears, and there I am in the middle. It is like a game. And it is. I played the game and clung to my luck, and now it won't elude me again.

"If they had seen you, what would you have done, comrade?" Culatra asks.

"I'd open fire. I was all ready to do so, when they looked over in your direction. So I waited, to see what they'd do. Even if I'd killed a few, it would have been hard to get away from where I was. There would have been no other solution, I would have died in combat."

"Yes, you were in a tight spot there," Mukindo comments.

"But when they discovered my boot prints, I was ready to open fire. Vitória ou morte!"

"Wow! You kept your head, comrade," says Strong Blood.

"I don't know what I would have done," says the fighter who had led him there. "I honestly don't know. Weren't you scared, comrade?"

"A bit, why not? Who isn't frightened in a situation like that? The problem isn't fear. You have to go beyond fear, not allow fear to dominate you. Otherwise you're finished."

"If you don't want to eat any more, let's start walking then," says Strong Blood. "It's very near. Just one last push and then you'll be able to rest properly, where it's dry."

"Yes, let's go, I can take it. A vitória é certa!"

They make their way for about an hour along a narrow path. Worldly follows close on the heels of the fighter in front of him, so as not to stray from the path that is invisible in the darkness. The pains in his body and from the cold are becoming unbearable, now that the possibility of rest is approaching. When you know your march is nearing its end, the last few moments are frightful, he thinks. By the time they leave the path, he can barely contain his despair and desire to just lie down on the ground and give up. They cut through the bush for about ten minutes. Then they reach a clearing in the forest, where there are traces of someone having slept recently. There are the remains of a fire and signs that the sand has been prepared for beds.

"We slept here yesterday," says Strong Blood. "Quickly light the fire for our comrade. Mukindo, prepare a place for him to sleep. He hasn't got a blanket, and he's wet. Mukindo, you sleep with Dynamite and lend him your blanket."

Worldly takes off his uniform and wraps himself in Mukindo's blanket. He, in the meantime, goes to get a bundle of dry grass. He gathers together the residue of some firewood from the previous night and lights the grass with a match. The flame immediately grows bigger. The most beautiful thing, Worldly thinks, a fire at night. They don't have any coffee, but Strong Blood gives him a cigarette. He lights it eagerly. He takes a deep draught and holds it in his lungs for as long as possible. He smiles as he exhales the smoke.

"A smoker suffers when he can't get tobacco," says the section chief.

"You can say that again! I don't know what's worse, hunger or lack of tobacco."

"I once went a week without being able to smoke. I thought I was going to go crazy. My fighters said afterwards that I picked on them for every tiny thing, and I wasn't even aware."

Strong Blood is a talker, Worldly thinks. All the better, it is so long since anyone has spoken to him. Soon, the heat of the fire increases, because the other fighters came back with more wood. Mukindo brings him a backpack to lean back on, while he spreads his legs near the fire. The heat gives him a pleasant tingling in his legs, which gradually spreads to the rest of his body.

"Mukindo here is a relative of mine," the chief confides.

But he stops what he is saying because Dynamite emerges from the forest with another backpack hidden there. He opens it and pulls out pieces of dried meat and a little bag of cornmeal. Another fighter appears with a saucepan and hangs it over the fire.

"What do you prefer?" Strong Blood asks. "Roast or stewed meat?"

"Roast is quicker," Worldly says. "The problem is the sauce."

"That's no problem. We've got tomato paste. We're well stocked. It's going to be an important mission. Commander Muxima is behind it. This is the first time I've come on a reconnaissance mission without going hungry."

The fighters sit down around the fire. There are seven of them, and they look at Worldly with admiration. He senses their respect and finds his self-confidence return. Life is beautiful. It is better like this. I didn't need to surrender. I'll always be able to do it if things don't get any better.

"How are things going round here?"

"Badly, very badly, comrade. All they do on the border is argue, hold meetings, and then more meetings, while our fighters run away. There's no population left in the bush, so all food has to come from outside. No one believes in this war anymore. They're tired and scared. The good thing is that there are still courageous commanders."

"Who?"

"Well, you for example. Not everyone can go through what you went through, and still want to fight."

"I'm not as good as you think."

Little do you know that I'm being honest, Worldly thinks. The best way of not making yourself believed is to say the truth. The guerrillas smile amiably, showing that they accept his modesty because they are polite. One of them offers him a whole packet of cigarettes. "Keep it, comrade."

"How are things going up ahead?" Mukindo asks.

"Like here. The people retreated, our fighters too. It's a troubling situation. But what are these meetings about?"

"To resolve issues, it would seem," Strong Blood answers. "So far, we haven't seen any change. This attack on Ninda has already been delayed twice because of these meetings. If only they led to some decisive action being taken … But all they do is attack one another."

"Are these meetings going to solve problems?" Mukindo says. "The people have spoken on numerous occasions, and no one heard or cared about what they said. Are they going to start caring now? When they called a meeting for us to speak, I didn't go. We've already said what we had to say. Everybody knows who's ruined this war. Now what's needed is to get on with it."

"How, if there are political problems?" Worldly says.

"Bring us food and stop this business of one or two people having everything, and them the only ones with any say, and let's see if the war doesn't progress. Give the people what was promised and they will fight even harder than before."

"But that's all due to the political problems which need to be resolved," Worldly says. "How do you want to end the inequalities you're talking about, without discussion, without getting organized?"

"Don't worry, comrade," says Strong Blood. "This fellow Mukindo doesn't know what he's talking about. He's just like that."

"I don't know what I'm talking about, Comrade Chief? I know very well. And I'm just saying what the people say, the very same thing."

"How are you going to improve things, then?" Worldly insists.

"It won't be with meetings, that's for sure. What we need is to rid ourselves of the one or two who are undermining the war effort. By force."

"Mukindo!"

"Sorry, Comrade Chief, but I mean it. I know Comrade Worldly is a commander. If he wants, he can go and tell them that's exactly what Mukindo said, it doesn't matter. All I'm saying is what the people and our fighters are already saying. If they want to arrest me or shoot me, well then, they're going to have to arrest a lot of people. We've had enough of talking behind people's backs. Now, we're talking openly, and one of these days, we're going to use force, because it's gone too far. Why not speak out?" He turns to the others. "Because he's a commander? But I don't know what you people are thinking. Do you think things get done without commanders? We can shout, protest—it won't change anything. But if there are commanders who listen to us, our commanders, not the outsiders, then things will get better. Why don't you speak out now so that Comrade Worldly can listen and accept our ideas. He's not Muxima. He's one of us."

"How do you know I'm one of you?"

"You can see straightaway, muata. One of them wouldn't have endured what you put up with, comrade, nor would he talk to us like you. They're haughty, they're the lords of this war, they think they know more than we do just because they know Portuguese. I know Mbunda; I can't even speak Portuguese. If you're going to learn a white man's language, then English is better. And no one is going to force me to speak Portuguese. Whoever wants to talk to me had better learn my language."

"Give me a break, Mukindo," says Culatra. "If I could, I'd learn Portuguese. Without Portuguese, you won't get beyond being section chief, you'll never get anywhere."

"I'm not here to be director of some committee," said Mukindo. "I'm defending my ideas, my people. The people don't speak Portuguese. I don't care if I'm not promoted. The Movement only promotes those who're already privileged, those who know Portuguese. Do you think I'm going to prostitute myself just in order to be a leader?"

"If you're a leader, you can defend your people better," says Worldly.

"I don't know how to be a leader. I'm fine as I am, a guerrilla fighter. When people start climbing, all they think about is their bellies. They forget the people. Even some of our people who were good when they were at the base. But then they were promoted because they knew how to speak Portuguese; some had been in the Tuga's schools, others were even teachers. They got promoted. They spoke to the people in our own language and promised to end exploitation. But they lived on the crumbs the leaders left on the table after they'd eaten their fill. Some of them mobilized against the leaders, against the Kamundongos. When it came to it, they also tricked us. They just wanted to profit from power."

"There were only a few of those," Strong Blood says.

"There were only a few, yes. Because there were only a few of our people who got promoted. But they also contributed to the damage. They didn't carry out what they said they'd do."

"They couldn't because they never had any real power," says Worldly. "So what do you think can be done? You seem to be against everyone and everything."

"Yes, I'm against everything that's bad. And everything is bad. They made a mess of the war, tricked the people, and now they spend their time in meetings attacking each other. Do you believe this action against Ninda will ever happen? No, never. At the last moment, they'll say things are bad further east in our rearward sector and it's better we all return to the border. The muatas will go to the border and send their fighters off to the bases out in the bush. But the fighters won't stay in the bases by themselves. They'll also go across the border, and who can blame them?"

"Well then, the chiefs need to be changed," says Worldly. "Only those who want to wage war should be leaders. That's why we need to meet, debate, and get ourselves new commanders. These meetings are vital if the militants want to choose the chiefs. I don't know what's going on at all. Out there on the front line, no one gets told anything. But I think that if these meetings are for electing new leaders, then it's a good thing, and it's time to make some changes in the organization."

"That's what I'm always telling Mukindo," one of the fighters says.

"Mukindo believes that whoever is chosen will behave exactly like the others," says Dynamite.

"What I think is that we're going to make the wrong choices," Mukindo says. "Why? Because the leaders ought to be those who want to make progress in the war. And who knows who those people are? We think this or that person is a good combatant, he'll wage war. Let's make him a leader. When he gains control, game over, he won't wage war; all he'll want is to enjoy his power. Comrades say the leaders should be men from the Eastern Front. I agree, not because they're from here, but because the Kamundongos have already demonstrated that they're not interested in the war. And the people think the same. But I know the ones who are going to be promoted. They're just like the Kamundongos. They won't do anything. Just because someone's Mbunda or Chokwe, that doesn't mean he's good, you'll see."

"A struggle without leaders?" Worldly says.

"The ones from here are better than the others," says Strong Blood.

"Are they better?" Mukindo persists. "Those we keep saying should be promoted, weren't they the very ones who started all that trouble with the Kamundongos? They said we needed leaders from the east. What was their reason for saying that? Have you never asked yourselves? They would be the ones chosen, that's why they're so active. I don't believe in them. If they'd thought we barbarians were the ones who'd get promoted, they'd have stopped running around like headless chickens, they might even have lost their tongues."

"As for you, you don't believe in anything," Strong Blood says.

"I don't, no, not anymore. Take Linyoka for instance. Everyone says Linyoka must become a leader, he'll move the war forward. What has Linyoka done recently? All he does is get drunk on moonshine. How long has it been since he left the front? He's never been back, much less shown any leadership. And what about Adriano? He was a good commander for a while; he made his name. Then he took his chance to get out and hasn't been back since. If he gets promoted, do you think he'll ever come back? Dammit, they're all the same . . ."

"It's not going to happen like that," Culatra says. "These men are really good leaders, they want what's best for the people. If they're promoted, you'll see how the people will back the fight."

"Because they're from here. The people back their own kins-men. Then they'll discover that they'll deceive them as well. After that, no one will be able to mobilize the people."

"They're not going to deceive the people," one of them says.

"That's enough, Mukindo," says another.

"Can't you see no one agrees with what you're saying?" Strong Blood asks.

The rest of the fighters tell Mukindo to keep quiet. He lowers his head and contemplates the fire, muttering, "You people think tribalism is good. Fair enough, you'll learn."

"Tribalism, tribalism," Strong Blood shouts. "Who's a tribalist?"

"All right, Comrade Chief, I won't say any more."

"No. Now, you're going to tell me who the tribalists are here. Come on now, you're going to tell me . . ."

The section chief is looking at his kinsman menacingly. The fighters watch them closely in an atmosphere of growing tension. Mukindo doesn't take his eyes from the fire. He says quietly and sadly, "We're all tribalists. Why deny it? We all want to be leaders here. But I don't say Muxima is a bad commander just because he's a Kamundongo. I say he's a bad commander because he hasn't done anything to encourage his guerrilla fighters, because he lives well outside the country. At least, that's what they say. But it's not because he's from the north. Kudila was from the north, and he was the best commander the Movement has ever had. Even today, we still mourn Kudila. Kimbari's from the north, and he was a great commander. The people still mourn Kimbari, even now. They sent him away from here, goodness knows why, to study."

"Muxima is just like the others, that's all," says Culatra.

"What others?" asks Worldly, giving him an encouraging smile.

"He means the Kamundongos," Mukindo says. "Why don't you say what's on your mind, Culatra? Are you scared because you know that's tribalism? Come on, talk, say what you usually

263

say, Muxima's a Kamundongo and has got to be removed. I think he should be removed, too, but not because he's a Kamundongo. And when force is used against them, it's because it's needed and not because they're from the north. But come on, out with it, what are you frightened of? The muata's one of ours, he's not a Kamundongo. You can say what you want."

The conversation is interrupted because the food is ready. They put the saucepan down next to Worldly. "There's no water to wash your hands," the chief explains apologetically.

Worldly puts his fingers in the saucepan, rolls a ball of cassava polenta between his thumb and index finger, dips the little ball in the sauce, and puts it in his mouth. With his left hand, he picks up a piece of roast meat. The others wait for him to swallow the chunk. The chief puts his fingers in the saucepan, and then the others follow one by one. Soon, the saucepan is empty.

"Mukindo has got a point," says Worldly, leaning back against the backpack once more and smoking a cigarette. "We shouldn't see the problem as involving the Kamundongos on one side, and us on the other. But we do need to see that most of the leaders and commanders assigned to this front committed many mistakes, and they didn't want to fight. All they wanted was to profit from the struggle. These, unfortunately, were from the north. That's why there is this confusion now. The people are unable to distinguish clearly. For them, they're all bad. On the other hand, the situation needs to change. And without being a tribalist or regionalist, I think that, in any case, we need to lessen the power of those leaders who made mistakes and replace them with other more capable people. If there are also northerners who deserve our trust, we shouldn't be scared to elect them. But let me ask you this: are there really any northern comrades who are capable of being leaders, at least from among the ones we know?"

"There aren't any," they all answer except for Mukindo.

"There is," Mukindo says. "Kimbari."

"He's far away," the others say.

"Wisdom," says Mukindo. "He's from the same zone as you, muata."

Worldly is unsettled by Mukindo's observation. Why the hell did he have to come up with that name? It reminds him of his past. He pretends not to hear and speaks, "So it's not tribalism if we want to put our people in positions of leadership. Really, they are the only ones capable of sorting out our problems. If there are one or two northerners, that doesn't matter..."

"Exactly," some murmur in agreement.

"Seen like this, no one can accuse us of tribalism. Those who do only do so in order to defend themselves. They know that this kind of accusation gives everyone a fright."

"Exactly," everyone says, with a round of applause.

"Comrade Mukindo, don't you agree with me?"

"More or less. That's what I was trying to say."

"So that's what we think, then," Strong Blood says.

"Deep down, in practice, we all agree, only the words are slightly different," says Worldly.

"I don't know," says Mukindo. "I don't know whether they understood what you said, but for me, it's not the same thing. They don't say what you said, muata. There's a difference..."

"Yes, we all agree, Mukindo," Worldly repeats. "We all want to put people in positions of leadership who know and respect the people. These leaders have to be our people. That is what's crucial."

"Not Linyoka or Adriano," Mukindo persists.

"Listen, Mukindo," says Worldly. "This is a very important moment for us, so we should all be united. What they want is to divide us, so that they can maintain their grip on power. As was the case with colonialism and imperialism. For years, they taught us that tribalism is bad, even though they themselves practised it. We absorbed these lessons so well that nowadays the worst insult that can be hurled at us is to call us tribalists. And they take full advantage. Every time we demand justice, they accuse us of tribalism. And we back down. And they go on doing whatever they want. They're the ones who are tribalists. We should demand justice, justice being that we should be the ones directing the war and the Movement here on the Eastern Front. We don't want to go and direct things up in the north. Right?"

"Exactly," Culatra says, clapping his hands.

"That's not tribalism; that's the language of revolution. We mustn't be separated from one another by the words we use, playing their game. It's the ideas that matter. And as you can see, Mukindo, we all have the same ideas."

"Maybe, maybe . . ." Mukindo says.

Worldly turns to the others with a smile and says, "It looks as if I've managed to bring everyone together."

"Yes, muata, you're a proper politician," Strong Blood says.

"We need a lot more like that at the top," says one of the fighters. "But they're all Kamundongos . . ."

The conversation comes to an end. Before they turn in for the night, the chief seizes Mukindo by the arm and admonishes him harshly in a low voice. Mukindo doesn't reply, but just shakes his head. As he lies down in his place near the fire, Worldly hears him muttering to himself, "Everyone talks about the people, but no one thinks about them. The people are like the trunk of a tree. Everyone leans on it, or climbs it to pick the fruit up above. They're not interested in the people but in the fruit."

Well, in any case, I managed to get consensus, even Mukindo the anarchist agreed. But a precarious consensus, he thinks, as he nestles indulgently under his blanket warmed by the fire. What's important is that the idea should stick. That I managed to make them agree with one another. Tomorrow, they may resume the debate and become divided again. They'll say, what we need here is a muata who will bring us together in agreement. The idea won't go away. I'm capable of drawing up a line of action that all can buy into. They will spread the rumour, and oh, how the rumour will fly. Then I'll be just one step away from being their representative. A step that he will take with relish, by now half-asleep, lulled by the flames of the fire crackling playfully.

10

When he wakes up, Worldly has already elaborated his plan of action. It involves persuading the section chief to allow him to continue to the border, without passing the guerrilla base, where the attack on Ninda is being planned.

After a breakfast of milk and manioc, he says to Strong Blood, "I need to get to the border urgently, as I have to deliver various reports. If I go to Tundombe with you, I'll be wasting time. I'm not going to discuss the situation in F Zone with Muxima. And if I go there, I'll have to stay for a few days. I've already lost a lot of time. They must all be worried that I died or was caught."

"Yes, that's true. But I have to take you back to base. It's the law. It's not because I suspect you, comrade, but you have to be checked. You don't even have a travel permit."

"That got left in my backpack."

The other fighters have their packs ready for departure and have camouflaged all traces of their presence in the place. They are listening to the two commanders talking, and Worldly winks at Mukindo.

"Is Muxima the one who is going to check me? The chief of this section is you, not Muxima. Unless you suspect me . . ."

"No, no, it's not that," Strong Blood protests. "But the law is the law."

"And what is the law? That the chief should monitor the people who pass through his sector. Well, you're the chief and you yourself monitored me."

"The commanders may want to speak with you in order to discover things . . ."

"They'll see me when they return from their mission. What I've got to do right now is make it to these meetings because I'm already late. I'll be taking them the opinions of the most advanced sectors of the guerrilla front, Zone F, and I'll be upholding the views of the people."

"That's good," says Culatra.

"Just pass through Tundombe, comrade, it's not a big detour," says the chief.

"I'll lose a day. If not more."

"The commanders are going to want to talk and he'll lose two days," Culatra says. "It's better if he makes straight for the border."

"You're just talking," says Strong Blood. "But I'm the chief here, and I'm the one the commanders will curse, not you lot. Comrade Worldly is a commander and understands, but you just talk for the sake of it."

It occurs to Worldly that he should circumvent the other man's bureaucratic misgivings. He speaks in a mild, friendly tone. "You're right to follow the law so vigilantly, comrade." The fighters mutter a complaint. "But I'll write to Muxima to explain why I needed to go directly to the border. He won't come down on you. There are times when rules aren't of any use, because quick decisions need to be made. I don't want to force you to let me proceed, comrade, because it's your sector. But I also know that you, Comrade Chief, appreciate the special circumstances in which we all find ourselves. So I'm asking you to help me, because I have a lot I need to say at these meetings, and I need to defend the ideas we were discussing yesterday. And if my discussions go well, then Muxima will soon no longer be a commander."

"Exactly!" Mukindo says. "You, chief, are scared of Muxima, that's what you are. How can you stop the muata from proceeding by the shortest route?"

"I'm not at all scared. You should all learn from Comrade Worldly, you don't even understand what he's saying. He knows the meaning of responsibility. You people talk like women, for the sake of it, without thinking. That's why you never get beyond being just guerrilla fighters ... I'm going to allow the comrade to proceed, but in so doing, I'm taking risks you can't even understand."

"I'll write to Muxima, so there won't be any risks. But there's one more thing ... I can't go alone."

"Two can accompany the muata and then come back," suggests Dynamite.

"How am I going to explain that?" Strong Blood says, scratching his head. "I set off with a reconnaissance unit for an attack. I come back minus two fighters, because I sent them to accompany the comrade to the border. A reconnaissance unit is top secret. The men can't leave the sector just like that."

"If you allow me to go, comrade, but don't give me two men as an escort, then it would be better if you said I couldn't go. I'm very tired and don't know whether I'll make it. And I don't know the way. I'll probably get lost again."

The chief sighs. He lights a cigarette to buy time. The guerillas chat among themselves quietly. Strong Blood knows that he is losing the respect of his men, who will accuse him of being afraid of Muxima. But he has learned that he has to maintain the maximum secrecy when it comes to military operations. He sighs again.

"Okay, I'm going to get chewed out for this. They'll criticize me. If only you were one of them, comrade, they might accept it. Okay. Dynamite and Culatra will go with you. Leave the comrade on the border and come straight back, without talking to anyone. If you're not back at the base in three days, I'll make sure you catch it. Don't mess around with me. Take a bit of food. And if you meet anyone, don't give away anything about the mission. Otherwise, they'll even go so far as to say that I sabotaged our attack. Three days."

Worldly writes a note to Muxima and gives it to the chief who, as they take their leave of each other, says, "You understand my position, muata ... It's not a time for games and it involves an attack that mustn't fail."

It has already failed, thinks Worldly. When the commanders find out that the Tugas suspect something, they'll drop the idea, and with justification. I would have to defend their position if I went to the base. And that's what I don't want. The fighters will think the attack has been cancelled because the Kamundongos aren't interested in the war.

"You're right, comrade," says Worldly. "The attack must be a success. We need to take the Ninda post and destroy it. If there weren't so many important matters to resolve, I'd take part as well, not as a commander, but in an assault party. You can rest assured that if there's a problem, I'll defend you against Muxima and his ilk."

They say goodbye and begin to move forward. Worldly turns round and raises his fist. "We need to take Ninda, comrades. A vitória é certa."

The guerrilla fighters and the chief raise their fists in response. They won't go anywhere near Ninda, Worldly thinks. If they do, they are stupid. And Muxima is anything but stupid.

Though Worldly aches all over, he sets the pace for the two fighters accompanying him. There is an added reason to reach the border quickly. Even if he has to fly. He has left behind his admirers, who would pass the word on to others. The two going with him would do the same on the border. They might not talk of the attack being prepared, but they wouldn't be able to resist the temptation to pass on the message about him. And Worldly isn't going to stop them, just because of Strong Blood. Soon, his reputation would be established. The situation is more timely than he had expected. There are some murky points that would soon be clarified. But he needs to get where he is going quickly. His excitement eventually gets the better of his aches and pains which, as the warmth increases, become positively pleasant. Once again he feels the lightheartedness of the old glory days, when nothing got in his way, giving him the reputation of a man with an iron will among his companions. In those far-off times when, fool that I was, I pursued a collective dream. When ideology caused him to face up to everything with the zeal of a missionary.

They stop at noon for some tinned meat and milk. There is a little left over for that night, but they would go hungry the following day. And thirsty as well, because there is no water on the savannah in the border area, during the misty season. He immediately gives the order for them to continue their march. Culatra asks, "Don't you want to rest, muata?"

"No, we need to get there quickly."

"But you're weak and tired, muata ..."

"No. Come on. The war won't wait for us, comrades. If we keep up this pace, when will we get to the border?"

"Tomorrow, when the sun is like this," and Culatra sticks his arm straight up in the air to indicate noon.

They stop at four o'clock to drink water from a pool. They fill their canteens. That will be their last ration. As it is late afternoon and few people passed that way during the day, the water is fairly clean. It is worse at night, for the animals come to drink there. They go on until it becomes dark. They light a fire and eat what they have left. The fighters are exhausted; they marched for twelve hours almost nonstop. Worldly seems refreshed. Dynamite gives him his blanket and says, without being able to conceal his admiration, "You really do fly, muata."

"I can see you're tired, comrades. Otherwise, we could go on through the night. The savannah starts here, right?"

"Yes, it's savannah from here on."

"I know you don't want to walk at night. But it would be better. We could get there by morning, or even before."

"Mm, but it's best if we get some sleep," Culatra says. "We're tired and it's good to be alert as we walk. The Tugas sometimes sleep around here."

"I won't insist. Let's sleep right here. But you'll grant I have a point. If the Tuga sometimes sleeps here, then it would be better if we crossed the savannah at night. The Tuga doesn't sleep out on the savannah . . . But tell me, you two, is Strong Blood a good fighter?"

"Like the other chiefs," Culatra says.

"What does that mean? That he's good or bad?"

"So-so. There are better ones."

"Why was he appointed section chief then?"

"It was Commander Linyoka who appointed him."

"Are they related?"

"All Mbunda are related."

"And you, aren't you Mbunda?"

"No. Me and Dynamite are Luchazi."

"So what about Mukindo?"

"His father is Mbunda. His mother is Nkangala."

"So aren't most of Strong Blood's fighters Mbunda?"

"Most? Not all of them are. Only Strong Blood and the unit leaders are Mbunda. The fighters are Luchazi, Nkangala, or even Chokwe. So weren't you aware, comrade, that here the commanders are the Kamundongos, and the chiefs Mbunda?"

Worldly laughs, although he is familiar with the joke. He continues his inquiry: "So what about the Ovimbundu?"

"Some are commanders, others are chiefs," Dynamite says.

"But you two are exaggerating," Worldly says. "There are Mbunda like Linyoka, who are commanders."

"Yes, of course," replies Culatra, the more talkative of the two.

"But this is what we say, the Kamundongo is a muata, the Mbunda is a chief, and the guerrilla fighters are Nkangala or Luchazi."

"But what about Mukindo?"

"Oh, him . . . It's his Nkangala blood that does the talking."

"Strong Blood told me they're related."

"Mukindo's father is Mbunda and all Mbunda are related. They look out for each other. But Mukindo doesn't care much about that. And he always tells the chiefs what's on his mind. Maybe he's a little crazy. He once ambushed a group of GEs on his own and captured two guns. He got a citation. That's why he can say what he likes. He was always with Commander Kudila and still talks a lot about him. He says Kudila was the greatest commander he knew. Mukindo was by Kudila's side when he died. Kudila liked him, and that's why Mukindo says he can never be hostile to the Kamundongos, because the moment the others attack the Kamundongos, he sees Kudila's face. He was a great commander and a fair man."

"That Mukindo is a funny fellow! I'd liked to have talked to him some more but didn't have time. What does he think of the Ovimbundu? You know I'm Ovimbundu, don't you?"

Culatra smiles. He pokes the fire with a stick.

"He says we're all united against the northerners: Umbundu, Mbunda, Luchazi, Nkangala, all together. But there'll be turmoil later. When we get rid of the Kamundongos, the Mbunda and Ovimbundu will engage in a fight for power. And up there in the north, there are the Chokwe and Luvale . . . He says we're busy being tribalists and that later tribalism will divide us. The Luchazi and Nkangala will be dominated by the Mbunda and Ovimbundu, as they were before. He says we're forgetting who brought the Tuga here. The Ovimbundu. And in the old days, the Mbunda dominated the Nkangala. The old rivalries will return, because we're stoking up the ashes of tribalism."

"That Mukindo is curious. Who taught him all this?"

"He studied at the CIR in Zone A. But now he says he doesn't speak Portuguese, though he really can. He studied politics, and Kudila talked with him a lot about it."

"Let's get some sleep," says Worldly. "Tomorrow, we've still got the savannah. The savannah, the chana, the savannah . . ."

A shiver runs through him, despite the fire. It would be his last trek across the savannah. The last! Afterwards, he would find an excuse to never set foot on that monstrosity again. What was it Wisdom used to say?

"There are two worlds, that of the savannah and that of the forest. The former is all about anguish, the interference of different worlds, discomfort, mobility, instability. The latter is the world at one with itself, the indivisible world of tranquillity, ease, quiet. The former is that of the gazelle—the duiker or the doe—the latter, that of the bee and honey. Eventually, the latter, the world of the forest, is the more dangerous, like its honey wine you drink, unconcerned, because it's sweet, without realizing that it makes you drunk. The former is a world in which any surprise is pleasant, because you always expect the worst. The latter is where every surprise brings change, danger, an unlucky encounter, a painfully novel situation for a sedentary spirit. The former is a world of mysterious life bubbling in the tiny shadow of a blade of grass: insects, droplets of water sucked up by the narrow stems, scorpions, or duikers. The latter is a world of seemingly conspicuous life, the vigorous green leaves sprouting from the bare trees, the noise of the wind thrashing the branches. Is it really as simple as that? In both worlds, everything is ambiguous."

Wisdom can say what he likes, Worldly thinks, but I prefer the forest. And he falls asleep.

II

The noise of a plane flying along the line of the border had delayed them, and at ten o'clock, they are still four hours' march from their destination. Hunger, which had never left him, is now more unbearable, because he knows they are close.

The savannah stretches out ahead of them. At first, it had only been ahead when they left the forest where they had slept. Afterwards, the savannah extended away to their right, then later, to their left, and finally, behind them. Only the occasional bush with leaves similar to those of a palm breaks the horizon. The ocean, the hated, feared ocean, thinks Worldly. The fighters walk ahead of him, more leisurely the nearer they get to the end of their trek. For him, it is always the opposite.

Suddenly, he remembers Elias, the Protestant who was an expert on Fanon. Could he be in this part of the world? They had escaped together from Portugal, along with all the others. In Paris, they split up. Elias and one or two others joined UPA and later the FNLA. Worldly had lost track of him. He must surely have left the FNLA and helped form UNITA, like all the Ovimbundu from the old UPA. He might be there in the east. There were little-known groups living semi-clandestinely in Zambia, occasionally making incursions into Angola. Elias might be among them. What would happen if they met? In Zambia, there would be no problem, and they might even talk. Out here in the Angolan bush, the only conversation would probably be an exchange of gunfire, even if that seemed absurd.

At noon, there slowly emerges into view, there where his gaze grew tired, a tenuous blue smudge indicating the Kaxamissa forest. Beyond that, they would reach Sikongo, in Zambia, the capital of illicit liquor. Two hours' march, Worldly estimates. He can't yet make out the huge, isolated evergreen that marks the border. The sun is overhead, which means that he trod unthinkingly on his shadow, his mind elsewhere.

The sound of a shot ahead of him causes him to start. He instinctively throws himself flat on the ground and undoes the safety catch on his gun. Not now that they are so near, he begs.

"It's escaped, it's escaped," he hears Dynamite shout.

The two fighters run off to their left.

"What is it?" Worldly shouts, half raising himself.

The others don't reply and continue running. Worldly looks both ways. Fear gradually gives way to puzzlement. He gets up cautiously and hears another shot. This time it is Culatra who has fired. Then they both start to run again. Dynamite stops suddenly and shoots. Then he starts running again, off to the right at an angle, followed by the other. Worldly is now standing up straight and with his gun in a firing position, when he sees a duiker pass by in front of him at a distance of some fifty metres. It is pursued by the two fighters. Worldly moves off to the right and soon catches up with them.

"It's injured," Culatra says.

They can't see the duiker. They walk for about five hundred metres and lose track of it. They turn back toward the path, where Dynamite discovers a blade of grass spattered with blood. He starts moving forward again, followed by the others.

"Where is it injured?" asks Worldly.

"In the leg," Culatra says.

"First shot?"

"Yes, it was right in front of me."

"And the other shots?"

"Looks as if we missed."

Dynamite keeps on, pointing at signs that Worldly didn't even spot. But Culatra nods in agreement. A kilometre to the right of the path, Dynamite stops short and raises his gun. Worldly only glimpses the animal when it jumps up, hit by the shot. But it dashes off, giving little skips every half-dozen paces.

"Come on, we hit it," Culatra says.

And they run in pursuit of the duiker, which is getting further away. Soon the animal disappears.

"It's lying down to rest," says Dynamite. "It won't last long now."

And off he goes, following the animal's bloody tracks, which are by now much clearer. Your fate's sealed, Worldly thinks. You'll run and leap, and in the end you'll drag yourself along, but perseverance will win. You'll leave your blood behind you, and as you shed your last drop, you'll find the strength for one last run. But blood runs out, too, my old friend. He didn't say it with malice, but tenderness. It is the execution of a law known and accepted by everyone: they are hungry, they are bound to kill the weaker creatures in order not to die.

The duiker raises its head when it senses their approach. Culatra, who was second in the line, shoots. The duiker leaps toward the right and Worldly shoots. The animal rolls in the sand, gets up, and runs off, but now with greater difficulty.

"Good shot, muata," Dynamite says.

They are now heading back toward the path. The duiker, some two hundred metres ahead, keeps hiding. But it gets up the moment it senses their steps. In order to lie down again a hundred yards in front. The fighters, implacable, won't give up their pursuit. Worldly has already forgotten to listen for the sound of planes, completely absorbed in the regular appearance and disappearance of the little yellow head. Yellow against the yellow of the savannah. Suddenly, the duiker jumps up in front of him and veers off to the left. The three fire point-blank, but the animal gets away.

"It lay down right there," says Dynamite. "Let's go more slowly."

Their camouflage shirts are soaked in sweat. Their very vision is dimmed by the drops of perspiration running down from their hair, their forehead, and their eyebrows. Their eyes burn. They advance cautiously, fingers on triggers. The animal emerges, raising its head some twenty metres away. Three shots echo in the noon stillness. The duiker disappears into the grass.

"Got it," Culatra shouts and runs forward.

Dynamite is on the point of firing a shot but stops himself in time as his companion is in the line of fire. Worldly sees the duiker jump out almost from under Culatra's feet and run off to the right. Culatra fires but misses. Worldly takes careful aim and fires, so as not to hit the other man. The duiker rolls over, but gets up again and enters a tuft of thicker grass. What tremendous resistance, Worldly thinks. That's what creatures do to cling to a wretched life. The blood is now thick and sticky on the glittering grains of sand. The tuft is ten metres away. The men advance three abreast, each step punctuated by a groan from the animal. Worldly glimpses the head sticking through the grass, its eyes staring at him, wide with terror. There is no hatred or recrimination in those gentle eyes, only fear. The tongue, dripping with blood, has become too swollen to find refuge inside its mouth.

The three men fire and fire again. The head droops. The duiker is dead, its eyes staring up at the sun, perhaps seeking some explanation. Its belly, torn by the bullets, has released the fetus germinating inside it, now a blood-soaked, pulsating ball.

Was Mussole also pregnant when she died? Worldly asks himself, his eyes fixed on the still living fetus. With his boot, he crushes the fetus's head, and it stops palpitating. Then he turns to one side and retches. Only liquid.

"Let's take it to where there's wood," Culatra says.

"Where are you going to find wood?" Dynamite says. "Here, it's all savannah."

"I'll carry it. You gather up any sticks you can find."

Culatra heaves the duiker up onto his shoulders and heads back to the path. Dynamite and Worldly gather all the sticks they can find. There are few, only the remains of bushes. After some time, they have accumulated enough. They sit down by the path, and while the others butcher the animal, Worldly lights the fire.

There, in the middle of the savannah, about two hours away from the border, they eat the ragged pieces of meat roasted over the fire. The flames are weak and the meat is half cooked. The sounds of the savannah are imperceptible, except for the liquid murmur that seems to emanate from the duiker's eyes, whose severed head has been thrown aside on the white sandy soil. Worldly eats without any joy, unable to avoid the animal's eyes that stare fixedly at him. And the duiker's eyes remind him of those of the unknown Mussole, or the eyes of Marilu, which he knew so well. Above all, they remind him of Wisdom's eyes.

No, nothing matters anymore. The past has been buried in the sand of the savannah along with all the promises and collective ideals. What matters now is what he is going to find in the blue haze of the future, his future. He, Worldly, is now safe, he has a future. What about Wisdom?

Epilogue

He got his answer two months later, from the last refugees from the most forward sectors. Wisdom had died, surrounded, two months before, because he hadn't been willing to retreat without receiving orders.

Two months earlier, at one in the afternoon. He couldn't be sure of this, but an anguished foreboding seemed to tell him that it happened on precisely the same day as he, Dynamite, and Culatra had hunted the duiker. A duiker that had given them enough strength to continue their trek to the border.

Had Wisdom been a duiker, or the trunk of a tree that no longer has any importance once one has reached the fruit?

It was a coincidence, it was a superstition, but this foreboding, which caused everyone to fall silent and brought a chill to his heart, never abandoned him. And it was made all the sharper by the bouts of heavy drinking and the xinjanguila ring dances on the border.

THE
OCTOPUS
(APRIL 1982)

I

The open sea was rough. Waves crashed against the rocks that marked the entrance to the little bay before losing their strength. The waters were still choppy as they washed over the line of reefs. However, on the sandy beach, yellowed slightly by the clayish soil that had fallen from the cliffs, the little waves faded and died as they always did, merely causing the algae growing from the rocky bottom to sway to and fro. Only the booming of the waves on the rocks further out from the shore gave any hint of the oncoming tidal surge. It was April, still the season for strong tidal surges. The last one had been in February and had lasted for three days. The waves had managed to sweep past the barrier of rocks and reefs to lap against the base of the cliffs. They had carried away sand and clay, the remains of fish and crabs, and brought clean sand. Nature looking after my beach, preventing it from getting polluted, the man thought.

He dipped his left foot in the water to feel the temperature. Colder than usual. "It's the rough sea that has brought colder water to the coast," he said out loud. Like that, the Benguela Current justified its reputation as being cold, but it was only when there was a swell that this became noticeable. During the rest of the year, the water was only slightly less warm than in Luanda. He only had his goggles with him and his snorkel, together with the indispensable flippers and harpoon. He had left his wetsuit at home. He looked up at the top of the cliff, where his house stood. He was too lazy to climb the steep path just to get his suit. Dammit, the water was bearable. He sat down on the sand and put on his flippers. He had decided, upon waking, that he wasn't going to do any extravagant dives, but just catch a couple of fish. That was why he had left behind his wetsuit and oxygen cylinders, which he seldom used. The cylinders were being kept for the great day. He had salvaged them from the abandoned fish sheds at Baía Farta six months ago. The fishermen had laughed. "What do you need that for?" But they were a godsend, because he would be able to explore the underwater cave he had discovered. He had once dived down about eight metres and looked into the cave from the outside. For a long time. He hadn't dared to go on. The entrance was wide, but further in, it seemed to narrow. He needed a special flashlight. It took him two months to eventually unearth one at a friend's house in Benguela. "Take it, I don't have any use for it. I don't even know what it's doing there." He dived again with his oxygen cylinders and now his flashlight. He confirmed his suspicion that the cave got narrower. But he didn't go in. He just remained there admiring the red tones of the rock, rendered green by deposits of silt and sparkling with quartz and silicates cleaned by the waves. The octopus was somewhere inside, he was sure. He didn't have the courage to confront it and returned to the surface. The time had not yet come.

He entered the water, and a shiver ran through his lean body. He swam out, just kicking his feet, looking down at the seabed and breathing through his snorkel. He turned to the left, where the bed was rocky, with thousands of little crevices where fish rested. There were hundreds of little fish, grunters, striped sea bream, the occasional red snapper. He observed his underwater world of rocks, algae, fish, and crabs, unhurriedly. Sooner or later, he would come across a large fish, one that was worth catching. Sometimes they appeared quite near the beach. Otherwise, they would be out near the reefs. Everything about his world was reduced in size. The bay had a perimeter of two hundred metres of sand. The reefs were fifty metres from the beach, and the rocks that enclosed the bay to the south were seventy metres away. Only the fish were abundant here, along with the odd grey shark. On the northern side of the bay, there were neither reefs nor rocks, because the very cliffs themselves stood out like a cape to enclose it. The large fish would enter the bay from the north and then seek protection behind the reefs in the south. The week before, he had caught a stone bass there that had weighed nearly a hundred kilos. Catching it was easy, but it was hard work dragging it back to the beach. And he had to ask for help to transport the fish to Caotinha, less than a kilometre away, where he sold it to a couple who had come from Benguela for a romantic outing in their car to contemplate the magnificent sunset. It was a good bit of business, but he would have sold it for ten times the price in Luanda. It was good because he had managed to sell the fish. If he hadn't, it would have ended up like so many others, given to the war refugees to prevent it from rotting and going to waste. The refugee village was growing for all to see at Caota, between the bay here and Baía Azul. Agriculture wasn't viable there because there was no water. They lived on fishing, which they were obliged to learn how to do, but above all they depended on the food received from one or two organizations. That happened only rarely, which was why he would give them fish he couldn't sell or couldn't eat himself. It was no more than a crumb for the famished mouths of those refugees from a war they were still unable to fathom.

The shoals of fish fled before him, but the man wasn't concerned. He knew he would find the fish he was looking for near the bulwark of the reefs. He chose in advance. I feel like a sea bream today, a big red porgy, grilled over the embers. Sometimes he couldn't find the meal he wanted and had to make do with something else. But that didn't happen often. He had the whole morning to look. He was master of his own time, the only freedom worth having. He deliberately avoided the far south of the bay, where the cave was located. He didn't even want to think about it; his nightmares of a lifetime were quite enough. He turned right in an arc, still exploring the rocky seabed, without getting as far as the reefs. He noticed a barracuda on his right, the noblest of fish. It wasn't the biggest, but it weighed at least fifteen kilos. No, I've had enough whitefish. I had one a few days ago. Today it's got to be a bream, my mind's made up. He left the barracuda to itself, slowly wending its way along the seabed, swaying like a serpent. Suddenly, he felt colder. He raised his head and looked at the sea. Of course, he had left the area protected by the reefs and was on the right hand side of the bay, where cold water flowed directly in. The barracuda was therefore heading out to the ocean. He turned back and swam toward the beach. He enjoyed the change in the temperature of the water, which grew warmer. But the seabed was now sandy and white, and bream were rarely seen there. He had learned from practice all about the behaviour of fish right there in his bay. They probably had different routines elsewhere. He had never bothered to study this scientifically, much less to come to general conclusions. In rare conversations on the subject, in his previous lives, he had learned things that didn't happen there. For example, that giltheads only liked to swim among debris, in particular the residue of rushes carried on the currents of rivers. That might be so in Luanda. But in his bay, he had already come across giltheads among the cleanest stones. He didn't catch them because he didn't like to eat them. They were merely trophies, and he wasn't after trophies. And the gilthead was a beautiful fish that he liked to watch in peace. Was his bay a unique ecosystem in this world, so very different from neighbouring Caotinha, or the more distant Baía Farta? That's how he saw it; that's how he wanted it. At least something in life had turned out as he wished.

He looked at his watch. Ten. He'd been in the water more than two hours. He got out of the water and lay down to warm up in the sun. He felt like smoking. But he had deliberately left his cigarettes at home, to see if he could get rid of the phlegm in his throat. When he woke up, he coughed more and more every day. Sometimes he even puked, liquid of course, as his stomach was empty. And so he imposed a further strict rule upon himself: he only allowed himself a cigarette after lunch. While he swam, he didn't even give it a thought. But when the hunting was over, the yearning returned. The answer was to go into the water again.

He now swam out to the reefs on the south side of the bay. In the beginning, he had swum casually, carrying out an inspection of his world, not worrying about the result. Now his hunting instincts came to the fore, and he was more impatient, closely watching the seabed with its rocks and weed. He reached the area of the reefs where the water was rougher because of the swell on the other side. He couldn't see the usual grouper hidden among the stones. They must be more to the left, protected from the turbulence by the great rocks that framed the entrance to the cave. He scared a group of cuttlefish that shot off squirting their dark ink, just as planes might leave a vapour trail. The water became less clear, and it reminded him of the presence of the enemy. Deep down, to the left, waiting in ambush. He sensed its presence, just as before, out on the savannahs, he used to antici- pate the arrival of Portuguese helicopters in attack formation. As before, on the savannahs, he gripped his weapon more firmly in his hand. And he experienced the same sensation of insecurity.

Two croaker were hovering, immobile, in front of him. He aimed his weapon at one of them. An almost unconscious gesture. But he didn't shoot. I want to eat bream. But then again, he was almost out of dried fish, and croaker was good for drying. It was a good idea to always have a stock of dried fish in case of an emergency. He shot. The harpoon pierced the body, and he felt the tug of the fish on the end of the line. The other croaker fled. He grabbed the harpoon handle and swam to shore, with the fish in tow. Once on the beach, he loaded the harpoon again into the shaft, breathed in a few times facing the sun, and plunged back into the water. Let's go and find this bream.

He swam decisively toward the reefs, avoiding the far south where the cave was. He spotted more croakers and one or two skipjack tuna. They would be good to accompany a funje, preferably when dried. He ignored them. With the turbulence, the waters were less transparent, with a lot of plankton being stirred around. But he could see clearly enough down into the depths and among the reefs. A few young bream appeared, but they were too small. What he liked were the big ones, with plenty of pearly flesh, which had to be well oiled before barbecuing. A tiny little grouper swam off at great speed after nearly bumping into him. The man had now stopped, only his feet maintaining the horizontal position of his body, as he searched among the reefs. From time to time, a wave broke over the barriers and caused him to shift. Later, as evening began to fall, the swell would be at its strongest and the waves would crash right over the reefs. Tomorrow would be a bad day for fishing; the boats will stay in harbour and Ximbulo's pirogue will be pulled up on the sand. It would be prudent to build up a few reserves today. The swell could last for days. If it was really strong, the waters could be so rough that it would be difficult to hunt. He could always resort to hook and line fishing, but he didn't have the patience to fish while seated on a rock. He was a hunter, not a fisherman. There was a huge cultural difference between them. Although economists mix them all up in the same group under the heading of extractive activity, the attitude, he thought, is different. The fisherman doesn't enter the habitat of the fish, either on the beach or in a boat. He invades the fish's abode with a weapon, a net or a hook, and only the weapon enters this milieu. The hunter penetrates the maritime world, risks bodily combat, and uses his weapon against a determined adversary or victim, which he sees and respects. Both of them kill, but the fisherman kills without even thinking about it. The hunter kills, fully aware of what he does. Who is the crueller? Ximbulo, one day when he had spoken to him about this, just laughed in that calm way of someone who has seen many a rough sea and answered, "Don't worry yourself about it, chief. The result is the same—fried fish or baked fish or fish soup."

At last he saw a large bream. He came face to face with it between two rocks, looking at him with its gentle eyes. It would be a very risky shot, his weapon was not very precise, it was all he had been able to find. Only if he managed to shoot it in the mouth, which opened and closed as it breathed. He waited a little longer, his harpoon at the ready. If the bream moved, it might expose its flank, and it would be an easier shot. But the fish was observing him, choosing not to move. Come on, start feeling scared, try and escape. He could make some abrupt gesture, make the bream move away. But then it would escape, because he would have to take his chances and aim left or right, carried by his intuition. And the harpoon might hit the rock and break. He only had one spare. It was harder to find harpoons in that neck of the woods than the Kingdom of Heaven. Just as it was hard to find food, cigarettes, clothes, or any other product. Everyone had to get by however they could and use their imagination in order to survive. He shot in anger. Not at the bream, disturbed in its abode, harmless, but at his past full of dreams that had brought him to this absurd present. The harpoon pierced its mouth and penetrated it lengthways. Beautiful shot, he told himself, devoid of emotion. Feeling cold, he took the fish back to the beach. If he didn't have to save the harpoon, he could have cooked the fish just as it was, turning it over the fire as if on a spit.

He pulled the harpoon out, which wasn't an easy operation. He took off his goggles and flippers, took his knife from its sheath on his right leg, and descaled the fish. The sun began to warm him and caused his anger to pass. He gutted the fish and washed them in the water. Tiny, almost transparent fish came to fight over the remains of the gills and intestines of their murdered kin. He stood watching the silent struggle in the clear water. Ever the fight for survival, such is the law of nature. Only man kills for pleasure, or for some other objective than to eat his defeated adversary. Cannibalism still gets a bad press, but at least it respects the law of nature. He smiled in the midst of these bitter thoughts. I'm exaggerating too. Animals don't generally eat their equals. Only fish do. Or some insects. The lion and the panther don't eat their dead partners; they leave them for the hyenas. But neither do they fight each other to death, as men do. Yes, man is his own greatest predator. So as to leave his beaten enemy to rot under the sun.

In view of the coming swell, he ought to go back and do some more hunting. The croaker was going to be dried, so it wouldn't be ready for a week. The bream would be eaten today. If the sea's rough tomorrow and I can't fish, I'll have no reserves. But the water was cold and he didn't feel like going back in. Dammit, he'd come up with something. He put the two fish in a net bag, picked up his gear, and climbed the cliff, just in his swimming trunks. The path was rough and very steep, for it was a tall cliff. From down below, he could hardly see the house above, even though it was almost on the edge of the cliff. The climb certainly warmed him up. Even his fingers quickly lost the wrinkles produced by the cold water. Now in July and August, during the season of night mists, that was when the water was cold. But it's not because of the cold that I don't hunt. The fisherman is luckier: he remains outside the water during the cold season. And he catches more fish. I'm a martyr. He laughed as he overcame the last obstacle separating him from the top of the cliff and his house. A solitary martyr who laments the life he has chosen. If I was ever free in any choice I made ...He dismissed this thought as he caught sight of his house.

He stopped, put the things he was carrying down on the concrete doorstep, and looked around. Just as he always did when he came from the sea. To the north, a kilometre away along the strand, but nearer if approached by way of the cliffs, he could see the fish sheds, which now belonged to Ximbulo. He could see the tile-covered annex where, in colonial times, the fish had been filleted before being put out to dry on racks in the sun. The annex still preserved its white lime-painted walls, and from afar, it looked as if it had just been painted. Two houses, also painted white, completed the complex. When the fishery had been fully operational, there were many huts in the immediate vicinity for the workers. Ximbulo lived in one of these. Before independence, the owner left for South Africa on his fishing trawler, and the fishery closed. One by one, the workers abandoned the place as well. Only Ximbulo and his family, or rather what was left of it, remained. He took over the main house and started to fish from a pirogue. Merely to survive. The State wasn't interested in taking over the fishery, which was very isolated and unprofitable. Ximbulo never put his occupation of the premises on a legal footing, nor did the law permit him. It didn't make much difference to him; he lived on what he caught in the place where he had been born.

Beyond the fish sheds, there were cliffs and more cliffs for twenty kilometres, as far as Benguela. Parched cliffs with only rare rainfall, which produced one or two timid blades of grass. Less and less of this as the desert spread north from Namib. To the east, the horizon was far nearer, limited by arid hills. The only signs of life seemed to lie to the south. A kilometre away, one could see the restaurant at Caotinha and the white house of an Italian architect, who had built it on a rock overlooking a small cove. After that, one could just make out a plain that extended as far as Baía Azul which, like Caotinha, attracted pleasure seekers. On this barren plain, the refugees had established themselves in a village, invisible from where he stood. And even further south, almost completely out of sight, Baía Farta, the main fishing centre for the region, which seemed to extend into the sea like a huge prong.

He salted the croaker and laid it out to dry on a little frame next to the house. He unplugged the water tank and filled a bucket. He watered the mango tree he had planted three years before and which was growing fast, despite all the warnings he had received. Even Ximbulo, the only person who didn't seem to regard him as crazy, warned him, "A mango tree up here on the clifftop won't grow. Not even a baobab." But he stubbornly planted the mango tree there and watered it every day. The soil soaked up the water so quickly that there didn't seem to be any left for the tree. But the truth was that it grew abundantly and already provided him with shade. That was why he had placed a deck chair under it, where he would sit and reflect or read during the day. A bucket of water for a mango tree was a luxury that Ximbulo would never understand. But for him, it was crucially important to have a tree that provided shade. This need had remained with him since the days when he had crossed the savannahs as a guerrilla fighter on the Eastern Front. The mango tree grew even better because he stroked it, confessed his most intimate thoughts to it, and read important passages of books to it. The mango tree had a human name, Mussole, but he would only call it that on special occasions. And never in front of strangers, for they would be bound to say, "He's gone cuckoo, he's completely unhinged, poor fellow, he even gives trees names."

Then he entered the house. The unfinished house which he saw one day and fell in love with. And which he fixed up with the help of Ximbulo.

2

The story of the house began a long time ago. During the war of 1975. They had sent him to the Soviet Union to do a military course, yet another one, this time for the high command. Perhaps to allow him to recover from his bad experiences on the Eastern Front during the collapse of the guerrilla campaign. Such bad experiences that on a number of occasions, his death had been announced. The stories were eventually shown to be false, but he ended up being forgotten out on the front. No one remembered to recall him, and he refused to retreat without receiving the order to do so. Until there were only three people left in his unit—him, a guide, and a lame guerrilla fighter who had nowhere else to go and didn't have the courage to march for a month through hunger-ridden lands and get across rivers in order to reach Zambia. At that point, he decided to retreat, for his group had ceased being an effective combat unit months before. The lame fighter stayed behind; nothing would persuade him to make the journey.

For a month, he and the guide managed to break through various military defence lines, living on honey for food. The guide could always find honey, without ever revealing the secret, whether he heard the bees or could smell the honey or some other way. He was a Musekele, a surviving member of the so-called Bushmen people. There was no danger of dying of hunger with him. He could not only discover honey but also attracted prey by whistling through certain leaves, and he could also smell an enemy from afar. When they reached the border, which was in a state of full-scale rebellion, there had been so many rumours about his death that he was almost taken to be a spirit, a cazumbi, of his own self. They should have treated him badly, for they were rebelling against the northerners, but they didn't dare touch a cazumbi. So he caught the first truck to Lusaka, where the leadership of the movement was based. That was the hard bit, because they began to suspect him for having managed to pass through the entire rebel zone unharmed. They more or less ignored him and didn't even summon him for their important meetings. When the new leadership was elected, someone remembered him for the course in the Soviet Union. He didn't want to accept, but they almost forced it on him. A lot of things had changed in Portugal in 1974, and the war was going to end. They needed to think about creating a regular army, which was why the most able had to study appropriate structures and strategies.

He returned to Angola in 1975, in the middle of the war against the rival parties. He was immediately chosen to lead a column to halt the South African advance at the River Keve. That was when he met Paulino, Ximbulo's son. The boy had survived the Battle of Catengue, where his elder brother had died, and had retreated with the troops from Benguela in the direction of Cuanza Sul. Paulino became a kind of mascot, whom he took everywhere. And during the night watches before battles, Paulino told him his father, Ximbulo, was a fisherman near Caotinha and that he and his brother had volunteered to fight when war began in the area around Benguela. The name Caotinha evoked childhood memories. He had gone to Benguela for his holidays, and he had been taken to that beach, where a huge octopus had given him a fright, a creature that then appeared in his dreams on the eve of battles. Paulino eventually died a stupid death, stepping on a mine when they reoccupied Benguela and the South Africans withdrew to their peaceful safe havens. He felt a duty to go to inform Paulino's family of his death. So this was how he came to that arid place, where there was an unfinished house, almost ready for habitation. He recognized the beach as the place where he had swum as a kid and come across the octopus. He spoke to Ximbulo and tried to provide expressions of comfort to someone who had lost two sons in the space of three months, knowing how useless his words were.

Two years later, in an attempt to forget the past and now free of all commitments, he decided to go to live in that house and hunt his childhood octopus. Ximbulo was his nearest neighbour and helped him finish the roof. He never managed to get hold of anything to paint the house, so it remained as it was. It had electric light, which was a miracle. Before the owner had abandoned the place, he had managed to build an access road from the highway, but he probably never used it. There was no water, and he had to get hold of a fibre-cement tank. A friend, who had a house at Baía Azul and who sent for a truck every two weeks to refill his cisterns, agreed that the truck should continue along the cliffs as far as his house, to fill up his water tank. It provided enough for him to cook, wash himself and the clothes he wore, and to water the mango tree. The rest, he gave Ximbulo, who would take it back to the fishery in demijohns. In that wilderness, water was gold, and Ximbulo was prepared to become his slave for some.

He lit a fire and put the bream on a metal griddle over the red-hot embers. He thought of Paulino, a smart kid, who had only been in school until second grade. How was he to study any further in a place like this? He attended classes in Baía Farta, but only when he could get a lift, not on any regular basis. Soon after they had met, Paulino addressed him as Commander Wisdom, and he tried to make a joke out of it. "Look, just call me Commander or Comrade Wisdom. Commander Wisdom is no good. Don't you see that a guy is either wise or he's a commander?"

Everyone called him that, Paulino noted. "Yes, but they're the stupid ones." Paulino became pensive, went for a walk, and came back with the answer. "Commander, what you said shows you're wise, so that's why I'm going to call you Commander Wisdom." Smart kid, a senseless death at the age of eighteen. Does any death make sense? Some do, the ones that don't affect us directly.

He recalled the death and looked at the mango tree. He had placed the grill in the sun at some distance from the tree, so that the smoke wouldn't disturb it. He hugged the trunk, stroked it. He said tenderly, "Does any death make sense, Mussole? And can you really hear me? I felt that on the day I gave you your name, your leaves began to stir as if to music." The far-off spirit of the woman killed out east had found its way here. It's so tired that it doesn't even speak or reveal itself. You grow and grow, with that spirit on top. You don't give any fruit. I know that time hasn't come yet. But from time to time, you could shake your leaves when there's no wind to show me you're there and that you're not asleep.

The mango tree didn't shake, in spite of the wind coming off the sea, where the waves were getting ever choppier outside the bay. Are you holding in your leaves? Is that a sign? It may be. The day of the octopus is near. It's April already. He went to turn the bream and drizzle a little more oil over the parallel slits he had cut in its flanks with his knife.

Only then did he go and put his fishing gear away in the little hideaway next to the bathroom. Next to it, he had a kitchen with a gas stove. Beyond that was his bedroom, with a bed and a built-in wardrobe. Some books scattered on the floor, an AKA propped against the wall, with a magazine next to it, left over from the war. Then there was the living room, the jewel in the crown. It was spacious, full of light because the whole of the front of the house was covered in glass or transparent brick. Wherever you were, you always had a view of the ocean. Only a metre separated the front wall of the living room and the edge of the cliff, which was why the entrance to the house was at the back, through the kitchen. He watched the waves, growing bigger and bigger, crashing against the rocks. In spite of the sunlight, the colour of the sea was leaden, only tempered by the foamy white horses. Out at sea, a trawler was making for Baía Farta, and shelter. It appeared and disappeared in the midst of the waves, pitching and rolling. He tried to read its name through the binoculars that he had also brought back from the war, but the trawler's movement made that impossible.

He remembered the bream and dashed outside. If it's burnt, there goes my meal. He got there in time to turn it; it was almost ready. That was when he heard the sound of a motor on the other side of the hills. His trained ear told him that the vehicle was a jeep and was coming in his direction. Along the track that the water carrier came down after leaving the paved highway that linked Baía Azul and Benguela. Occasionally, he would get visitors, mainly Marília. But it wasn't the right time of day for Marília, as she was working. Or was it Sunday? He hadn't the faintest idea. He knew it was April. He had heard some reference to it on the radio. Not that he needed to hear it, because his whole body told him it was April. But the days of the week had long ago lost any meaning for him.

3

The green jeep came to a stop next to the mango tree. It was driven by a white woman. She got out of the vehicle, and he barely recognized Sara. They hadn't seen each other during fifteen years of war, she lost somewhere in Paris, he on missions elsewhere. When Sara returned to Angola at the end of 1974, he was in the Soviet Union. Then he went straight back into the war. They only met once in 1977, when he went to Luanda to settle a difference of opinion between him and the army high command, and to request retirement from his commission. They didn't agree to this—there was no law allowing them to do so—but they let him leave the army, because he was just trouble. He had a right to a pension that gave him a living allowance, and no more. On that occasion, they had met at the hospital where Sara was working; they had arranged to visit each other, and she gave him her address. But, having resolved his military situation, he then hit on the idea of living in the abandoned house. He was in such a hurry because he feared others might remember him, and he forgot all other matters. Or rather he went out of his way to forget. He jumped at the first chance of a lift down to Benguela, busied himself with finishing the house and getting hold of the most essential bits of equipment with which to fish. He often thought of Sara and how he owed her an apology. Now she was coming to get even with him, that was for sure.

They gave each other a long hug. Then he remembered he

was wearing his swimming trunks, and he went and put on some trousers. He returned straightaway, and taking the bream off the grill, he said quite naturally, "You've arrived just in time for lunch. You mustn't refuse this bream. It was caught less than two hours ago; it couldn't be fresher."

"I must have guessed right. I've brought drinks. And a cold salad."

She went to the jeep to fetch two bottles of wine, one of whiskey, and a Tupperware box of salad. He brought a folding table and two chairs from the living room. They opened the table under the mango tree; it was cooler there than in the living room.

"Whiskey?" he said. "What luxury? Here, the only liquor I've got is kaxipembe, which is what they call kaporroto in Luanda, and which my friend Ximbulo, who distills the stuff, pompously calls brandy. It has the advantage of not requiring ice. But sorry, I'd forgotten that doctors disapprove of kaxipembe because it contains aldehydes."

"You know perfectly well that whiskey is easier to find in this country than a sewing needle. And you can drink it without ice."

"Easy for you with your card that allows you to buy in special shops. On the black market, there's plenty of the stuff, but it's much too expensive for a poor hunter. Of course, if I had a car, I could exchange fish for whiskey in Benguela. It would just involve a bit more work, catching a few more fish. They promised to get me a bike, but sadly, the regional delegate for industry who made me the promise was transferred. Twenty kilometres on a bike into the city would even be good exercise. But I've got to wait until some guy who remembers me gets transferred down here."

"Plenty of people remember you, Aníbal."

"In order to label me a madman, I know."

They sat down at table. He had two plates and forks, and even a dish to put the fish on. They helped themselves to the bream, which was steaming, its fragrance wafting upwards toward the clouds. He suddenly remembered he didn't have any lemon, nor anything that might serve as an alternative. Lemon was important for grilled bream, but that was too bad. They opened a bottle of wine.

Sara spoke, "You must agree that your disappearance from the political scene surprised many people. It would seem they offered you various roles. Vítor told me you could even have become a minister. And you came down here, far from everything, without telling anyone. At the very least, that's strange behaviour. After a lifetime of struggle . . ."

"Vítor, Worldly . . . he's still a minister, but he changed portfolio some time ago. I heard that on the radio. So you can see, I'm up to date. I've got a radio, and at night, when I've got the patience, I listen to the national news. But not always, because it's hard to stomach so many slogans and empty speeches. Any village secretary within the party, or the delegate of a mass organization in a municipality, simply has to make some vacuously boring speech, and it's broadcast straightaway on the radio. And the listener has to endure these slogans, without being able to contest them, because they are supposedly important declarations. Just as any meeting is a decisive one, even if it's a meeting of the local fat cats, for some in-depth analysis that grabs their attention, as if they were all looking down a well, just as all the leaders have a special level of excellence and a clarity of vision, et cetera, et cetera. I'll spare you the endless litany of the most commonly used adjectives in this country. You hear them every day, a disciplined militant like you, or like you should be."

"I am."

"Well, all right. I don't condemn you. You were always very dedicated. And I wouldn't want to offend you with any term I might use. I swear that's not my intention. I know very well how to draw distinctions between people. But you brought up the subject of my disappearance from the scene, and you've backed

it up by alluding to the authority of Vítor, a bastard who promised to send me coffee and some socks when I was deep in the
bush. He got mixed up in all that commotion at the border, and
I'm still waiting for my socks ... Between you and me, I never
understood how Worldly deviated from the Eastern Revolt at
the last moment. In 1972, when he left for the border, he was
fed up with them all. They couldn't deceive anyone. But then he
sensed which way the wind was blowing, or he had a prophetic
dream. Later, I began to fit things together from what people
told me. He kept his distance from both camps, while keeping
a hidden finger in both pies. When he had to make a decisive
choice, he cut his links with the rebels. And of course, he began
his ascent within the organization. I have to admit he was hugely
skilful. The so-called cat that leaps and always falls on its feet."

"You don't like him."

"Maybe because I was once too fond of him. You know, dis-
illusionment is the worst feeling one can have. He was like a
younger brother, and I felt great affection for him. I forgave him
all his little faults, defended him when necessary, trusted him.
In the end, he turned out to be no more than an opportunist."

"You're exaggerating. He's a talented leader."

"As they all are, while they are leaders. They're all talented
and honest, without exception. When one of them ceases to be
a leader, then we discover that he was, after all, incompetent
and corrupt. The mythology of power, or the mythologizing of
men in power. It happens in any religion or sect. The chief of
the sect is a saint, selfless, adored by the faithful. When he falls,
they discover that he was the devil incarnate, with a Swiss bank
account worth millions. All this is as old as the hills and repeated
without change from one regime to the next. But people don't
see it, because they think their experience is special and better
than the others. A kind of religious faith. Well, one cannot contest
a faith, even by recourse to logic."

"You remind me of Marta. After you left Portugal, Marta told me you only had two routes to go down: either you would die in the war, which would be better for you, or you would become disenchanted. She guessed right. Because you were in pursuit of a utopian dream of revolution. In the end, you became thoroughly disillusioned."

"Marta . . . I never heard from her again. Do you know what happened to her?"

"No, when I was in Paris, I eventually lost contact with her."

"She was wrong about one thing: she gave two different alternatives. I died and became disenchanted. Two paths in one."

"Disenchantment is always a kind of death, isn't it?"

He absent-mindedly caressed the trunk of the mango tree. Underneath its gnarled bark, he sensed the sap flowing voluptuously.

"This thing about utopia is true. I often think that our generation should be called the utopian generation. You and I, Laurindo, the Vítor of the old days, to mention only those you knew. But so many others, who came before or after, all of us at a particular moment were pure and wanted to do something different. We thought we were going to build a fairer society, without differences, without privileges, without persecution, a community of interests and thought. In short, what Christians call paradise. At a particular moment, even though it might have been fleeting in certain cases, we were pure, selfless, thinking only of the people and struggling on their behalf. And then . . . Everything got corrupted, everything went rancid, long before power was achieved. When people realized that sooner or later, their rise to power was inevitable. Each one began to prepare the springboard for their bid to power, to defend their own particular, selfish positions. Utopia died. And today it stinks, like any decomposing body. All that remains is empty rhetoric."

Sara helped herself to some more fish. And she added a little more to his plate, which was still full. She also poured some wine into his glass, which was empty.

"You still eat so little. You find energy elsewhere, as Marta used to say."

"I've always eaten little. No one ever understood my lack of appetite. That was good during the war, when there was hunger, because I hardly noticed it. No one criticized me then; there was more left over to share out. But today no one understands my lack of appetite, it's funny. And they condemn me because I dropped everything—didn't want cars, houses, or numerous women, as they, the possessors of voracious, insatiable appetites, all have. I made them feel awkward. At a cannibals' banquet, all I took was a tiny pastry. You must acknowledge that that type of behaviour makes those who are stuffing themselves with so much food feel uncomfortable. This way, I at least spare them my embarrassing presence. And I spare myself from puking with disgust at seeing so much food wasted when the people are dying of hunger. I'm sorry, this isn't a conversation for the dinner table. What do you think of my bream? Isn't it marvellous? All it needs is some lemon to complete a masterpiece of natural, refined flavour. And they say the French know all about cooking. You who lived all those years in la douce France, did you ever eat a bream as good as this?"

"Only in Benguela."

"How did you get here?"

"I'm on holiday. I decided to spend a few days in Benguela, even though I no longer have any family here. I don't know, maybe I have—my mother's family must be scattered everywhere because of the war. But I didn't manage to make contact with any of them."

"And what about your parents?"

"My parents and my brother went to Portugal before independence. By the time I got to Luanda, they had already left.

Three years ago, I went there as part of a delegation from the Ministry of Health. I was included because I was the director of a hospital, and it was then that I saw them. After twenty-four or twenty-five years. They're well. My father managed to take a lot of money with him. He was very quick off the mark, straight after the April twenty-fifth coup in Portugal. He realized what he had to do long before the others. He sold all his businesses and managed to transfer the money to Portugal. They left here before the end of '74. They live off their investments, my father blaming the Communists for everything. You know the old story, that the Communists stripped him of everything, they're only not living at death's door because he took precautions. My mother has a very different story. She yearns for her homeland. This year, I'll go and visit them as I've got the means, and I'll introduce them to their granddaughter, whom they've never met."

"Ah, of course, how is your daughter? Did she come with you?"

"No, she had classes. She's in the Faculty of Medicine. It seems she's got the family curse; she wants to be a doctor."

"She's twenty-one and her name is Judite, right?"

"You've still got the memory of an elephant."

"Only for those things that interest me. I try and forget the rest. Sadly, all too often without success. But how did you manage to get down here?"

Sara laughed. She finished eating her fish before answering. While she spoke, he finished the food that was still untouched on his plate.

"I knew you were somewhere down this way, near Caotinha. In Benguela, they gave me directions, but told me straightaway that it wasn't easy to find you. Very few people knew the way. The delegate for health lent me the jeep. And it wasn't easy to get here, because I missed the turn at first. I went to Baía Azul, and from there made it to Caota. At the restaurant in Caotinha, they told me I couldn't get here directly. I had to go back to the highway and look out for the lamppost. I eventually found the place, but after I left the main road, my heart was in my hands. What if this wasn't the right track? You really have hidden yourself away very well. There's no risk of undesirable visitors."

"That's where you're wrong. Last year, Worldly turned up here. Just imagine, in the middle of all this peace and quiet, three jeeps full of bodyguards and a delegation from the authorities in Benguela. They had been visiting Baía Farta, and on the return, someone had told him the nutcase lived around here. He left a few bottles of whiskey they were taking to some banquet, which was the only bonus. Bottles I polished off in the company of Ximbulo, while badmouthing Worldly, of course."

The meal had ended. And what was more, he had finished his share of the fish; only a bit of salad was left. He finished the bottle of wine, noticing that Sara could hold her own when it came to drinking.

"Now some good news. I've got coffee, and I'll go and make some. Fruit is the only thing I don't have."

"Don't worry, I'll make the coffee, Aníbal."

They both went to the kitchen and started tidying up. While the water boiled, he showed her the house. Sara was delighted with the living room and its panoramic views. It was indeed impressive to be able to watch the surges of water beating against the rocks, breaching the reefs, and lapping against the sands of the beach. The sun was starting to shine fully on the windows of the living room, all its colours refracted by the transparent bricks. "A cathedral," Sara murmured, fascinated. "My cathedral, the only one I have," said Wisdom.

They went back outside. They accompanied their coffee with a neat whiskey, sitting there in silence, each one clinging to the clouded shreds of their memories. He noticed Sara had aged. She must be about forty-six, like him. No, she was a year younger. A lot of white hairs, and lines on her brow. But it wasn't so much that. The way she dressed, sat down, smoked her cigarette, all gave her an air of negligence. Very different from that elegant but unaffected Sara he had known in Lisbon. Was it her stay in Paris? No, it wasn't that. When they had met in Luanda four years before, she still had that air of sober refinement, dressed in the white coat of a hospital doctor. And now she wore glasses all the time. These last few years of her life must have been hard, with its trail of disappointments and difficulties. I'm noticing how she has aged and I don't even look at myself; the mirror must tell me something.

"How do you think I look, Sara? Physically, I mean."

She looked at his shoulders, his bare chest, his head. Slowly. He could feel a caress from beyond her glasses; Sara burst out laughing.

"You're looking really good. You look like an Ethiopian. True, I'm not joking. That enormous mass of hair, like a lion's mane, and then your thinness ... But at the same time, you look healthy. Lean as always. The look of someone at no risk of heart disease."

"A frugal life, that's the secret. Lots of fish and never any meat or butter, or things like that. And the kaxipembe to burn up any fat. Lots of time spent in the sea, sun, and wind too."

"If you went around leaning on a staff, with a cloth round your midriff instead of trousers, people would take you for a saint. A prophet!"

"I don't need that. People already view me as a kind of prophet, except that I'm a prophet of the apocalypse. God's madman! Once a month, I go into the military warehouse in Benguela to pick up the food allowance the army gave me. I load up with sugar, rice, beans, oil, stuff like that. It's the only time I ever leave here. And the younger soldiers laugh, I can tell they're laughing behind my back, 'There goes the nutcase.' But when I speak to them, they're all ears, taking in every word I utter. Isn't that the attitude of people when in the presence of a prophet?"

She didn't answer. She discarded the remains of her cigarette. She turned around and contemplated the parched escarpments along which she had come. He was secretly caressing the trunk of the mango tree. Sara turned toward him once again.

"Don't you feel too lonely?"

"But I'm not alone. I'm surrounded by things I love. The hills, the house, the tree, the fish, the sea, the algae, the reefs, the crabs, the birds, and the ants. Do you know anything about the life of ants? Do you know the different species and the relationships they establish among themselves? I've studied them. I've continued the study I started on the Eastern Front. Here, there are no white ants. In the east, the white ants were a plague; they ate the roofs of the huts. I had to find a way of avoiding this. I spent a huge amount of time studying the movements of the white ant, you know, the types of clay tunnels they make in order to move around safely inside and eat the dried-up sticks and grass that they find. Then I invented an ecological weapon to combat the white ant. Don't laugh, it's true. I discovered that black ants, the same ones you can find here, of a medium size and glossy black, but with smaller jaws than a kissonde driver ant … Anyway, these black ants, if they can get into the tunnels, controlled the white ant. They killed some and enslaved most of them. So, the remedy was a simple one, namely to attract the black ants up onto my roof. Not many, because, apart from anything else, they weren't very abundant. Result: the white ants stopped devouring my grass-thatch roof. I taught this to Worldly, but he laughed and went and told everybody about Wisdom's latest antics. Until there was a particularly strong downpour, and he got soaked to the skin because it was raining as hard inside as it was out. He came to me all humble pie, for instructions.

"And do you know the best way to catch crabs on the beach, those little crabs? By luring them with any dark material, a piece of coal or a casuarina cone, further and further away from their hole. When you've done this, you run and block the hole before it can go back in. It gets lost, defenceless, because each crab needs to return to its own hole. If it enters another one, it gets into a fight. To discover these things, I need to carry out genuine scientific research. So I don't have time to get bored. And if I want to see someone I like, I go along to Ximbulo's fish sheds, or to the refugee village. Lonely? The worst form of loneliness is to be among a crowd of people with whom you no longer have anything in common."

"But don't you sometimes feel the need for a more constant human presence, I don't know, a woman for example?"

"Ah, do you mean the loneliness of a male without a female or a female without a male? I've solved that problem, though not in the manner of a saint. There's a girl in Benguela who took a shine to me in the old days when I was a commander. She sometimes comes and spends the night here. When she feels like it. Without any kind of commitment. I amuse her, and we've spent some good times together. I play the part of the guy who's a bit dotty. I tell her strange stories. I don't need to use much imagination because my life has always consisted of strange things. In fact, just like the life of everyone here in this land of every miracle imaginable. Except that people aren't aware of the strange nature of these things and are astonished when they're told things they in fact witness on a daily basis."

"But doesn't this girl want to stay here?"

"That's the last thing she wants! She's got her own life in Benguela. And I wouldn't want it either. So, the occasional rendezvous suits us both. When she comes, I'm the one who talks. In fact, it's one of my worst defects. I end up being the only one talking. That's why I got called Wisdom. At first, it was a way of teasing me, irony and nothing more. Eventually, I adopted it as my nom de guerre, and it lost its comedic side. I had noticed this when I was a kid. If they gave me a nickname and I got annoyed, well, I got stuck with it. The best thing to do has always been to accept the nickname, and eventually it loses all its original meaning. In fact, the word *Black* here in Angola underwent the same process. Whites called us Blacks in order to humiliate us, to belittle us. When we embarked on the struggle and began using the term as an assertion of an identity, calling ourselves Blacks, the whites were at a loss, even the progressive ones, and no longer knew what to call us. Then they started calling us Blacks not as an insult but as a neutral term, almost as an acknowledgement of our emancipation. I don't even know whether they were conscious of this, but it was the first gesture that announced an unconscious acceptance of our independence ... If Marília lived here, she'd get fed up listening to me talking after three days. And I would get fed up talking to someone who doesn't have much to say."

"You don't have much respect for her. Don't you think you're being a bit of a male chauvinist?"

"Well, I don't know, I've never thought about it. But I respect her and have never asked her for anything. She turns up whenever she wants. I've never asked her whether she's got a man in Benguela, but I imagine she does. A pretty young girl isn't going to be satisfied with an old wreck like me once every week or two. I know about her problems, and if she asks, I give her some advice. Not about her love life, because she never tells me about it. It's not a subject of any interest when we're together. Male chauvinism? Maybe because I don't let her share more of my life? But she doesn't want to. Neither would I want it. Can the absence of any kind of dependence be seen as chauvinistic? Why not feminism on her part?"

"No. It was just the way you said she doesn't have much to say."

"And she doesn't. It would be paternalistic if I denied it. Even though I'm old enough to be her father, I don't treat her like a daughter, and I acknowledge her limitations. What's wrong with that?"

Sara didn't answer. She lit another cigarette. It was two o'clock. Under the mango tree, it was cool, but the sun was baking the hilltops. She came out with an idea:

"Do you feel like going for a drive? We can go as far as Baía Farta. It's many years since I last set foot there, and I won't have another opportunity for quite some time."

"I'll go and get a shirt."

He put on a shirt and some sandals, and he combed his hair, which was knotted because he hadn't had a freshwater bath. He was almost unable to stick the comb in, and it was even harder to get it out. Sara's right, I look like an Ethiopian. With this huge, unruly hairdo, my thin face and the sharp nose, almost like that of a white, I could be taken for an Ethiopian or a Somali. Without any offence meant to those distinguished people. He left, shutting the door on the latch. He never used the key, which was unwise, because there were occasional spates of theft in Baía Azul. But his confidence in humanity was far too strong.

He got into the jeep, and Sara drove off. She drove along the track, crossing the hills with caution and in silence. When they reached the main road, she asked, "How do you go and get your supplies if you don't have a car?"

"I get a lift on the truck that brings water on one of its journeys along the track. At the military store, they give me a lift back here. When it comes to that kind of thing, they're still great. And I know that if I asked them for other stuff, they might get it for me. A fridge, for example. Even a beaten-up old military jeep, there are so many of them. But I don't want to ask for anything. It's a question of pride. And then again, how would I do up the jeep, where would I get the parts? It would be a devil of a job, and I can't be bothered."

"I'm sorry, Aníbal, but I find this pride of yours hard to comprehend. It doesn't prevent you from accepting the food allowance, which must be minimal, I imagine, but in any case ..."

He wasn't offended. Sara could tell him anything, be really hard on him, he'd never get offended. It wasn't in her nature to say things deliberately to offend, he knew that. And he could understand her puzzlement. Hadn't he asked himself the same question umpteen times?

"Let me try and explain. I find it hard to understand as well sometimes. When someone cuts himself off, cuts himself off from everything and doesn't depend on the smallest handout, is that the basis of your doubt? I accepted this illegal pension because there's no law governing the retirement of military personnel. It wasn't because I thought I had a right to it after having fought for so many years. So many others think they've got all the rights in the world because they fought. They justify the privileges they invented for themselves on the grounds that all they ever did was their patriotic duty. My point of view is that Angola doesn't owe me anything. So, in cutting myself off completely, I should also have refused the pension. On the other hand, without it, I couldn't survive, because they invented a system in which everything works through schemes and favours. There's no place for the marginalized. I could sell fish to the nearest restaurant and survive like that. But the restaurant belongs to the State and can't buy from me; it has to buy fish from the State. And I don't have a shop where I can buy all the products I need. The shops are empty and require coupons. What to do then? It wasn't me who invented this system, nor did they seek my opinion, and even if they had, they wouldn't have taken the slightest notice. The State is the father, the State is the one who knows, the State sustains you. As its son, I accept the pension my father gives me. I have no other. A man can never choose his father, isn't that so?"

"There's one thing I don't agree with. The people who fought really do have a right to some acknowledgement. Dammit, you people delivered independence to this country."

"That doesn't imply special privileges. What they should have

313

is a retirement pension, all the greater depending on the years people served. And special treatment for those who were left without their legs or were disabled in some other way or were left widows and orphans. And special treatment for the illiterate who assumed important roles and today clearly have nothing more to offer, because they can't learn the skills to administer a state. They keep them on in roles because they don't know what to do with them, but they're dead weight. That was the pension I requested, and I must have offended them, because they kicked up one hell of a fuss. 'If you don't want to stay with us, it's because you're against us.' All I wanted was to remove myself, to be independent. I'm not against them, nor is there a viable alternative. In the end, they suggested this type of pension, which may end at any time, depending on which way the wind is blowing and who's in charge."

"All right, you might seek your independence, that's okay. Other people have done so. But they stayed on and worked within the system. And you've got a degree. You could get a job anywhere you wanted. This is what people find hard to understand—that you've buried yourself here, cut off from the world. That means a radical severance from the system, a voluntary exile, and it leaves people feeling uncomfortable."

"I know, oh, I know that only too well! Tell me, Sara, can't I have my own private reasons to bury myself here? Do they always have to be political reasons?"

"People don't know your reasons."

"It's none of their business. And that is the problem: the State behaves like a father, and the son has to tell him everything. He has no right to any privacy. The people you speak of so fallaciously aren't people; they are merely the roles they fulfill in the apparatus of the State. There's no place for sentiments, human relations, only relationships of power. Men have ceased to be men, with all their virtues and defects, and are merely comfortable chairs, machines, screws, assets that can be put to use. Or more complex machines who make use of these assets. These people you talk of aren't people, Sara. They are the State, the system. To a person like you, who is still a person, even though you're the director of a hospital—"

"Not anymore. I asked to be relieved of my position in management. I had disagreements with the bureaucrats. Now I'm just a doctor, responsible only for clinical matters."

Aníbal burst out laughing. It was his first true belly laugh in a long time, he remembered clearly, ever since a discussion he had had with Ximbulo about the sex of fishes. He choked and coughed hard. He coughed and laughed, until tears came to his eyes. When he eventually calmed down, he said, between laughs, "As you see, in some way, you, too, have escaped the system. That proves you're still a person. It's not exile, but you're on your way there . . ."

They had passed Baía Azul without noticing and were now on their way to Baía Farta. In a dip in the terrain, there was green grass, where some cattle were grazing. This piece of lowland always had grass, even after the cacimbo, the misty season and despite all the droughts, one of nature's mysteries. The water table must be very near the surface, he thought. He always reflected on this each time that he passed this way, so much so that he barely noticed it anymore.

"To someone like you, I could confide my reasons for coming to live here, which are strictly personal. But I'd never give the State that privilege. At first a young lad would often turn up, sent by big daddy, to find out what I was cooking up here, but nowadays that seldom happens. They're all alike, carrying a little briefcase, asking the neighbours. How I live, what I do, et cetera. These kids never ask me directly, because they'd get an earful. They must imagine I'm developing a secret weapon . . ."

He fell silent. He'd dropped the hint, but Sara hadn't taken it up; she would never dare ask him what these personal reasons were. She drove on, itching with curiosity but without saying a word. Good old Sara, the pillar of discretion. Aníbal hadn't decided yet whether to tell her or not. If she were to ask, he would answer straightaway. He had nothing to hide from her. Although he had some qualms as to what his friend's reaction might be, precisely because she was a friend. He would also tell Ximbulo. He had even suggested why at one point, but Ximbulo had other concerns. He enjoyed having him living nearby and that was enough, each one knows his own heart. Marília had broached the subject a number of times, but he had always avoided telling her. Sara was probably right: Marília was merely a body he made use of. But she made use of him and all his stories as well, so they were quits.

They arrived at Baía Farta. The village was almost lifeless, nothing that recalled the old days when it was the fishing capital. The shops were closed, many with smashed windows. Most of the beer halls where one could eat the best shellfish were also as good as closed. He noticed that António's was open. One or two other facilities were open, too, but there wasn't much activity. A few people in the streets, many of them dressed in rags, revealing their condition as war refugees, who packed the surrounding villages. They continued down the main street as far as the tip of the promontory that enclosed the bay and along which the fish sheds were situated. The trawlers were all at anchor, sheltered from the powerful waves of the open seas, which rocked them gently. One or two fish sheds were in operation, but never enough to satisfy demand for orders. They reached the end and Sara turned the jeep around, without a word. Nor did she have to say anything, for Aníbal could guess her melancholy thoughts. Yes, Baía Farta was like a ghost town, although it still showed a few signs of life. Still?

As they were driving back, Aníbal told her to stop in front of António's beer hall. "Let's see if he's got some cool beer." Sara complied. A cool beer was always welcome.

António was a tubby, amiable mixed-race fellow, who got up sluggishly from a stool, the moment they entered. He had the piping voice of a child. "Down this way, Commander? It's been a long time."

"I've brought a good friend of mine. She's dying of thirst, poor girl. She's come all the way from Benguela just for a nice cold beer."

António laughed. He glanced at the door and then out the back. He winked and spoke in his high-pitched tone, "Keep your voice down, Commander, keep your voice down, the walls have ears. I haven't received any beer for ages. I haven't sold any since last month. That's why the bar's so empty. But for you, Commander, I've got my little stash I was saving for tomorrow's lunch. But you'll have to take it in the room at the back. A few shrimps to go with it? Or some crab?"

Aníbal looked at Sara for an answer. She said, "Shrimps. We've just had lunch."

António led them to what he called his back room, which was in fact a veranda at the rear of the premises, with a table where the family ate their meals. The yard was paved with concrete and attracted the sun. The front room, though closed, was cooler. But Aníbal realized they would have to have their drink there for reasons of security. If the thirsty inhabitants of Baía Farta saw him welcoming customers, they might smash up his establishment. And he might be legally charged with embezzlement of his products, which meant he would be fined and his beer hall closed down. Every time Aníbal went there, he always drank at the back, because it was very rare that António had any beer for the public. And the little he did receive was via a secret contact in Lubango. Three bottles of N'gola beer appeared; António served them with two and sat down at the same table with the third one. He sent one of his sons to fetch a dish of shrimps from the fridge.

"They're fresh, home cooked, don't have any qualms about eating them. The crab is good, too, just like the old days. They're easy to get hold of. I buy them for the bar and my friends. What's the point of buying more? Without any beer, there are no customers. All the crab goes to Luanda, via secret deals."

"Have you known each other long?" Sara asked.

António laughed his childlike laugh. He patted Aníbal on the shoulder. "Ever since Cuanza Sul. When the South Africans took Benguela, I withdrew along with my family to Sumbe, and from there, we had to flee to Porto Amboim. The commander here appeared in due course, at the head of a unit that later took back Sumbe and Benguela. You were one of the first people to enter liberated Benguela, isn't that so, Commander? I was following behind the soldiers, with the family and household possessions, yearning to get back to this bay after three months away. On tenterhooks, because I thought the house and shop might have been completely trashed. In the end, I was lucky. All they took were the deep freezers. Your friend, lady, worked so hard. Everyone was grateful. One day, he turned up here telling me we were neighbours, as he now lived near Caotinha. We celebrated with plenty of beer. I had some that day, I remember. The customers were the ones who suffered, but it was a good reason for closing the shop and commemorating."

"Lots of people think he's round the bend, gone mad," Sara said.

"Let them talk, they don't know what they're saying. Nor what they're doing. They're the ones who are mad. Haven't you seen how this bar is deserted? Anyone who wanted to preserve their sanity and didn't want to fill their pockets at other people's expense would do what the commander did and send them all to blazes, so as to live in the best place in the world. Much better for a man called Wisdom."

More beer came. And another round. Aníbal kept quiet and let António do the talking, recounting the little dramas of the place, all the red tape that exasperated him, the approaching season of tidal surges, his children's school which functioned irregularly, the colonial times, which he didn't want to see again but when life was better. After the third round, Aníbal said, "Let's go, Sara, before we empty his stock completely." She got up. António refused to charge them. The commander had limitless credit at the beer hall; he was a liberator who hadn't made use of the liberty given to others. He stood on the doorstep waving goodbye when the jeep pulled away.

Aníbal suggested they head home by way of Baía Aul, so that he could show her the refugee village. As they approached it, the children left their games or domestic tasks to come and welcome the arrival of the jeep. Aníbal got out and the children surrounded him, shouting back to the huts, "Wisdom, Wisdom." The adults came out straightaway to greet them. Aníbal was laughing and telling jokes, occasionally greeting people by name, and introducing them to Sara. She asked them about their problems, hunger, and illnesses. Sometimes food was delivered to them; now and then some doctors would appear with vaccines for the children, not much else.

"Isn't there a doctor who comes to hold a regular clinic?" she asked.

"No, never," an older man said. "He turns up . . . kind of."

"Two or three times a year," Aníbal translated.

Their provisions were almost at an end, and they were eating sweet rice pudding, but without milk, which was reserved for the children and was becoming scarce. Sweet rice pudding was boiled rice with a bit of sugar, Wisdom explained. They were all thin, but the children displayed distended bellies, the result of too little protein and worms. Sara was concerned and felt that something could always be done. It was she who asked to leave. The cries of the children and the salutations of the adults accompanied them for a good way along the track.

"They all show signs of severe malnutrition," Sara said. "And with a sea so full of fish."

"Fish gives them their dose of protein. This will strike you as strange, but they were in a far worse state some time back. Okay, they eat a tiny amount of fish, but they don't have cornmeal to make mealie porridge."

"Can't you do anything for them?"

"No. If the appropriate organizations do little for them, who am I to be able to do so?"

He didn't mention that he gave them fish from time to time, because it hardly counted. Nor did he mention the complaints he hurled at the relevant authorities in Benguela, demanding that they take drastic measures on the various occasions famine had set in at the village. What for? Nothing moved. He alone couldn't change the world, and he no longer had the strength to try. The refugees had come from all corners of the province; they were peasants without good soil or enough water to plant crops. Their clothes were decent, for they had received bundles from a Danish humanitarian organization. The problem was hunger and illness, just as they had said. Aníbal looked at them and recognized the same type of faces and attitudes as those he had seen fleeing to Zambia ten years before. The languages were different, but the look in their eyes was the same, with the bloody reflection of war on their tail.

"That's so sad," Sara said. "I'm going to speak to the delegate for health. A medical team has got to visit them at least once a month. I heard some coughing there that suggested the possible onset of tuberculosis."

"They're all fully aware. They always promise to send people and medicines. Then either they really don't have the means or they just forget. And it's no good me turning up to badger them continually. They just give me sideways glances now."

Aníbal pointed to a track that cut through the hills and was quicker. Sara examined the new trail. It didn't seem any more dangerous than the others. She turned the jeep onto it.

"So, you are doing things for them. You must be, judging by the way they welcomed you and talked. There was one thing that was immediately recognizable, and that was the confidence the people appeared to have in you. They like you, they trust you."

"I think so. That's why I didn't tell them you were a doctor. Otherwise they would think I was promising them a regular visit from you. I've never made them any promises, even when I go to Benguela to push their case. But they always end up knowing."

"You felt at ease among them. If I hadn't asked to leave, you would have sat down on a stool and stayed to talk to them. You seemed like another person, more open. I'd even say more joyful."

"Perhaps. I sometimes go there for a chat."

"Because you're an outcast like them?"

"It's a kind of fate. I always seek the company of the victims of a process. Maybe it's pride, but I never feel good in the company of the victors."

"You can't do anything for them here. Nor for the thousands and thousands of others like them throughout the country."

"I can't do anything here, nor anywhere else in the world. I've stopped being a fighter. I know you understand me. I haven't lost many battles, but I'm still a loser. Deep down, we're all losers. We have no future, even those who think they've found a safe anchorage. All that's needed is a larger wave and they'll be cast adrift."

"Vítor?"

"For example. We don't have a future. We don't represent the future. We're already the past. Our generation has exhausted its resources. It did what it had to do at a moment in history: it fought for and won independence. After that, it was left worn out. We need to know when to withdraw, when we have no more to give. Many people don't know that. They cling to a more or less glorious past, but they are fossils."

"So who is the future?"

"The Malongos of this world."

"What a delightful prospect!"

"No worse than the present. What's he up to now?"

Sara didn't say anything for a few minutes, as she focused on the way ahead. They were already near the house, except from this side, it would appear quite suddenly, as there was a slight rise in the ground between it and where they were. Then she spoke. "You're like a wizard. I heard from him recently. He doesn't sing anymore and is mixed up in some sort of business dealings. I'm not quite sure, but they are firms that do business with Angola. It looks as if he's becoming some kind of a middleman. He said that he'd show up in Angola one of these days. He wrote to his daughter and sent her clothes. Useful stuff. He always had a very real affection for his daughter, and in that, he was absolutely sincere. On a couple of occasions, he paid for her trip to Brussels, where he's been living for quite a while now, and she went and spent her holidays with him. When it comes to his daughter, he's almost the perfect father. Sooner or later, he'll make a breakthrough over there, selling useless things and filling his pockets. That's his style."

They got home. He all but leaped out of the jeep and went and greeted the mango tree. She got out more slowly, with a certain reluctance, her hands appearing to try to straighten her somewhat crumpled dress. She glanced at her watch and sighed. "I've got to go."

"It's only five o'clock," he said. "Have you got to return the vehicle now?"

"No, I've got it for the whole day. I'll only return it tomorrow, before I leave for Luanda."

"Well, then? How can you leave without going for a swim in my bay? Isn't it beautiful? It's really begging you for a dip. And by now, in the afternoon, the water's warm, despite the swell further out."

They gazed at the bay, the reefs, from the top of the cliffs, in silence. Then Sara tittered with laughter. A nervous laugh, he noticed.

"I didn't bring a bathing suit."

"That's a fine excuse, honestly. Go in your underpants, or naked. What's the difference?"

She chuckled nervously again. She adjusted her glasses, playing for time. "Yes, it's a feeble excuse. You're giving me a pretext to stay a bit longer. Are you coming too?"

"I'll go down with you, of course. But I won't go in. I went for a long enough swim this morning. I'll bring you a towel."

He went and got his largest towel and, on his way back, a bottle of whiskey. They climbed down the path, he taking the lead, occasionally helping her at the hardest parts. Sara giggled quietly when he had to hold her arm to stop her from slipping. On the beach, he sat down, leaning against the cliff in his usual spot. He put the towel down next to him and unscrewed the top of the whiskey bottle. "A mouthful before your bath?" Sara shook her head. He drank straight from the bottle. He sat there looking at her standing in front of him. After an endless few minutes, Sara made a decision; she took off her glasses, which she placed on the towel, and lifted her dress up. She tossed it onto the towel. She stood there in her underpants and bra. She turned toward the sea, undid the clasp of her bra, and threw it onto the towel without turning round. She ran to the water. Aníbal glimpsed her still shapely white body plunge into the waves. At that particular moment, and without looking at her face, she seemed to him like the young girl of eighteen he had met in Lisbon. Time had not taken its toll on her body.

He watched her swim. She took a long time. She would swim back to the shore, look as if she was going to get out and come toward him, but then she would decide not to, and she would dive back in, swimming away in the direction of the reefs, where she would turn back toward the shore again. It lasted as long as it took him to finish the whiskey, one sip at a time. All of a sudden, Sara apparently summoned up the courage and left the water. He imagined she would cover her breasts with her hands in the usual gesture of female modesty, but he was surprised to see her walking slowly toward him, so slowly that it seemed like some deliberate ploy, her arms away from her body, her small round breasts, dark nipples still erect, her white underpants, now transparent, revealing her golden pubis, the dying sun beating down on her back, her whiteness standing out against the violets and orange of the west and the ocean, approaching him, breathless despite the slowness of her walk, gazing at him fixedly and frontally, her tongue between her teeth, languid. She stopped a metre from him and stood there open-legged like a statue, her arms still away from her body, which now shivered in strange, almost imperceptible convulsions, until he banished away the mists before his eyes caused by the alcohol. He leaped to his feet, towel in hand, wrapping it around her and pulling her into the warmth of his body. Now sitting again, he leaned back against the cliff, she in his arms, his arms around her, his breath caressing her elegant neck, as time passed lingeringly, so slowly that the sun sank into the sea almost under the force of their eyes staring at the star's daily demise. She furtively opened the towel and guided his hands so that they touched her still-cold naked body, and then he slowly, and oh so gently, moved his hands up over her belly and over her breasts, pausing there, squeezing them softly, while words sprung as if by magic from his mouth, unbidden.

"Out there, right in front of us, to the left of those reefs, there's a cave where my lifelong enemy dwells, a gigantic octopus that terrorized me on this very beach when I was a child, and I swore and swore again that I would one day kill it, not out of vengeance, but out of the inevitability of destiny that made our paths cross one fine day, and that's why I'm here, putting off the day of our encounter, putting it off, knowing that it's there but without taking a step to meet it, feeling its presence, its existence, every day, every second, and yet delaying the fateful day when everything must end, it or me, although I know it's got to be in April, and it'll be this April, just as before I delayed our encounter, in the knowledge that you were always ready for it, but it would have to be very special, which is why it's been worth this twenty-five-year wait, just to feel the nipples of your breasts so hard they are almost exploding under the slight pressure of my fingers, which deep down is only one explanation, for the other truer one would be to say that they're as hard as they are for having waited twenty-five years, just as I sense your repressed desire being unchained, a desire that I can sense in the sweet smells you release, and at this very moment I could ask everything of you, this world and the next, you would promise it to me, because you no longer have the power to decide anything, only to consume yourself in pleasure, and nor can I decide anything, except that we must fulfill our fate of dying together for some moments, forget the world and your sick patients, forget myself and my octopus, and descend into the depths of your very self, kiss the rose that is hidden beneath your pubis, but no, don't kiss me there, your tongue is splitting me in two, just as I was always split in two in relation to you, the woman who loved you while at the same time desiring another, because you took so long to take this step, took so long to suck my soul with that never-ending kiss, exhausting me and announcing new sensations that were ever my desire and fear, divided, as I have been all through my life." Sara was lying down, still quivering from her first burst of pleasure, and Aníbal lay on top of her, slowly tearing into what he had languorously kissed before. Soon, she began once again to lose her power of reason, imploring in barely coherent phrases, while her body convulsed, arched, and wept in an endless orgasm, as she fruitlessly sought in a few minutes to regain all those lost years.

4

Later, in bed, while Aníbal attentively explored her now tranquil body with his eyes and hands, she said, "When you suggested a swim, I realized that if I accepted, what I had waited for so long was finally going to happen. What's more, I knew I'd have to take the initiative for it not to be lost again. That's why I hesitated. When you said it wouldn't make any difference if I swam naked, you were showing me that this time, you would help make things happen. So I accepted, but I was nervous. My nervousness turned to panic when I saw you sit down, getting ready to quietly enjoy the spectacle of me getting undressed, without any warning. After all, I was the one who was going to have to take the initiative. I imagined it would happen differently, I didn't know how, but I was sure you'd help. You didn't help. You sat down with the bottle. I don't know how I got undressed. It was like a dream, trying to overcome the psychological impasse that left me standing there motionless, in front of you, no doubt with an air of a vulnerable little girl. As I ran down to the sea, I felt free, I was escaping your gaze. I calmed down a bit as I swam, but then I had to face another problem. I knew those underpants of mine were completely transparent and my breasts were uncovered. How should I behave when I got out of the water? Defend my modesty, which might inhibit any progress, or openly surrender? It could only be one of these, but in spite of these twenty-five years, I hadn't overcome the barriers. That's why I swam out again, further delaying what I had put off for so long. And as I did so, I thought of what was going to happen, and I burned inside while I froze on the outside. I paused for a moment and watched you. You were looking at me with undisguised desire. A powerful desire that excited me so much, I began to get spasms and a pain in my belly. I swam out again, feeling colder and colder, and knew I had to make a decision. This couldn't go on any longer. And so that's how it happened, when you throw the last dice, taking a deep breath and hurling yourself into the abyss. I walked toward you, making it obvious I was ready to give myself to you, but you didn't produce the expected reaction. You sat there stock-still, just eyeing me with lust. I stopped in front of you, without knowing what to do. I was me but I was someone else, an actress in some erotic film or a streetwalker, and I would have wept for sure if you hadn't gotten to your feet at last and wrapped me in the towel. When you hugged me and I sat down on your lap, you were at last beginning to take the initiative, and that allowed nature to take its course. I could feel your excitement under me, waiting to burst through the towel, and your hot breath on my neck. It was good but not enough. You were on the brink of coming, and that would have been shameful in the circumstances. That was why I opened the towel, and your hands and words invaded my body. Your words smothered my first orgasm; I died and made love with an octopus that sucked me and penetrated me at the same time. It was devilish and it was powerful. Why was it I who had to initiate things? Why did you never bring things to that point before? Was it pride?"

He continued to caress her body and study each millimetre of her skin. Sara was lying back, her legs open, hands behind her head, letting him do whatever he wanted. No one had ever given herself to him with such trust.

"Call it pride if you want. But everything has its time. It's no use sitting under a mango tree and waiting for it to give you fruit. It will give you them when it is time. Wisdom involves knowing the right moment for each thing, and that's all there is to it. That's when you enjoy things best. If we had reached this point when we were young, we wouldn't have appreciated it in the same way. Like any other young person, we would have merely consumed the moment, consumed it in fire. Little would be left. Ashes. When I saw you get out of the jeep, I knew that the moment had come. I just made the moment stretch a little. If you hadn't taken the initiative, I would have taken it. Just as I did without you realizing it. Introducing you to António, the refugees, wasn't that a way of telling you I'm not mad, that I can be trusted? That there are still people who understand me, outside the circles you move in?"

"The strategy of a serpent? Or an octopus?"

He was nibbling her nipples gently, while curling the hairs on her pubic mound with his fingers and inhaling the smells emanating from her. He murmured things to her breasts, her navel, the light down covering her belly.

"Maybe, maybe that of the sekulo, the village elder. Those old men we scorn, imbued in our urban Judeo-Christian culture, have a lot to teach us about the management of time, the rhythms of life. They drank this from the fountain of knowledge. They transmit their teachings through fables, oral poems, riddles. Although these appear in books, we don't know how to read them. What they tell us, with their words we don't understand, is that nature has its own rhythms, and we should reconcile ourselves with these in order to adapt nature to our needs. Now, what do we do, as hybrid products of two civilizations? All we do is impose the model of industrialization and foreign developmental values, whether we are socialists or capitalists, all of which imply other rhythms. And then we're surprised when nature doesn't follow us, and it plays tricks on us at every turn. They know this and tell us, but as they are illiterate, they are reduced to silence by our prejudice and intellect. We have the sacred knowledge of Marxism-Leninism or the ultra-liberalism of the IMF, we studied in the finest universities. How are we going to lower ourselves, waste our time, trying to understand what they teach us? And if things go badly, as must happen, we blame outside factors. We never see our own blindness."

"We were talking about ourselves and there you go seeking refuge in a more general analysis, with even some politics in the mix."

"Everything is linked, everything explains everything else. I was talking about time, which determines everything. The time of the seasons, the time for planting, the time for young grass to sprout, the time for the species to mate, the time to die. Love, too, has its time. It's just that modern man has lost this notion of rhythms. He thinks he can modify them with impunity. And you, who are a doctor, know that the body has its own cycles, determined by our ancestral nature, and that current changes in the rhythm of our lives are the number one cause for stress. Isn't that so?"

"Maybe the octopus you seek isn't a monster," she said. "It's just become magnified as the result of a childhood trauma. It may not even be in the cave."

"It is. I feel it's there. Waiting for me."

He fell silent, stopped observing and caressing her body. He got up, naked, and went outside. It was midnight. He saw the leaves of the mango tree rustling. There was a wind, and the sea was roaring. But the tree was sheltered by the house. There was no reason for the leaves to be so merry. He approached it and gave it a few pats on the trunk.

"Are you happy, Mussole? Are you expressing yourself at last, showing me your joy? Has the time for you to talk also arrived, after so many years of silence? Everything has happened in a rush this month. It's like some universal cataclysm. That's always the way of things. Everything seems to be in stasis, nothing happening. Suddenly, a change in the weather is heralded by a lightning flash or a tidal surge. And things begin to happen, that which was written in the air and in the depths of the sea. Just like the prophecies of old."

The tree calmed down, indicating that he should go back inside. He agreed and closed the door. He went to the kitchen to drink some water and then went back to bed. Sara had sat up, alert. She was now looking at him, unsure.

"Who were you talking to—the mango tree?"

"Yes," he said casually, as he gave her a quick kiss.

"And you called it Mussole. Wasn't that the name of your woman who died on the Eastern Front, according to Vítor?"

"That guy always was a busybody. But yes, it's true."

"Haven't you got over it yet?"

"Oh, that's in the past. It's stopped being a scar that kept opening up. It's now just become a good memory. Her spirit is sitting quietly up there on top of the mango tree. It came straight after I planted it. And just now, she told me of her joy at what had happened between us."

Sara looked at him strangely but didn't comment. Aníbal understood it would be hard for her to grasp; it would be too much to expect. Now, for sure, she's going to think I'm crazy. And he had absolutely no way of explaining it better to her. He had explained things as clearly as he could. He felt he was in the same situation as the village elder, who doesn't know how to make himself any clearer and still sees that the other person doesn't understand him. That's the problem: wisdom means being misunderstood, even by Sara. He shrugged. He started caressing her body again. She, for her part, didn't open herself to him as trustfully as before, one leg resting on the other. The moment of total communion was over. Time had gone by too quickly, he thought to himself bitterly. It would be stupid to try to stretch it like a piece of elastic; time would break it because it was more tenacious than steel. He continued to caress her but now as a means to provoke her sexually. Sara wouldn't broach the subject again. She would bide her time as well, or perhaps she would take the whole thing as a joke. Let's not make too much of it. She has a great gift for accepting things. Either his optimism was justified, or Sara had made an effort to cast off her bewilderment, because she did indeed begin to respond to his moves and they were soon in each other's arms again.

When the morning light shining through the window woke them, Sara nestled closely against his body and, licking his shoulder, said, "You smell of the sea, you taste of the sea, you love like the sea."

She kissed him, licked him, bit him, until she was at the peak of her excitement. Then she mounted him unceremoniously, spending herself in cries and tears, of pleasure and farewell.

They washed, dressed, and made coffee. She had to leave to catch her flight to Luanda. Near the mango tree, hesitating before getting into the jeep, she said, "Give me an excuse to stay."

He shook his enormous mane of hair. He looked at the sun rising above the hills, the mango tree, Ximbulo's fishery, over beyond where the jeep was parked.

"You belong to another world. You've got your daughter, your patients. Come and spend your holidays here. Come whenever you can and feel like it."

"Would you get tired after three days?"

"You know that's not true. We've got so much to discover together...You lived so long in exile, you're not ready for another one."

She sat behind the wheel of the jeep. She waved goodbye with one hand. The leaves of the mango tree rustled again, as of one. Sara looked at them for a few moments, astonished, then at Aníbal. He smiled and shrugged. Maybe Sara would now believe that

Mussole was talking and wishing her a speedy return. Maybe she would think it was an effect of the absent wind. However, she said nothing, fired the engine, and sped off, waving again. But the mango tree didn't stop rustling until the dust raised by the jeep was merely a smudge on the skyline, beyond the parched hills.

5

During the night, the tidal surge had grown in intensity. The waves were now crashing over the reefs and breaking on the beach, reaching as far as the base of the cliffs. That's good, it means I can't go into the water. He still had the scent of Sara permeating his body and in his brain, and he wanted to preserve it. If he went for a dip, the scent would disperse and sweep away the memory of it preserved in his mind. It was good to sit there, at the top of the cliff, looking at the sea crashing against the rocks and smelling Sara. It wasn't perfume, she didn't use it, except for a vague whiff of deodorant. It was a female scent, powerful, magnified by excitement. When they climbed back up to the house after making love on the beach, she wanted to have a bath. So he poured water over her from a bucket, while she soaped herself. Then he poured more water over her. When he helped her dry herself, rubbing her with the towel, he could smell the scent emanating in waves from her body, bathing him. It was enough to touch her for her to release her female scent. Years of waiting had turned Sara into a formidable armoury of desire. She could control all of its manifestations except for the release of her scent. He had been aware of this at lunch, when she asked him whether he was in a relationship with a woman. From under the table, something was given off, which he now knew had been provoked by the thought. He had had the same sensation in the jeep, on their way back from Baía Farta. A heady odour stimulated by something that was said. The whole time, she was thinking about making love to him but was struggling with her doubts. Her body betrayed her inhibition. But Aníbal only understood it completely when he suggested the dip in the sea, and he was suffused in its emanations almost immediately. He had to restrain himself, almost agonizingly, from not embracing her there and then, and taking her off to bed. The ritual had to run its course slowly, with the dip in the sea and all that ensued. And now it was over, leaving him with the smell and a pain in the pit of his stomach. Would she still be able to smell him on the plane?

At about ten o'clock, he decided to go over and visit Ximbulo. He took with him the second bottle of wine, left over from the previous day. He went barefoot, dressed in his bathing trunks. It was an easy path, downhill, along a gentle slope. With such a choppy sea, Ximbulo hadn't gone fishing and must be at home. If not, Maria, his wife, and Nina, his only daughter, would be there. They had had only three sons, the first died at birth, the other two in the war. And a girl, much later, who was now seventeen. They called her their belated, yearned-for little girl. So that when they registered her birth, she was simply called Nina. The path to their house was full of lizards, from tiny geckos to the largest blued-headed ones. They darted across the white sandy path, fleeing from his steps. Aníbal didn't even notice them, so absorbed was he in his thoughts about Sara.

Ximbulo was at home and shouted a greeting when he caught sight of him. He walked down the ramp that led to the fish sheds and saw the wooden racks upon which they dried the fish, a reasonable quantity of them. There would be more if Ximbulo had been able to mend the outer frames that dated from colonial times. One could still see, in front of the fish sheds, the racks and some of the buoys, where the net between the frames had been installed. But the net had rotted away and a new one was needed. How to get hold of one? That was Ximbulo's dream. To get the racks fully operational once more, employ a few war refugees to help him pull the nets, and gradually get the fishery up and running again. Even get hold of a trawler. Bourgeois dreams, Aníbal teased him. Ximbulo didn't understand and he wasn't into further explanations. What for? He encouraged him to pursue his dream, knowing full well that, for the moment, it would be hard to realize.

Nina came running toward him. A beautiful girl. Breasts of a young virgin, pressing against the cloth of her blouse. Her wide skirt wrapped tightly around her legs, allowing one to picture the shapeliness of her thighs. Under her blouse and skirt, she wore nothing more; she had revealed this to him when he visited one morning and she got into the water with her clothes on, precisely to show him she was bare underneath. That was last year. Or was it two years ago? He no longer knew. Ever since the age of fifteen, Nina had given him provocative looks and would lean up against him casually, whenever she had the chance. She never disguised her intentions, even in front of her indulgent parents. There was a kind of unspoken pact within the family. Nina was destined for him; their neighbour needed a woman, and he would be the best possible husband for her. All that was needed was for him to want her. But Aníbal was fond of Nina as the forthright young daughter of his best friend, and nothing more. He didn't want any ties. That was why he knew he would never touch her.

The only thing he feared was if he left the fishery one night very much the worse for wear from kaxipembe, drunk in the company of Ximbulo, and she were to appear on his way home bent on provocation. He couldn't promise that in such a moment he would have the strength to evade the advances of that sensual little gazelle. And that would be tiresome. How would he explain what had happened to Ximbulo and Maria, okay, but didn't he want her in his home? It would be a serious enough offence to destroy the great friendship that existed between them. On a number of occasions, he had hinted to his friend that Nina's obvious interest made him feel uncomfortable. But Ximbulo appeared not to understand. Or rather he understood but thought it was only a question of time. And that might be the case, who knows? But now it would be harder because of Sara. He wanted to be free for Sara, when she appeared unexpectedly. This year, next year? It didn't depend on him, which was why he shouldn't be impatient. She would be back, that much he knew.

"Yesterday you had a visitor, I saw. A white woman in a car. And she only left today. Did you sleep in the same bed?"

"You're very cheeky, Nina. Don't you know that a young girl can't ask a man that kind of question?"

She burst out laughing. They were walking along side by side as they reached the tiled annex where the parents were waiting for their visitor.

"Go on then. You've only got one bed, so how did you sleep?"

"In that same bed. She's my wife. She lives in Luanda." He blurted it out without thinking. But wasn't it true? He hadn't even asked Sara whether she had a man, they hadn't talked about that, time had been so short. But he considered her his wife. It would even do Nina good to lose her illusions. She took the hint, for she told her parents crossly, "It was his wife from Luanda."

Ximbulo greeted him. Maria shook his hand after having wiped her hand with the cloth rolled up over her gown, as always, her head bowed. They had just finished cleaning out the empty annex.

"With these swells, we're not going to catch any fish for a few days," Ximbulo said, changing the subject.

"I know. I didn't have the courage to hunt either. I've brought this bottle of wine."

"Well, you'll have lunch with us then!" Maria said. "Or is the wine to have now?"

"You people decide," said Aníbal. "Whether you invite me or not..."

Ximbulo laughed. He accepted the bottle and passed it to his wife. He invited him to sit down and then followed suit.

"It's best if you stay for lunch. Maria's going to make calulú. Yesterday we got palm oil and flour. I was even going to invite you yesterday, but I saw you had a visitor..."

"I could have come; there wouldn't have been a problem. All the more so if it was an invitation to eat calulú. But did you manage to get some sweet potato?"

"Hey, yes everything!" Maria said. "And jindungo as well, which had run out."

"Mateus came to get fish," said Ximbulo. "He bought it cheap, daylight robbery. Then he left the products he'd brought as a gift."

"And he probably made a pile, I bet," said Aníbal.

"Of course, a black marketeer never makes a loss. But what can we do about it? They're the only ones who come and buy fish. We've even got to be thankful to them. Otherwise, everything would just go to waste here."

Nina went into the house, bored with the conversation. Her mother followed soon after. "Hey, excuse me, I'm going to cook." She shouted to her daughter, "Come and light the fire." The girl appeared; she crouched in front of the stove in a corner of the shed, some twenty metres away from where they were sitting. Her skirt was bunched between her legs, revealing her bare round thighs. She blew on the coal and glanced sulkily at Aníbal. He pretended not to notice, but he remained closely aware of her reactions. The fire caught and she shouted inside, "It's alight, Mother, what else should I do?" Aníbal didn't catch the reply, but Nina got up and disappeared into the house. Casting him one last murderous look.

"Have you still got water, neighbour? Ours is nearly finished."

"You can go and get some. I must still have half a tank. The truck never comes on the right day, but it must be nearly time for it."

"Yes, it's more than a week since it last came," Ximbulo said.

Aníbal had no notion of the days passing, but Ximbulo always knew. Which was a good thing, for his friend was his calendar and reminded him when it was time to go to Benguela to pick up provisions.

"Would you like a drop of brandy?"

"Not for me, thank you. Only after lunch. Yesterday I had too much to drink. Sara brought a bottle of whiskey, which I finished. And in the afternoon, we went and had a few N'golas at António's. Kaxipembe now would be the end of me."

"You never told me you were married. I thought you only had that girlfriend, Marília."

Ximbulo was like Sara, the soul of discretion. For him to mention this meant that he must be really perturbed, and this merely confirmed the existence of their family pact. Aníbal no longer knew quite how to proceed. He opted to make things a little more clear, for it could only help.

"She's a friend from many years ago, and we have just started seeing each other again. She's a doctor and lives in Luanda. She'll only turn up here occasionally, but she's my wife. Marília is to pass the time, you know that, neighbour."

Ximbulo merely nodded. He would never touch on the subject again; the case was closed. And he might have a word with his daughter, so that that she would stop behaving in such a brazen way. Free of her obsession for him, Nina would give herself to the first black marketeer to appear and get her into trouble. Her future was already clear; one didn't need to open up a goat and read its entrails. What alternative did she have there, so far from anywhere? At least if there were some young man in the refugee camp...But the young men and youths were snapped up to fight for one or other of the warring armies, leaving only the elderly, the children, and one or two men of a mature age in the villages. In the camp, the birth rate must be decreasing with the absence of young men, Aníbal thought to himself, veering away from the subject somewhat. And rapidly growing in the cities. But there were no studies on the topic, or at least none that he knew of.

Nina returned, carrying a saucepan, which she placed on the stove. That must be the fish and vegetables, which Maria had prepared in the house. Ximbulo started to explain the advantages of trap-net fishing. He loathed the fleets of huge foreign fishing vessels, which hoovered up the seas, dragging up smaller younger fish. Along with the dwelling places of shrimp and lobster, nets and all, even our pirogues if we're not careful. Especially the Soviet and Japanese ships, which approach the coast and suck everything up right under the nose of the government, and no one does anything. Only the other day, he had been talking about the problem with fishermen from local companies, and they all agreed that if there was a lack of fish, it was because of these foreigners who don't respect the laws of the country and ravage other people's waters after having laid waste to their own. Aníbal listened while also observing Nina, who would come and watch over the saucepan, glance at him out of the corner of her eye, and then go back inside, almost muttering her indignation. Ximbulo explained that in colonial times, it wasn't like this, the boats were monitored, those vast monster ships couldn't even come near the coast, because they'd be caught immediately. That's why there was more fish in those days, despite all the small trawlers out working every night.

After some considerable time, the calulú was ready. Nina placed another saucepan on the stove, obviously with water to make the porridge. When it began to boil, she called her mother to come and beat the funje. Which Maria did. She took the saucepan off the stove and added the flour to the water, gripping the saucepan between her feet on the ground and beating the pap with a special stick. As he watched the food being prepared, Aníbal felt an unusual hunger. Maybe because the aroma of the calulú mingled with Sara's scent, still on his body. They immediately sat down at table, right there in the fishery annex, where it was cooler, and Ximbulo opened the bottle of wine. Aníbal managed to consume the pile of food that Maria had put on his plate. This was itself notable, and they all rejoiced in his healthy appetite. That's not quite true, because Nina kept her eyes set firmly on her own plate.

When the meal was over, Ximbulo told his daughter to fetch the bottle of brandy. He meant, of course, the kaporroto, with its deadly aldehydes, according to the doctors. No one took any notice of this. The fisherman had learned to distill kaxipembe even during colonial times, but in secret, because it was prohibited. Not because the law was concerned with Ximbulo's health, but because these home-brewed drinks competed with colonial wines and beers. Afterwards, with the almost complete disappearance of other drinks, he devoted himself to the art of distillation, which he now did in a more sophisticated way. He had been astonished when Aníbal explained to him that in Luanda, manufacturers added dry batteries to accelerate the process, which increased the danger of poisoning. He didn't understand the scientific explanation, but he had learned his lesson: that place Luanda was beyond redemption, all that's bad comes from there. They were capable of killing a family member simply to make a few quick kwanzas. Sometimes he joked, "This brandy of mine is pure; there are no batteries in it." Nina might well think, too, that with Sara's visit, all bad things came from Luanda, Wisdom mused.

They sat drinking and talking the whole afternoon. There wasn't much else to do. By now, Aníbal was somewhat inebriated and took his leave as the colours of the dying sun began to spread over the sea. He didn't see Nina. As he approached his house, he found her sitting on a stone. She got up straightaway. Just as I feared, he thought. Thankfully, I'm not roaring drunk. And I have Sara's scent to protect me.

"Is it really true she's your wife?"

Nina appeared to be distressed, wringing her hands together. Maybe it was something stronger than the mere whim of a young girl who had hardly met any other men. He stopped in front of her, so as not to invite her to come into the house. He looked at the mango tree, which was silent and still. In expectation.

"Yes, it's true."

"Mateus keeps saying he's going to take me back to his home in Benguela. He's got a car and a big house."

"And how many women?"

"He didn't say. I don't care. The other day, he tried to feel me up. I ran away. Next time, I won't."

Aníbal needed to say something. Even if her fate was sealed and it wouldn't change anything. Should he resort to past habits and lecture her on morality? Explain Mateus's motives by embarking on a class analysis, if necessary, in order to show that this type of savage, razor-toothed petit bourgeois would stop at nothing to get what he wanted? And in due course, it would become a ruthless bourgeois who sooner or later would bleed the people dry, by putting into effect the laws of quick profit. He could do this by using simple words, for he had a vast experience of explaining things in a straightforward language that even a child could understand. But he had also learned in life that people only accept advice that reinforces the decision they have already made. And they don't listen to opinions that go against their desires. Nina might just be trying to blackmail him; she knew his ideas about black marketeers. Blackmail in order to bend him to her desires. And he was terribly tired of giving advice and making moralizing speeches that no one ever followed.

"He just wants to take advantage of you, and then he'll kick you out."

"So what am I going to do? I need a man."

She went into the house without being invited. That was normal; she often did so. She switched on the light and went to the living room. Aníbal followed her. Nina went and reclined peevishly on the only sofa. He chose to remain standing, next to the window, looking out at the turbulent sea below.

"You need a man who respects you, who'll always treat you well. If you bide your time, he'll turn up."

"Round here, there's no one. Only you."

"He'll turn up. You're still very young. Time's on your side. There are single men at Baía Farta."

"I don't want a fisherman. And it's a long way away. Why go so far just to get myself a fisherman?"

"Your father's a fisherman, and that's nothing to be ashamed of. He's one of the best people I know. Ask your mother whether she's not happy to be married to a fisherman."

"My mother's never known anything else. I got as far as fourth grade, so I know about other things. The world isn't just these hillsides and this sea. I'm sick of it."

He still had his back to her. Then he suddenly remembered he hadn't smoked the whole day. He had deliberately left his cigarettes behind at home, and he had only felt like one after lunch. He turned round to look for the packet, and he saw her, completely naked, lying on the sofa. He contemplated her for a few moments. Her only sign of modesty was her hand covering her pudenda. He lit a cigarette and took two quick draughts. He thought about the choices facing him. The first was to give her an earful, force her to get dressed, and kick her out, followed by a visit to Ximbulo to tell him what had happened. The second was to take off his shorts and mount her. He sniffed his right arm and recognized the smell of Sara. He sat down in a chair in front of her, gazing at her alluring young body. He spoke calmly, "These hills and this sea have something you are unaware of: peace. Over those hills, out in the countryside, there's war, and every day people are dying. And in the cities, there's another kind of war: some people trying to dominate and trick others, and many people dying as well. You'll only value this tranquillity when you lose it. That's how it is always. But it's no use trying to provoke me because I love my wife. I already know how pretty you are. Thank you for showing me your beauty. Now you can go."

She didn't move but stared at him with her liquid eyes. Aníbal continued to smoke and to appreciate Nina's body. Just as a painter admires his model, studies her in order to reproduce her on his canvas, so he thought.

"I want the first time to be with you. After that, I can go with Mateus."

"There isn't going to be a first time. I respect you too much for that, although it's not how you see things at the moment. And forget Mateus, he'll abandon you with a baby in your arms. Ask your mother, she'll tell you. The city is an illusion, and Mateus is a liar."

"I know, but I don't care anymore. I don't care about anything."

After some time, she got up. She pulled her skirt up over her legs, and he noticed the almost complete absence of pubic hair. Then she put her blouse on over her firm round breasts. She walked out of the door, from where she shouted tearfully, "Next time Mateus comes, I'm going with him, I don't care."

Aníbal remained sitting in his chair, looking out the window. It was dark now, and he could no longer see the ocean. All that could be heard was the hollow roar of the sea crashing against the rocks. Everything happens suddenly, everything that had been heralded before, was happening now, like some universal cataclysm. He got up slowly and went out to stroke Mussole's trunk, and then went back inside. He was very tired. The sleep-

344

less night and the kaxipembe had left him exhausted. He went to bed and fell asleep, dreaming of octopuses and Sara opening jar after jar of intense smells, and Nina lying naked on the altar stone of the Cuvale, ready to sacrifice her virginity.

6

He woke up as day began to break. Then he heard the crash of the tidal surge. He didn't feel like getting out of bed, for there was nothing he could do if the sea was so rough. But neither could he go on sleeping, so he got up, wondering how to fill the day. He washed and had coffee. He was going to smoke, but then remembered his cough. It was much better, because the night before he'd only had one cigarette. It was worth maintaining the discipline he had set himself. This reminded him of lunch. He went to see what he had in his rather scanty reserves. It must be time to go to Benguela to fetch his provisions. He had a little rice, some beans, and tins of meat and tuna. He immediately put the beans aside; they had to soak and then cook for a long time, and he couldn't serve them up for lunch. Maybe tomorrow. He'd make some rice with tuna. That would be the easiest. He found some leftover onions to fry up, but he didn't have any tomatoes. He'd make it even so. He decided to put the beans in the Tupperware that Sara had left behind. If they soak for a whole day, they'll cook more quickly tomorrow.

He sat down under the mango tree, contemplating the sun rising over the hills through its leaves. He sat there half-awake, allowing his thoughts to run freely. Suddenly, he got up and went to get his notepad and a pen. He wrote feverishly, "The human race is always looking back to the past in search of the lost trail of evolution. This is why Man doesn't look to the future and clings to what was (and what wasn't but he thinks was, or what he would like others to think was)."

He put the pad and pen on the ground and lay back, gazing at the sun. Later, he grabbed the notepad again and reread what he had written days before, finding it hard to make out the scribblings jotted down so frantically.

"The regimes inspired by the experience of the October Revolution constantly rewrite History. Not only in the better-known sense of altering information in accordance with the needs of the dominant group of the time, but in a subtler, more important way. This enables them to refuse to promote more radical modifications that might call into question previously held principles. If there is a change to be made, dictated by necessity, the change is not assumed as such; it is an 'adjustment' that emerges within the previous line of thinking, based on unchanging, sacrosanct principles, a piece of cloth that serves for any manner of clothing. Even if what is being done today flies in the face of what was done yesterday, it is merely an adjustment to new conditions. The regime is like the Pope: it never errs because it has never erred and never will. We must have blind confidence in it, faith in the leaders, the parties. They are like God. The funny thing is that people don't see that these atheist parties are the ones that have copied most closely the teachings of the Church. The rewriting of History, in this case, is to transform it into a straight line, prophetically dictated ever since they took power. It's the biggest kick in the shins dialectics has ever received, which is why Marx must be spinning in his grave in an underground dance. Poor old Marx obliged to dance such a lively samba."

He put aside his notepad because he heard Ximbulo's voice getting nearer. He was carrying the demijohns and was accompanied by Nina. They filled four of these from the tank, which was in fact emptier than he had thought. This reminded him he hadn't watered Mussole. He went to fetch his bucket and watered the tree, before Ximbulo's customary look of disbelief. But he didn't say anything; they had already talked about this, and he had to admit that the mango tree was growing well and might even give some fruit next year. Nina stood some distance away, next to her two demijohns, eyes on the ground. Was she ashamed of last night's scene? Aníbal didn't think so. It wasn't shame, for she didn't have problems with that kind of shame. Not even rejection. She was sulky and wanted him to see.

"I don't know whether we can take any more. The tank is very low. This water's enough for today's food. I needed some for making liquor, but I'll wait."

"Take some more, neighbour. The truck should be along today or tomorrow."

"And by the way, it's the twelfth today. You've got to go to Benguela to pick up your supplies. Don't forget."

"I'd noticed food was getting low. Let's see if the truck comes today or tomorrow."

"It won't come today," Ximbulo said. "I've still got a drop of liquor left. We didn't manage to finish it yesterday. If the truck comes tomorrow, we'll fetch more water."

Ximbulo picked up two of the demijohns, and he and Nina started to leave. Then the father remembered and, over his shoulder, said, "In three days, Mateus is coming to pick up the rest of the fish. Do you want him to bring you anything?"

Nina looked at Aníbal for the first time. Her look challenged him: See, you've only got three days. He pretended not to notice. He said, "If you can get him a message, a few onions and tomatoes would be useful. They don't always have them at the military store. All they have is tomato paste."

Ximbulo took his leave and set off. The little things Ximbulo ordered from Mateus for Aníbal were a way of paying him for the water. It wasn't the value of the things exchanged that counted, but the gesture. The same went for the kaxipembe he often offered him. If they added everything up, the water was worth much more. But friendship is always nurtured by the exchange of small favours, as important as the words that are exchanged.

Today is April twelfth, Wisdom thought. Not long now before the inevitable happens. Let's hope tomorrow is the last day of the surge. Then the prophecy foreseen in the convulsions running through Mussole's trunk will be fulfilled.

He swept and tidied the house and made lunch. From time to time, he would go and peer at the sea, looking for signs that the surge was lessening. But the waters were still breaching the reefs and crashing against the base of the cliffs. The occasional cloud passed overhead, though not dense enough to produce any rain. This year, he remembered, it had rained only once. The grass hadn't even sprouted on the hilltops, which happened when there was a lot of rain. And April was the last month when it might rain. In the interior, drought was tightening its grip, aggravating the suffering of people already driven to despair by war. The Cuvale, further south, must have settled around the few places where there was water, but the waterholes almost dried up with so many cattle and men using them to drink from. It was going to be a year of severe famine. Yet another one.

He had lunch in the shade of the mango tree, occasionally talking to it. It didn't reply, and it seemed that Mussole's spirit was sleeping again. He let the afternoon drift by, the notepad still next to him. From time to time, he would read one of the many passages written during his years of solitude, here or in the various wars in which he had participated. He knew them almost by heart. He picked up the pad and opened it at random. He read the reflection on the second page.

"Before the 1789 Revolution, there were three Estates in France: the nobility, the clergy, and the people, this latter including the bourgeoisie. Here, too, there are three Estates: the ruling bureaucracy, the black marketeers, and the people. Unlike

France, the forces that will seize power will not come from the Third Estate. Here, it is the black marketeers who are growing in the shadow of small enterprises that are more or less legal, active in the field of transporting people and goods, unequal trade with country people or small-time urban commerce, diversion of money and robbery, falsification of documents, accumulating capital, and establishing themselves as a ruthless class of entrepreneurs. Within the First Estate, there are also black marketeers, usually connected by family ties. When the surface appearance of utopia is no longer any use, they will shamelessly create the most brutal form of capitalism that has ever existed on Earth."

He went to bed as soon as the sun had set. For a long time, he lay listening to the sea, thinking about the octopus sheltering peacefully in its cave, waiting for calmer waters in order to sally forth and hunt. The octopus also belonged to the Second Estate: it had tentacles that reached everywhere, grabbing squid and unsuspecting smaller fish, in order to swallow them greedily. The bed smelled of Sara. He focused his spirit on the scents she had left behind. He inhaled them eagerly, forgetting the rough seas, only recalling in his mind the image of Sara slowly, very slowly emerging from the water in a universe of potent scents. He fell asleep.

7

The surge had clearly abated during the night. He got up and went to check through the living-room windows. Although the sea was pretty choppy, only the occasional wave washed over the reefs and it no longer had sufficient strength to break against the base of the cliffs. He could go diving again if it was absolutely necessary to catch a fish. He went to the kitchen and saw the beans soaking in the water. No, he didn't need to go diving; he had his day's meal. It would be better to wait until tomorrow, when the waters would be even calmer, even more so than usual. The sea also gets tired and for some time would be as languidly smooth as a mirror.

Midmorning, he heard the water truck negotiating the track over the hills. He lifted the lid of the tank and used the rest of the contents to water the mango tree. The driver drew up right alongside the tank, and they began the task of filling it.

"I'll go and get dressed," said Aníbal. "I need to go to Benguela."

The driver nodded. He continued, while Aníbal went and put on a more or less clean shirt and some trousers. He only remembered his shoes once he was outside. He dashed back inside to wash his feet and put some sandals on. He was so used to wandering around barefoot that he was once again about to forget to put his shoes on; he would have shown up in the city like some labourer. It had happened before, which only served to reinforce people's opinion on his fragile mental state. In the hall, he glanced at the mirror. He really was looking more and more like an Ethiopian.

He tried to flatten his hair but to no avail. When I get back from Benguela, I've really got to wash this mane three times, or even cut it beforehand. I can't even get a comb through it anymore.

The tank was full, and they set off for the city. Ximbulo must have heard the truck and be preparing to go and fetch some water, he thought to himself. There'll be kaxipembe later. The truck rattled along the track until it reached the paved highway. The driver was talking about the hardships of life in Benguela. The same complaints as always: lack of food, lack of clothing, potholed roads, lack of building materials for housing—he had a little house that was half-built, while he waited for a few sacks of cement in order to finish it—there were continual ambushes along the roads, especially at Canjala, which cut traffic links with Luanda. Aníbal just listened to these lamentations and didn't respond. Not that this concerned the driver, who simply wanted to be listened to, as he was talking to a former commander, even if an eccentric one, true, though one with real links to those who had the power to change things. He even said as much after a while. "You know what the situation's like, comrade, you should go straight to the top and explain what's happening, the people are suffering too much." Wisdom didn't think it worth explaining to him that it wouldn't resolve anything. The machinery of bureaucracy was arranged in such a way that even honest guys still in positions of responsibility didn't know how to take any initiative of their own.

They entered the Baía de Santo António and saw the salt pans with heaps of salt yellowing under the film of dust covering them. The salt wasn't sold commercially and remained there, growing yellow, because they were unable to organize an efficient system to transport it. Meanwhile, out in the country, there was a desperate need for salt, and the inhabitants were burning a special herb that contained tiny amounts of sodium chlorate as a substitute. And Luanda sometimes imported salt from overseas. "See that?" the driver was saying, and he knew what he was thinking. They took the road to Casseque as they entered the city. The adobe houses clustered at the base of the hills, sheltering refugees from the interior. The roofs were made from whatever material they chanced upon, awaiting the promised fibre cement sheets. Districts housing the displaced were expanding fast, their jobless inhabitants living off mysterious reserves.

The driver dropped him off at the barracks, where he stocked up with provisions, and Aníbal tried to speak to the commander. He wasn't there, but his substitute, a young lieutenant Aníbal knew from the war and who'd once been a member of his unit, was.

"The comrade captain has gone to Ganda, as there are problems there. Haven't you seen we've got no electric light? They've sabotaged the electricity cables again."

He hadn't noticed the absence of light. I went to bed early yesterday, that must be why. They were going to be without electricity for some time, which represented a huge problem for the city's inhabitants. Aníbal had no sympathy for the bureaucrats; they'd be without air conditioning in their offices, but apart from that, they always managed to get by. But for the people, it was a disaster: devoid of means to preserve food, having to queue interminably to purchase gasoline, which was always scarce, even though the country was a major producer.

"This month, we're low on supplies," said the lieutenant. "We're out of one or two products. Let's go and see what we can fix you up with."

He led him over to the warehouse and spoke to the person in charge. Two soldiers set about bagging up what food there was. There was no shortage of sugar, which was good, as Aníbal also gave some to Ximbulo to distill his kaxipembe. There wasn't much tinned food and nothing fresh, not a single onion. For him, the tins of tuna, sardines, meat, or sausages weren't really a necessity, because he had the fresh fish that he caught.

"So how do you feed the soldiers?" Aníbal asked the lieutenant.

"It's been hard. Rice and beans, sweet rice pudding, that's what they're eating. The soldiers are complaining, but they didn't send us anything last month. The boats never came, and the road is very unsafe. Two convoys of trucks got ambushed at Canjala and were forced to turn back. UNITA has increased its military activity ever since the last South African invasion. Now, Cunene and part of Cuando Cubango are under South African occupation. And from there, they can arm the groups in the interior. The war is more intense than ever. Not to mention the acts of sabotage."

The soldiers finished bagging up the rice, sugar, beans, flour, and macaroni and placed the sacks by the entrance to the warehouse. The lieutenant said, "I'll get a jeep to take you home."

"Wait," said Aníbal. "I've got to do something in town. I'll come and pick up my things when I finish, in a couple of hours."

"Well, take a jeep. I'll get you a driver. Then pick the stuff up and go on to Caotinha."

"It's not worth it, thanks. I'll walk. It's not far."

The lieutenant was amiable and insistent. But Aníbal wouldn't budge. He wanted the fewest possible favours. This was his strange pride, which Sara had talked about. Yes, that's what it was. He knew he was indulging in the most complete contradiction. What difference would an extra lift make? But the idea of a driver hanging around outside while he went about his business irritated him. On the other hand, he had no qualms about obliging the driver to take him all the way to Caotinha and then back on his own. And no driver would worry about that; it was an excuse for an outing, and these soldiers love to drive. And, what's more, fast. Putting many lives at risk: theirs and their passengers, along with those of the poor souls who happened to be on the road when they came along. He said goodbye to the lieutenant, who promised to have the vehicle ready for him in two hours' time.

He had lied: the health department wasn't close by. He set off on his walk, contemplating the changes that had been made in the city since the last time he was there. For the worse, they were always for the worse. The houses unpainted and without any plaster, many roofs in a clear state of deterioration, the potholed streets, the paving on the sidewalks broken, the empty shops, and queues of people waiting to be blessed with the chance of purchasing some product. Near the market, there was some sign of life, which he avoided and dodged past on one side. As he did this, he found himself in front of Honório's bar, its door half-closed. But Honório was inside and saw him pass. He rushed outside and called him.

"Long time no see, Commander! I've got some cold beer. Come and have one, because tomorrow I won't have any more cool ones, we've got no electricity."

He went into the empty bar. Honório went and got a bottle and poured it for him.

"Last night, the light went. So, this morning I put some bottles in the freezer, which still stays cold for some time. I need to make use of it."

"It'll be just one for me. I've got a few things to do."

"What have you been up to, Commander? Still out at Caotinha?"

"Yes, still there."

These Benguela people would never kick the habit of calling him "Commander." He was no longer one, and the rank had long disappeared from the army. But for them, Aníbal would forever be one of the commanders who entered the city at the head of the army that liberated Benguela from the South Africans. Honório looked him in the eye with some sadness, Wisdom thought. I must really look pretty wretched.

"The war is becoming more and more fierce. Those guys are crawling out of the woodwork with the South Africans here again. We need the commanders from the old days back. Aren't you thinking of returning to the army?"

"No way."

Honório shook his head in pity. He clearly wanted to ask him how he lived, what he did, but he didn't have the courage. They had, in fact, never been on intimate terms, as he was with António, for example. The bar owner changed the subject while Aníbal savoured his ice-cold beer.

"Life is getting more and more complicated. Now we've got no light, goodness knows for how long."

"It'll take time. It was sabotaged."

"Bastards! I hoped it was some sort of a breakdown. Don't those sons of bitches realize they're just fucking up the lives of the people even more? And then they say they're freeing ..."

Aníbal nodded in agreement. He was going to say everyone wants to free the people, that's all they think about, before they go and take a dump on them. But he restrained himself, preferring to drink his beer.

"Today there's no light. But if there was, it would still be about the same. Beer is delivered from time to time, but all the rest disappeared a long time ago from the market. How can I keep a bar going on just a trickle of beer? And everyone knows that a good bar depends on having beer on tap, not in bottles. But I haven't seen a barrel in years. As for other drinks, well, no chance! In days gone by, this bar was famous for its steak sandwiches. A steak in a roll or served on a plate with an egg on top. And lupin beans, peanuts, and fried whitebait and shrimp ... In short, everything that makes a good bar. Now, it's empty. There's no meat for steak sandwiches, and if there was meat, there'd be no bread, and as for eggs, no sign of those even in a hen's ass, and as for lupin beans ...What a fucking life!"

Honório wasn't a man for mincing his words, even with a bar full of customers. Maybe the residue of an education received from his Portuguese father, a country bumpkin, as the social elite of Benguela used to say in the old days. The country bumpkin had run away before independence, leaving his mixed-race son in charge of the bar. But the social elite also ran away at the same time, and they all mingled democratically on the ships taking people and their crates to Portugal.

Aníbal finished his beer and asked how much he owed. "You must be joking, Commander, I'm the one who invited you, and please have one for the road. It's always a pleasure to have you here." He declined the second beer, said a friendly farewell, and left. Honório accompanied him to the door and watched him walk away. Aníbal sensed his eyes on the back of his neck, turned round, and there was Honório watching him. He waved and went on his way. Yet another one who thinks I've gone bonkers once and for all. I even turned down a second beer in these times of crisis.

He arrived at the provincial health department for Benguela and went in. He headed straight for the office of the director, whom he knew from various other fruitless visits. If Sara had spoken to him, he might show greater diligence. He approached the secretary, but she was busy with a disabled man who was talking in an excited fashion. He was dressed in very worn military fatigues and was supporting himself on a pair of crutches. He had lost a leg. A mine, Aníbal thought to himself. The secretary merely listened to what the man was saying in Portuguese that was typical of someone from the east.

She raised her voice and interrupted him, "I've already told you twice, that's an issue for the Department of State for War Veterans. We are only concerned with health. The Department of State for Social Affairs may also be able to do something. It's there you've got to go."

"I've already been there, I've been to the Veterans, I've seen the Comrade Commissioner, I've been everywhere. It's always the same story: you've got to wait."

"We can't do anything. And there's no point in your talking to the Comrade Director. He's very busy and doesn't have anything to do with your problem."

The man shrugged, defeated. He turned and saw Aníbal. A ray of joy lit up his tired eyes. "Comrade Commander ... Comrade Wisdom!"

Aníbal didn't remember him; he just recognized his way of talking, which marked him as being from the east. A former guerrilla fighter, no doubt. The man propped himself on the table so as to free one of his hands, which he offered Aníbal, saying, "You don't remember me, muata. I'm Mukindo. I was in Zone C. I was with Commander Kudila."

And he looked at him, smiling. Then Aníbal remembered him because of his mention of the dead Kudila. Yes, a clever young fighter whom Kudila had taken to heart. How many years ago had it been? Well over ten. But now the former kid looked old, his thin face deeply lined. The war, with all its horrors, was standing there in front of him.

"How did you lose your leg?"

"A mine. In '79, in Cuando Cubango. They cut my leg off in hospital. I was there for a long, long time. Last year, the army sent me here, I don't know why. They haven't forgotten me; I still live at the barracks. I'm going around trying to get an artificial leg, but no one wants to give me one here. Is that how they treat veterans? My family's in Moxico, I can't even get there. Everyone gets an artificial leg—why not me? Am I going to be on crutches for the rest of my life?"

"I've already told the comrade that Health doesn't have anything to do with this," the secretary told Aníbal.

He was irritated by the self-important way she spoke, refining her voice in what she thought was how they spoke Portuguese in Lisbon. And she seemed to have more influence than the director. Carefully painted nails, expensive clothes, and nothing in her brains, he noted. He spoke in an abrupt tone, "I heard you. Is the director there? I want to speak to him."

She looked down, intimidated by Wisdom's reputation, said,

"I'll go and see," and went into the adjoining room. Not long afterwards, the director appeared, holding an envelope, the secretary behind him.

"Dr. Sara Pereira gave me this letter for you. I was just wondering how I would get it to you. But come in, come in."

Aníbal took the letter and put it in his pocket; he wasn't going to read Sara's letter there and then. He signalled for Mukindo to enter as well. The secretary was about to stop him but backed down when faced with Aníbal's glare. Mukindo hopped into the office. The director closed the door.

"Sit down, sit down. What can I do for you, Commander?"

"Firstly, the matter of this comrade here. He has been trying to speak to you, but the poker-faced policewoman next door stopped him. He's a former guerrilla fighter, and he's been fobbed off by one secretary after another. Who deals with artificial limbs and who can take charge of this?"

"Well, I really don't have—"

"I know you don't. But you're familiar with how things work and you can help him. Maybe by writing a recommendation to your colleague in Social Affairs or someone else. You're a member of the provincial government, comrade."

"Yes, I can do that. He should be evacuated to Luanda. It's much easier to get a prosthesis there. I'll do a letter right away."

He pulled out a card and wrote a few lines. He put it in an envelope and told Mukindo where he should go. "They'll resolve your problem there." Mukindo accepted the envelope as if it were gold. He got up from the chair and shook Wisdom's hand. His eyes were full of tears. "Thank you so much, Commander." Mukindo shook the director's hand and hobbled out of the room on his crutches.

"What are the chances of him getting a prosthesis?" Aníbal asked.

"There are many amputees. He's got more chance than others

because he's a former guerrilla fighter. I think they'll see to him in Luanda. If you know someone there . . ."

"The matter that's brought me here is the same as ever. I took Dr. Pereira to the refugee camp, and she was shocked by the general state of health of those people. She said she would speak to you. Apart from malnutrition, she noticed suspected cases of tuberculosis."

"She brought that up. In fact, between you and me, she took me to task. But we have neither the means, nor doctors nor material. I'll speak to the Red Cross, maybe they can give some more regular assistance. I promised Dr. Pereira that I would bring the Red Cross on board in this matter."

"So, when are you going to speak to them?"

"Today, tomorrow. I promise I'll try."

"Next time I come to Benguela, I'll come and hear how you got on."

He got up, impatient to read Sara's letter. How important was the message she wanted to send him? They'd said goodbye in the morning, and she was going to catch her plane. Only something really important would have made her write to him before leaving. And the letter would have stayed with the director for another month if he hadn't by chance remembered to go and speak to him. He said a hurried goodbye and tore open the envelope as soon as he was out of the office. He walked down the street, reading as he went. Sara was writing from the airport, waiting for her flight, in order to tell him she would never forget what had happened between them. That she would visit as soon as she could. It was indeed important, and she was right to send him a letter.

He saw Mukindo hopping along further down the street. He quickened his step and called him. The amputee stopped and waited for him.

"Look, I've remembered something. The director is sure they'll send you to Luanda. When you get there, it's going to be hard. No one knows anyone in that jungle. But I know someone who'll help you. Tell her I sent you. She's a doctor who knows Worldly, and he's a minister. She'll help you."

"Oh, that guy ..."

"I take it you don't think much of Comrade Worldly. Is that because of your time on the Eastern Front?"

Mukindo was probably a supporter of the Eastern Revolt and had infuriated Vítor for having pulled out of the revolt at the last minute, he thought. That was why he was surprised when the other man said, "We found that comrade when he was heading back to the Zambian border. He came out with this great tribalist speech about how the easterners should be in charge of things, and he was going to the meetings of the war council to talk about it. Full of talk and conviction, he spoke like a hero. I was the only one who disagreed. I didn't think tribalism would get us anywhere. In the end, he didn't join the rebellion. One day, in Cuando Cubango, I went to guard the airport because a minister was going to be flying in. He was the one who got off the plane, Worldly, an MPLA minister. He saw me; I accompanied him as a bodyguard. But he didn't want to talk about anything to do with the east for fear I might spill the beans about what he'd said. I didn't say anything. What was the point?"

This merely confirmed what he had always suspected. He could remember quite clearly Worldly's retreat to the border and the conversations they had had at the time. It always was a struggle between opportunists, and Vítor was an opportunist. And now he's a minister. He said, "If Dr. Pereira asks him, he'll do it for you. Even if only to ensure you keep quiet. And she will ask him. Just say I sent you."

He gave him Sara's address and insisted again, "Go and speak to her, you'll get your leg." Another handshake, and he had done his bit. He headed back to the barracks. Sara would help

Mukindo; he was more certain of that than he was of meeting the octopus next day. If Sara ever failed, then he might lose faith in everything. The world would be shrouded in darkness forever more. Her note to him was burning his leg, and he wanted to reread it. He would discover her scent once more. But he quickened his pace in a hurry to get home, to see his mango tree and his bay again. He would have plenty of time to reread her note, soak himself in her perfume and her promise to return.

8

The morning of April 14 began differently. He could gauge it by the colour of the sky, which was more luminous than ever. The sea was especially calm, and from the top of the cliff, he could see the rocky and sandy seabed. He could even make out the slim shapes of the fish as they swam among the stones and algae. The hills seemed more golden and stood out more clearly against the lustrous blue sky. Aníbal went and greeted the mango tree, which rustled its leaves. He placed his hand on the trunk and sensed the spasmodic convulsions of its sap. You're excited, Mussole. Today's the day, you know it. During the night, it had shed all its old leaves, which now lay on the ground. You've dressed in your best, you've only got fresh green leaves now, you're a beautiful young girl.

He had his coffee and resisted smoking a cigarette. He decided to clear the dead leaves from around the mango tree. If it had shed them, it wasn't so that they should spoil the surroundings. He swept the leaves into a hole he had dug some time ago, where he also threw the organic leftovers from cooking. Then he covered the hole with a thin layer of soil. With the remains of his food and the mango leaves, the ditch would soon be ready to accommodate another tree, which would grow still more quickly with the help of the natural compost. He hadn't yet decided what tree he would plant. A strangler fig would be the best, for it was sacred. But there weren't any in the region, so it would be hard to get a shoot. He had only ever seen one, the sacred tree of the Cuvale, much further south, beyond Dombe Grande. Maybe a kapok tree from Cabinda, which was also a sacred tree and inhabited by spirits. Still more difficult to come by a shoot. When the ditch was almost full, he would have to decide. It would be good to have two trees for Mussole's spirit to be able to choose her home. It would be a kind of game, she would change trees and he'd have to guess where she was hiding. He smiled at the idea. Mussole would enjoy playing hide-and-seek.

Then he remembered, But when is it that mango trees shed their old leaves? Is it at this time of year? Surely not. Nor did they ever do it suddenly, during the course of one night. Only through the special willpower of the spirits that inhabit them. This was yet another sign that the time had come. Mussole was getting impatient. Calm, keep calm, today's the day.

He prepared his hunting gear; he loaded his reserve harpoon on his belt. He picked up his two oxygen cylinders, checked they were working, all as it should be. He did the same with his special underwater flashlight. He was about to set off down the cliff when Nina called him. She was bringing two bottles of kaxipembe. Ximbulo had distilled some the night before, making use of the fresh supply of water. He put the bottles in the kitchen and brought out two sacks of sugar. "Give these to your father."

"Can I help you carry your things?"

He agreed and gave her his weapon and flippers, while he carried the cylinders. They climbed down the steep slope. She stood on the beach, watching him put on his flippers and then fix the cylinders on his back. As he was washing his goggles, she said, "Mateus should be here tomorrow. I'm going with him." Casually, just as she might say it wasn't going to rain anymore this season.

He adopted the same detached tone. "Have you told your parents?"

"No, of course not."

She lifted her skirt and entered the water. She lifted it high enough for him to see her perfect round buttocks. She stopped, the water round her waist, her back to him. Was she peeing or what? Might be. Maybe a spell to bind him to her. But when Nina left the water, Aníbal didn't give her the pleasure of asking her the reason for her gesture. And he wasn't going to dive anywhere near where she had peed, if that is what she had done. He said calmly, "Now take that sugar home. When I'm hunting, I don't like to be seen. All the more so today. Okay?"

She looked at him slowly. Then she turned her back and started to climb the cliff. From up above, she shouted, "I'll come back after lunch."

He didn't bother to answer, concentrating on the sea near the entrance to the cave. He entered the water, dived down to test the oxygen cylinders. Perfect. It couldn't be said it was the same as breathing fresh air, but it was bearable. He had read that the effect of decompression could be dangerous when one dived to great depths. In those cases, it was necessary to return to the surface in stages, so that one's blood pressure could adapt gradually to the lower ambient pressure. But it wasn't the case here, as he was only going to dive down eight or nine metres, something he could easily do even without cylinders. Of course, when he returned to the surface, his ears seemed to explode because of the lack of pressure. But nothing else happened. And with the cylinders, he didn't even have to return to the surface so fast.

He swam out toward the reefs, propelling himself with his feet alone. There were a lot of fish around today, possibly because they had been swept in by the waves. No, it must be the other way round: they had sought shelter behind the rocks because of the turbulence of the sea. And they hadn't yet found their way back out into the ocean on the right-hand side of the bay, or had decided that this bay, which had appeared at such an opportune moment, was a much pleasanter place than the high seas. Croakers, meagre, and sea bream mingled with barracudas. He also saw two or three giltheads and a shoal of bonito. The bay was overpopulated; it was just a question of choice. And he hadn't even got as far as the reefs, where the water was deeper and there were consequently many more fish. He suddenly noticed a shark, and in an instinctive gesture of defence, he pointed his harpoon at it. The shark looked at him, or seemed to be looking at him—he could never tell what was going on inside a shark's head—and then it turned to the right, uninterested. Or scared of him but too proud to show it. One day, he would kill a shark, just for the pleasure of it. Don't be stupid, he immediately thought. Am I going to follow the example of trophy hunters, who afterwards allow themselves to be photographed with one foot on the victim?

Sharks weren't dangerous in those waters. Ximbulo had told him that when he was a kid, he would dive off the pontoons keeping the trap nets in place and swim among them. They prefer fish and there's an abundance of fish, Ximbulo had said. He wasn't so sure, perhaps because he had read books about sharks. That they were attracted by blood and they would then attack whatever was in front of them. He recalled a film in which an underwater hunter was attacked by a shark because he was carrying a fish he had harpooned on his belt. The shark was attracted by the blood of the fish and tried to seize it. Along with the fish, it also came away with half the hunter's stomach. He never trusted them: those teeth were no joke. Angolan sharks are peace-loving, we all know, just like Angolan men are. But Angolans have been fighting wars for centuries, and over the last twenty years, not a day has gone by without people dying. That's why it's pointless believing in the pacifism of sharks.

He forgot the creature and contemplated the seabed. He was approaching the reefs, and some grouper appeared. There were enough varieties for all tastes. Today of all days, when I'm not here to hunt fish. All he had to do was shut his eyes and shoot, and he'd be certain to harpoon a fish. But like that, there's no enjoyment. It's got to involve some effort in order to be worth it. With Sara, there was no effort involved, he didn't even stalk his prey, the prey stalked him, and yet it gave him so much enjoyment that the mere act of remembering brought it all back. No, in that instance, it was different. The enjoyment came from having waited for so long, while knowing that it could happen at any time. The enjoyment came from the effort of waiting. Bullshit, with Sara, there was no prey, neither one hunted the other, I've no right to mix things up. Completely immersed in the water, his chest almost brushing the rocky seabed, he couldn't inhale the scent of Sara. But it was in his mind and it came when he recalled it.

To his left, he saw the sudden depression indicating that he was near the cave. The bed suddenly fell away, almost sheer, deepening from two to eight metres. He entered the depression and peered downwards. Today, the water was so clear that even with the nine o'clock sun still shining obliquely, he could see the bottom perfectly and the fish of all colours and sizes that inhabited it. A little to the left was the entrance to the cave between two gigantic rocks, which rose thirty metres above sea level. So what if the cave wasn't closed but were just a passage that provided access to Caotinha Bay under the cliff? It might be. Nature sometimes contained these unpredictable phenomena. No, it couldn't be. That would spoil everything. If a cave were open, a passage, then it wasn't a cave—it was a tunnel, and it couldn't be used as a refuge. And it had to be the refuge of the octopus. Otherwise, nothing would make sense.

Sara had cautiously suggested, "Maybe it's not a monster." She was afraid he'd be disillusioned once the hunt was over, or did she mean that the never-ending hunt had no raison d'être?

He didn't even attempt to speculate further on the root of her thought. Out of pride, of course. He knew, he felt it in every pore of his skin, that it was a monster, the same one that had challenged him when he was a child. He had spent his whole life preparing to combat it. And there had been no shortage of training opportunities, even extending to his being sent on a course by the high command at the best military academy in the Soviet Union.

The Soviets didn't know, nor did he at the time, but the course was not for him to learn how to direct soldiers and armoured troop carriers and artillery, to devise tactics using rulers and set squares. Only later did he understand the meaning of the training he had received, there and in North Korea before, to direct groups of guerrilla fighters. Every night, for nine months, they had shown him war films. Films of the Korean-Japanese war, and the Korean-American war. They would place bets at dinner: today is the film going to be against the Yankee imperialists or against the Japanese militarists? They would bet beer. And the funny thing was that the Yankees or the Japanese or the Korean reactionaries appeared in these films with their faces painted white, the faces of Korean actors smothered in talcum powder. In order to distinguish them, there could be absolutely no doubt in the mind of the spectator. The good guys had natural facial tones; the bad ones were white. The good guys had deep, luminous gazes, contemplating the future, and filmed from below so they could be perceived as the giants of justice. The bad guys had aloof, rancorous expressions, tight lipped, and filmed from the front so that all the villainy they harboured could be clearly seen. The good guys always won, but one of them, or a girl, had to die, so that they could see that the struggle involves sacrifices, but that everything is worth it, because the future is rosy and Daddy watches over us. He mocked the films but discreetly, just in case some companion were to send in a report denouncing his heretical ideas and his petit bourgeois nihilism. In the end, much later, he understood why he had had to endure nine months in North Korea, and it was so that he could today see his enemy painted white, the horrible marine monster with its thousands of tentacles. That was it: today he needed to be unequivocally Manichean, he the good cowboy, the octopus the bad Indian.

He swam down very slowly, propelled only by the slightest pressure of his back muscles. He watched the black hole that he could just make out. He had all the time in the world; he shouldn't rush things. He saw himself in the water through an effort of his imagination, moving in slow motion, as in the movies. And he wanted to appear to himself and to his enemy, as well as to all the aquatic creatures who were witnesses to the drama, as the calm, determined, justice-seeking hero who represents the strong arm of fate. There were no fish to be seen in the vicinity of the hole. This reinforced his certainty that the fish sensed the proximity of the octopus and kept away from its lair. It only emerged at night in order to hunt. That was why they had not yet met, although he had once sensed its presence. And on the other occasion, more than thirty, almost forty years ago. It wasn't by chance that the octopus had left its den forty years ago. It emerged for the sole purpose of making itself known. And again a second time, when he was fleetingly aware of it, merely to confirm its presence and lure him in. Nothing in nature happened by chance: men were the ones who didn't understand the deep motives and called them fortuitous twists of fate. In nature, there are only fateful occurrences, he thought. And men stubbornly seek to operate in ways that are contrary to such fatefulness, until they stupidly destroy the planet.

He was one metre above the crack in the rock and three metres away from it. His ears began to feel the pressure of the water. The seabed was especially white, just sand. As if the octopus, every night, cleaned the entrance, sweeping it with its thousand tentacles, clearing it of algae and stones in order to leave an area of pristine sand in a semicircle some six metres wide. He descended until his feet touched the ground. It was a strange sensation to be standing under the water and looking at the entrance to the cave. He tried to walk toward it, very slowly, but it was exceedingly hard. At each instant, his feet would leave the ground, and he had to wave his arms upwards. With his flashlight in his left hand and his weapon in his right, it wasn't an easy thing to do. He was now a metre away from it. Are you there, you disgusting beast? Are you cowering in fear against the rock, hoping I don't see you, or are you quietly readying your suction pads? Don't disappoint me, I'd rather you were waiting to pounce, like a Comanche with his axe at the ready. I'm the sheriff here to do justice, against those who killed my sweetheart, or my parents, in order to add to their collection of scalps. Don't you recognize me? You knew I was coming, that's why you're painted white, the white of fear, but also the white of hatred and death.

He took a final step forward, and he was at the entrance. He flicked on his flashlight, and the yellow ray swept over the glimmering walls of quartz, which were reflected in bluish hues. The chamber was about two metres wide and three in height, and it was empty, absolutely empty. He flashed his light around once more, trying to overcome his disappointment. It couldn't be. Wasn't the octopus there? So many years dreaming of this moment, yearning for it and fearing it. And in the end, was it all for nothing? He felt his heart beat more strongly, because he caught sight of a hole above him, almost in the roof of the cave. There was another inner chamber. But supposing what he feared were true, and this chamber provided access to Caotinha, under the cliff? No, it's a cave; it's got to be a cave. He kicked with his flippers and glided up the rock face until he reached the hole. He first introduced his weapon into the hole, which was only just wide enough to allow him to pass through. Then he inserted his left arm with the flashlight. And he remained parallel to the ground, in order to see ahead. It was a kind of narrow tunnel, which widened out further ahead.

He penetrated the hole with caution, swimming straight ahead. As he advanced, he began to take in the cave in front of him. He reached the end of the tunnel, and his flashlight revealed that he was in a chamber measuring some twenty metres in length and five metres in height. But it was full of water, so the roof of the cave must be below the waterline. He made his way into the cave, waving his flashlight around somewhat at random. Suddenly he saw it, above and to his right, hanging there, suspended. His instinct hadn't deceived him: the enemy was there.

He leaned against the left-hand wall of the cave, so as to give himself as much space as possible. The octopus was too far away for him to shoot. The harpoon line was only ten metres long. Aiming his weapon, he looked at it, all his senses in a state of tension. The world stopped, his ears no longer buzzed, Sara hid away in a corner of his memory. The monster waved its tentacles away from its body and grew ever larger. It wasn't painted white; rather it looked more like a reddish black, with the pink dots of its suction pads. The creature then shook its tentacles and began to descend. Do you want to put yourself on the same level as me? How are you going to attack? From the front, like an equal? From above, wouldn't you have the advantage, because it would be harder to shoot you due to the gravitational pull underwater? But does gravity count underwater? I don't know, nor do I care. You're still a long way off, come and attack me, I'm waiting for you. I came to meet you. It was I who took the first step. Now you take the second, surely that's only fair.

The octopus continued to float downwards, shaking its tentacles more rapidly, so that they appeared to occupy the whole cave. It stopped level with him, without touching the bottom.

Aníbal straightened himself until he was almost standing. He could now clearly see its round head and eyes. His weapon was pointing at it, held only in his right hand. As the water was completely still, it wasn't hard to keep his weapon straight, his finger on the trigger, nor did he have to use much strength to sustain it. Come nearer, come on. He calculated the distance, which wasn't at all certain under the water, as he had learned from experience. It seemed to be within reach. But he decided to wait; he couldn't waste his first shot. If he missed, he wouldn't have time to reload the weapon with his spare harpoon, before being grabbed by a tentacle. You're not scared. Otherwise you would have squirted out your ink to darken the water. And you're not ready to attack either. Otherwise you would have pissed your red liquid. What are you waiting for? You want me to be the one to advance. That's not fair, all you did was to take a few tiny steps forward with your clumsy leggy arms. But really that would be too much to expect: when were the Indians in those cowboy films ever loyal, or the Vietnamese, or the reactionary militarists? I'm the good guy in the story, which is why I've got to take the initiative again. You don't have the courage for that.

He inched forward about a metre from the rock. While he was doing this, very slowly, he conjured up an image from his childhood in Luanda: in a sudden flash, he saw the body of a Black man lying on the asphalt being beaten by white and Black policemen. He wasn't a thief, he was told later, but a young worker who had complained to his boss because he had had three days' worth of wages docked. The boss called the police, and they began to beat him, pushed him out into the street, and continued to beat him there. Aníbal had been quite small, maybe only five years old, and he saw the bloodstained body lying in the road and four men bludgeoning him. This was the fleeting vision that came to him, just like the very moment when he gave the order to attack in the battles he had been through in his life.

He knew, the vision always came in a flash of light, a lightning strike and never in slow motion, as in a movie.

The octopus must have guessed, because it made a slight movement upwards. By this time, the harpoon was shooting through the water to pierce it underneath the eyes. The cave became suddenly dark, with the liquid released by the creature. All Aníbal could feel was the pressure on the line attached to his weapon. He thought about reloading it with his spare harpoon, but in order to do that, he would have to let go of his flashlight because he didn't have three hands. The octopus could see in the darkness, but he couldn't. Nor could he put the flashlight in his mouth and grip it with his teeth, because of his breathing tube. This was an empirical situation, he thought just as he had before engaging in combat, and in guerrilla terminology, this meant a complicated situation. He still felt the weight of the octopus on the end of the line. As long as he could feel it, all was well, because it was trying to get away. When he could no longer feel it, that was when it could be bad, because it meant an attack might be imminent. He tried to control his panic within reasonable limits. He should have found a way of attaching the flashlight to his head, like miners do. He would then have had both hands free. But it was too late now; all he could do was to wait and see. He remembered his dagger, which he always wore on his leg. Holding the flashlight in his left hand, he managed to pull out his dagger. It wasn't very easy to use it in the current conditions. He switched the flashlight to his right hand, which now held this as well as his weapon. His left hand was now free to use the dagger, his weaker hand for such an occasion because, to make matters worse, he wasn't left-handed. Better than nothing. At that moment, he felt the pressure slackening on his weapon. Was this the attack?

Pressure stopped completely. He tried frantically to point the flashlight down the length of the line, but he couldn't see more than two metres. Beyond that, everything was dark, a kind of dull, bloody liquid. He would only see the octopus when it was on top of him. For the moment, he had no thoughts, nor even a feeling of panic. He awaited the inevitable. How long did it last? He had lost all sense, but he sensed he had been there a long time. He had little experience of swimming on compressed air, but now he began to feel breathless. The cylinders must be near their end; he had to get out of there. And then he suddenly understood. The octopus was no longer tugging at the line because it was dead. It wasn't because it was preparing its assault; it was because it was lying on the sea floor. He made for the tunnel on his back and once again felt pressure on the line; of course, he was dragging it along. He swam into the tunnel, overcoming the resistance the creature's body put up as it bumped along the seabed. He got to the first chamber and pulled the line toward him. He then saw the shapeless mass on the end. He swam down the cave and out into the open. The octopus followed obediently. He swam up to the surface, all the time feeling he was running out of air. Fortunately, the line was long; he didn't have to haul the creature up before reaching the surface, taking the tube out of his mouth and breathing. That's when his ears popped. But he almost failed to notice this, so busy was he taking deep gasps of fresh air.

He swam toward the beach, sensing through the juddering of his weapon, that he was dragging the octopus along the bottom. He reached the sands and stood up, freeing himself at once from the empty cylinders. He left his weapon on the sand, tossed his flashlight down with it, and lay down on his back, breathing in the sea air. The octopus had remained in the water, on the end of the line. He didn't want to think about it; he didn't want to pull it out. All he wanted to do was breathe. And rest.

For a long time, he lay sleepily enjoying the sun, allowing his thoughts and memories to flow, without ordering them. He began to feel hot and sat up on the sand. He took off his flippers. He looked at the water. He seemed to make out a dark stain and a shoal of fish. He got up and walked toward the water. He had to pull the creature out and remove the harpoon. He pulled on the line and the octopus appeared, first a round mass and then its tentacles all bunched together, turned toward the sea. Dozens of tiny fish flocked around, nibbling it. He pulled it out of the water and then saw that it was an insignificant little octopus, not the marine monster he had fought against. He easily pulled the harpoon out of the blubbery mass. He spread the tentacles out with the shaft. The distance from the tip of one tentacle to the tip of the tentacle at the other extreme can't have been more than one and a half metres.

He sat down again, looking at the creature. A tiny ripple occasionally reached it and caused the tentacles to stir. It could be an illusion, but the octopus seemed to be shrivelling up in the sunlight before his eyes. It looked like a faded flower, a welwitschia from the desert of Namib. And ugly, he thought to himself. He never should have taken it from its element: an octopus belongs to the sea. With his foot, he nudged it into the water. It remained floating, its tentacles all tangled, nibbled at by fish and crabs. I didn't kill you out of hatred, he told the remains of the creature. I just killed you. Was it death that made you shrivel, or was it the thirty or forty years it took me to kill you? Today, you're not a monster, but merely the body of an insignificant octopus, certainly the largest in these waters. But you're still a tiny, insignificant octopus. So many years, so many years ...

He grabbed his things and started to climb the path. Halfway up, he turned and looked down. The waters were seething frantically. The fish and crabs were finishing off the octopus. Maybe the shark was joining in the feast as well. He climbed back up to his house, exhausted. He knew he had aged that morning. Nothing would ever be the same as it was before. The octopus would no longer be there. He would go on diving and occasionally enter the cave, waiting for it to come back. An act of fate had been fulfilled, yet another, but he felt no pride. The mango tree rustled its leaves in greeting. He didn't respond to its call and went into the house.

9

He threw himself onto the sofa in the living room. He didn't make any lunch, nor did he even think about eating. He lay there a long time, empty of any thoughts. He felt completely and utterly drained. He remembered the kaxipembe and struggled to his feet to go and fetch a bottle. He drank straight from the bottle, making a face as he did so. The first few drops were always horrible, because of the taste of burnt alcohol. That then passed, and the next ones tasted better. He returned to the sofa, bottle in hand. He let time pass, taking occasional slow sips. The effect of the kaxipembe would soon be felt and give him the peace of indolence. Only the indolent are happy, they content themselves with the little they manage to obtain, he thought. Thirty years ago, it was a huge monster; today it was a shrivelled-up little octopus on the sand; and now it's just a few shreds of skin and flesh. He drank again. He was still far from feeling at peace.

At that point, Nina entered the house. He was aware of her approaching the sofa. Through half-closed eyes, he noticed the colour of that eternal blue skirt, much worn but always clean. She stopped in front of him, without saying a word. She just stood there eyeing him. He didn't move his eyes, but he had already lost the little peace he had gained. The blue skirt shimmered in front of him. Like the red rag in front of the eyes of a bull. He got to his feet and placed the bottle, which was still almost full, on the table.

"Come to the bedroom."

He led the way, she followed. He took off her blouse and tossed it on the floor. Her young breasts blossomed, challenging him. With one stroke, he pulled down her skirt. Nina stood there, completely naked, and instinctively defended herself by covering her pubis with her hands. He pushed her toward the bed. He fell on top of her, opened her legs, still hesitant in their parting, and penetrated her. He didn't do so brutally, but merely with firmness. She screamed as he deflowered her. And then she was quiet, allowing him to get on with it by himself. He finished and stayed on top of her, almost asleep. Then, for the first time, he fondled her firm breasts. He felt no palpitations in her breasts that might show any desire. He kissed her lightly on the lips and lay down beside her. His hand descended over her smooth belly. Then she spoke, "It wasn't any good, after all. It just hurt."

Aníbal felt he should do something. He knew what had been missing and what was missing now. Giving her some tenderness, so as to erase the initial bad impression that would accompany her for the rest of her life. But he was too tired. Not even her youthful body excited him now. The hand on her belly conveyed no heat; it merely caressed her mechanically, something owed her as an afterthought.

"See? I'm not the only one with a right to be disappointed. You also have a right to disillusion, and it's the only true right we have."

"I didn't understand you. But you weren't talking to me, were you?"

"You're right. I never talk to others."

They lay there, side by side, his hand paused on her belly. For a long time. Then she got up, looked at the bed, and said, "There's blood on the sheet."

He didn't reply. Nina must know that's normal, or hadn't she been told? He felt he should give her an explanation, a bit of a talk, not to teach her anything but just to establish some kind of human contact. She put on her blouse and skirt. She stood there for some time, contemplating him, no doubt waiting for something more. A word of affection, at least. He didn't move.

"Tomorrow, I'm going with Mateus."

She left the room. He was aware of her slamming the front door. You're just going to ruin your life, he thought. There's nothing I can do.

Some considerable time after she had left, he felt like a drink. He saw the two drops of blood on the sheet that she, herself, had washed so often. She was going off with the black marketeer, and she would never have to wash the sheet with her blood on it. He pulled it off the bed and threw it into a corner. He had another clean one, and he'd change it later. He went into the living room and drank from the bottle. He flopped onto the sofa again, now drinking more quickly, seeking some peace.

He had nearly finished the second bottle when he heard a car pull up by the tree. He didn't even check to see what time it was, but it must be nighttime. Sara? This mad idea imbued him with a residue of lucidity. What a state she's going to find me in. The car started up again. Someone opened the front door. He panicked. Sara couldn't see him like this. But his thoughts dimmed again because he heard Marília's voice. "Still in your shorts at this hour?" Stupid, he was always in his shorts. That's just talking for the sake of talking.

"Haven't you eaten anything?"

"I don't feel like it."

He had made a huge effort to reply, and his voice sounded gruff. He remained in the same position, his eyes closed.

"Do you want me to make you something to eat?"

"Fuck."

"What?"

"Leave me alone."

She saw the almost empty bottle next to the other one. She sniffed it and made a face.

"What a lovely state you're in. Kaporroto!"

"Leave me alone."

"If you don't want to see me, tell me. That's no way to receive people."

"Beat it, then."

"You're drunk, you don't know what you're saying. The kaporroto was bad for you."

"So what? Are you going to lecture me?"

"That's not my intention."

"So beat it, then."

"Look, I will. And I won't come back."

She went to the door. Waiting, maybe, for him to ask her to stay. Just as Nina had done in the bedroom, already dressed, with one last hope of tenderness. He was empty and tired, incapable of thinking about the needs of others. Marília, her hand on the doorknob, said, almost tearfully, "Am I going on foot? I got a lift and the car went on to Baía Farta. I can't go out there like this. It's dark."

"You turn up here as if you had a room booked at a hotel. Now deal with it however you can. The hotel's closed."

He was drained from having talked so much. He swore to himself, I'm not opening my mouth again. Talking kills me. He sensed Marília coming closer again.

"Has something happened?"

He didn't answer. She sat down in the chair. She didn't say anything for a long time, and he felt at peace again. He forgot she existed. But then he heard her voice again.

"Has something happened? What was it?"

He didn't answer. He was furious at her for depriving him of his tranquillity again. But too weak to show his anger.

"Can I do anything for you? Some food for example?"

"Yes, you can. Die."

She jumped up. She almost screamed, which showed the level of her despair, for Marília was normally very calm.

"I'm going to your room. Sleep here on the sofa if you want, I don't care. But I've had enough of your foul-mouthed behaviour. Anyone would think you're a drunken old souse."

And she took herself off to the bedroom. Making a supreme effort to think clearly, Aníbal remembered he hadn't put a clean sheet on the bed. Did Marília know where he kept them? She might see the dirty sheet on the floor and wrap herself in it. The sheet that still preserved Sara's scent, and now had Nina's drops of blood. Too bad, she'll find a clean one. Everything was happening suddenly, it was the foreseen cataclysm, what could he do? He managed to stretch out his arm to the bottle, tip it up, and finish the rest of the kaxipembe. He dropped the bottle and lost consciousness, with the light still on.

He woke up as the morning light flooded into the room. He tried to get up and stumbled over, falling to the ground. His head ached, and he felt sick. He was puzzled to find himself in the living room. He saw the two empty bottles. Dammit, I had a skinful. He got up again and stumbled toward the bathroom. He noticed the half-open door to his bedroom and peeped in. Marília was sleeping in his bed, on top of his mattress and in her underpants. He admired her body, golden brown in the morning light. He washed, and feeling sick, he vomited into the lavatory. Then he went and drank water. He felt better and drank some more. He had a general burning sensation in his insides. And he felt dehydrated. He drank another glass of water. He knew that until he had eliminated all the toxins, the dryness and nausea wouldn't stop. He put some water on to boil for coffee. A good strong coffee would help. He opened the front door and looked at the mango tree. Mussole wasn't shaking her leaves. She looked even smaller, all bowed down over herself. That was the impression he got because of the early morning half-light.

He went and made coffee. He drank two cups and left the rest for Marília when she woke up. Then he remembered, Yesterday, all I had was coffee, nothing else. But he wasn't hungry, only nausea and dryness in his stomach. He drank some more water. He sat down on the front step and looked at the mango tree, waiting for some signal. Marília woke up. He was aware of her going to the bathroom. She appeared soon afterwards, fully dressed. She was wearing a loose blouse with a flowery pattern and a white skirt. He hadn't noticed the blouse yesterday; it was very pretty. She had dolled herself up for him. Today she had a saddened air, with rings under her eyes, which were proof she had had a bad night. He spoke softly, "There's coffee in the kitchen."

She went and got some, and he got to his feet. He leaned on the kitchen doorpost. When she had finished her coffee and was preparing to light a cigarette, Aníbal said, "I was horrible yesterday, and I apologize. I had no right to treat you like that."

He saw her eyes come alive. Marília was rapidly preparing herself for reconciliation. But she waited for him to continue. Her self-esteem couldn't allow her to surrender so soon. She would forgive but in her own time. He was supposed to explain the reasons behind his behaviour before anything else; he was supposed to take her in his arms, speak loving words to her, after which they would end up in bed, the past definitely behind them. Wasn't that how it went in the movies? He spoke again, as before, in a very gentle tone, "The way I said things was unkind, but in its essence, I meant what I said. It's over, Marília. Please don't come back again."

She looked down, no doubt seeking to hide her disillusion. She took a nervous drag on her cigarette. She left the kitchen, swerving past him to avoid his body. Once outside, she smoked again and tossed her barely smoked cigarette onto the ground.

She crushed it carefully, in silence. She glanced quickly at Wisdom and started to walk back along the track in the direction of the highway. Without turning back. And she didn't even ask why, he thought. He stood watching her walking away down the track, with such a lightness of step that she didn't even raise the slightest cloud of dust. Her blouse gave colour to the track and the yellow hillsides, now bathed in sunlight. Flowers fluttering gracefully, and with pain. Something of his carefree past accompanied those flowers, a past of laughter and sensual pleasures, innocent games and half-true, half-imagined stories told. With Marília's mischievous bursts of laughter.

Epilogue

He hugged the trunk of the mango tree and caressed it with his hand. The sap was not flowing, the leaves didn't seem so green and tender as the previous morning, but it retained its scent and its low purring, which indicated life and pleasure.

"Are you sad? You seem quiet and motionless just as you did before Sara came. Yesterday was April fourteenth, the anniversary of the death of Mussole and of the Hero, and you were happy. I know, the Hero went to his burial, and all the speeches they dumped on top of him, killed him for good, and one day, he'll no longer be remembered. Such is the injustice of men. As for Mussole, I did what I could. I planted you so that you could receive her spirit. Did I leave something out?"

The mango tree didn't answer. Could it be because of the octopus or because of Nina? Or Marília? The spirit was slumbering again. Perhaps it would be like that for years, while it waited for some new universal cataclysm. And yet he knew that he would go on watering the mango tree every day, caressing its trunk and talking to it, as he grew ever older and weaker, more unbelieving, too, in the hope of awakening the spirit of the eastern savannahs—the chanas—that dwelt at rest within it.

THE TEMPLE
(From JULY 1991)

I

Thirty years.

In a person's life, that's enough to produce a load of kids. Complete a degree, lead a stable life. For a soccer player, it's nearly the end of his career. For war, well, that's just too long.

During the final years of his period of residence in Europe, he became really annoyed by the endless question: But when is that war going to end? He also felt like asking the same question to whoever was qualified to give an answer, and he had even done so, but in this case, it was different. What he didn't accept was that Europeans should come and lecture to him. They had once fought a war that was even called the Thirty Years' War. And another was called the Hundred Years' War, which must be a world record. So they shouldn't come and present themselves as experts in pacifism, just because there hadn't been a proper war in Europe since the bloodshed of the middle of the century. What they had learned to do was wage wars far from home, dumping all their shit into other people's backyards. And there were European countries, nowadays considered second rate because they had been cast adrift east of Eden, which couldn't wait to tear each other to pieces in homegrown conflicts. No, Europeans didn't have lessons to teach anyone, not least because the thirty years of war had largely, or mostly, been caused by them.

But the war was finally over. And he had been preparing for the peace for a long time. He started off by getting involved in small-time business ventures. He became an intermediary for medium-sized Belgian, French, or Dutch firms seeking to sell their products or technology. As he was an old friend of important leaders, especially Vítor Ramos, a long-time buddy of his, he managed to push through his first business deals. Little things, because, apart from anything else, the firms didn't have much faith in his abilities. But with his first successful outcomes, his reputation began to grow. He visited Angola more and more often in order to push through ever more important deals. He never got involved in politics, he was everyone's friend, all doors were open to him. All he had to do was to open the first one, Vítor's, and then he had access to whoever he wanted. He would talk a lot about soccer and music, maybe play a few tunes on his guitar to make people relax. In the middle of the banter, which was by now all very lively, "My friend, tomorrow I've got to talk to you about a thing I've got going, not now, man, work is work, whiskey is whiskey, a little thing, but something I'd like to seal, you know what it's like to earn a living, and life over there in Europe isn't easy, everything costs the earth, see if you can get me an audience tomorrow, not now, that'd be annoying, you're having fun here, family and friends around you, I'm not going to talk to you about work in your own home, but, well, if you're really sure, it's about that little matter I talked to you about some time ago, we're waiting for a decision from you, of course we know it was open to public tender and there were other bids, but ours was obviously better, it's more advantageous for the country, in fact the country's progress is the only thing we're interested in, so everything is waiting on your decision, it's enough for you to say that your preference is for our firm and that's it, we'll do the rest, but of course, it hasn't yet been settled because the director of your department told me yesterday that the matter's in your hands, so you decide tomorrow, that'll be cool, man, that'll be fine, let me play you that little samba we used to dance to in Lisbon, I bet you remember, you going out with Ermelinda, and me after Joana, that's right, the girl from the firemen's ball you ended up screwing, you old rogue, there wasn't a local chick who escaped your clutches, you must have flooded that country with little coffee-coloured kids." And in this way, his friends ended up settling issues in favour of the firms he represented.

He had started this seven years ago. More recently, he only got involved in bigger deals and turned down the little firms he had begun with. Now he was swimming among the sharks and received great big portions of game fish; the occasional sardine was no longer enough for him. Of course, his affairs now involved other risks. Because friends were no longer happy with a bit of music and friendly chat, with recollections about the good old days. When it came to these big business deals, his friends also had to be prudent, in case they got found out by the people, that ungrateful crowd, who regarded them all as corrupt and thieving. To protect themselves, his friends demanded special conditions not only for the projects, which needed to be well planned and minimally trustworthy, but for themselves. They ran the risk of being hurriedly rushed into retirement if they were found to be favouring the firms he represented. And these special conditions no longer involved a trip to a luxury nightclub in Paris or Brussels, all expenses paid, or a fortnight's holiday in the Alps for the family to learn to ski. They wanted other special conditions that wouldn't melt away under the sun in Switzerland. He had to share his commission. But in spite of this, he was earning a lot of money. He earned ten times more in one year than in the whole of his previous life. He was well prepared for the peace everyone was waiting for. And it came just in time because he was beginning to feel the gusts of racial intolerance blowing through Western Europe, stemming from its perceived future as a global power.

Peace found him now living back home. He bought a villa paid for in foreign currency, in the Alvalade district, not as big as he would have liked, and it didn't even have a swimming pool, but it was enough to start with. He had to pay a lot of money for it, a scandalous amount, but there was no other way. It was harder to find a house in Luanda than it was to find water in the Namib Desert. Taking advantage of the recent lifting of bureaucratic restrictions, he registered his import-export firm. Now he needed to choose the products and technologies he wanted to introduce into the country. Thinking randomly about what he could sell overseas. That was a secondary consideration for the time being as the country needed to import everything and wasn't producing anything for export. On the other hand, this was a transitory state of affairs, and he was making a list of things he might sell overseas at competitive prices. Torch ginger, for example. It was an old idea of his that came from his having seen the market for tulips in Holland. He could even take advantage of that writer's crazy idea about the east of Angola being torch ginger's birthplace, giving the flower mythological significance. Publicity could be based on myths, flowers along with Chokwe masks, allusions to the Lunda Empire, that kind of thing. By the time some son of a bitch of a botanist turned up proving the plant was from somewhere else, even from another continent, the thing would have stuck in people's minds; it would be just another myth. And the myth could make a healthy profit. What a lucky fit of madness had gripped the writer, who was probably gnawing fishbones now that his books weren't selling. The idea was going to make him fat, he who only swam with sharks and no longer knew what it was like to gnaw a fishbone.

The genius of an entrepreneur lies in sniffing out money concealed in other people's ideas, he thought, shaking the ice cubes in his glass of twelve-year-old whiskey. What a devil of a place! This must be the city with the highest consumption of twelve-year-old whiskey in the world. Only the other day, a bureaucrat he invited home for a drink in order to push through a business deal, on seeing the bottle he was opening, a good whiskey that would have made many a middle-class European's mouth water, frowned and commented, "It isn't a twelve-year-old one, is it?" What a bastard! A guy who's little more than an office boy, playing the smarty-pants. Upstarts like this would drop out of sight once the market economy got underway: the price of whiskey would get so high that these pencil-pushers would show their little asses just to get a sniff at the shoddiest brand of new whiskey. Blessed be the market economy, for it'll keep people in their proper places, the cook in the kitchen, the servant cleaning lavatories, and the magnate on his yacht. He didn't have a yacht yet, but he was on his way.

He looked at his watch: Vítor was late. They'd arranged to go over to Viana, where a nightclub had opened that was getting a reputation for the quality of its service, and above all because there wasn't another one in Luanda. He had been there before and had to acknowledge that by European standards, it was of the seediest kind. He suspected that Vítor had a stake in this nightclub, but he didn't ask him. One doesn't ask about such things. He saw the glint in the other man's eyes when he spoke about the place, and that was enough. And if they bowed and scraped to him at the entrance, it would be hard to distinguish where the obligations due to a minister ended and those to their boss began.

The doorbell rang. He jumped up from his armchair to open the door; it must be Vítor. But no, it wasn't, it was Judite and her boyfriend, Orlando. His daughter kissed him affectionately.

"We decided to drop by and see how you are, Father. Were you on your way out?"

"Actually, I'm waiting for Vítor Ramos so we can head out together. But that's no problem, make yourselves at home. Now that you've come to see me for once, I won't kick you out, not even to receive the Pope."

The couple settled down on the sofa in the living room. He served them drinks. Judite was still a beautiful young woman, now thirty years of age, and he was very proud of that only daughter of his. They seemed very much in love, forever holding hands. Orlando felt a bit awkward; it was the first time he had come to visit him at his home. They had met each other only twice before, once at the airport and the second time at Sara's house, where Judite still lived with her mother. He decided to tease him, as a way of breaking the ice.

"So, when's the wedding?"

"What kind of a joke is that, Father? Have you gone all old-fashioned now, with stories of marriage? I'm no longer of an age to turn up with a sprig of orange blossom. Or are you after a bride price?"

He laughed. His daughter always had an answer for everything. A doctor brought up alone by her mother, an independent spirit. But they still got on like two friends. There hadn't been any other way to foster a different kind of relationship. Orlando appeared to relax, for he chipped in, "In fact, we've already talked about it. I would like children, but Judite isn't interested in that kind of conversation. Do you know how she dealt with the question? She just said, 'Go and get us a house.' At the moment, I still live with my parents, because I haven't managed to find an apartment. And she lives with her mother. If we only get married when I get an apartment, it's not going to happen this century. You know how hard it is."

"This house is big enough for you. I live on my own, and I'm not thinking of getting married."

"Don't even think about it, Father. We're fine as we are. So let's change the subject. Or are you now so old that you want a daughter to make you your little bowl of pap?"

"Wow! I'm not old yet. I'm not even fifty-five. But the house is big. There's enough room for everyone. Find another excuse not to get married, Judite."

"Okay, I don't want to get married, and that's all there is to it. We're fine as we are. As for children, we'll see later, when the situation improves. It's all very difficult now, all the more so with children."

"Others do it," said Orlando.

"That's their choice."

He noticed the conversation was beginning to irritate his daughter, which made him think it must have been an exhaustively debated topic between the young lovers, so he changed the subject, for fear it might provoke one of those annoying arguments between them. He deliberately turned to Orlando, a tall thin fellow with a wispy beard that made his chin seem even more pointed. Judging by his facial lines, there was probably some remote white blood flowing in his veins, for his appearance was fairly typical of a traditional Luanda family.

"So how's your work going?"

"You know how it is, same as ever. They are now going to create some new private banks. So there will be some changes in my prospects. But I'm not thinking of leaving the National Bank for the time being."

Orlando was an economist. From what he had heard, he was competent and had a future. He must be the same age as Judite, and they had been sweethearts for a long time. He suddenly realized he didn't know anything about them. He had never lived with his daughter, except for holidays, which they occasionally spent travelling abroad. Now he had come back, they saw more of each other but not enough to deepen the merely friendly relations they enjoyed. And when it came to Orlando, Judite was very reserved. She seemed to want to bar him from any inclination he might have to interfere in her life.

"The National Bank maybe provides greater stability, but the new banks probably provide more chances to get ahead quickly and offer better salaries."

"Maybe," Orlando said. "But I have no intention of working for the private sector."

"Socialist bias?"

"Oh no. Not anymore. I think the State has an important role to fulfill as a regulator. And it provides other guarantees to its employees. At least, I don't have much cause to complain."

"That's true, Father. The banking sector always benefitted from better conditions than the others. For example, Orlando has a much better food allowance than I have. And other benefits, such as a courtesy car or frequent overseas missions."

"But those perks are going to come to an end. The State is going to have to shrink in order to save money. Work trips and cars will end. Public monopolies and orders from above will finish. The private companies will determine economic activity and provide better prospects to talented employees."

"Do you really believe that, Malongo, sir?" Orlando said. "In the first place, do you think the role of the State will be reduced to a minimum? I don't believe it, because we are in Africa. That's just the demagoguery of one or two politicians who say they'll limit state intervention to near zero, imitating ultra-liberal theorists. Even in the United States, these theories are once again being contested. Now it's the fashion, but like all fashions, it's limited to a decade. The nineties will have other fashions, not that one. Our politicians, as always, are behind the times. They are trying to imitate the language of Reagan and Thatcher, though the world has taken another turn on its axis without them even being aware."

"Do you think the apparatus of the state will continue being the monster it is at present?"

"It might be rationalized. There are a lot of services that will completely disappear. But it won't be the radical squeeze that some people promise. That's not possible, because we're in an underdeveloped country, where either the State does some things or they just don't get done. Education is a case in point. It's fashionable now to talk about private education. All the politicians have suddenly discovered that the magic solution to the problem of a lack of schools and teachers is privatization. When it comes down to it, how many schools are going to open funded by private capital? The thousands that we need? Not at all. There might be the odd group of teachers who try, but they can only do it with the financial backing of the State. That's because if I had enough money to establish a school, I'd more likely go and open a restaurant or a snack bar, which provides a more immediate return. And our entrepreneurs only think of a quick profit. They're primitive entrepreneurs, at the earliest stage of capital accumulation. The few entrepreneurs with a creative spirit, whom we could consider as contributing to the formation of a national bourgeoisie, can't satisfy every commission. As the Europeans say, one swallow doesn't make a spring. One or two energetic industrialists, with a vision for the future, don't make a national bourgeoisie. In a country without a national bourgeoisie, either the State guarantees some essential services, or there's a complete vacuum. A gap easily filled by foreigners. That's why this ultra-liberal discourse isn't just theoretical or innocent. It corresponds to an invasive strategy on the part of those propagating it. And those are, as always, the same invaders who have been around throughout the modern period but who now have an open field."

"Well, when it comes to politics, I don't understand a thing. My field is business."

"That's the same thing. When you say the State should be trimmed down, you're talking politics."

"Careful, Father, you don't know what you've got yourself into. Orlando's a professor of politics. Sooner or later, he'll persuade you to join a party."

Judite's boyfriend didn't pay attention to her joke. He only stopped talking to finish his glass of whiskey. Then he continued enthusiastically, while Malongo attentively poured him another.

"It's also not true that private companies pay better than the State. Nor will they abolish the so-called perks of their managerial employees. There are lots of examples, in Africa and elsewhere, which manage to reconcile capitalism with huge privileges for their chief executives. In opposition to this, we have to listen to the demagoguery of the one who aspires to be none other than a chief executive himself, preferably the most important of all, president of the Republic or prime minister."

Judite was absorbing her boyfriend's words. Was she interested in politics, too, or was this just love's fascination? Malongo thought to himself. She had imbibed politics since she was a baby, through her mother's influence. But sometimes that served as an antidote rather than encouraging the addiction. He knew of many cases.

"So, what do you think, Judite? Or are you like me? Is your politics your profession?"

"What a horrible way of putting it, Father. I'm sorry, I don't mean to offend you, but that's a tremendously reactionary turn of phrase. I'm fed up with hearing things like that, precisely from people who didn't want to change anything, or who were frightened of doing so. Politics for me is my work, politics for me is my family, politics for me is soccer, et cetera, et cetera. That's the discourse of paralysis."

"Judite is right. Those who advocate an apolitical stance are those who help keep things at a standstill, without any progress of whatever type. And totalitarian regimes love these apolitical statements, even though they don't recognize them."

"Poor me, what have I said," Malongo moaned, trying to make a joke out of it. "Soon I'll be accused of being responsible for all this shit."

"I wasn't referring to you, Father. I just said that the way you put it was unfortunate, because it's too ugly and time-worn. But I know that your lack of interest in politics is sincere and complete. Mother sometimes mentions that you used to fall asleep if friends began discussing politics. Because you're not interested, you like practical things, you're a pragmatist who thinks politicians are always talking in the abstract. But it's still true that this kind of indifference favours the established order, whatever that may be."

The doorbell rang again. Now it must certainly be Vítor Ramos. Malongo went and opened the door, preparing to curse his friend for being late. But he stood there lost for words because it was Vítor's wife, Luzia, who appeared first. She walked straight in. Vítor followed, shrugging impotently at him. Luzia plonked two kisses on his cheeks and shouted, tuning up her voice to imitate someone from Lisbon, "Ooooh, look who's here, Judite . . ."

There was no real reason for such surprise at finding a daughter at her father's house, but Luzia had to call attention to herself in any way she could. Malongo was fairly harsh in his opinion of his friend's wife, but he kept it to himself and had no wish to cast judgments about the matter. Worldly had abandoned the wife he had brought from the bush, along with their two children, a year after establishing himself in Luanda. Six months after he had been made minister, he noticed Luzia, a typist in his office. She had soon been made his secretary and become his mistress. But Luzia wanted more and succeeded: a marriage ceremony with lots of guests and a grand wedding banquet supplied by a foreign company. She stopped working, for it didn't look good for a minister's wife to also be his secretary. But she imposed changes in his office staff, so as to ensure no rivals would appear. And she would often turn up to keep a close watch on the minister's relations with women in the ministry and keep herself informed of any rumours circulating. One day, when a pretty woman was appointed as the head of a department, she kicked up such a fuss that the other woman wasn't in the position for long. Malongo searched Vítor's face to try to understand why he had brought his wife along. Luzia's presence was going to spoil their night out, goodbye to any fun and games.

"Just imagine! Luzia was moaning that we two were going out to a rave. I told her we weren't, we had matters to discuss, and we were just going to have a drink. But she wouldn't believe me. She wanted to see for herself that we were going to be here at home."

"What a girl, Luzia!" said Malongo, ushering her over to the sofa. "That's the spirit, keep a good eye on him. It's not as if there are many ministers, and we've got to hold onto the ones we have."

"Of course," she agreed. "And I know there are young girls out there, always ready to hook one."

Malongo noticed Judite and Orlando were uncomfortable. Judite was certainly embarrassed by Luzia's presence. She had once remarked, "She's stupider than a chicken," which had brought protests from Sara, her mother, always ready to forgive everything when it came to friends and their families. But he agreed with his daughter. Luzia, poor girl, was even quite pretty, but that head of hers was hollow, something that was quite common among certain people who seemed to be ever-present in the ministries and at official receptions. And without the slightest sense of occasion. To come to the house of one of her husband's oldest friends, she was wearing a heavy blue velvet dress. A beautiful long dress, but something to be worn in some European ballroom or at a ceremony presided over by the president of the Republic. And she wore her hair long, with undulating curls right down to the middle of her back. All she needed was for her wig to be blond for her ridiculous appearance to stand out even more. Malongo served them whiskey with a lot of ice, for he knew their tastes and didn't need to be asked.

"Before you arrived, Orlando was giving me a lesson in politics. You know him, of course."

"Actually, I haven't met him," Luzia said. "I mean, I have heard all about him at Sara's house."

"We've met, we were at a meeting together," said Vítor.

"More than one, sir."

Orlando was very formal, Malongo noted. He needed to break the ice but couldn't think how for the moment. And it would have to be a hell of a joke if he was to break it once and for all. But Vítor Ramos took the lead in the conversation.

"I've heard you're thinking of forming a party."

"Oh, it's too early to talk about forming a party," Orlando said, measuring his words. "Let's say there's a group of people with similar ideas and concerns, and that they're coming together to express their thoughts. It might or might not compete with the party in power. It's not necessarily going to evolve into a party, but that possibility hasn't been dismissed out of hand. What I find surprising, sir, is that you have already got wind of something when we don't yet know the outcome ourselves."

"In this country, we get to know everything. It's always been like that. When it was a one-party state, and the Central Committee met, didn't we already know all the decisions taken? Rumour is part of our political culture. Most of our politics is conducted through rumour. And there are specialists, those who exploit rumour. Now more than ever, rumours are manipulated in order to sully the names of the leaders, with fairy tales about corruption, for example. And this causes damage, tremendous damage."

"In what sense are you using the term *rumour*, sir? In the sense of gossip, which is now the most common use of the word, or in the sense of information, its original meaning?"

"It depends on the context. I use it in both senses, depending ..."

Orlando now seemed amused. Judite was right: he only woke

up when talk turned to politics. Thank goodness she doesn't want to get married, just think what a tiresome son-in-law I'd get. But the bastard's enjoying himself, he's being ironic. I hope Vítor doesn't notice.

Orlando returned to the fray. "In the case of corruption, are you using the term in the sense of false gossip or true information, sir?"

"Gossip, of course, it's just gossip. No one can prove anything. But these rumours cause damage, moral damage in the first place. There are even people who want to step down from government or as directors of companies; they say they can't take any more unfounded suspicion. So I ask you, if everyone leaves, who takes charge of the country?"

"Well, I don't think there's any danger of that. There are always people willing to risk a bad reputation throughout their lives, even if only for a single day in power. Power attracts more than the sun. The problem is that when a regime is created on the basis of secrecy, society can only respond by means of rumour. And there may be injustices, with the just paying the price for the sinners. But as for the existence of sinners, that is undeniable. And it has nothing to do with whether their sins can be proven or not ... The proof must exist. It's just kept in the hands of the accused, those who hold power. There's a change of power, and the proof emerges. And there's a lot of false proof, too, invented by the newly empowered just in order to burn their adversaries, who held power previously. These kinds of things have happened before, so it won't be the first time."

"But it's annoying, annoying."

Malongo noticed Judite squeeze her boyfriend's hand to try to shut him up. But he was on a roll, and there was no stopping him.

"Have there been any rumours with respect to yourself, sir?"

"You're the ones who should know. The interested party is always the last to know, isn't that what they say of the cuckold?

It's the same with these rumours. But I have one rule of thumb, and it's something I've always had, oh yes. People who work for me have to tell me all they hear about me, good or bad. That's how I remain aware of what people are saying. And recently, everyone has been talked about, left, right, and centre. Why should I be an exception?"

"Nothing serious, I hope," said Malongo.

He intervened in the conversation, just so as not to leave the two of them at each other, which might prove dangerous for the evening's friendly atmosphere, for Orlando could barely disguise his enjoyment at the punishment he was dishing out.

"Same things as always. Always the same accusations: huge commissions, money in secret bank accounts, contracts that are ruinous for the country. You know the kind of thing."

"I'm not talking about you, sir, with all due respect," Orlando insisted once again. "But there's no smoke without fire."

"Come on now, I'm not one to put my hands in that fire of yours either. If even among Jesus Christ's closest companions, there was a traitor . . . and they were all saints . . . Why shouldn't there be one or two more ambitious members within the government? That's why I'm only speaking for myself, not for others."

"Which doesn't suggest any great solidarity within the government," Judite commented.

"Not that there ever was," replied Worldly. "Each one always did his own thing. I always said it was a coalition government and not a one-party administration. And one or two who were with us until recently are now forming opposition parties and blaming us for all manner of evil. As if they, last year, weren't milking the same cow they are now spitting at. The most blatant form of opportunism . . . Why should I show solidarity with guys like that? Or someone like Arnaldo, my colleague in the government, whose wife and children are now in Portugal waiting to see which way the wind is blowing? As she has no work skills, that's an expensive stay. Paid for by whom? If it's the State, that's wrong. If it's him, how did he get the money?"

Luzia finally saw her chance to chip in. It was with obvious pleasure that she unleashed her blow: "And it's not as if his wife liked cheap things. She only goes for luxury ..."

You're a fine one to talk, Malongo thought. He remembered the time Luzia spent her holidays at his house in Brussels, alone with her children because Vítor was unable to go at the last minute. Her expenses almost bankrupted him; he swore it would never happen again. What's more, at the time, he hadn't yet started doing business with Angola and hardly had enough to get by from one day to the next. It wasn't just that she liked luxury, but she only had the vaguest notion of how much things cost. She bought the most expensive items, because she had nothing to compare them with. Later, he noticed this was a general characteristic of people who were able to travel abroad at the expense of the State. They went to the most expensive restaurants, and when someone told them with that amount of money, you could eat more and better elsewhere, they were all astonished. Luzia worked her way through his scarce savings, but she also gave him his idea as to how to make his bit from his homeland, when she talked of rumours about business deals and how things got done. She knew all about these schemes from the inside. So then he thought, Why not me? As if purely by chance, he introduced Luzia to one or two acquaintances who owned medium-sized companies. Just to demonstrate that he had good contacts. Sometime after that, he started acting as middleman for these very firms in their business dealings with Angola. That's when he set out on his road to fortune.

"You're saying these rumours are justified, or at least some of them, sir," Orlando said. "Why don't you condemn these cases publicly, given that the government or the party in power doesn't?"

"Are you crazy?"

"Coming from you, such a condemnation would have repercussions. You would gain popularity, sir. And the party in power would at last have to do something to clean up its act."

Worldly stroked his long beard, which he had had ever since his time in the guerrilla war. There were a lot of white strands in it. The gesture served to give him time to reflect. Also to control his emotions. Malongo was already acquainted with it.

"Come off it, what do I want popularity for? Some are thinking about doing this, that's true. To gain a reputation now by creating a few ripples, support a few public works in their home region, and then run as deputies, counting on their regional base for votes. But I certainly don't intend to run for office in the elections."

"So you're depending on your party's victory in the election. And if it loses, will you join the opposition and lose your job?"

"Oh! Come on! You're not a long-serving minister for nothing. You learn a lot of things. I can make a career in business. I've got a lot of contacts. I know all about procedures. I'll always find a job."

"But don't you then fear justifying those rumours? Spread by people who accuse you of having private links with foreign interests?"

"I don't see why."

"Many people would tend to follow this line of thought. 'When he was a minister, he favoured certain foreign firms, and that's why he maintains good relations with them, what's more on the basis of capital created by the commissions he received when he was a minister in the government.' All kinds of speculation will be possible."

"One thing I've become sure of," said Worldly, discreetly indicating to Malongo that his glass was empty, "people will always talk. And they believe in rumours. They need them."

Malongo poured him another whiskey. On his way, he also poured another thimbleful in Luzia's glass. You can never talk about business without ending up in politics, he thought. No matter how hard you try, it's unavoidable. Even I, who was careful never to get my feet wet, ended up in the middle of these conversations if I wanted to do business. But they're much more interesting than when I was young, when they all wanted to change the world and only debated abstract things, like freedom, equality, social justice. In those days, it was tedious; people would come up with terms no one understood: capital appreciation, exploitation, struggle here, revolution there. Now it's better: it's always about how to trick the other guy, or the State, to get rich quicker. At least that's clear and positive. It's the only kind of politics capable of interesting me.

"So when he leaves the government and I invite him to become a partner in my firm, what happens then?" Malongo said to Orlando. "Does that mean he favoured me when he was a minister?"

"People will probably think that."

"You're done for, Vítor, the invitation's off. I don't want people to start talking about me."

"You'll lose someone of considerable managerial experience," said Worldly, laughing but unable to hide a certain nervousness. "I think our friend Orlando is exaggerating, and he'll discover later that this isn't so important. The people forget things and become interested in other matters."

"Careful, Uncle Vítor, don't delude yourself," said Judite, who had been unusually silent during the whole conversation. Malongo also noticed a habit that had come through from her childhood, of calling her parents' friends uncle and aunt, a habit that was common among the younger generation. "Some of you people, who grew rich illicitly, will have to explain how you did it. Uncle Aníbal says you all came out of the forest the same, each one of you with one hand covering your front and the other your back, so as to conceal your nudity. Then some of you amassed fortunes. How did you manage that if all of you had more or less the same salaries?"

"Trust Aníbal to enter the conversation," mumbled Vítor.

"Isn't he the crazy fellow who lives on a beach in Benguela?" Luzia said. But then she looked at Judite and covered her mouth with her hand. "Sorry, it just came out."

Malongo burst out laughing at silly Luzia's embarrassment. But also because he wasn't displeased at the odd snide remark about Wisdom, who had despised him when they were young. And everyone knew about Sara's strange relationship with him, consisting of once or twice yearly encounters during the holidays. But Judite wasn't at all shocked by Luzia's comment and even laughed. She said, amused, "By the way, he sent a message that he's coming up here one of these days. He's hitching a ride on top of a truck, to celebrate the peace, which will allow traffic on the roads."

"He really is soft in the head," said Vítor bitterly.

"Why?" Judite asked. "Because he travels like the people do? He doesn't have a car, and we all know how chaotic travelling by plane is, unless you're a VIP, of course. I think it's great to come like that, on top of a truck. And you get a much better view of the landscape from up there."

"We visited him at Caotinha last year," Orlando said. "I enjoyed meeting him very much. He's not crazy, far from it. But he's far too clear-headed for some people's taste. He saw the whole film unroll before it even happened. He's bitter, without a doubt, but that just shows he's clear-minded."

"He's just showing off, that's what he's doing," said Vítor. "He wants to appear purer than all the rest, more dispassionate."

He signalled to Malongo again, who came over with the bottle. Luzia didn't have any inhibitions and insisted he top her up as well. The other couple also accepted another drink.

Judite took a mouthful and then answered, "No one lives

for thirteen or fourteen years as he does just for the sake of appearance. He's purer than the others, period. And it's precisely because of this that some people can't forgive him."

"Is that directed at me?" asked Vítor, aggressively.

That was it: the night had been spoiled. Nothing was more likely to enrage Vítor than someone talking well of that madman, Aníbal. They must have had a major falling-out during the guerrilla campaign, thought Malongo. Vítor well and truly hates the guy. And there was I thinking that things would explode because of some political argument, and in the end it was mention of Aníbal that wrecked everything. Judite, unflustered, answered, "I'm talking in general terms. You can interpret it as you like, Uncle."

Malongo felt duty bound to intervene, for she was after all his daughter, irritating a prestigious guest who was making visible efforts to contain his anger.

"Let's change the subject because this is getting tedious. What about going out for a drink somewhere? There are some nice clubs, and as it's a weekday, they won't be full."

It was a way of telling Judite it was time to go, because she hated nightclubs and the loud music that inhibited any conversation. This was ideal for such a heterogeneous group, for whom any conversation ran the risk of ending in blows. She understood, for she quickly finished her whiskey and said, "You people go. We've still got one or two errands to do."

They said a formal but hurried goodbye and left. Malongo got as far as saying, "Drop by more often," but they didn't even respond. But then Worldly also said, "Thanks for the invitation, but I don't feel like it. That conversation put me in a bad mood. These young people nowadays. First, it was your son-in-law—"

"Wait, hang on a minute, he's not my son-in-law. They're not married."

"It's only a question of time. The guy was making fun of me. I acted like I wasn't aware so as not to make trouble. That ironic little bastard...He's a subversive! If he weren't your son-in-law, he'd be arrested tomorrow for insulting a leader."

"Cool it, my friend. He didn't say anything that could offend you. Asking doesn't constitute an offence."

"Fuck off. Those questions were full of venom. I repeat, he can count himself lucky he's your son-in-law."

Malongo patted him on the knee and poured him another whiskey. Of course, Luzia held out her glass and didn't say stop until it was almost full. And she didn't wait for the whiskey to settle in the glass before upending it. This dame's going to get completely plastered, but maybe that's the best thing that could happen. If she falls asleep, we can still get to the club out at Viana, and she'll never notice our absence.

"Those times have passed, Vítor, when you could put a guy behind bars for a real or imagined insult."

"That's the shit, that's the shit we've got ourselves into."

"Now there's democracy. Everyone can have their say."

"Democracy . . ." Luzia said. "Fill my glass, that's all you've got to do, and I'll toast to democracy, urra!"

"Urra is Russian, not very suitable for drinking a toast to democracy," Malongo said, filling her glass and deliberately forgetting to add ice.

He winked at Vítor, who was going to grab his wife's glass to stop her from drinking whiskey neat. Vítor then understood his friend's intention and smiled. Luzia polished off her drink in five seconds. She made a face and put her glass down on the table. Malongo stood, bottle in hand, looking at her and then the glass, hesitating.

"Fill it, fill it up," Vítor said. "When Luzia starts drinking, she never stops, isn't that so, darling?"

She fleetingly fondled his knee. She rolled her eyes and said, by now slurring her words, but still in her affected tone of voice,

"It's been such a long time since you last called me darling! Ever since ... since our youngest was born, ten years ago. Don't argue, it was then ..."

"But I'm not arguing about anything. Come on, drink and be quiet, because I'm talking to Malongo."

"When I drink, I talk a lot. I argue like hell."

"Nonsense. When you drink, you go straight to sleep."

Malongo watched the scene, highly amused, noticing the impressive speed with which Luzia got drunk. Vítor was now apparently very calm, stroking his beard.

"I sleep, don't I? I can't drink, and I fall asleep straightaway, isn't that so, darling? Like that dinner in Moscow, when all those Russians drank vodka and mineral water, and I drank vodka neat and didn't want mineral water, that was some scene, an official dinner for the delegation Vítor was leading, and I shouted urra and fell asleep on the table."

"Exactly, that's what happened. Now have another glass and sleep. We'll sit here and talk."

Malongo filled her glass, she drank and then fell to one side, without another word. Her wig slipped, and Vítor tore it off unceremoniously. He laid it on the sofa, with a wide theatrical gesture.

"Incredible," said Malongo. "I've never seen anyone fall asleep so fast. How long will she sleep?"

"The whole night. A doctor once told me it bordered on a comatose state. But it's probably not dangerous. We can leave without any worries. I'll wake her up when it's time for us to go home."

"It might be better to take her to the guest room."

Malongo took her by the feet and the other by her armpits. The former soccer player was still well-built and could have carried her in his arms. But as her husband was present, he also had to participate. They took her up to a room on the second floor and left her on the bed. Vítor slipped her shoes off and put them next to the bed. "Sweet dreams, darling."

After that, they went and drowned their sorrows at the night-club in Viana.

2

The night wasn't going as they had hoped. Luzia's obstinacy had considerably delayed their departure from the house, and the two girls they had arranged to take to the club were no longer free. They went by themselves, and despite the special attention afforded Vítor by the proprietor of the club, they were unable to arrange any interesting company. The ladies were all with men, and they themselves were no longer of an age to get involved in contests. There were a few girls who would occasionally approach their table, but they would send them away. They didn't want anything to do with prostitutes, who only created problems and gave them a bad reputation, and then there was the spectre of AIDS hovering over them.

They drank their whiskey steadily, unwilling to talk because of the booming music. In this, Judite was right: dance halls and nightclubs, quintessential sites of African conviviality, were no good for conversation. Conversation in traditional societies was a supreme pleasure and the highest form of art. This meant that in the cities, electronic music was destroying the soul of African culture, the trade in words. It destroyed it in the name of African culture, which is supposed to be rooted in music. People were dancing or thrashing about in electronic pop movements, but they weren't speaking. The girls chewed gum, ruminating, so as to give their mouths something to do. The men turned their eyes inwards, so as to feel the stereophonic vibrations inside their skulls, intoxicating themselves with emptiness and the cadence of their movements. Malongo pursued these thoughts; he had been a musician after all. No, it wasn't the same thing. He played the guitar and sang, without any special electronic backing to cover up the song's lack of melody or poetry with its beat. And he had never allowed himself to be influenced by Congolese music, mistakenly assumed in many places to be a prototype for all African music. In fact, in Brussels and Paris, when people thought about Africa, all they knew anything about was that part where French was spoken. The same went for music. As if there weren't many Africas, all of them distinct . . .

Vítor had been in a state of tension for quite some time, observing a man dancing by himself in the middle of the dance floor. And he had muttered exclamations that Malongo didn't catch because of the music. He tugged at his shirt, and Malongo strained to hear him.

"That guy in the green shirt . . . Don't you recognize him?"

Malongo shook his head. On closer inspection, the man wasn't alone. He was just dancing so far away from the lady, and without any apparent interest in her, that he seemed to be absorbed in himself, swaying to his own music. His partner was a woman in a red dress, with dark stains on it from perspiration. The man was rotund, short and fat, with large glasses and almost completely bald. Everything about him accentuated his tubbiness.

"It must be the ghost of Elias. It looks just like Elias. I haven't seen him for thirty years, I might be mistaken."

"Which Elias?" Malongo shouted. "The one who fled Portugal for Paris with us?"

"That one, yes. The one who then went to the United States with the help of UPA."

Malongo tried hard to remember. He hardly knew the other guy. It might be him, he had no idea. Vítor continued to watch the dancer, and from time to time shouted, "Yes, it's him." Malongo was surprised, because he recalled that at the time Elias had been a Protestant and a very serious intellectual of the really annoying kind, who only talked about the most important things in the world. He found it impossible to associate him with the fat little bald guy, and a dancer to boot. But he wasn't arguing. Vítor was the one who had been his friend back in the time of the Casa dos Estudantes. The music stopped, and there were a few seconds of respite for their ears. Worldly took advantage of the sudden silence and shouted to Elias, over the murmur of conversation that resumed throughout the dance hall. And sure enough, the other guy reacted, looking around him in all directions. The music started up again, and Vítor didn't waste any time. He got up from the table, strategically situated in a dark corner, and, at the risk of being recognized in public, went over to Elias. Malongo saw them say something to each other, embrace, and then walk back to the table. He didn't hear what Vítor was saying, but he was probably introducing him, and he found himself embracing the bald, bespectacled fellow, who was bathed in sweat but smelled of recently applied deodorant. Elias sat down at their table, but soon Vítor gave up trying to talk, which they could only do by shouting at each other. He called the manager of the club, said something, and the other nodded. At a sign from the minister, they got up and left the dance hall through a side door. They entered a small room with two tables. There was no one else there. The sound of the music was now muffled.

"We can talk here," said Vítor. "Bring us something to drink, Mr. Gomes."

"Wait, let me go and fetch my lady," Elias said.

He made as if to get up, but Vítor didn't let him, squeezing the other fellow's fat shoulder.

"Let her dance, we must talk. She's not alone, is she?"

"That's the problem, she isn't. There's a young boy there, and I don't trust him not to lust after her."

"Don't worry, you can go and get her in a minute. But tell me, what have you been up to? How did you turn up here without telling your friends you'd come back?"

"Oh, that's a long story."

"You went off to the United States in 1961. After that, I never got any more news from you."

"I was with UPA and then the FNLA. I got a scholarship to study in the States, philosophy of course. Psychology later. Afterwards, they founded UNITA, and I joined them. But then I lost faith in my fellow countrymen from Bié who led it. Disagreements that are not worth going into now. I distanced myself from politics. I did a doctorate in social psychology and started teaching. In 1975, I was on the point of coming back here, but was discouraged by the war and I stopped in Nigeria, where I stayed on as a teacher. I settled there. But then I got news that things here were changing, and I came back. There's now enough freedom for me to spread my message, whereas before, I would have encountered problems."

"We're well and truly fucked, another one who's turned up to create a political party," said Malongo. "You guys spent all this time living overseas, thinking we were fast asleep here, and now you come and teach us all about democracy. Do what I did, which was to come and do business. Those who stayed behind are the ones who know all about politics. Vítor, for example, has more experience than all of you people put together."

"Hey, wait a minute. Who told you I've come back to form a political party? It wasn't me, was it?"

Malongo sat there, his mouth hanging open, not knowing what to say. Indeed, Elias hadn't said anything of the sort, but he had suggested he had a message to impart. The manager returned with a bottle of whiskey, ice, and glasses. The table back in the dance hall was still reserved for them, he said, whenever you gentlemen feel like returning...Vítor poured them their drinks.

413

"So what have you come back to do?"

Elias put on a solemn face, extinguishing his amused grin as if flicking a switch. He drank his whiskey in a single gulp and with a more serious air. Vítor recognized the student of thirty years before, a good few years older than himself, who gave him lectures on the need for violence, even total violence, for the psychological liberation of people.

"I've come to teach what I have learned. I know I'm taking a risk in telling you this, because I imagine you are the same disbelievers and disparagers as before. But I'll tell you all the same. I'm a bishop of the Dominus Church of Hope and Joy."

"What the hell is that?" Malongo asked, almost shouting. "And who is this guy Dominus?"

Elias smiled condescendingly, like a grandfather or a village elder who has seen many things. He spoke like a medium, for his voice emerged more deeply from his throat, without moving his lips and with his eyes fixed on some future: "It's a Church of God. *Dominus* means *Lord* in Latin. And it is a church of hope because it is the only church which always has a word of stimulus, encouragement, for people. The other churches are repressive, they threaten, all of them influenced by the Jehovah of Israel, who is a cruel god. Believers live with the sword of Damocles forever above their head, fearing the final judgment, paying for an original sin they didn't commit. Dominus is the God of kindness, who forgives, who never threatens, for whom life is always one of hope and sweetness. And of joy, because Dominus wants people to enjoy themselves, within certain limits of course. That's why you shouldn't be surprised to see the only bishop of the church dancing and drinking in this club right now. Dominus appeared to me in Nigeria, when I was in Ibadan, unwell and abandoned by my latest wife, and He cured me by placing His hand on me and teaching me the religion of hope and joy. As health is important for joy in life, He taught me to treat some illnesses, concentrating hidden energies in the hand that cures."

"What kind of cures do you administer?" asked Vítor. "For mental illnesses?"

"Those too. But they are the easiest. Any impostor with an ability to convince people can cure many of those illnesses. It's a question of belief. Psychiatrists will tell you that. Above all, I cure radical illnesses that doctors don't know about, or don't want to know."

Malongo tried hard not to laugh. He knew he had to contain himself, just as Vítor was doing with apparent ease. What a great buffoon, this guy Elias! But what a flair for deceiving others he sensed in him! This, at the same time, Malongo found intimidating. He asked, "Come again, what illnesses?"

"Radical ones. The word comes from *radix*, or *root*. They are the illnesses that lie at the root of all other ones. The doctors cure the other ones, those that manifest themselves. They don't realize that these illnesses that show themselves are merely epiphenomena of the radical illnesses, those of the basic structure. To make all this clearer: you have AIDS, which manifests itself through other illnesses such as pneumonia, influenza, infections, and so on."

"Is AIDS radical?" Vítor asked. "Can you cure AIDS?"

"No. You don't understand. I just gave the example of how a disease like AIDS manifests itself through others. AIDS isn't radical, and unfortunately I don't know how to cure it yet. But I can attack the root of AIDS. I cure illnesses that facilitate the appearance of AIDS if they are not countered. Do you understand? I attack the depths of a person's being, in its predisposition to have an illness. I cure the most intimate part of an individual, the most intimate part of his constitution, not illnesses of the mind. I intervene in the basic energy flows of the body, the essential metabolism and its exchanges with nature. By curing the most intimate part of his organism, he can then defend himself more effectively against the aggression of bacteria, viruses, et cetera. Normal illnesses belong to the realm of doctors, who have managed to unveil some of the mysteries of Dominus, the most superficial ones. The deepest secrets, He has only revealed to me, and it is obvious that I cannot unveil all of them at once. The world is not yet prepared for that. But this treatment administered by my hand, which I usually carry out in public ceremonies, is only one facet of our religious practice. The most important part is the teaching that man is good, just as Dominus is good. This is very different from other religions, which state that man is bad, only because God is severe and impenetrable. As man convinces himself that he is bad, he goes on to kill and maim, driven by these gods of war. Dominus is transparent, and ancient civilizations were able to assume some of His essence. For example, Dionysus for the Greeks and Bacchus for the Romans are partial manifestations of Dominus, as are Aphrodite or Venus. Some African cultures also assumed aspects of the essence of Dominus. This god Nzambi who leaves us alone, without pestering us in our lives, is, of course, Dominus. The problem is that no civilization has assumed him in His totality."

"What a guy!" Malongo commented, ironically.

Elias lowered his eyes in modesty. He sat for a few moments in silence, possibly for the others to notice his humble attitude. He spoke with the cavernous voice he must have picked up from some circus-performing ventriloquist.

"Dominus chose me to reveal Himself. But I may not have been the only one. The existence of fragments of His essence, such as Bacchus and Yemanjá, are proof that He once revealed Himself to others. But these perhaps never had the ability to assimilate Him in His totality, or maybe the historical period did not favour it. So it has befallen me to take on the onerous but gratifying task to be His messenger."

"In Bantu culture, the messenger is often the creator, because the word creates," Vítor said.

The bishop of the Dominus Church unleashed a loud cackle of laughter, not in keeping with his previous behaviour. And his voice changed, as he began to talk normally, moving his lips.

"What you don't realize is that is precisely Dominus's revelation to the Bantus and Moses. That is why the Bible states that in the beginning was the Word. Given that today we know that everything began in Africa, we can say that it was the Africans who taught it to the first Jews. But I see what you're trying to get at. And I'm telling you in spite of your malice. Obviously, as the messenger of Dominus, I embark on a process of recreating Him. He created me, and I recreate Him. By speaking of Him, by revealing Him to the eyes of others, I recreate Him. What other God agrees to be recreated? None. All other gods have created us, and that's over and done with. They are unmovable, and we are their inferiors. Dominus lives on our love and the affection with which we give Him form. His superiority is absolute, you have to admit. He is so superior that he consents to be recreated by a humble prophet."

"So you're a prophet then?" Malongo said, looking aghast.

"That is what those selected by Dominus are called. Buddha, Jesus, Muhammad—"

"And Elias," Malongo concluded with a laugh. "Go to hell, dammit. You're having us on. And, what's more, with the air of a saint."

"I may be enjoying your astonishment, that's true. Enjoyment is the main obligation of my religion. Enjoyment without any malice, I stress. But I'm telling you the truth. I don't know whether that proves anything before your incredulous spirits, but look here."

He took two business cards from his pocket and handed them to Malongo and Vítor. On them, was written "Elias Mungombe, Bishop of the Dominus Church of Hope and Joy," followed by a telephone number. In the upper left corner, there was an emblem, a tottering triangle on an oblique line. There weren't even any hieroglyphics or any other cabbalistic signs, Malongo noted.

"If it was just to poke fun at you, I wouldn't have had cards printed. Although I acknowledge that the pleasure of poking fun at you might merit having them printed, above all in the case of Vítor, who is a minister in this government of atheists and sinners. Let me make it clear that I don't blame you for that. Better atheists than believers in those tired old religions that can no longer produce anything new."

Vítor was decidedly quiet, maybe even intimidated, Malongo thought. He hadn't joined in his laughter and was now closely examining his visiting card. And then he spoke with all the naturalness in the world: "Many have quickly shed the shirt of atheism, which is no longer appropriate. But are you making a living out of this?"

"No, not at all. Fortunately, I managed to build up some savings over all those years I lived abroad. I brought foreign currency with me, and you know what it's like, a guy can get by comfortably for a while, using the parallel exchange rate. But everything comes to an end. I haven't yet managed to build a church. I organized one or two religious services in premises belonging to clubs and managed to gather in some believers who are beginning to make a financial contribution. But not much. Things will get hard if I don't receive any financial backing."

"Give me a break!" said Malongo. "Who is going to finance you, the World Bank, the European Community?"

"No," Elias replied calmly, the shadow of a smile at the corner of his mouth. "You, for example. I know you're a millionaire. And Vítor, who may not have much money to risk but has influence. With that kind of support, I can build a large church. But the most important thing is to expand the organization far and wide and conquer the love of men. With the love of men, it's obvious that the Church can then access some of its members' money. That's what love is: to know how to share. In a nutshell, I'm looking for partners with power and money. I'll do the rest."

The conversation was becoming more interesting. Malongo stopped smiling. For the first time, he felt that little shiver in his belly that indicated that he was in the presence of a business opportunity, the uncertain thrill of a risk. In the face of Vítor's apparent lack of interest, he asked, "Are you saying you intend to build a sect like those that crop up all over the world and sequester people's assets, indulge in dodgy business activity, torture their followers, and so on? They earn a shedload of money, but they're always against the law. And occasionally their leader goes to jail or disappears from circulation."

"Those are demonic sects. Mine is a church, not a sect. And it will be subject to the laws of the country. No violence or extortion. People contribute to the Church, and it lives on these proceeds. But the contributions are completely voluntary. And those who are cured can pay something if they want, but they are not obliged."

"From what I understood, you don't cure known illnesses," said Vítor. "You cure what isn't felt. So people don't feel that you have cured them. And so they don't contribute money."

Elias shook his head at the other man's inability to comprehend. But without showing any impatience. Like the teacher who knows that the student will understand, sooner or later, if he remains calm enough to press forward and explain in a different way. He filled their three glasses.

"People feel better, more joyful, more willing. They feel able to communicate; they're more optimistic. That is what they feel. And also that they have gained greater resistance in relation to common illnesses. That is the important thing. In their faith in Dominus, people feel full of joy, strong, and hopeful."

"Okay, one more thing," said Malongo. "How does the show work? With electronic instruments? Or don't you use the show as the central focus of your activity?"

"Presumably, you're talking about the church service. Call it a show, if you like. It is very reminiscent of a spectacle, you're right. Psychology explains the need for the cult, or service, in order to make the faithful commune together with the divinity. The priest plays a fundamental part, because he creates the link. The better the priest as an actor, the greater the emotion he can harvest, and the stronger the thread between the mass of believers and the divinity. Here, electronics help a lot. The volume must be very high, and there are rhythms that must be maintained, rhythms that accord with the people's original culture ... Here, it's drum music. In Europe, it'll be something else. A litany structured in ancestral cadences provokes an effect close to hypnosis, which facilitates their understanding of supreme truths and the strengthening of the power of the hand. All great religions have grasped this, hence the importance of chants and certain repetitive movements of the body to induce an ecstatic reaction in the faithful. In Africa, the rhythm must be different, faster, acting on the pulse by accelerating it. Even the Catholics have begun to change their cadences; otherwise, they would just be left behind. The introspective, languid litanies of Asia Minor, transported to Europe by Judeo-Christianism, clash with the extroverted, happy nature of the African. The Protestants understood this very early on and gained ground. But they remain anchored to the gloomy ideology of the Bible. We have cut all links with Asia Minor. We are an African church, the first to proclaim the virtue of love and joy and to take the guilt out of pleasure-seeking, which joins God and revelry. Dominus is a unique God, but he is pagan, in the sense that he represents the sensual force of Nature."

"Sounds great," said Malongo. "A church that encourages bacchanalia. Tell me, in the cult are there any of these scenes of collective orgy, everyone with a leg over each other?"

"No, you don't understand anything at all!" The exclamation was powerful and censorious, for the first time unleashing a breath of divine fury. "You have been corrupted by your lax life in Europe, by materialist capitalism, which sullies everything. Enjoyment doesn't necessarily have to be licentious, perverse. Everything should be within acceptable limits."

"Acceptable to whom?" Vítor asked. "Who establishes the limits? The moral of the Bible?"

Elias nodded in approval, like the teacher upon hearing an intelligent observation from a pupil. He finished his whiskey and held out his glass to Malongo, who refilled it.

"That is a good question, you're as smart as ever. The other prophets who received revelations said that we are mere intermediaries. They didn't create anything; they just interpreted the teachings assimilated directly from God. With us, it's different. We are the first to claim sincerely that we have received a revelation. Dominus taught us things, but there is a huge grey area in which we have to operate, by improvising and inventing. And so our culture of origin has a huge influence, for it is on the basis of this that we invent answers that the divinity didn't provide. Hence my perfectly sincere answer to your question that the limits are those prescribed by our common sense, by the way we imagine that the average citizen would react. Of course, we may get things wrong. For example, we are now against polygamy, because before we arrived in Angola, we were influenced by what we had seen in Nigeria. At the time, we were in favour of polygamy as a manifestation of man's freedom and a symbol of African family traditions. But here, we saw that it's not a very popular cause. Women have more influence in Angola than in Nigeria. The regime's propaganda in favour of women's equality has become embedded in some people's spirits, and the monogamous churches have also had an effect over many years. So we altered our position. In this case, we didn't even have to change our position publicly, because we hadn't even gotten round to touching on the subject. But I'm telling you about it now. As you see, it is common sense that guides us in those matters that Dominus has kept from us."

"So the doctrine evolves in accordance with what people think or wish. Like the politicians in Europe who first sound out opinion and then adopt positions depending on the wishes of the electorate."

"No, Malongo, you still don't understand. That would be opportunism. The great principles of our doctrine are unchangeable, because they stem from the revelation of Dominus. But in those areas that have not been revealed, we have to find an answer, and our answer is influenced by our culture, our common sense, which does not mean that we follow what people want."

"Oh! Come off it! You were quite clear in the case of polygamy. You changed your opinion because you saw that polygamy wouldn't be a popular cause. Those were your words."

Elias shook his head, disappointed in his lack of understanding. But he didn't lose his patience. Like any servant of the Lord, he was bound to put up with everything, to explain and explain again. Men always find it hard to understand things. He used his guttural tone to give greater formality to his speech. "Things are perhaps too subtle. I'll give you another example. Dominus didn't tell me what title I should use, but I had to have one. I thought of *soma, soba, muata, mfumu,* all of which mean chief in the languages of Angola. Then I turned to the titles of priests, such as *tahi, kilamba,* and others. They wouldn't do, because it was always a case of having to privilege one region or culture over others, and it detracted from the national character of the Church. It had to be a title in the language of all and therefore in Portuguese. Or Latin, which could be explained and here in the acculturated areas is immediately recognized as a language of religion. I ended up choosing the title of bishop, which is the easiest and something everyone is familiar with. I already explained this at one of the services, and the faithful agreed that it was the best option. The difference in relation to the other prophets is that I proceed on the assumption that not everything is decided through divine inspiration, but merely through social and cultural inspiration and therefore subject to correction and improvement."

"Wait a moment, let me speak," Malongo cut in. "You've got to defend that opinion, I understand perfectly well, and if we get bogged down in that kind of discussion, we'll never get out of here. You don't need to convince me of anything, nor is it your aim. You want a partner, and what you've got to convince me of is whether the business is viable. As a business. The show may work, but I would need to see you on the stage, that is, the pulpit or whatever you call it. That business of rhythm, I liked, I liked it a lot. There must be hand-clapping or drums, or something like that, and an electronic synthesizer helps. I saw the Pope in the Vatican square, receiving the faithful from all over the world and speaking in all languages. There, what made the show were the big stone buildings, the grandeur of the square with all that space and some very thick columns, the ponderous nature of things, and the theatrical performance of one person able to speak dozens of languages. That's the trick. That's what works there. The heat was scorching, and people stood there for three hours in the sun waiting for him to say something in their language. And when this happened, they collapsed from the sun and the pleasure. It was as if God had addressed them directly. The current pope is an artist, who has carved out a role as the pope of communication, with all his languages and trips to all corners of the world. You, too, can be a great artist. That trick of talking like a ventriloquist could even work well. The rabble love circus acts like that. People will also like this whole pleasure thing and freeing pleasure from guilt. Of course, you're going to be accused of inciting vice. At this time, when people are scared of AIDS, such an accusation might be damaging, given that AIDS is associated with vice. But some of our youth will like the idea."

"In all services of worship, I advise every precaution in relation to AIDS, and I explain how best to avoid it. I would like to distribute condoms, but that's very expensive."

"I don't know whether that would go down well," commented Vítor, at last breaking his silence. "Distributing condoms in a religious cult..."

"Now it's you who are seizing on a morality of the Bible. You're making a very simplistic association between the Church and the Catholic Church, between cult and mass. Of course it would look bad for a priest to be distributing contraceptives as people left mass at the Church of Nazaré. They are against contraceptives, because in their innermost selves, and without being able to confess it, they are against the sex act and generally against pleasure. They want people who are always sad, dragging their feet. They don't affirm it openly, because it would be a sin against charity, but they secretly rejoiced at the appearance of AIDS, because it's like God's vengeance against the sexual abuses encouraged by the freedoms of the 1960s revolution. My church has nothing to do with any of that. We are the apostles of healthy joy and shared pleasure."

Vítor stroked his beard, while Malongo poured some more whiskey. They had run out of ice, and he went to get the bucket replenished. He noticed that the couples were not dancing, for the second show of the night was about to start. Gomes took the bucket with multiple apologies. "I'll bring you some more, I'll bring you some more, but don't you want to see the show?" Malongo was going to answer, "It's always the same one," but he shrugged and returned to the private room.

Elias was talking again, but now in his normal tone of voice. "Of course we should take a position, but we haven't yet decided. Obviously, Dominus didn't enter into such detail. Abortion nowadays is an important problem, and we shall soon make public our thoughts on the subject."

"Tell me something, Elias," Malongo asked as he sat down. "What language did Dominus use when He addressed you?"

The bishop laughed. He patted him on the knee. He drank some whiskey without ice, made a face, and answered happily, "That is a question I get asked straightaway. People are very curious to know what the language of God is. Look, I don't know. He said many things to me, but it was just one voice and light. I understood everything, but I cannot distinguish what the language was. Most probably the radical language, the root, the first language used by humanity. I sometimes think about these things and it is as if He spoke in Umbundu, my mother tongue, or other times in Portuguese, or again in English, the language I've used a lot in recent years . . ."

The manager appeared with the ice and also announced the start of the second show of the night. Elias fidgeted on his chair. Vítor asked if there were any changes, and the manager told him there weren't. When Gomes left the room, the bishop raised his glass and emptied it in one go.

"I'm sorry but I have to go. There's a sensational striptease, a dame from Zaire."

"We've seen it," Malongo said. "It's not worth it. The dame's cross-eyed, and to make matters worse, she's a lesbian. And it's not starting now. First, there are some songs."

"I've got to go and see how my lady is doing. You understand, our relationship is still a bit tentative, and the young boy who came with us may take advantage of my absence and the darkness in the room to stick his hand somewhere he shouldn't. These kids nowadays haven't the slightest degree of decorum."

"Isn't he from your church?" Vítor asked.

"No. She dragged him along plus a girlfriend of hers. Only my lady is a believer, but she has just joined recently and isn't very well prepared."

"Wait, I just want to ask you one last question. A guy who was with me during the guerrilla campaign, Aníbal, better known as Wisdom, I don't think you ever met him ... Well, this guy used to say that the gods of the Earth were residues in mankind's memory of extraterrestrial beings who colonized the planet, or at least influenced its evolution. They were beings from a far more advanced civilization, masters of advanced forms of energy, whom men feared and worshipped, and for that reason deified them. All gods would come from these, because all cultures would have borne these traces of a memory that came through from the beginning of time. Well, have you never tried to integrate UFOs and extraterrestrials into your religion? It stirs up people's imagination."

For the first time, Elias appeared perturbed. He filled his glass with whiskey again, drank a bit, and then added some ice. He sat pensively, shaking his glass. Then he spoke in a very quiet voice, as if he were revealing the most hidden secrets.

"Dominus never spoke to me about that, and I didn't think to ask Him either. I wasn't very concerned with questions of history. I wanted to know more about Him. And He never appeared to me again. However, He did say that in the event of my having some fundamental doubt, and only in that event, I could invoke Him and talk with Him. I never tried; there was never any need. I'm asking myself if this time ... A notion of the cosmos and its creation is important. Every religion has its answers to these questions about space and the universe. It's probably where it has made most mistakes, because science, in its progress, has shown the incongruences of its various answers. The religion of Dominus is centred in Man, in the happiness of Man. But is Man the only thinking being in the Universe? There are so many signs that indicate he isn't ... I have to decide whether this is a radical problem before I invoke Him or not."

Once again, Malongo had to stop himself from bursting out in a loud peal of laughter. What a sharp customer this guy Elias is! An artist, no doubt about it. It was staring him in the face, the guy had clean forgotten the UFOs, Vítor blindsides him, one of those feints politicians are good at, the guy's thrown off balance, caught on the hop, he knows we've noticed he's been trapped, he can no longer give us a clear answer in his beyond-the-tomb voice, but he wriggles out of it admirably by coming over all sincere and leaving open the possibility of using Vítor's suggestion. That's how you construct a religion, which obviously is going to include extraterrestrials, it's as plain as day.

"You deserve some support. As a conjuror, you're top dog. But find a way of introducing all the UFOs you can in the show. I can see it now: multicoloured lights over the stage and you rising up to heaven without a balloon or anything. A first-rate show, Angolans are going to pay loads to see it. They're going to call you the greatest witch doctor of the century."

Elias didn't modify his humble tone of speech. He turned to face Malongo and asked, "Are you really going to support us? It would be important for the Church to gain the backing of such a prestigious figure in the business community. Of course I shall try and ensure, as much as I can, that you don't see serious things merely as a show. But the grace of Dominus will only enter your spirit, given time."

"Stop the claptrap, nothing enters me, who do you think I am? I may back you. I've still got to think about it. But for the time being, I don't want anyone to know. That condition is binding."

"Of course, of course. What about you, Vítor?"

"Me? Damn it! In these changing times, what would be the point? My colleagues and I in government are already accused of corruption, repression, over everything and for no reason at all. Every day, new opposition parties appear wanting to dig up shit, and I go and get involved in an electronic church? What I need is the support of a good prestige church, Catholic or Protestant, but one that carries weight with it."

Elias had already forgotten his lady friend, who must be inside playing footsie with the young lad, while the fifth-rate show got underway. The bishop of Dominus had now turned all his attention to Vítor, his beggarly eyes hidden behind his thick glasses. His voice gained the sensual tones of certainty.

"A church gains prestige and power from the support it receives. Ours can have as much strength in society as the ones you have cited. Its message is far more modern and accords more with the very soul of Angolan man. From here, it will spill over to other parts of Africa and then to all the African diaspora. Imagine the global market of souls at our disposal. With economic crises, with the loss of the utopia of political liberation, with the disappearance of the enemy who was on the other side during the Cold War, with the foreign debt that deprives our countries of any possibility of development, our young jobless and starved of instruction, delinquency and galloping insecurity—all these things will lead people to view religion as the only salvation. Everyone appeals to a god capable of showing them a way forward in life that they no longer have, or never had. Politicians will come courting us, too, one day, because we shall be a force to be reckoned with. But for the moment, we need a modicum of discreet support from a political figure. A little word in the right person's ear so that the Church can be legally recognized. That's the problem: we're not yet recognized, which limits us. A little word isn't much to ask. It doesn't commit you to any extent. And you will have our support when you need it, which won't be long in coming. One doesn't need to be a witch doctor to hazard a guess. You will be the only communist to have the support of a church."

"I've never been a communist."

"Your party was and the government as well. That isn't an accusation, but merely to show you where you'll be attacked in future."

"They never were. Everyone knows it was all talk. No one believed in the theory that was parroted, nor did they practise it. Everyone knows, starting with the KGB and the CIA."

"You will have our discreet and effective support. Think about it."

Malongo was fascinated. The bishop had once again turned the tables and was now presenting himself as an unforeseen internal powerhouse. Having totally abandoned his humble air, he was exerting pressure on Vítor's weak point, without any need for threats but hinting at a disastrous future for him if he didn't adhere to his project. And Malongo knew that the bullet had hit the target, because Vítor was terrified by the incriminations that were being shouted from the city's rooftops, and which had been the central focus of the conversation with Orlando. Worldly sensed that the power he had controlled for years and years was slipping away between his fingers like fine sand. His world was disintegrating, and he might not have enough time to accumulate enough foreign currency to live out his days elsewhere. Malongo understood this because he was his friend. But the bishop of Dominus hadn't had any contact with Vítor for thirty years. Yet he had immediately managed to grasp the other man's weak point and was even using it to get what he wanted. And no one could call it blackmail. No, this guy Elias is no lightweight. It's worth going into business with him, but with great care, because one might get bundled over.

"He's going to think about it, of course he is," Malongo said. "Didn't you want to go and see your cross-eyed Zaïroise? She must be starting."

"You've discouraged me with that story about her having a squint and being gay. But I'll go and take a closer look."

The bishop got up, leaned a little on the table to gain his balance, and went off to the main dance hall, his rotund body rolling rather more than usual. Then Vítor spoke, "What an incredible transformation! That guy was a serious student, full of serious ideas, a religious man. He had radical political ideas. I always assumed he'd be some big cheese in UNITA, or that he had died. I often asked about him, but no one knew anything. Just look how he's turned out. No wonder we lost track of him."

"So you see, my friend, it's not just politics that attracts people's talents."

"Do you think he's got talent? That swindler?"

Malongo unleashed one of his famous guffaws. He slapped Vítor heartily on the shoulder, and his friend recoiled, in self-defence. If it weren't for the white strands in Vítor's beard and Malongo's extra few kilos, one wouldn't think thirty years had gone by since they first became friends at the Casa.

"I understand this sort of thing. I did a lot of shows in seedy clip joints, earning my keep, as you know, singing, playing, but above all living off the women I was with. And I learned a lot from contact with lots of different people. This guy has got bags of talent. A swindler? Yes, okay, but for that you need a gift. And deep down, he's still a religious man. He hasn't changed much when it comes down to it. Except that he has changed his religion to that of pleasure. He's getting his own back on the Protestants for all the trauma they must have caused him with that moral puritanism of theirs. This guy's a gold mine."

"Were you serious? Are you going to back him?"

"I haven't had time to think about it, but I'm going to do a deal with him. And you as well, my old friend. Let's go into this together. Give me a few days to figure things out. Before I bring him any proposal, I'll talk with you. Let's make some dough out of the gullibility of the rabble. And without anyone knowing. We'll put the bishop out in front; he's the front man. We'll just rake it in. This church is going to be popular and earn a stack of money. What the mob wants is to dance, drink, fuck, without feeling guilty about anything. And if there are any cures performed as it goes along, all the merrier. And a show with music, noise, and lights. But before we're in it up to our necks, Elias will organize a show for us. Let's see what he's like when he's on stage. It may be that when people see him, he'll fall apart, he won't have strong enough nerves, and he'll lose his charismatic skills. Apart from anything else, his physique doesn't help him—short, tubby, bald ... He's not exactly an Apollo. But if he's got a bit of spark, that may compensate."

"I'm not having anything to do with it."

"Are you so sure of your political future? Or have you got a pile of dough stashed overseas? Look, anything could happen here. A guy has to start thinking about tomorrow. Some ready cash and the support of a dynamic church, I don't think that's something to turn your nose up at. Just imagine the young fanatics Elias might have under his control. It would be enough for him to tell them, 'Back that guy,' and they'd smash everything else up. In Africa, the winner is the one with the greatest potential for smashing things up. At the very least, it'll gain enough time for an orderly retreat, while his fanatics let themselves get killed."

Vítor didn't answer immediately. He looked at the empty bottle. Shook the remains of the ice in his glass and drank the drop of water left over in the bottom. He got up, he, too, leaning his thin body against the table.

"Let's go and see the rest of the show and order some more drink. All right ... think about it and we'll talk then. But I've had enough of churches for one day. When I remember how intimidated I felt when I spoke to Elias, who was older and had read so much ... From that time I went and invited him to the dance at the Casa, I was shaking because I was so certain he had been involved in the UPA violence. He spoke with such conviction that I began to doubt our ideas. Yes, you're right, he's an actor. Maybe ..."

They entered the main dance hall and took their seats at their reserved table again. The manager signalled to a waiter who came over and asked whether they wanted anything to drink. The Zaïroise had done her number, and now someone was singing, accompanying himself on a guitar. The music was low, and they could even talk. Malongo surveyed the room. All the tables were occupied. A significant proportion were foreigners, both men and women, and judging by their skin tone, Europeans who were only temporarily subjected to the heat of the tropical sun, very different from Sara's dusky whiteness, for example. The only cabaret in Luanda was becoming popular. Eventually, he glimpsed Elias at a rear table, hard to make out because the bishop and his lady were as one, kissing and embracing on the same chair. The young boy, as Elias called him, and the woman friend were laughing.

"Our priest isn't wasting any time putting into practice what he preaches," he said to Vítor, gesturing with his head in their direction.

The other looked over to where Malongo had indicated and smiled. "Wasn't there a saint who said do what I say and not what I do? Our saint Elias is the opposite: he does precisely what he says. That's radical coherence for you."

Malongo's bark of laughter drowned the sound of the music and caused heads to turn in their direction. Vítor recoiled into a corner in order to hide from prying eyes that see everything and then spread malevolent rumours all over the place. Malongo noticed this, and the bishop also heard them from across the hall and waved with his free hand. The other remained clutching his neophyte's ample bosom.

3

Malongo breathed in the fresh morning air with delight. He had lived too long in Europe, and he found the cold agreeable. He even found the heat in Luanda during the rainy season very hard to endure. He took shelter anywhere that had air conditioning, which fortunately was abundant in the circles he frequented. Now they were in the misty season. Even so, once the sun came up, he had to turn on the cooling system in his Volvo. Yes, I've become a white man. I just don't notice it here in my homeland. He stepped out onto his veranda and stretched. The houseboy was serving breakfast at the table on the veranda, where he liked to take it, gazing at the movement in the street and the plants in the garden. The house lacked a woman. He didn't like getting involved in the domestic tasks of managing the servants, choosing what meals the cook should prepare or sorting out the clothes that Dona Maria was supposed to wash and iron. He didn't mind shopping, which was easily done in a supermarket that took foreign currency. The problems would arise when they stopped taking foreign currency, as the government was promising. Any barefoot riff-raff would be able to go there, meaning kilometre-long queues and products quickly sold out. Clearly things couldn't continue like that. Better to raise prices so much that the loafers would stop going. They've got to learn that egalitarianism is over. There are places for some people, and there are places for others, those with the means can go in, those who don't can feed themselves by window shopping.

433

The table was set, and he sat down on one of the matching white wrought-iron chairs. It was the usual veranda furniture to be found in the houses of the bourgeoisie in Alvalade, uncomfortable but fashionable. He split open a croissant and smeared it with butter. He drank a glass of orange juice as an appetizer and then helped himself to a plate of scrambled eggs and bacon. There was bread, milk, coffee, and fruit still to come. The breakfast of a four-star hotel, he thought to himself, satisfied. He didn't know about a five-star hotel because he'd never been in one. That would happen next time he travelled abroad, if business went as he predicted. He tasted the eggs. Shit, not enough salt. The cook had taught the houseboy, João, how to do the eggs, so that he wouldn't have to come to work so early. But nine times out of ten, João either forgot the salt or added too much. Malongo's shout brought him running, terrified. He had the appearance of a restless eighteen-year-old.

"You never learn, do you, you Black jackass? You've forgotten the salt again, you son of an old bitch. Come here, come and taste it."

Malongo grabbed his head with both hands and forced it down into the plate. "Taste it, you bastard, taste it so you can learn." João struggled, but the boss was too strong for him, and his face only left the plate when a gigantic slap threw him against the wall of the veranda. The houseboy lay on the ground, dizzy, rubbing his face. Two small boys who were walking down the road stopped to look. The gardener heard bellowing and came round to the front garden, but when he saw what was happening, he withdrew strategically. João shook his head and got up. His eyes were narrowed with rage, and he shouted, "Do you think the colonists still run this country?"

Malongo stepped toward him menacingly. But he stopped a couple of metres away when he noticed that the scene was being watched from the street by a woman who had joined the two boys. How tiresome, the wall wasn't high enough to guarantee domestic privacy. Moreover, the hedge above it had been mistreated by the previous tenant, and there were gaps in it, which were only gradually being filled.

"Shut your mouth, or you'll get some more."

"We're independent, do you hear? No one has the right to hit me."

"Go and get your things, and get out of my sight. Otherwise I'll beat you to a pulp. There's no shortage of people like you for housework here. I gave you a slap so you'd learn, because Black jackasses like you only learn if they get a good hiding. You don't want to learn? That's your problem. Scram!"

"Aren't you Black too? You're like a colonist, worse than a colonist."

Malongo went into the house, embarrassed by the people gathering on the sidewalk, listening to the lively description from the little boys who had heard the houseboy's cries. He went to the backyard and spoke to the frightened old gardener.

"João's leaving. He lacked respect. Go and tell him to get his things together quickly and beat it. Before I smash his face."

The houseboy had been living in the room in the backyard for the last two months, at the request of the gardener, who was his uncle. At least that is what he called himself when he had asked him whether he would give João a job. He must be from the same village; he's just become his nephew, Malongo thought. Bloody kid, always talking about independence. A yokel from the backwoods now feels big enough to complain to an elder. Of course, he did fourth grade at the school in the bush and then came to Luanda to try his luck. And at school, instead of learning how to work, all he learned were these puffed-up, empty political slogans, because we're independent. They've been independent for donkey's years, and they work less and less. That's what the problem with them is. He went back to the front room but didn't dare go out onto the veranda. Through the window, he could see that João was holding what was almost a political rally on the sidewalk. There were now more than twenty people. The gardener was trying to pull his nephew inside, but he was seething with anger, explaining that the colonists were coming back to take over the country, now helped by one or two Blacks who had been in Europe all these years learning how to better betray their compatriots.

The gardener finally managed to drag João back into the garden, and the crowd gradually dispersed, arguing among themselves. That's why this country doesn't move forward. People don't have anything to do. In Europe, you'd never see a scene like that, a gathering of such layabouts, all quite happy to while away some time when there was something unexpected to engage their interest. Certainly not, because there, time matters. And now because of these cretins, I'm under siege inside, with my food getting cold outside. Fuck them! He went out onto the veranda, looked at the half-dozen people who still lingered on the sidewalk, and sat down at the table with an air of indifference. He pushed aside the plate with the eggs into which he had shoved João's face. He poured himself some coffee and milk and ate the croissant he had prepared.

"Give us some bread, mister colonist," shouted one of the kids on the sidewalk, holding out his skinny arm.

Malongo choked because of the sudden fury overwhelming him. He spluttered coffee over the tablecloth, and the people on the sidewalk burst out laughing. He got up, coughing, and went back inside, followed by the flies and the kids' guffaws. He stayed for a good few minutes inside the bathroom, waiting for his coughing to subside and for the mob to disperse outside. But of one thing he was sure: they had spoiled his breakfast, and he no longer felt at all hungry. As he left the bathroom, he bumped into the gardener, with his meek air.

"I'm sorry, boss. João wants to speak to you."

"He'd better make himself scarce. I don't want to see him."

But the houseboy came in without asking permission. He was

carrying a bag with his things. He looked at Malongo fearlessly but without any defiance. The left side of his face was starting to swell.

"I've come for my money. This month, I worked for two weeks."

"I'm not paying you anything. Go and complain to the union."

Domestic staff weren't protected by the union, Malongo knew that. If he'd wanted, he could have paid him the money, as it was a derisory amount for someone of his means. But João was the author of all his misfortunes, and to cap it all off had made him retreat from his veranda and go without breakfast. He wasn't going to pay him, that was that, and nothing in this world was going to force him. And don't let them come with that story of social rights acquired as a result of the Revolution, that was over and done with. No more populism and egalitarianism, which had ruined the country.

"You've got to pay, boss. I worked."

"Either you get out of here or I'll give you the beating of your life. And you'll end up in prison as well."

The gardener grabbed João by the shoulder. "Go now." The boy shook himself free with a shove. His eyes narrowed again. He put his bag on the floor and faced up to Malongo. This guy is going to force me to give him another beating, the savage bastard. But the gardener placed himself between them and pushed his nephew. "That's enough, go away. I'll speak to the boss later." João picked up his bag again and let himself be led out by his uncle. Malongo heard him still talking in the front garden: "That colonist is going to pay for this, Uncle. These gents come back from abroad and think they can order us around, rob us, and beat us up. Colonialism is over."

Then he heard the garden gate shut and the old man chiding the kids on the sidewalk, "What are you waiting for?" Silence fell. Malongo sat down in an armchair to calm down. After a while, the gardener started to use his shears on the bougainvillea, which was destined to reinforce the hedge on top of the garden wall,

437

turning the house into an impregnable fortress. The monotonous sound of the shears as they did their pruning made him feel a drowsiness that caused his anger to abate. He sat there for a long time, concentrating on the sound.

He looked at his watch: nine o'clock. The cook hadn't yet arrived, but he wasn't going to wait. He would know what to prepare for lunch by himself. He would have to look for another houseboy. Maybe a woman would be better, preferably from the cook's family, who were from Cuanza Sul. Serious people. He didn't want any more spoiled brats with populist ideas about independence.

He told the gardener to open the garage door and left in his Volvo. He drove along slowly, breathing in the cool of the car's air conditioning, a CD of Caribbean music playing. With the music and behind the smoked-glass windows, Malongo felt secure inside his car. Very different from the sensation felt by those walking along the street, permanently plunged into a climate of war. The pavement in the Rua Marien Ngouabi was as potholed as ever; over the last seven years, he'd learned where they were. Occasionally, they would disappear, because they would get filled with asphalt. But as the burst water pipes were never repaired underneath, the holes would reappear after a couple of weeks. He avoided the potholes, dodged past the kids selling cigarettes and bread along the street, and continued on his way toward the downtown Baixa area. He was making a wide detour in order to get to his intended destination, which was Cazenga. But there was no hurry, and it was always pleasant to pass through the Baixa, in spite of the dilapidation of the buildings. He could feel it: one day it would be the business centre, the Wall Street of Luanda. That was why he had established his firm there. A small apartment with two rooms, his own office and that of his secretary. The secretary didn't have anything to do, but an impresario had to have a secretary. His business really hadn't yet got off the ground; he was at the stage of settling in and making contacts. He had also been obliged to buy the apartment with foreign currency, but it was worth it. Not everyone could boast a head office in the Rua Rainha Ginga.

In squares and on street corners, women and children were selling cigarettes and beer. Some had set up shoeshine operations and were sitting on dried-milk cans. He suddenly remembered Horácio, the poet from his time in Lisbon, a tiresome fellow who wanted to force literature on everyone. Horácio said that Angolan literature was shot through with shoeshine boys, because they were the most succinct image of colonialism. That may have been true, but even so many years after independence, kids still skipped school to shine shoes, if they wanted to earn a living without resorting to stealing. An image of colonialism? Those people were going to do things differently from other African countries. When they passed by his house in Paris or Brussels, during the time of the war against the Portuguese, they'd say, "Such-and-such country, a disaster, they don't even use scales in the market; another country, shameful, there they go sucking up to the Europeans." In the end, it turned out the same. Even the sale of products in little heaps, without any scales, the result of an economy based on penury. And prostitution, small-scale illegal businesses, side hustles. Not to mention the mendacity of their leaders in relation to the World Bank, the European Community, and all the aid organizations. Such a noble people turned into beggars…Shit, those were Aníbal's words, according to Judite. A friend had confided in him as a form of self-criticism: we wanted to make this land into a country in Africa; in the end all we made was just another African country.

He passed the building where he had his firm; the secretary was probably there, contemplating the furniture. Too bad. What's important is to have a legal firm at a prestigious address. Business deals take place elsewhere. That was the case with the current project he was involved in, with the divine pastor of Dominus.

He had imposed his conditions on the rotund Elias: he would invest capital, above all for the sound systems, the thousand-watt columns, strobe lights of all tones and sizes. And for the construction of the church at Cazenga, which is where he was heading now. Vítor would give his political backing. But he, Malongo, was the financier, and profits were to be divided into two halves. One half for the bishop and the other for them. It was fair that Elias should keep half, for it had been his idea and he was the front man. The two friends would share the other half equally. Elias sighed, argued, sighed again, complained that he was being robbed, but there was nothing he could do about it. He needed help urgently, because he didn't even have enough money to hire a movie theatre to put on his show on a Sunday morning. He had chosen a vacant plot in Cazenga and began to build a church, thanks to the work of a few volunteers among the faithful, but he couldn't get hold of enough cement to continue with it. Worst of all was when he was summoned to the commissariat for building without authorization, and they wanted the whole thing knocked down. The servant of Dominus eventually accepted the conditions and even the final demand: whatever happened, he didn't know them; they had no business ventures together. In the best African fashion, the agreement was celebrated with a bottle, without any paperwork or witnesses. Two days later, Vítor entered the fray and legalized the Dominus Church of Hope and Joy. And in a week, Elias received the papers authorizing the construction of the temple and ownership of the huge plot surrounding it, which had previously been destined to become low-income housing. It was a long way from the centre of the city, but there was nothing more that could be done about it for now. With the predicted liberalization, they might be able to buy another more central plot of land, with a loan from a bank.

He drove up the zigzag road to the Alto das Cruzes Cemetery, overtaking trucks loaded with products coming up from the docks. But soon the traffic was blocked because a ten-ton Mercedes, loaded down with demijohns of wine, had driven off the road on a curve and rolled over. Half of its cargo had fallen out. Many of the demijohns had smashed and the wine was flowing back down the road. Passersby took advantage of the situation to grab whole demijohns of wine and run off with them. Judging by the number of people who immediately turned up to pillage the truck, it looked as if there had been some prior arrangement with the driver. He had already heard about this stratagem: the truck was deliberately rolled over, always on the same tight bend, and its contents pillaged before the police arrived. The driver could easily justify the accident on a bend that was too tight for such badly loaded large vehicles. As the products belonged to the State, no one worried too much about finding out how the accidents occurred. Malongo saw some people loading a van with bottles taken from the top of the truck. And the van sped off right in front of everyone. The wine would be sold straightaway on the parallel market. Business done Luanda-style, in broad daylight.

The traffic started moving again very slowly. The vehicles which managed to draw level with the truck would stop, because everyone wanted to gape at the scene. And also get the chance of grabbing a demijohn of wine. It took Malongo half an hour to break free of the traffic snarl. The driver of the truck had a look of resignation as he spoke to two policemen who had arrived, in the meantime, on motorcycles. The pillaging had been completed, which was why the police had an easy job of keeping people away. That's the result of a state economy, Malongo thought. No one is ever responsible, and the mafia take advantage. If the driver knew that the boss would punch him in the face and take him to court, he would never roll his truck over. Nor would he risk taking that route, which everyone knew was unsuitable for heavily laden trucks. But the boss is the State and doesn't give a fig for the loss incurred.

He advanced through the Miramar district as far as Sambizanga. Once again, he had chosen a longer route, but he needed to drive in order to dispel, once and for all, the bad feeling caused by the houseboy. The young son of a bitch, thinking he was so smart. Then his thoughts changed as he saw people, in particular children, who were crowded around piles of trash, looking for remnants of food, clothes, or things they could sell, competing with the rats and birds. The trash heap was once small and the area uncrowded. But with the growth of the city, it now stretched almost as far as the centre, right next to the diplomatic quarter. When the wind blew from the north, the stench invaded the embassies. Shameful. People moved around on top of the steaming trash, as dirty as the trash itself. And residential areas had grown up around the trash, breathing in ever more closely the putrid vapours emanating from it. A doctor had told him the whole population of the area suffered from respiratory problems. There had often been talk of moving the trash heap outside the city, but garbage trucks continued to unload their contents into the gullies there. He turned off the air conditioning so as not to fill the car with pestilent fumes and drove past as quickly as he could.

Straight after this, in a wide open space that dominated the whole bay, he came to the Roque Santeiro market, the largest in Luanda. In recent years, when he had regularly visited the country, he had been able to witness the unstoppable growth of the market, which had first been resisted and then accepted with resignation by the authorities. Thousands of traders set themselves up on the ground selling vegetables and then later clothes, shoes, medicines, domestic appliances, motorbikes, car parts—in a word, everything. What couldn't be found in the official shops appeared at the Roque. Stalls had been erected, and now there were bars and restaurants under shades made of palm fronds. This was fast becoming the place where all business transactions were taking place, almost on the periphery of the city, right in the area of the musseque, or shanty town. The musseque laying down the gauntlet against the colonial Baixa. He pulled to the side of the road up on a slope, but relatively far from the market. He contemplated the azure sea, the verdant Ilha opposite, the red of the gullies, the yellow and grey of the buildings back along the Marginal, the boulevard running along the bay in the city centre. From there, Luanda looked like a rainbow inside a shell. This image had been ever-present in his youth, ever since he had come to Luanda from Malanje to study and play soccer. Far from his homeland, he had often opened the shell of his memory, and that rainbow had emerged to provide him with comfort.

A woman knocked on the car window. "Haven't you got anything, friend?" Of course, a car parked there, outside the market, attracted attention. They immediately thought he was bringing beer to be resold. He shook his head, without lowering the window. He had to get going, otherwise more people would come and pester him. But his attention was drawn toward a seething crowd on the left-hand side of the market, where the women sold vegetables and coal. A man emerged, running away from it, chased by dozens of people. He saw the man grabbed by someone, fall to the ground, and then smothered under the weight of a mass of bodies. People were converging there from all corners of the market. And they were also making their way toward the scene from the highway, running past the car and shouting. The woman who wanted to buy beer from him also ran off. Malongo rolled down the window to hear what was happening. The shouting revealed that a thief had been caught. A small boy ran right next to the car, shouting back to others, "A thief! They're gonna singe him."

It was impossible to see what was happening, but they must have been on the point of lynching him. As in a film, Malongo saw the throng open up in a circle, leaving a body in the middle struggling to get up. Then someone threw some liquid over the body, which must be gasoline, and seconds later an orange flame flared up from the fallen body, which got up, ran toward the people who quickly moved apart, only to collapse again on the red earth of the musseque, where the flame and the body's life consumed themselves, in the solemn silence of the market. A police car arrived, its siren wailing, and people ran off in all directions, diluting collective responsibility in the labyrinth of market stalls and huts and leaving the body sprawled on the ground.

Malongo started the engine, trembling slightly, and drove off through the middle of Sambizanga, turning right toward Cazenga. He'd had enough driving around; his day really was ruined now. Only the peace and joy of Dominus can bring me any serenity, he thought to himself ironically. He drove at speed, even forgetting to roll the window back up, down the long thoroughfares leading to Elias's temple.

This time, he had a pleasant surprise, when he reached the square where the church was being built. About a hundred people were working, dancing and singing, making cement blocks, placing the dry blocks on the walls of the building being constructed, with an effort and a joy that he had never seen before. In their midst was Elias, bubbling with energy, shouting, dancing, going from group to group. Malongo saw the devotee who had been at the cabaret and whom he now knew was called Micaela. A mature woman and a widow, she was holding a builder's shovel. The two loudspeaker columns he had got hold of provisionally, until the equipment he had ordered from abroad arrived, were bellowing out music by Mory Kanté. Another hundred or so people were standing around in a circle, admiring the spectacle, their bodies moving to the rhythm of the music. He got out of the car and walked over to the bishop.

"Lots of energy, and the work is moving forward quickly."

"Hello, Malongo. As you can see, the love for Dominus can bring about miracles. Who said these people don't like working? Here, they know they're participating in the work of redeeming the world, so they've got motivation."

"Don't give me that," whispered Malongo. "It's because of the music."

"That helps, but it's not everything. Work should be a joyous thing, and music brings out the joy. But hang around for a bit, and you'll see the main reason."

Elias climbed up onto a platform where the sound system was placed, grabbed a microphone, turned the volume of the music down a little, and began to speak, his words wafting over the sound of the music, while he made use of the musical backing and its rhythm. He spoke and danced, up and down the platform from one end to the other.

"These are the people of Dominus, the one and only lord. These are the people who defy Evil, the only loser. Evil is sadness, Evil is lovelessness. Dominus is joy, Dominus is Love. We have Hope, we belong to Dominus. We have Joy, we belong to Dominus. The future is ours, we belong to Dominus. The World will have Peace, we are its builders. No illness will defeat us, we belong to Dominus. We are building a temple, the temple of Dominus. We are putting the world to rights, a World for us. Pleasure is not a sin, to love is not a sin. We work with joy, we dance with Dominus."

Malongo listened to Elias in full flow and unconsciously fell in with his lively litany. And he watched the people smiling adoringly and working even harder. They carried the heavy blocks, stepping along in time to the music, laughed with one another, giving each other hugs as they passed by. One or two people in the circle of bystanders crossed the square and offered to join in the work. And a constant stream of people came from the

445

adjacent streets to swell the ranks of onlookers and workers. Elias didn't stop walking up and down the makeshift stage and addressing the crowd. The music ended and some more began, and he, without so much as a second's hesitation, kept up his patter, merely changing its rhythm in accordance with the new song. Yes sir, an artist. Swaying his bulky body to the rhythm of the dance, Malongo felt proud: he had invested in a winner. Elias really was a gold mine.

The pastor ended his speech, exhorting everyone not to slack off, turned the music up again, and came over to Malongo.

"I do this from time to time in order to encourage them and to attract more people. At midday, the square will be full. Yesterday, it was the same, except that the blocks weren't dry and the walls couldn't be built. Today, there are more people working. At the end, I explain to the newcomers that it's the Church of Dominus, and I concentrate all the energy in my hand before placing it upon them. They feel much happier and come back the next day."

"You should place your hand on the market traders at Roque Santeiro. I saw them kill a thief. They set him on fire."

The bishop made an anguished face. He examined Malongo with his myopic eyes and noticed that he was perturbed. He reflected for a moment. Then he spoke in a very gentle tone. "Society is sick. People have lost their moral values. As far as they are concerned, another person's life doesn't count for anything. We need to work hard so as to give them new values."

"The problem is that they don't trust the authorities. The State has become well and truly discredited. So they take justice into their own hands, because they don't trust the State to administer it. To kill someone because he stole something..."

"That's a good topic for a sermon. Here in Cazenga, it's usual for thieves to be burned, or singed, as they call it. It's a polemical subject and needs to be approached with care. But maybe it's worth it. A society based on joy doesn't do that. But take courage, brother, our temple is growing. And without any specialist architect or workmen."

"That's what's worrying me. Won't it fall down?"

"The hand of Dominus is cradling it. How is it going to fall?"

"I'd be more reassured if an architect came and took a look at this. Do you mind if I arrange for one? Because if there's an accident, and people get killed, that's it, we'll have to invent another enterprise."

Elias looked at the walls that were now more than two metres tall. He himself had marked out the lines on the ground for the foundations. He shrugged and said, "If you want to bring in an architect, okay, that's no problem. Even though I don't think it's necessary. Dominus isn't going to let his temple fall down."

"Oh, come off it! You said yourself that Dominus doesn't intervene in things. He's like Nzambi."

"All right, all right, do as you wish. I don't mind."

Malongo turned his attention to Micaela, who was encouraging a group of followers. She was sweating, in spite of the fresh air of the cacimbo. She was reasonably fat, the fruit of a lot of religiously ingested funje. Speaking with her some days before, he had noticed her strong breath and its smell of meat. Maybe that was what the breath of a lion was like after it had eaten a buffalo. He drew the attention of Elias to Micaela's activity. The bishop smiled, and his eyes revealed the virtue of licentiousness.

"That's one great woman. All flesh and energy. She has given herself to Dominus with great verve and devotion."

"Or to his pastor," Malongo said, laughing as he got into his car.

He had left behind him the resentment caused by the house-boy, by the potholes in the road and the garbage, and the violence that ranged freely through the slums and markets. Dominus had touched him, too, with his grace. The future now looked full of hope and joy.

4

Aníbal, the man called Wisdom, arrived. He came sweating dust and happiness, recounting the long two-day journey on a truck carrying produce for the markets of Luanda, he and another ten people sitting on top of the cargo, sharing the food and drink that each of them carried in their bags. The truck belonged to Mateus, the black marketeer with whom Nina had gone to live almost ten years before and who, proving all Aníbal's prophecies correct, had got her pregnant and then kicked her out. Nina had given birth to her baby at Caotinha and remained there for a bit, before leaving her child with her own mother and vanishing from sight in some city. Sara knew the story. Each of the travellers paid a fortune for the lift on top of the truck, but Aníbal got a free ride, a courtesy of the black marketeer.

The journey had been interrupted countless times, either because of the poor state of the road, blown up by mines, or because they were held up by some armed groups, who got paid with some of the produce before allowing them through. Groups from either one of the former contenders for power, now at peace—no one could distinguish them one from another, nor did they identify themselves. They could just as well be bands of deserters. Who knows, perhaps they had mingled together in their pillaging, forgetting their former antagonism from another age. The truck drivers were used to this and had separated the merchandise with which to pay the warlords for their right to

448

pass through. A country of highway robbers, this is what we've become, Aníbal declared without emotion. They may even be true soldiers who have become unsettled. They sense that peace is going to make them less important. The cigarettes or part of the food supplies they demand is an affirmation of the power of their weapons, but at the same time an anticipated compensation for their future loss of power. For an individual to be alive and to feel that he has become a mere exhibit in a museum is always a disconcerting sensation. The important thing was that the war was over and that people and goods could circulate, rebuilding the fragmented nation. But it was beautiful, you just can't imagine, after so many years, I was able to pass through Canjala, looking across to the magnificent escarpments of Pundo on the horizon, and on the other side, the gentle gorge that fades away when it reaches the sea at Egypt Beach. Then we crossed the Quicombo and climbed the Xingo, the hills where so many battles had been fought in past wars, where the skeletons of forgotten people and the rusting remains of vehicles still lie for history to tell. We passed the mythical Keve, imagined on our right the Gabela Mountains in their eternal green, then entered the Kissama Park of all the lions, which, one must add, are no longer there, nor are the elephants or buffaloes, all eliminated by heroic weekend hunters, some of them even ferried there on helicopters. A country of plunderers, that's what we have become. Then Aníbal's eyes lit up involuntarily when he described the crossing of the bridge over the Kwanza, the people singing on the truck because Luanda was near and they could already smell the sea. That's where his narrative came to an end, and Sara knew why. Aníbal avoided talking about his arrival in his native city, which he had abandoned so many years ago and which nevertheless was an irresistible attraction to him, lulling him with childhood songs, legends of the Kianda and races across the red sands of the musseques. Love-resentment, passion-rejection,

449

Luanda. There was always a Luanda in the past of any native of Benguela, which Aníbal now considered himself to be.

Judite and Orlando were also in the sitting room. It was night and Aníbal had washed and eaten. He was wearing his eternal shorts and plastic sandals, just as in his house at Caotinha. But as he was a guest, he was wearing a loose shirt, a present from Sara, with the word *peace* emblazoned across it. His hair and beard were still long and tangled, with one or two grey strands. I must get him to have that mane cut, Sara thought. Otherwise people really will classify him as completely crazy.

"It's getting to the point when the history of this whole thing will have to be told," Orlando said. "How a generation embarks on a glorious struggle for independence and then destroys itself. But it seems that the people of your generation aren't capable of telling it. And I'm not sure whether my generation, people who are now thirty, can either. We were castrated at birth. I was just thirteen when Luanda mobilized en masse to greet the heroes of liberation. I was a member of a pioneers' base at the entrance to the Ilha, where I lived. We lived for that. We would march, listen to the stories told by the elders who had come from the forests; we would sing revolutionary songs; we invented that march-dance that spread throughout the country, which was a mixture of patriotic fervour and our creative imagination. Afterwards they wanted to organize us. They told us we should march like soldiers. 'You are the future soldiers.' We were no longer allowed to do those crazy steps that brought applause from everyone, a step forward, one to the side, a step back, a funny joke in the middle. Even at Carnival, years later, we could only march like soldiers, our groups stopped dancing. They destroyed our imagination in the name of a militaristic set of values, based on the discipline of the barracks or the convent, I don't know which, and we could no longer be critical, say what we thought. We had to think before we said anything. There were internal rifts, palace coups that no one understood, the removal of guys we regarded as heroes, others ended up in prison. And my generation, which was youthful and enthusiastic, gradually lost its enthusiasm, began to think of politics as something forbidden and dangerous, the only thing we were expected to do was to blindly carry out orders. That's what our generation has come to, thinking only of having a car and going on foreign trips, soccer and parties. Without a purpose in life."

"You're right," said Wisdom. "The most important thing for a generation is to pass on something good to the next, a project, a banner. Essentially, it's about the father leaving his son an inheritance. And it's sad to feel that our generation, which after all, and in spite of everything, gave you independence, deprived you of a chance to enjoy it straight afterwards. Like the father who gives his son a toy and then keeps it for himself, with the excuse that his son is going to ruin it. Isn't it all just so tragic and absurd?"

"You're too negative about everything," said Sara. "Okay, there were mistakes. But not everything was bad, as people say nowadays. And if we weren't allowed to do what we wanted, there were always external pressures that prevented it. From one side and the other, let's face it."

Aníbal went and got the bottle of whiskey he had brought from Benguela, which stood forgotten on the table. There was no shortage of whiskey in Luanda, but he couldn't think of a better present, and he had to bring some sort of a memento, apart from the dried fish which he had caught himself. He freshened his own drink and poured some more for the others.

Then he said, "To tell you the truth, the wrongs originated long before. This country had an intellectual elite that was the envy of any other African country. It was an urban-based elite, which transitioned quite happily between European and African culture, reconciling them successfully, in a process that lasted for centuries. But this elite never learned how to ally itself with the traditional rural elites. Last century, this was the reason why various attempts to gain autonomy failed. Because when the colonial power attacked these traditional power structures, the elite greeted the wars of conquest as the bearers of progress, for new territorial gains gave it opportunities for business and administrative roles, without understanding that in this way its own position was weakened. Then, later on, during the course of this century, despite a lot of talk about links with the countryside, the urban elite remained selfishly aloof and alone, considering itself superior to the rest of the country. Hence the so-called division within Angolan nationalism, which eventually came out into the open in this civil war, which no one wants to admit as such. I'm not saying mistakes have only come from our side. But we were the most aware of the problems, the most open to progress, which is why we had a greater responsibility to take decisive steps in order to call others to join our ranks. And when a part of you excludes the other, it will end up splintering into successive waves of exclusion. And that's how this slow agony of coups and counter-coups occurred, which Orlando referred to, continually excluding those who thought differently at a given moment, and as often as not over questions of tactics. This created an attitude of ostracism and intolerance. Those holding power at a particular moment couldn't accept an opinion that differed from their own, even though that opinion might later change, but without their admitting it, and without summoning back those who had been sidelined in the interim. We intellectuals always had beautiful ideas, but we were never capable of defending them in a serious way. And absurdly, we created an anti-intellectual populism, which we didn't even realize was self-destructive."

"So, Uncle Aníbal, what you're saying is that everything can be explained by the history of what some people call the Creole elite," Judite said. "Isn't that a bit too easy?"

"If we only limit ourselves to that . . . Of course, there were external factors that complicated things, above all the East-West ideological conflict. But these factors merely fed on our inability to unite. The term *creole* invites confusion, which is why I don't like it. Maybe the adjective *Angolese* is more precise. Whatever the case, this culturally and even racially mixed social stratum was the only one capable of looking forward and uniting the country, because it was the only one with an idea of nationhood. But it was too tainted by its own ambiguous trajectory. These people had been intermediaries in the process of colonization, while at the same time protesting against it. They proclaimed the defence of the Black race and scorned the rights of the populations of the interior because they considered them uncivilized. They demanded autonomy, but at the same time benefitted from their situation as dependants. And of course, this created a climate of suspicion between the urban class of ruling families and the traditional societies, which felt that they were merely pawns in the game. And even in the midst of these elite families, there were social divisions between those who had been slave owners and those who were the descendants of slaves, between the sons of the big house and the sons of the shanty. They were the subject of talk and argument throughout my whole childhood in the Bairro Operário, so I know what I'm talking about. All this left an atmosphere of resentment, marked patterns of behaviour, and divided the elite. A practice of exclusion is the inevitable outcome. It's obvious that these processes are not clearly perceived by people. However, the intelligentsia had an obligation to understand them from the beginning and to overcome them. Instead, they were weighed down by their original sin and their past privileges. And like all Christians, they had to chastise themselves because of the sin they carried through from their ancestors. They became intellectuals, while feeling ashamed of being so. They didn't carry out their role of intellectuals, those

who show the way ahead. It got to the stage when they accepted being considered class enemies by some so-called leaders
because they had studied more than the others. And they beat
their breasts, mea culpa, mea culpa. When the intellectuals back
down, it's obvious that society loses its sense of direction, and
it goes and seeks other values, generally those associated with
uniformity. This is the problem we face at the moment."

"That is an interesting line of thought," said Orlando. "As
you know, we have created a group, independent of any party,
to reflect on these problems. Why don't you come and address
our group? It will provide for a lively discussion."

"If you promise not to invite the press. And at the end, you
don't hand me a paper from some party to sign."

"I've already told you, it's a circle that is independent of any
party, and it exists purely as a forum for reflection."

Sara had allowed Aníbal to talk, as she knew he loved to do
this. Poor thing, he spent months on end talking to mango trees,
because he now had four, all of them with names. It was very
rare for him to have an audience, and his sin was to need an
audience. Oh, he had other sins as well, she knew that perfectly
well. Deep down, she had never forgiven him for the scene with
Nina, which he had told her about with complete candour. Not
for the fact that he had made love to her. But for having been so
brutal, for having denied her the tenderness that such a moment
demanded. He, too, acknowledged his guilt, the violent male
there is in all men had surfaced with the alcohol. "I was cruel."

"You had to face the civil war," Sara said. "Was that also a
result of this rupture?"

"Of course. There are two Angolas, and they faced up to each
other. Two Angolas originating in the schism between the urban
elite and the traditional elite. This in a very basic sense, obviously, because there were always comings and goings between
the various sectors. Fortunately, this war resulted in a draw,

neither side destroyed the other. But there are still two Angolas. We have to fill the gap, once again build bridges. But the gap will no longer be filled by parties. Parties are made to divide, not to unite. What we need is an idea that goes beyond parties, an idea of a nation."

"And a religion?" Orlando said.

"Certainly not Dominus," Judite laughed.

Faced with Aníbal's confusion, Judite told him about the project of Malongo, Vítor, and Elias. Her father had confided in her, but in this group of people, she didn't feel particularly guilty about revealing secrets that, at heart, would sooner or later become public knowledge. Aníbal didn't make any comment. Sara was insistent. "What do you think?"

"I'd rather not say anything," he replied. "After all, he's Judite's father, and the other man is your good friend, Vítor. I'm not surprised they've discovered this. Today, when society is devoid of values, people have turned to religion, of whatever kind, because they need to believe in something. And just as has always been the case, there are religions that live for the people and others that live off the people."

"You can say what you like, Uncle," Judite said. "I've already criticized my father over this. Not in political terms, because I don't know, nor do I want to know, about these shameless struggles for power, but because of the moral question. They are going to make money off people's gullibility, which is dishonest, tantamount to robbery."

"The fundamental problem is that Malongo and Vítor are the new bourgeoisie, those who have grown rich or are planning to get rich in the shadow of the State, and behave like nouveaux riches, with all that's tragic and ridiculous about the term. Then there are the lumpen bourgeois, the black marketeers of every kind, the ones who began as street traders and are growing rich without any culture or ethical stance. Which of these classes will devour the other? They are classes born from different social origins, but both have an insatiable appetite. Will they ally themselves to each other and create a new entrepreneurial class? Will they sell out to the foreigner, or will they assimilate him? I shall follow this contest, which is set to dominate the last years of the century, with interest."

"By the way," Sara said, "Malongo is thinking of putting on a dinner for you at his house, where he'll bring together Vítor and some other old friends."

"I hope you'll have sufficient diplomacy to save me from that trap."

Judite went and joined Orlando on the sofa. She gave him a quick kiss and muttered, but in such a way that all could hear, "We've got to let the two lovebirds head off to bed. They haven't seen each other for a year and have got a lot of catching up to do." Everyone chuckled complicitly. Aníbal drank the rest of his whiskey and was about to get up. But Orlando still asked, in a last attempt to feed the conversation, "Aren't you thinking of taking an active part in politics?"

"To tell you the truth, I'd like to create the MPM, the Movement for the Politically Marginalized. Its only program would be to oppose the future elected government, of whatever persuasion that might be. Because the marginalized can only be in opposition; they never win elections, even though they are the overwhelming majority of the population. And if, by some quirk of fate, the move-ment managed to get the most votes, which would correspond to a massive display of consciousness on the part of the people, it would immediately disband so as not to become corrupted by the use of power. But like a good Angolan intellectual, I don't have the ability to put into practice such a wonderful idea."

"You're not going to relinquish your responsibilities as an intellectual, I hope," Orlando said. "At least accept our invitation to develop your ideas at our independent think tank meetings. Our group also brings together the politically marginalized."

"The past never justifies passivity," Judite said. "If everyone says it's not worth it, then we might as well die, or let ourselves wither away, because that's always more coherent than just vegetating."

Each couple went off to their bedrooms, smiling mischievously. The apartment only had the two bedrooms and the living room, because Sara had always refused to get a villa. From the other side of the wall, Judite shouted, "If you need some of that Cabinda bark, you know where it's kept."

"Let's hope you get to the age of fifty plus and are still as horny as we are," Aníbal, also known as Wisdom, replied. "Our generation was only ever good at this."

When they were in bed and waiting to embrace, pleasurably deferring the inevitable, Sara asked, "How long are you planning to stay in Luanda?"

"A week. I have to get the most out of my bay. Because with this savage capitalism on the way, they're going to stuff it with hotels and bars. They're going to destroy it along with my golden solitude. One of these days, I'm going to have to find myself another bay further south, ever further south. Could the south be my final utopia?"

Aníbal spoke in a drifting tone of resignation and loss of belief. It was like the monotonous succession of arid hills endlessly awaiting rain, the infinite dimension of the savannahs, the repetitive appeal of the sun sinking into the sea at Caotinha. Sara sensed in him the fateful abdication of the guerrilla fighter, lowering his weapon, his impotent gesture of revolt surrendering to the inevitability of fate. She had a vision of Aníbal swimming out into the open seas, as straight as a die, in the direction of Brazil, without the strength nor the will to struggle against the current that sucked him along. In despair, and with compassion, she embraced his thin body, seeking to infuse it with warmth.

5

The first major service of the Dominus Church of Hope and Joy took place at the Luminar movie theatre on a misty Sunday morning. Vítor managed to get the loan of the auditorium and Malongo saw to the sound system, hired from the State Cultural Institute. Within a few months, the equipment ordered from abroad would arrive, which would give the Church its independence. The plot of land in Cazenga was being prepared, entrusted to a team of architects and engineers contracted for the project. Plans for the temple were drawn up, which improved upon Elias's initial idea, taking in the adjoining area as well, with an open square for major celebrations among the trees. In this arid area, trees were planted and the means for watering them organized. The spirits of the ancestors gained the stature of divinities in the theology of Elias, which was why trees were needed where they could dwell. One of the side walls of the temple was built out so as to support a huge terraced stage, where he would officiate. In the meantime, worship would take place in movie houses hired especially for the purpose.

From seven o'clock onwards, the faithful began to assemble, dragging along with them friends and family who were curious to attend the worship, which was billed as a spectacle in which there would be cures and other surprises. The pamphlets for the meeting, printed with Malongo's money, had been conceived by a firm of talented young designers, the best in Luanda, directed by an old artist who looked like Buffalo Bill, and distributed throughout the city for a week by the ready and willing street kids who had learned to yell, "Dominus revealed at the Luminar, let's shake and shout for Dominus." In the newspaper, a half-page advert appeared, just with the words "Dominus at the Luminar." And people asked each other as they talked in diners and bars, "But who is this Dominus? Is it a new party?" There were many questions, and few answers. So much propaganda ended up being broadcast over the radio that on one very popular morning program they also asked the question, "But what is this Dominus? Go along to the Luminar on Sunday to find out." The word *magic* was heard all over the city. Dominus became a topic of general curiosity. And so, at nine in the morning, the advertised time for the service, the auditorium was full, and lots of people were still trying to get in.

Almost all the spectators had respected the request on the pamphlet and were not wearing black, a colour that was ill-advised because of its links with sadness, and they instead wore flowery tops and blue, green, or red trousers. The faithful wore the uniform of the church, which had been organized in a hurry because of the long debate about colours, and because Dominus had not pronounced on the matter. For this reason, Elias eventually chose loose blouses or shirts made from Congo cotton, with trousers or skirts of a yellow cloth. No loud printed cotton tops or Mao jackets, African gear connoted in Luanda with sadly recalled attempts at authenticity, but trousers and shirts in the European style, tropicalized with the help of the garish cloth churned out by the Africa Textile Company in Benguela. African and Caribbean music, the volume turned up several thousand decibels, had been attracting people from neighbouring areas ever since seven o'clock, and even some diplomats who lived in the area, torn from their beds by the power of the sound system, which seemed to proclaim a different kind of Sunday. Groups of Luandans, coming from Saturday night raves, invaded the theatre thinking their party was resuming after being interrupted by the rising sun.

While the publicity had been successful and the hall was more packed than the most optimistic forecasts, Malongo and Vítor, accompanied by the inquisitive Judite, couldn't hide a certain degree of nervousness. They had arrived in Malongo's car and the minister was wearing thick dark glasses and a cloth cap, so as not to be noticed. How would Elias perform in front of such a huge crowd? The hour of truth was nigh. They didn't know the details of the service, and they were particularly scared of the cures, because these constituted the weak point, which could easily expose their flank to accusations of skulduggery. They were more nervous still when they saw André Silva, a young journalist, with his notepad and pen, ready to jot down evidence for some scathing article. André Silva wrote in elegant, corrosive prose, a rare example among a new generation of journalists. They were in the last, most inconspicuous row, which had been kept under close guard by Elias's wardens ever since seven. But even so, Vítor shrank into his seat, hoping the journalist wouldn't spot him. "Can you imagine what it would be like," Worldly whispered to Malongo, "if tomorrow's headline was 'Minister Attends Electronic Cult Worship'? I'd be done for."

"Of course not," Malongo replied. "You could always just say that a minister has to be with the people, and that you came to see what this Dominus thing was all about. They're not going to catch you out because of this. But, of course, they could do a bit of investigating and discover you've been giving the Church a bit of a helping hand. That would cause a stir." Judite smiled as she listened to the conversation. She had accepted her father's invitation to observe the effect of Elias's cures in her capacity as a doctor. And she could see how nervous Malongo was. He had tried to convince Elias to drop the cures, but the bishop was adamant: "A religion that doesn't produce cures isn't an acceptable religion, and my mission is to make people happier." The contract between them was quite clear, and Elias reminded him of it: "When it comes to religious questions, I'm the one who decides. I'm the one who was chosen by Dominus."

The music suddenly changed from the Caribbean music by Kassav' to Bach. It was exactly nine o'clock, and a nervous murmur went through the packed hall, with all the aisles between the fully occupied rows of seats jammed with people standing. One minute of Bach and then silence. The silence was painful to the eardrums and intimidated all the spectators, with the result that there wasn't so much as a cough or a sigh to be heard. In the middle of this almost agonizing silence, Elias made his entry onto the stage decked with flowers. Extraordinary how they managed to get hold of so many flowers, Judite thought. They must have devastated all the city's gardens. They'll have the young ecologists after them.

The bishop of Dominus wore the same clothing as the members of his congregation, a loose multicoloured blouse, with motifs relating to national culture, chief among these the Thinker and Chibinda Ilunga, and yellow trousers. Around his neck, he wore a thick glossy necklace, from which hung a huge medallion, with the triangle and the sloping line. His bare head accentuated his gleaming baldness. He made his entrance with his arms held wide, walking with quick, dainty steps, and came to a halt in the middle of the stage, while the sound of drum music got louder and louder. As the volume of the drums increased, he began to accompany the ancestral rhythms. Then he began to speak, with the help of the hidden microphone in his shirt, making the cadence of his speech follow the rhythm of the drums.

"This is the Church of Dominus, all are welcome, the faithful are welcome, the curious are welcome, enemies are welcome, slanderers are welcome, disbelievers are welcome, because all

belong to Dominus, because Dominus loves you all, and at the
end, there will be no more disbelievers, at the end there will be
no more enemies, at the end there will be no more slanderers,
for in the end we are all brothers, we are all the children of
Dominus, and Dominus is the only father and mother of all
the gods, and he is father and mother of all the spirits, and he
is the father and mother of all the winds and of the Moon, of
the storms and the sun, of the animals and the plants, of those
who love and unlove, of those who are joyful and those who
are sad, of those who accept and those who are intolerant, of
those who love without fear and those who are fearful of love,
because Dominus created us to be happy, because Dominus
created us to enjoy pleasure, and there were men who did not
understand, there were men who wanted to make us sad, there
were men who created rules to keep us unhappy, and those
men created religions without understanding the message of
Dominus, of love and joy, and those religions oppress people,
they want people to suffer and weep, to feel guilty when they are
full of joy, feel guilty when they enjoy pleasure, feel guilty when
they make love, and people are unhappy, they lose their sense
of pleasure, and they become like those who hate, and kill and
maim, and wage wars and steal, all because they feel no pleasure,
all because they feel no love, all because they have forgotten the
message of Dominus, the one and only true god, the Nzambi
of our hearts, the Nzambi-Kalunga of our beliefs, the Nzambi
of our hope, and that is why we are teaching the doctrine of
Dominus, who revealed Himself to us in Nigeria, land of all the
gods and orixás, gods who crossed the Atlantic, all of them the
children of Dominus, the Nzambi of our joy, who said go forth
and teach my children who suffer in wars, my children who are
oppressed, my children who have forgotten about pleasure, go
forth and teach the truth." And at this moment the drumming
became frenetic and Elias started shaking his buttocks. "Go

forth and teach, Dominus said, go forth and teach, Dominus
spoke, so that women may hear, Dominus spoke, so that men
may hear, Dominus spoke, so that children may hear, Dominus
spoke, so that the deaf may hear, Dominus spoke, so that the
mutilated may hear, Dominus spoke, so that the crippled may
dance, Dominus spoke, so that the blind may dance, Dominus
spoke, so that the sad may sing, Dominus spoke, so that the
widowed may sing, Dominus spoke, so that the orphans may
sing, Dominus spoke, so that the spirits may dance, Dominus
spoke, let them dance in the leaves of trees, Dominus spoke, let
them sing in the crossroads, Dominus spoke, let the medicine
men sing, Dominus spoke, let witchcraft end, Dominus spoke, let
ingratitude end, Dominus spoke, let envy end, Dominus spoke,
let jealousy end, Dominus spoke." And the crowd began to clap
their hands, repeating the litany Dominus spoke, their eyes rolling, bodies shaking, the rhythm of the drums penetrating them,
penetrating them, their eyes looking into themselves, their words
more anxious, their breathing more gasping, until a woman got
up and ran to the stage, screamed "Dominus spoke," and started
shimmying and shaking, frothing at the mouth, her eyes rolling
around, shimmying until she fell to her knees, Elias still shaking
his buttocks this way and that, reciting, the people screaming
"Dominus spoke," and the woman shimmying until she fell flat
out on the wooden floor, in convulsions, her hips wriggling as
if in some frenetic act of love, and then Elias stopped speaking,
stopped shaking his buttocks, and pointed at her with his right
arm, his hand open toward the woman, and said, "My hand will
cure you, mine is the hand of Dominus, with Dominus I cure
you, your sadness will go to the sea, my hand will cure you," and
the woman lying there, quietly, breathing calmly, and the people
who were sitting got up so as to get a better view, Judite among
the first, and now the drumming was beating more softly, until
the woman sat up, looked at the people who were staring at

her, and smiled, that smile of peace, a bow of gratitude to Elias, and she stepped down from the stage with an air of happiness, her eyes no longer looking inside her but out at the world that was observing her, and Elias took up his litany again, "Because Dominus cured her, merely through the imposition of his hand, she had the spirits of her ancestors oppressing her heart, but now she is free and happy, she will never be the same person again, and illnesses will find it harder to assail her, because she has received the grace of Dominus," and then the drum beats speeded up once more and he began to shake his butt again. "Dominus spoke through this woman, Dominus spoke through her body, whoever wants to be free, Dominus spoke, should love Dominus, Dominus spoke, should love others, Dominus spoke."

At that precise moment, Judite heard a deep sigh of relief, and she looked at her father and saw him smiling, the first test had gone well, the hall was once again red hot with excitement, the rhythm of the drums once more frantic, people shouting in unison "Dominus spoke."

No one was listening to Elias's discourse any longer, all of them intoxicated by the hand-clapping and the drums, by the shouting and by the toing and froing of the great prophet on the stage, until a murmur ran through the audience and a man leaped up onto the stage, his eyes all but sticking out of their orbits, and ran toward Elias waving his arms, as if he were about to assault him, but he stopped abruptly and fell to his knees, kissing the prophet's extended hand, and acquired a beatific expression in his broad, happy grin, and then got up without a word and left the stage, a peaceful smile on his face, ceding his place to a young girl and then another and then one more woman, in an endless line of people going up to receive what might be some sort of blessing, but which, according to Elias, were the flows of energy coming directly from Dominus, which treated the radical illnesses through his hand, a humble instrument used by the divinity, while all this time, the people in the audience repeated the same litany, swaying to the rhythm of the drums, until their sound abated a little, and the bishop used the opportunity to speak, always in the same tone, explaining the main features of the doctrine, thundering against intolerance, speaking of the need to forget the resentments of war, and the need to believe in a collective future, not in the paradise after death but now, immediately, because the future was made in the present and the present should be lived with pleasure, with faith and confidence, for only happy people could create just worlds and not the opposite, as all religions and ideologies had hitherto always taught them, that a just future made men better, this was a mistake stemming from the failure of previous prophets to understand the words of Dominus, for Dominus taught us, in Nigeria the only truth, the future will only be just if we are happy today, which is why we must view life as the brief time of pleasure, without excess or wantonness, but with hope and faith, for Dominus is good and does not make us pay for any original sin, Man was born pure and pure he will remain if he follows the rules of a normal life in which love is natural, eating and drinking is natural, singing is natural, dancing is natural, and above all, above all—at which point Elias allowed a pause to settle over everyone in order to make himself clearly understood. "Dancing is the art of the gods, and that is why in all of the most ancient religions, the ones closest to the teachings of Dominus, the dancers were sacred and everything happened with dance, just as in our own traditional societies, because rhythm and pleasure in bodily movement are a manifestation of godliness, which is why it's no coincidence that Africans are the best dancers in the world, for man was born in Africa, and speech was born in Africa, the divine word, and dance was born in Africa, the divine art, and from Africa the true word of Dominus will radiate out into the world, from this, our Africa, right here, this land blessed with all the marvels, but forever crushed by all forms of oppression, which nevertheless have never managed to completely stifle our VOICE, which comes down from times beyond memory, THE VOICE OF DOMINUS, this voice through which I shall now address you all, just as I heard it one day in Nigeria."

And Elias once again paused, and all those shaking and shouting stopped in order to watch him and listen, and he began to talk in that special way of his, without moving his lips, a deep almost hoarse voice filling the auditorium, now in complete silence: "THIS is my voice, I am Dominus and I speak to you through my dear son, Elias, and everything he tells you, I am the one speaking, and everything he does, it is because I wish it, and those who follow him will be better, and those who follow him will be happy, and those who follow him will own the present, because THIS is my wish." And then Elias shook his head, went back to speaking in his normal voice, while the drumming started again with a low beat, making people sway gently. "This is what Dominus has said, and he is the light, and he is the voice, and he comes from the stars to visit us, and we never understand him, we never succeed in grasping the strange objects that sometimes pass over our heads, which not even the scientists can explain."

"That's it," Malongo said out loud. "He managed to stick the UFOS into all this crap, I knew he would, I knew it." But Judite noticed that her father was radiant, in wonder, and his dancer's gift was coming to the surface, as he couldn't stop himself from swaying to the rhythm of the litany and the drumming, he, too, caught in the trap, while Elias continued to speak and to increase his cadence, again shaking his buttocks and repeating "Dominus spoke," accompanied by his acolytes and then by the whole auditorium, even by the journalist, André Silva, who had jettisoned his notepad and was shouting like everyone else, his eyes gaping, his role as mordant critic forgotten, to the extent that the next day he would write in his column that the Luminar had lost its roof during the cult. He himself had seen the ceiling launch into space in a million fragments of light, and that is why the theatre is now an open-air one, a marvellous ruin which should remain like this as a testament to the great strength of Dominus, a ruin that was the equal of the Colosseum in Rome, which, according to recent scientific studies, had also had a roof before the lions ate the first Christians who at the time were faithful disciples of the theories of Dominus, though also deceived by the asceticism of the prophets who had failed to completely understand the lesson of tolerance.

And the only people to remain calm were Vítor, who remained curled up in his corner, and Judite, who had been strangely cast back to the time when she was fifteen, and she had witnessed the multitudes chanting independence slogans with the same fervour, for Malongo was now swaying to the litany, which was now reaching its fullest cadence, Elias now totally on the loose and with the spotlight on him, declaring "Dominus spoke," administering the cure with his hand on the line of people climbing onto the stage and shaking, imposing his hand over the whole of the auditorium, now singing, dancing, and laughing, in absolute harmony, and one or two witch doctors climbed onto the stage in order to cast off their charms, a chicken's foot, a little piece of bone, the remains of a human ear, nails or sticks, the carved wooden figures, repentant witch doctors now free, in a festival without precedent in Luanda, and the church wardens passed among the people with collection bags, while the bishop, bathed in sweat, his voice hoarse, kept up the litany. "Dominus spoke, no one is obliged, Dominus spoke, the unbeliever shouldn't give, Dominus spoke, the money is for the Church, Dominus spoke, Africa teaches the world, Dominus spoke, those who hate shouldn't give, Dominus spoke, the enemy of Dominus shouldn't give, Dominus spoke, we need your help, Dominus spoke, we shall teach the truth, Dominus spoke, but we don't want dirty

467

money, Dominus spoke, drug money is dirty, Dominus spoke, money from corruption is dirty, Dominus spoke, money from envy is dirty, Dominus spoke, money from theft is dirty, Dominus spoke."

And the audience filled the bags with money, the odd item of jewellery and even a few shirts, and the wardens went and emptied the bags behind the movie screen and returned for more, everyone dancing, kissing each other, touching each other, dancing navel to navel in the rows and the aisles, and later in the square in front of the Luminar and in the adjacent streets, stamping their feet and clapping their hands and repeating "Dominus spoke," on their way to the markets and their homes, the beaches and the musseques, in ever larger processions, as in Carnival, setting off happily from the Luminar to gain the World and to gain Hope.

Epilogue

It is obvious that a story that began with the word *so* cannot end
with an epilogue or even a full stop.

Berlin, February 1992

GLOSSARY

Andrade, Mário de (1928–1990): Angolan poet, politician, and founding member of the MPLA in 1956, and its first president in 1960.

anhara: Savannah.

A vitória é certa: "Victory is certain." A slogan and rallying cry used by the MPLA.

*bailundo*s: An ethnic and linguistic group from the Huambo region, who formed the core of migrant workers in the northern coffee plantations during the colonial period. See *Ovimbundu*.

Bairro Operário / Workers' District: An area of Luanda that, by the 1950s, was inhabited by many old Creole families pushed out of adjacent central areas of the city by incoming Portuguese settlers.

bica: A term common in Lisbon for an espresso.

cabrito: A light-skinned person of European and African ancestry.

cacimbo: Mist or drizzle prevalent during the dry season in Angola.

calulú: A stew of fish or meat that usually includes green vegetables, tomatoes, sweet potato and palm oil.

Casa dos Estudantes do Império: An institution founded in Lisbon by the Portuguese government in 1944 to provide a meeting place for students from the colonies. It was closed by the authorities in 1965.

chana: Savannah.

Chibinda Ilunga: Royal ancestor and hero of the Chokwe people.

Chokwe: One of the ethnic groups that formed the basis of the Lunda Empire in northeastern Angola.

Cimade: A French NGO founded in 1939 to aid the flight of refugees from Nazism.

CIR *(Centro de Instrução Revolucionária)*: A network of educational centres set up by the MPLA within and outside Angola during the war of independence.

Cruz, Viriato da (1928–1973): Angolan poet, political figure, and author of the original 1956 manifesto of the MPLA.

Cuvale: A pastoral people inhabiting southwestern Angola and northern Namibia.

Drummond de Andrade, Carlos (1902–1987): A major Brazilian poet of the twentieth century.

Eastern Revolt: A revolt resulting from the collapse of the Eastern Front opened up by the MPLA in 1966 in its campaign against Portuguese rule. The revolt expressed Ovimbundu dissatisfaction with the MPLA.

Fanon, Frantz (1925–1961): Originally from Martinique, Fanon joined the Algerian FLN and was an iconic figure in the interpretation of colonialism and in postcolonial studies. Best known for *Black Skin, White Masks* (1952) and *The Wretched of the Earth* (1961).

Flechas: Black paramilitary units under the command of the Portuguese political police (PIDE) and involved in counterinsurgency operations.

FLN *(Front de libération nationale)*: Algerian nationalist movement founded in 1954.

FNLA (Frente Nacional de Libertação de Angola): Angolan nationalist movement based in the north of Angola, which emerged from UPA and was led by Holden Roberto.

funje: A porridge or pap made from cassava flour, or in the south, cornmeal, and used as an accompaniment in Angolan cuisine.

GE *(Grupos Especiais)*: Auxiliary paramilitary units under the command of the Portuguese army in the 1960 and '70s and consisting of African volunteers.

ginjinha: A cherry liqueur popular in Lisbon.

Hero, the: A reference to Hoji ya Henda, one of the MPLA's most charismatic early guerrilla fighters, who died in combat on the Eastern Front on April 14, 1968.

Ilha / Island: Ilha is a beach, residential, and leisure area of Luanda formed by a spit of sand that encloses the bay of Luanda on its seaward side.

jindungo: Hot pepper sauce.

Kamundongo: A derogatory term used to describe someone from Luanda and the Kimbundu-speaking area of Angola during the war of independence.

kaporroto: A term used in Angola to describe home-brewed spirit, traditionally made from maize.

kaxipembe: Home-brewed spirit, traditionally made from potato and cassava skin. Similar to kaporroto in Luanda.

Kimbundu: The language spoken in Luanda and in the northwest of Angola by the Northern Mbundu or Kimbundu people.

kissanje: A musical instrument akin to a thumb piano or lamellaphone.

kissonde: A variety of ant capable of attacking humans.

kwanza: The Angolan national currency.

Luchazi: A linguistic group affiliated to the Mbunda.

Lumumba, Patrice (1925–1961): A Congolese nationalist and pan-Africanist, who was imprisoned and executed in 1961.

maboque: *Strychnos spinosa*, a variety of citrus fruit, sometimes called the Napal-orange, spiny orange, or monkey orange.

makolo: The Mbunda term for the Kimbundu word *maboque* (see above).

Mbunda: A people located largely in eastern and southeastern Angola, sometimes referred to as Vambunda.

mestiço: A person of mixed descent.

Mestre Liceu: Liceu Vieira Dias was a member of Ngola Ritmos and an active member of the MPLA. He was arrested in 1959 and sent to the Tarrafal prison camp.

MPLA *(Movimento Popular de Libertação de Angola)*: The main Angolan nationalist group, founded in 1956 and centred in Luanda and the surrounding area. The party gained power upon independence in 1975.

muata: A traditional term for a chief in Eastern Angola.

mulato: A term commonly used in colonial times to describe someone of mixed African and European parentage. Feminine form: *mulata*.

musseque: A shanty or shantytown in Luanda.

Mussolo: An island just south of Luanda, popular as a weekend destination.

Ngola Ritmos: An Angolan musical group set up in 1947 and associated with the nationalist movement and the MPLA.

Nkangala: A linguistic group affiliated to the Mbunda.

Nova Lisboa: The colonial name for the city now known as Huambo.

Nzambi-Kalunga: Nzambi was a name to describe a supreme god in the Kongo tradition, and Kalunga was a god of water.

OAS *(Organisation de l'armée secrète)*: French right-wing paramilitary organization responsible for a number of atrocities during the Algerian war of independence.

orixás: Deities of Yoruban origin, common in the religious beliefs of communities of the African diaspora in the Caribbean and South America.

Ovimbundu: The largest ethnic group in Angola inhabiting the southern and eastern region of the country. See *bailundo*.

PIDE *(Polícia Internacional e de Defesa do Estado)*: Portuguese political and state security police during the dictatorship.

Salazar, António de Oliveira (1889–1970): President of the Council of Ministers and dictator of Portugal from 1932 to 1968. The regime he created was finally overthrown on April 25, 1974.

Tuga: A derogatory term for a Portuguese person.

Turra: A slang term for a terrorist, used by the Portuguese.

UNITA *(União Nacional para a Libertação Total de Angola)*: A nationalist party that split from the FNLA in 1966. It was based in the south and east of Angola. Led by Jonas Savimbi, it continued, with the military support of South Africa, to fight the MPLA after independence in 1975.

UPA *(União dos Povos de Angola)*: Union of the Peoples of Angola. An early nationalist group based in the north of Angola.

Vitória ou morte: "Victory or death." A slogan and rallying cry used by the MPLA.

xinjanguila: A ring dance from eastern Angola.

Awarded the Camões Prize, the Portuguese language's highest literary award, for his life's work, PEPETELA is the author of twenty-one novels that have won prizes in Holland, Spain, Portugal, Brazil, and Angola and which have been published in more than twenty languages.

Born in Benguela, Angola, he fled Portugal as a student and studied in Algeria, where he wrote a literacy manual that won a prize from UNESCO. From 1969 to 1975, Pepetela fought as an MPLA guerrilla, seeing front-line service against the armies of Portugal and apartheid South Africa, as well as rival rebel groups. After Angolan independence, he was deputy minister of education (1976–82) and taught sociology at Agostinho Neto University (1984–2008).

Pepetela lives in Luanda, Angola.

DAVID BROOKSHAW's translations include many novels by Mia Couto, such as *Woman of the Ashes*, *The Sword and the Spear*, *The Drinker of Horizons*, *Sleepwalking Land*, and *The Tuner of Silences*. In addition to his translations of Lusophone African writers such as Couto and Paulina Chiziane, he has translated widely from the literatures of Lusophone Asia and the Azores. Brookshaw is professor emeritus of Lusophone studies at the University of Bristol, England.

BIBLIOASIS INTERNATIONAL TRANSLATION SERIES
General Editor: Stephen Henighan

1   *I Wrote Stone: The Selected Poetry of Ryszard Kapuściński*
    (Poland)
    Translated by Diana Kuprel and Marek Kusiba

2   *Good Morning Comrades* by Ondjaki (Angola)
    Translated by Stephen Henighan

3   *Kahn & Engelmann* by Hans Eichner (Austria-Canada)
    Translated by Jean M. Snook

4   *Dance with Snakes* by Horacio Castellanos Moya (El Salvador)
    Translated by Lee Paula Springer

5   *Black Alley* by Mauricio Segura (Quebec)
    Translated by Dawn M. Cornelio

6   *The Accident* by Mihail Sebastian (Romania)
    Translated by Stephen Henighan

7   *Love Poems* by Jaime Sabines (Mexico)
    Translated by Colin Carberry

8   *The End of the Story* by Liliana Heker (Argentina)
    Translated by Andrea G. Labinger

9   *The Tuner of Silences* by Mia Couto (Mozambique)
    Translated by David Brookshaw

10 *For as Far as the Eye Can See* by Robert Melançon (Quebec)
    Translated by Judith Cowan

11 *Eucalyptus* by Mauricio Segura (Quebec)
    Translated by Donald Winkler

12 *Granma Nineteen and the Soviet's Secret* by Ondjaki (Angola)
    Translated by Stephen Henighan

13 *Montreal Before Spring* by Robert Melançon (Quebec)
    Translated by Donald McGrath

14 *Pensativities: Essays and Provocations* by Mia Couto
    (Mozambique)
    Translated by David Brookshaw

15 *Arvida* by Samuel Archibald (Quebec)
    Translated by Donald Winkler

16 *The Orange Grove* by Larry Tremblay (Quebec)
    Translated by Sheila Fischman